6-16

D1360186

MESSENGER BY MOONLIGHT

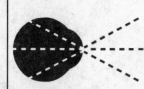

This Large Print Book carries the
Seal of Approval of N.A.V.H.

MESSENGER BY MOONLIGHT

STEPHANIE GRACE WHITSON

THORNDIKE PRESS
A part of Gale, Cengage Learning

WELLS PUBLIC LIBRARY
54 1ST STREET SW
WELLS, MN 56097

GALE
CENGAGE Learning·

Farmington Hills, Mich • San Francisco • New York • Waterville, Maine
Meriden, Conn • Mason, Ohio • Chicago

Copyright © 2016 by Whitson, Inc.
All scripture quotations are from the King James Version of the Bible.
Thorndike Press, a part of Gale, Cengage Learning.

ALL RIGHTS RESERVED
This book is a work of fiction. Names, characters, places, and incidents are the product of the author's imagination or are used fictitiously. Any resemblance to actual events, locales, or persons, living or dead, is coincidental.
The publisher is not responsible for websites (or their content) that are not owned by the publisher.
Thorndike Press® Large Print Christian Fiction.
The text of this Large Print edition is unabridged.
Other aspects of the book may vary from the original edition.
Set in 16 pt. Plantin.

LIBRARY OF CONGRESS CATALOGING-IN-PUBLICATION DATA

Names: Whitson, Stephanie Grace, author.
Title: Messenger by moonlight / Stephanie Grace Whitson.
Description: Large print edition. | Waterville, Maine : Thorndike Press Large Print, 2016. | © 2016 | Series: Thorndike Press large print Christian fiction
Identifiers: LCCN 2016015527 | ISBN 9781410488855 (hardback) | ISBN 1410488853 (hardcover)
Subjects: LCSH: Pony express—Fiction. | Large type books. | BISAC: FICTION / Christian / Historical. | GSAFD: Love stories. | Christian fiction.
Classification: LCC PS3573.H555 M49 2016b | DDC 813/.54—dc23
LC record available at https://lccn.loc.gov/2016015527

Published in 2016 by arrangement with FaithWords, a division of Hachette Book Group, Inc.

Printed in Mexico
1 2 3 4 5 6 7 20 19 18 17 16

Dedicated to the memory of the women of the Pony Express:

Mrs. Tom Perry,
Kennekuk Station, Kansas
Mrs. John E. Smith,
Seneca Station, Kansas
Mrs. George Guittard,
Guittard Ranch, Kansas
Mrs. Sophia Hollenberg,
Hollenberg Station, Kansas
Mrs. George Comstock,
Thirty-Two Mile Creek Station,
Nebraska
Mrs. Molly Slade,
Horseshoe Station, Nebraska
Mrs. Moore,
Three Crossings Station, Utah
The "three English women,"
Green River Station, Utah

Mrs. David Lewis,
Ham's Fork Station, Utah
The "French Canadian Wife,"
Muddy Creek Station, Wyoming
And those whose names
were not recorded,
but whose labor fueled the men
who ran the race

ACKNOWLEDGMENTS

Thank you, Christina Boys, editor extraordinaire, for never losing faith in this story . . . or in me.

Thank you, Janet Kobobel Grant, for your continued encouragement and guidance.

Thank you, Daniel, for sharing my passion for history, for listening to countless read-aloud sessions, and for allowing my imaginary friends to become yours, too.

Thank you, Judith McCoy Miller and Nancy Moser, for faithful prayers, treasured friendship, and brainstorming brilliance.

Thank you, Katherine McCartney, Site Administrator at Hollenberg Pony Express Station Historic Site in Hanover, Kansas, for your encouragement, knowledge, and selfless enthusiasm for this project.

I, _____, do hereby swear, before the Great and Living God, that during my engagement, and while an employee of Russell, Majors, and Waddell, I will, under no circumstances, use profane language, that I will drink no intoxicating liquors, that I will not quarrel or fight with any other employee of the firm, and that in every respect I will conduct myself honestly, be faithful to my duties, and so direct all my acts as to win the confidence of my employers, so help me God.

— Pony Express Rider's Oath

. . . the driver exclaims:
"HERE HE COMES!"
Every neck is stretched further, and every eye strained wider. Away across the endless dead level of the prairie a black speck appears against the sky, and it is plain that it moves. Well, I should think so! In a

second it becomes a horse and rider, rising and falling, rising and falling — sweeping towards us nearer and nearer — growing more and more distinct, more and more sharply defined — nearer and still nearer, and the flutter of the hoofs comes faintly to the ear — another instant a whoop and a hurrah from our upper deck, a wave of the rider's hand, but no reply, and man and horse burst past our excited faces, and go swinging away like a belated fragment of a storm!

So sudden is it all, and so like a flash of unreal fancy, that . . . we might have doubted whether we had seen any horse and man at all . . .

— Mark Twain, *Roughing It*

PROLOGUE

Buchanan County, Missouri, 1855
After five years of hoping, fourteen-year-old Annie Paxton had finally stopped waiting for Pa to come back from wherever his soul had gone the day Ma died. Hunkered down in the lean-to, she pulled her pillow over her head to shut out the noise. In the next room, Pa yelled and swore while Emmet and Frank tried to calm him down, Annie willed herself to take in a deep breath while she recalled the sound of Ma's soothing voice reciting the Shepherd's Psalm. Annie knew the entire passage, but she focused on the first few words, emphasizing a different word with each repetition. *The Lord is my shepherd. The Lord is my shepherd. The Lord is my shepherd.*

A thud in the other room signaled what Annie hoped would be the end of tonight's confrontation. She pulled the pillow away to listen. Emmet — always the peacemaker, always calm and quiet — was talking in low, mellow tones, and while Annie couldn't quite catch the words, she could imagine them. *Let us help you to bed, Pa. Annie's already turned in. We don't want to wake her.*

But Pa was bad tonight. Really bad. "*We* don't want to wake her? What you talking about, *we*? You don't speak for me. You got no idea what I want!" Pa blathered on with cursings Ma never would have allowed. Then again, Annie didn't remember Pa ever cursing when Ma was still alive.

The Lord is my shepherd. Shuffling footsteps approached the doorway between the cabin's all-purpose main room and the lean-to. Annie pressed herself as close to the log wall as she could manage. Pa was standing in the doorway. She could smell sweat and whiskey. She pressed her eyes closed, willing the tears away. They leaked out anyway. She held her breath.

"Pa." Emmet's voice again. Closer, this time. "She's asleep, Pa."

Pa mumbled something about a "poor little motherless gal" and how she didn't deserve to lose her ma.

Frank spoke up then, agreeing. They didn't deserve to lose Ma, he said. Frank wasn't like Emmet. Given a choice between backing down or fighting, Frank would fight.

Annie relaxed a little when she heard Pa moan, "I don't deserve you kids. Didn't deserve my Tennessee belle, and don't deserve you-ns."

A shard of bitterness pierced Annie's heart. Maybe Pa didn't "deserve" his kids, but couldn't he love them anyway? Couldn't he at least try? When Ma died, Emmet had taken up the farming Pa neglected, though he'd only been fourteen at the time. Nine-year-old Frank, Annie's twin, had helped, while Annie took on the cooking and cleaning and gardening and milking and chicken-tending. Neighbors had stepped up for a while, but Pa's penchant for drunken displays eventually ended that.

Pa began to cry, and Annie put the pillow back over her head. She didn't want to hear it. Didn't want to hear him say how sorry he was and how he'd do better. Sorry or not, he never did any better.

The Lord is my shepherd. Lately, Annie had focused on that phrase alone in the psalm, avoiding the rest, because all the questions she had about it made her feel guilty. Maybe she'd understand it better if they went to church. Maybe she could ask a preacher sometime. Emmet remembered going to church with Ma, but Annie didn't think he'd appreciate his younger sister questioning the Word of God. After Ma died, when Annie couldn't reason the answers to her questions about the Shepherd's Psalm, she just stopped reciting the whole thing. Instead, she clung to that first phrase, comforted by the vague notion of someone powerful being her shepherd.

She still thought about the rest of the passage, though, and the mention of *green pastures* and *goodness and mercy*. It would be nice if the farm wouldn't grow so many weeds. Both the mules and the milk cow would surely enjoy green pastures. But the phrase that caused her the most trouble was the one right at the beginning. The words *I shall not want* just flat-out haunted her, because she did "want."

She wanted Pa to stop drinking and to help Emmet and Frank with the farm. She wanted a real home, with a front porch and curtains at the windows — real curtains, not the flour sacks Ma had decorated with embroidered bluebirds. She wanted to live somewhere where people didn't think of her as one of those "poor Paxton kids." She wanted to go to a nice church with a choir and maybe even a stained-glass window like the one she'd seen the only time she'd made the twenty-mile journey to St. Joseph. And she wanted friends.

It was quiet out in the main room now. She turned onto her back, staring toward the rafters. *The Lord is my shepherd.* She closed her eyes. *Please don't be mad at me. I do want. So much.*

CHAPTER 1

Buchanan County, Missouri
March 5, 1860

Surprised by the emotion that welled up as she prepared to leave the ramshackle cabin for the last time, nineteen-year-old Ann Elizabeth Paxton hesitated before stepping across the threshold. Slowly, she turned about for a final look; at the rustic table where they'd eaten countless meals; at the two-burner stove she'd struggled with after Ma died; at the front door on the opposite side of the room, barred shut and perhaps never to be opened again. According to Frank, even the stock hands over at Hillsdale Farms lived in better places than this. Hiram Hillsdale wanted the land. He didn't care about the cabin.

Emmet and Frank had both said their good-byes to the cabin and its contents before sunup, wolfing down grits and gulping weak coffee before hauling their trunks

17

out back on their way to hitch the mules to the wagon. While they were gone, Annie laid her own things in the trunk that was hers now — the trunk Ma had brought to Buchanan County years ago and that still contained a faded silk gown, dance slippers, lace mitts, and a few other treasures that had been Ma's.

By the time Frank and Emmet had driven the wagon up to the back door and loaded Annie's trunk, the sun was up. Emmet said they'd wait for her outside. He patted her on the shoulder and said she should take all the time she needed. Pulling her threadbare shawl close about her thin shoulders, Annie looked about the room and summoned the memory of Ma. This morning, it wasn't the Shepherd's Psalm she remembered. This morning, as Annie looked at the pieces of the only life she'd ever known, she remembered Ma saying that *even on the darkest day, when all a body wants to do is cry, if she looks hard enough, she can find a sliver of light.* The tightness in her chest eased up. Taking one last look, she stepped outside.

Emmet waited beside the team, but Frank had already climbed up to the wagon seat. An unseasonably warm March breeze ruffled his shaggy auburn hair as he reached down to take Annie's hand and haul her up beside him. The minute Annie and Frank were settled, Emmet said something about taking his own last look. He went back inside.

Frank muttered, "I hope another gander finally convinces him we haven't lost much."

Annie was inclined to agree — at least when it came to the farm itself. The earth hadn't yielded much beyond weeds and poor crops for a long time now. She didn't really know why the neighbor, Mr. Hillsdale, even wanted it. Annie knew all about Hillsdale Farms, for working there from time to time had been part of Emmet and Frank's desperate attempts to save their home. Both men were good with horses. Neither could imagine Hiram Hillsdale's fine Thoroughbreds on Paxton land. *Paxton* land. She stifled a sigh. If only Ma hadn't died. If only Pa could have managed better. If only he hadn't become part of the trouble. If only he hadn't caused the worst of it.

Poor Pa. He never had recovered from losing the woman he called his "Tennessee belle." Oh, he'd determined time and again to "buck up" and "move on," but just when Annie and her brothers thought he might actually do it, Pa headed for town and one saloon or another. For ten years, she and her brothers had locked arms and kept things going. Somehow. But then, just two weeks ago, Pa had tried to find his way home through a late winter snowstorm — and failed. A few days after they laid him to rest beside Ma, the local banker knocked on the front door, and the three Paxton siblings learned that drinking hadn't been their father's only problem. He'd taken to gambling, too. And he always lost.

Thinking on it now while she sat beside Frank on the wagon seat and Emmet lingered inside invited a fresh wave of emotion. *Oh . . . Pa.* Annie flung another plea at heaven. *Help Emmet. Please.* All Emmet had ever wanted to do was farm. It had taken him several days to accept the truth delivered by the town banker. Earl Paxton had left his three children a farm with so much debt carried against it that the only thing to do was to sell it.

"That can't be right," Emmet protested. "We own the place, free and clear."

The banker shook his head. "I'm afraid not." He was sorry, but his hands were tied. Surely they could understand that under the circumstances, he simply could not give another extension. He seemed pleased with himself when he told them they were not left "without recourse." He was authorized to make an offer on behalf of their neighbor,

Mr. Hiram Hillsdale. A "generous offer" the banker called it — one that would not only cancel the debt but also free Earl's adult children to "explore the world."

They would of course be able to keep things considered personal. Clothing and the like. Whatever would fit in a trunk — three trunks, since there were three of them. The team of ancient mules and the farm wagon would also be "overlooked," since they'd need transportation off the property. Mr. Hillsdale would give them a full forty-eight hours to vacate the premises once they'd accepted his offer.

Annie had never seen Emmet lose his temper, but he came close that day. His face flushed bright red. He spun about and strode to the open door of the cabin, standing there for a long while, his body fairly vibrating with emotion. Finally, he took a deep breath and turned back around. "Forty-eight hours to pack up the only life we've ever known? You can't be serious. We need more time."

The banker grimaced. "I suppose I could speak with Mr. Hillsdale — if you insist."

Frank intervened. "Don't bother." He scowled as he said, "We'll not be begging crumbs from the table of the illustrious Hiram Hillsdale." Frank put one hand on

Emmet's shoulder and gave it a little shake. "Remember how Annie blabbered about St. Joseph that time Pa took her to the city? We'll go there. It's March. The ice will be breaking up on the Missouri and that'll mean a lot of business coming into St. Jo. We shouldn't have any trouble finding jobs." He winked at Annie. "What d'ya say? Shall we give St. Joseph a try?"

It was strange to look back on that moment now and realize that Frank had been the one to make peace with their situation while Emmet struggled. No one who knew the Paxtons would ever have called Frank a peacemaker. His auburn hair and deep brown eyes were visible indications of a dark, stormy temperament. Blond, blue-eyed Emmet was the quiet, steady one who never wanted more than what already lay within reach.

Weathered boards and rusty hinges creaked as Emmet finally exited the cabin and pulled the door closed behind him. When he climbed aboard and lifted the reins to signal the mules to move out, the team refused to budge. Slapping their rumps with the reins, he called out, "Come on, now, Bart. Git up, there, Bill. You can retire the minute you pull us up to the livery in St. Joseph. And that's a promise."

Frank muttered something about retirement "courtesy of Mr. Winchester."

Annie frowned at him. "You don't mean that." When Frank only shrugged, she appealed to Emmet. "He doesn't mean that, does he? You can't let anyone hurt the mules. They can't help being old."

Emmet flashed a warning look at Frank as he said, "No one's going to hurt the mules, Annie. Not as long as I have a say." He flicked the reins across the team's flanks. With a brayed protest, they leaned into the creaking harness. The wagon began to move. "Now don't cry," Emmet said as they pulled onto the road. "We're going to be all right."

"Darned right we are," Frank said. He nudged Annie. "We've got us a fresh start, and we're going to make the most of it."

Annie nodded. She rather liked the idea of a fresh start, although it sometimes made her feel guilty to admit it, even to herself. After all, but for Pa's dying they might have been able to hang on. Maybe she shouldn't be *glad* to be leaving, but still — there were good things about moving on, not the least of which was an end to being seen as one of "that drunken Earl Paxton's poor kids." From what she remembered of St. Jo., it was as different from home as one of Mr.

Hillsdale's fine Thoroughbreds was from Bart, the lop-eared mule. This time of year, thousands of travelers would be poised to begin spring journeys either to gold mines in the Rockies or homesteads in Oregon. The city would be bustling. If one job didn't work out, a body could try another and another and another, until finally he or she landed on whatever was just right. St. Jo. was the perfect place to get a fresh start.

Annie glanced over at poor Emmet, who wasn't the least bit interested in living somewhere different. All twenty-four-year-old Emmet cared about was farming, Luvina Aiken, and God — although probably not quite in that order. For Emmet, St. Joseph was only a temporary necessity. A place to earn the respectable living that would convince Luvina's father to consent to a wedding. A detour on a path that he hoped would lead him right back to farming — and to Luvina.

They'd been on the road for a while now, and Emmet had apparently mistaken Annie's silence for sadness. "I know things seem bleak," he said, "but God hasn't forgotten us. The Lord *is* our shepherd, and He still means everything for our good, whether we can see it or not. Thinking about our going to St. Joseph just now had me thinking about Joseph in the Bible. You remember that story? Ma used to tell it. I think it comforted her when she felt homesick for Tennessee."

"I remember Joseph," Annie said, although the memory didn't come from Ma. Compared to Emmet, she remembered so very little about Ma. She had a vague notion of warmth and feeling safe. A gentle voice. Sitting in church and liking the sound of Ma's voice singing hymns — although she wasn't sure if she actually remembered the part about church or if she'd just heard Emmet talk about it often enough that she thought she remembered. It especially bothered her that she didn't remember what Ma looked like. Emmet said if she wanted to know that, all she had to do was look in the mirror. Annie wasn't sure if that helped or hurt, because if Ma looked like her or she looked like Ma, then why didn't she remember her better? Then again, Emmet was five years older than she and Frank, and the extra years had given him more memories of Ma. Memories from a time when life was better and Pa was sober all the time. Sometimes Annie thought the hardness of the past ten years had put a jagged edge to her memories and cut away most of the good. Maybe that was why she couldn't remember Ma better.

"Joseph," Emmet was saying, "found himself in a far country because of terrible things he couldn't control. But God never lost track of Joseph." He paused. "He won't lose track of us, either."

Annie nodded. She remembered the story. She hoped it meant what Emmet said. She liked the way he could be counted on to share comfort from the Bible. Ma's Bible, actually. He read it morning and night. Sometimes he read it aloud, although most of the time he kept it to himself. Annie knew that was because Frank was like Pa when it came to religion. Neither of them had any use for it.

One thing she did remember clearly was the day after Ma's funeral, when Emmet brought Ma's Bible to breakfast with him, planning to read one of Ma's favorite passages to the four of them. One she'd underlined, he said. But Emmet didn't so much as get the Bible opened before Pa grabbed it and threw it across the room. Then he stormed out the back door, leaving his eggs and grits to grow cold. After that, Emmet did his Bible reading when Pa wasn't around. When Annie mentioned remembering Ma reciting the Shepherd's Psalm, Emmet helped her learn it — on the sly. Frank never showed any interest.

26

Emmet had also talked about Joseph and God's keeping track of him when he'd told his sweetheart about the Paxtons' losing the farm. Sixteen-year-old Luvina Aiken had promised to wait, but Annie had witnessed that promise, and while she knew very little about love, she knew quite a lot about emotions, and it seemed to her that pale, prim Luvina's were decidedly lukewarm. She hadn't shed a tear. It seemed to Annie that a woman in love ought to show a little more enthusiasm.

Annie hoped she was wrong. For all she knew, the girl was making quilts for her hope chest and counting the days until she could keep house for Emmet. In the meantime, Annie had her own dreams, and they revolved around keeping house, too — for her brothers in St. Jo. As the wagon creaked along the rutted road, Annie closed her eyes and envisioned it. Four rooms would do, one for living and cooking, and three for sleeping. They would paint the exterior white and the trim blue. She would ask Frank to build window boxes where she'd plant sweet peas to spill out and down like a blooming waterfall.

When she really let her imagination fly, Annie envisioned a front porch where she could sit and have her morning coffee and keep an eye on everything going on just beyond a picket fence nearly hidden beneath yards of rambling rosebushes. She imagined a vegetable garden and a medium-sized dog to bark and announce company, and a cat to keep mice out of the pantry.

Once they had jobs and a new home in St. Jo., Emmet would realize that losing the farm was for the best. He certainly deserved better than a battered cabin and a drunken father and land that grew very little besides waist-high thistles. In St. Joseph, he could work toward something better — the future he wanted with Luvina. They could all work toward something better.

Annie hadn't said anything about it to Frank or Emmet yet, but she'd decided that as soon as they were settled she would see about getting a job as a cook. Ma had been a cook at a big hotel when she met Pa, and while the Paxtons had never been able to afford much in the way of *cuisine* — Ma said that meant fancy cooking — still, Annie remembered her doing things like sprinkling cinnamon on grits. She remembered bunches of herbs hanging from twine strung between the rafters of the cabin. She remembered smiles around the supper table.

She would get a job as a cook and learn new things and one day she would gather

her family around the table and serve delicious food. Instead of gulping down whatever was before them for the sole purpose of staving off their ever-present hunger, they would take their time. They would smile and say things like, *Trying something new? We love your cooking, Ma. How come everything's always so good? We love you, Ma.* There was a shadowy "Pa" somewhere in that daydream, too, and now that they were leaving the farm, Annie let herself think about the possibilities. Maybe she'd meet "him" in St. Jo. She allowed a little smile. *The Lord is my shepherd.* As far as Annie was concerned, the farther they got from the farm, the more the future shimmered with bright promise.

The world seemed a little less "shimmery" as the day went on — mostly because of the growing concern that Bart and Bill might not make it to St. Jo. Annie felt bad for the poor mules, their heads hanging low, their hooves barely clearing the earth as they ambled along. What would they all do if Bart and Bill dropped in their traces?

Around midday, when Frank said they were going to have to walk, Annie immediately thought of the hole in the sole of her right boot. Emmet did, too. "You and I can walk," he said to Frank and proceeded to climb down. But when Annie moved to join her brothers, Emmet stayed her with his hand. "Those boots of yours won't take much walking. Besides, you don't add much to the load, little as you are. Bart and Bill can manage a few extra pounds."

Truth be told, there wasn't much to any of the Paxtons. They were a fine-boned, wiry lot, with twins Annie and Frank not quite five feet tall and Emmet not much taller. Still, with Bart and Bill almost on their last legs, Annie said that every pound would make a difference, and she wasn't going to be the reason they ended up stranded beside the road with three trunks and no way to move them.

"That's our girl," Frank said. He directed Annie to take off the boot with the biggest hole in the sole and then snatched up dried grass to provide a little extra padding over the folded paper that already shielded her stocking from the earth.

Emmet slipped his hand beneath the throatlatch at Bart's head and pulled to keep the team moving. The sun was sinking fast when the wagon finally topped the last hill. The mules seemed to know they were near the end of the journey. They didn't move any faster, but they lifted their heads and picked up their feet a bit.

Annie took note of the scarlet-rimmed clouds in the western sky and smiled. Colorful slivers of light, even as night descended. She began to pay attention to the city itself. What she saw as they made their way into St. Joseph fascinated her. In one candlelit room where the drapes were drawn back, a family sat around their dining table. As Annie watched, a maid wearing a white apron presented something to the man sitting with his back to the window. So enthralled was Annie as she watched that she nearly fell when she encountered a rut in the road. She would have fallen if not for Frank's steadying hand.

"If you lived there," he groused, "you'd be the one in the apron — not the one sitting at that fancy table. You'd have a tiny room in the attic and you'd freeze all winter and swelter all summer. And be at some stranger's beck and call every hour of the day and night."

I wouldn't care. I bet their cook doesn't have to make do with a tiny stove in a corner. She probably doesn't have to worry about stretching the grits or making the molasses last, either. If I worked there, I'd be able to set the table with china. And polish the silver. Real silver.

She thought those things, but Annie didn't

say them. It was pointless to argue with Frank when he was in one of his dark moods, and the set of his jaw and the way one corner of his mouth turned down were evidence enough that such a mood was fast descending. Poor Frank. Only nineteen years old and already sporting a permanent furrow between his eyebrows — a furrow that would only deepen if he didn't find a way to harvest happiness from life.

Tucking her hand beneath his elbow, Annie gave his arm an affectionate squeeze. "You're probably right, but once they tasted my apple dumplings, I bet they'd give me an extra day off and a bigger room, just to keep me on."

Frank snorted softly. "And plant you an apple orchard, I suppose." He was still grousing, but his downturned mouth didn't look quite so grim.

"Not an entire orchard, silly," she teased. "Just a couple of trees would be enough. After all, that yard wasn't all that big." She glanced behind them. "Although peach trees and a cherry tree or two would be nice."

A faint, lopsided smile appeared. "Don't forget the raspberry bushes."

"And strawberries," Annie said.

"And asparagus and a blackberry bramble.

I know."

"And —" Annie broke off when she caught sight of a massive brick building looming in the distance. Visions of blackberries faded, as she stared at the cupola reaching toward the sky. Four stories. *Brick.* Iron posts supporting a platform that served not only to protect the main entrance from weather but also to create an observation deck. Annie pointed at the dozen or so well-dressed people gathered there. "They must feel like royalty, gazing down on us." She peered down the hill. "I bet they can see all the way to the river from up there."

Frank harrumphed and muttered something about dandies looking down their noses at the pathetic rig he and Annie were following down the road, but Annie didn't pay him any mind. She was concentrating on every detail of what was surely one of the finest hotels in the country. Just look at all the chimneys. And the elegant trim just above the top row of windows. And the windows — at least a dozen on a side. Was this the kind of hotel where Ma had met Pa? A girl could surely learn to cook wonderful food working in such a place. Would she dare go through that arched doorway to ask about working there?

Again, Annie stumbled. This time she was

still holding onto Frank's arm. Unfortunately, it wasn't a rut in the road that had tripped her up, but a steaming pile of manure. And she'd stepped right in the middle of it. With the boot with the biggest hole in the sole. She crinkled her nose at the idea of removing the manure-soaked newspaper acting as a patch. Hurrying to the side of the street, she did what she could to free the shoe of manure, scraping the bottom and sides along the edge of the board-walk.

"Now the stitching's coming out across the toe," Frank said. He swore softly.

"It'll be all right. I'll stitch it with some cord. I think I have some in my trunk."

"Let me see the other one," Frank demanded.

"They're fine," Annie said. "Really."

Frank pointed toward the hem of her skirt. "Let me see the other one."

Reluctantly, Annie extended her other foot. The toe of her red stocking showed through a hole in the leather. "It's all right," she said. "It's not that hard to keep it tucked under my skirt." She pulled her foot back and tried to erase the frown on his face by teasing. "I hope you're happy. We've probably scandalized one of the fine ladies up on that observation deck."

Frank blurted out a response that included some not very complimentary things about "cads who'd never known an honest day's work and their primping paramours." Emmet, who'd come back to check on them when he realized Annie and Frank had stopped following the wagon opened his mouth to say something, but Frank held up a hand and apologized. "I know. I shouldn't talk like that in front of Annie. I'm sorry. It just bothers me. Hiram Hillsdale's daddy hands him an easy life and what do we get? A drunken father who can't even keep hold of a failing farm." He glowered at Emmet. "And I'm in no mood to hear all about how God hasn't forgotten us and everything's going to be just fine." He nodded Annie's way. "Our sister doesn't even have a decent pair of *shoes.*"

Annie squeezed Frank's arm. "I do, however, have two superb brothers. And from what I know of him, Mr. Hiram Hillsdale doesn't have a single family member who so much as speaks to him. That means we're better off. And I really don't care about the shoes."

"Well *I* do, and if it's the last thing —"

Annie tugged on his arm. "All right. I understand. Just — stop acting like everything is terrible. Terrible is behind us. Think good thoughts, Frank. Good thoughts."

CHAPTER 2

It wasn't easy, but Frank managed to keep "good thoughts" all the way to the bottom of the hill. For Annie's sake if for nothing else. But then they pulled up to the back door of a stone livery and Emmet begged the owner to buy the team and the wagon. Of course Emmet put it a little more subtly than that, but that's what they were doing. Begging. Frank could barely stand it. He was too embarrassed to so much as look the livery owner in the eye.

The spry old guy wasn't exactly rude, but he barely glanced at Bart and Bill before shaking his head. "Can't think they'd do me any good. I buy and sell some, but these two old boys aren't fit for much beyond —" He glanced Annie's way. Didn't finish the sentence.

At least the old guy had considered Annie's feelings before stating the obvious. Bart and Bill weren't fit for much beyond the meat market. The livery owner nodded toward a large corral where several other mules were lined up at a trough filled with fresh hay. "You can leave them for the night," he said. "I'd offer you stalls inside, but I'm full up."

Frank glanced over at Annie, wondering if she realized what a "good thing" it was for a businessman to so much as consider offering stalls at the livery to people like them. After all, the man had to realize the situation. Then again, only an evil so-and-so would have the heart to turn away blond-haired, blue-eyed Annie Paxton. Who wouldn't fall under the spell of a girl who could walk into a strange town with shoes so worn they were nearly falling off her feet and encourage her cranky twin brother to "think good things."

Annie. If not for his sister, Frank would have signed the farm over to Emmet, wished him well, and left the day Pa was laid to rest. *If not for Annie.* Guilt washed over him at the flicker of resentment. *It's not her fault.* He quieted the tug-of-war inside him and looked over at his sister. She shouldn't have to stand here in the chill of the evening wondering where she would lay her head tonight. Come heck or high water, he was going to see to it that life got better for Annie. Once that was done — well, then he would be free. Maybe he'd hire on with a wagon boss and see what California had to offer. Shake the last of Missouri off his boots and think good thoughts somewhere else.

Emmet thanked the livery owner for the offer regarding a place for the mules for the night, then pressed to settle the matter of payment. "If you don't want to give cash money for the team, would you take the rig in trade for board? The harness isn't too bad."

"To be honest, I heard you coming from up Patee House way. You're about to lose an axle." Again, the livery owner looked over at Annie and then back at Emmet. "Tell you what. I'll look it over in the morning when there's good light. You can set your trunks inside if you like. For now, though, you should find yourselves a room before it gets too dark. I'll see to the mules before I lock up. We can talk business in the morning." He offered his hand and introduced himself. "Name's Gould, by the way. Ira Gould."

Emmet introduced the three of them.

"What brings you to St. Joseph?"

"Looking for a fresh start," Emmet said.

Frank chimed in. "Our sister, here, has a hankering to conquer the big city."

The old man chuckled. "Well, you'd better get to it. Decent rooms tend to be in short supply these days." He suggested a few boardinghouses and then added, "You're welcome to just climb up to the loft for the night. It's a bit dusty, but there's plenty of fresh hay and the price is right."

"Thank you," Emmet said, "but I hope we don't have to take you up on it."

"Suit yourself. I'll leave the side door open just in case. And if you do come back, don't let my other boarder startle you. There's a bunk in one corner of the barn. I get paid to board freighters now and again. The season's starting and they're thick as thieves in St. Jo., competing for contracts to haul supplies west. Luther's as big as a bear, but he's harmless — except for snoring loud enough to raise the dead. I'll introduce you tomorrow."

As he and Annie followed Emmet toward the street, Frank decided that meeting Ira Gould might just be one of those "good things" Annie always insisted they watch for. If this "Luther" person was the least bit friendly, Frank would have a chance to talk to someone who knew what lay beyond the Missouri. He had a million questions.

Annie's stubborn optimism, which Frank

40

honestly thought of as a willful denial of reality sometimes, did nothing to help the Paxtons find rooms in St. Jo. As the evening wore on and the air grew chilly, even Emmet seemed discouraged when an advertised "room to let" proved to be one corner of a room already occupied by a family — husband, wife, and six children.

"The kids don't take up much room," the landlady said. "They can just roll under the bed when the time comes to sleep."

Frank didn't wait for Emmet to respond to that before retreating out the door and back to the street. He nudged Annie's shoulder and groused, "Got any more good thoughts for us?"

"Mr. Gould seemed nice," Annie said. "Let's go back to the livery."

As the three walked along, Annie tucked one hand beneath each brother's arm. The way back led past the fancy hotel again, and when Frank noticed Annie staring into the brightly lit hotel lobby, he murmured, "I'd like nothing better than to escort you inside and ask for the best room in the house."

"Two rooms," Annie said. "I wouldn't want to stay there alone. And I wasn't hankering to stay there, anyway. I was wondering if that's the kind of place Ma worked. You know — when she met Pa.

41

Maybe I'll see about getting hired on."

Frank sobered. If serving rich people was the best dream Annie could summon — the idea cast a pall over the relief he'd felt at finally getting free of the worthless few acres of dirt where Pa had ground out the last years of his sad life. "What happened to the little house with the window boxes?"

"I still want it," Annie said quickly. "I just figured I should do my part to earn it."

All right. That was better. It was probably a good sign that she expected to work. Even better if she could get work she thought she wanted. Emmet loved Annie, but he was focused more on Luvina Aiken these days. For Frank's part, Annie came first. He was going to see to it that she got her little house. And that she never again had to stick folded paper inside her shoes.

Emmet apologized to Annie. "I knew St. Joseph was a busy place, but I never expected this."

"Having trouble finding a room is just a sign that we've come to the right place," Annie said. "You said it yourself. God hasn't lost track of us and we're going to be all right. I believed it when you said it this morning, and I still believe it. We just need to stick together and work hard. It's one night in a nice man's barn loft. That's not so horrible, is it?"

"It's not horrible at all," Frank said. "Come on, Emmet. She's right. It's one night." He looked pointedly up at the night sky. "And it *is* night. Let's turn in." He didn't always understand the way Annie's mind worked. Sometimes it seemed to him that she was downright illogical, but this wasn't one of those times. Tonight she was being practical, and he loved her for it.

Annie started awake. She barely managed to stifle a screech. Thinking a mouse had just skittered across her feet, she jerked away from the critter. Just before she sprang to her feet to shake out her skirt, she caught sight of the offender. *Not a mouse. A cat.* More of a kitten than a cat. Black, with white paws, a white nose, and blue eyes.

"Hey you," she murmured. The kitten lowered its haunches to sit. As it inspected her, its white-tipped tail switched back and forth. A different kind of screech sounded from below as someone slid the huge double doors along a metal track. The kitten bolted, disappearing behind a wall of hay. With a sigh, Annie rose and shook out the blue-and-white blanket she'd wrapped up in the night before. Crossing to the open haymow door, she peered down into the back lot, smiling when she caught sight of Frank working the handle of a pump while Emmet cupped his hands to capture the water.

Frank caught sight of her and made a show of bowing before calling, "Is the Lady Paxton ready to descend from her chamber?"

Feeling guilty for sleeping later than her brothers, Annie hurried to descend and join them at the pump. She scrubbed her face as best she could, thankful that her morning ablutions were sheltered from public view by a row of wagons and carriages lined up beneath the livery sign: RIGS FOR HIRE. BEST PRICES, BEST HORSES. WAGONS. HARNESS REPAIR. BLACKSMITHING. IRA P. GOULD, PROPRIETOR.

Back inside the stable, Frank and Emmet kept watch while Annie "reconstituted" her hair. The key to her trunk hung from a length of velvet ribbon about her neck. Pulling it out, she unlocked the trunk and retrieved Ma's ivory-handled looking glass. Looking in the mirror confirmed her worst suspicions. No one would hire a girl who looked like she'd slept in a barn. Letting down her hair, she brushed through it, then pulled it back and twisted it into a tight, smooth bun at the base of her neck — well, as smooth a bun as a girl cursed with

44

natural curls could manage, anyway. She took another look in the mirror, turning her head from side to side. Not too bad. Respectable, at least.

After returning Ma's looking glass to the top tray, she closed the trunk and twisted the key in the lock. *The Lord is my shepherd. Please let today be a good one.* She dropped the key inside the front of her blouse, making certain the ribbon was tucked out of sight beneath her collar. "All right," she said, and stepped up between her brothers. "This is the day the Lord has made. Let us rejoice and be glad in it." She glanced Emmet's way, hoping it made him feel better about things to hear her quote a verse he'd taught her.

She doled out the last of the bread she'd baked before they left home the previous morning. They ate quickly, washing down the dried crusts with a shared cup of well water. Finally, Annie said, "While the two of you settle up with Mr. Gould, I'll go up to the hotel we passed on the way here. If I get work, I'll ask for written proof of the job and the pay. Knowing we aren't drifters might help us secure a room with that woman up on Oak Street."

"You mean the one who looked like she'd just eaten a lemon?" Frank pursed his lips in a hilarious imitation of Miss Eleanor Stanton, "proprietress" of the Oak Street Inn, as the sign in front of the two-story clapboard house had proclaimed.

Annie laughed at Frank's pantomime. "She wasn't very nice, but that house — that porch with the rockers — wouldn't it be nice to come home to a place like that?"

"She said she didn't have any rooms," Emmet warned. "There's no point in hankering after something you can't have."

Annie stood her ground. "She probably never has rooms for people she suspects of being drifters. I bet she'll change her tune if we go back with written proof that we have jobs."

Emmet shrugged. "All right. If you really want to, we'll try again — when all three of us have jobs. But you'll have to wait a bit to go back to that hotel. Frank and I aren't about to let you wander the streets of St. Joseph without an escort, and if Gould doesn't want the mules, we'll probably have to muck out a few stalls to pay for board."

"He said he'd look at the rig," Annie reminded him.

"And when he does," Frank said, "he's not going to want it."

Emmet chimed in. "Have patience, little sister. It shouldn't take us too long."

"But I can see the top of the hotel cupola from here. I can't possibly get lost."

"That's not the point," Emmet insisted.

Frank nodded agreement. "He's right."

Annie had just opened her mouth to argue some more, when the livery owner stepped outside — followed by a burly stranger he introduced as Luther Mufsy.

The stranger shook hands with Emmet and Frank and tugged on the brim of his hat by way of greeting Annie. "Ma'am." He spoke to Emmet: "I've done a little black-smithing in my day. Ira said something about the rear axle on your wagon. Want me to have a look? See if it's an easy fix?"

"We appreciate the offer," Emmet said, "but we need to sell the wagon — as is." He glanced over at Mr. Gould, clearly inviting the livery owner to make an offer.

Instead of acting on Emmet's invitation, Mr. Gould weighed in on the subject of Annie's heading off on her own. "As to the idea of your walking about St. Joseph unes-corted, Miss Paxton, I add my voice to the *nays.*"

"See?" Emmet said. "I'm right."

Annie glowered at him. "Then settle up with Mr. Gould and let's get going."

"If you don't mind my inquiring," Mr. Gould asked, "I didn't hear enough to know where it is your brothers don't want you going. Mind telling me?"

"Just up the hill to the Patee House. I want to see if I can get hired to work in the kitchen."

"As it happens, I know one of the ladies who works there. And I need to talk to Mr. Lewis at the Pony office just off the hotel lobby. I'd be happy to have you come along. I could introduce you to Fern. Can't make any promises, of course, but with business picking up, I wouldn't be surprised if they're hiring extra kitchen help." He nodded at Emmet and Frank. "If you two will help Luther mind the livery while we're gone, I'll consider us square regarding last night. Does that suit?"

Emmet accepted for them all. As he and Frank left, accompanied by Mr. Luther, Annie took Mr. Gould's proffered arm. "Just so you know," he said, "Mr. P-a-t-e-e pronounces his name *PAY-tee* — not *Patty.*"

"Thank you for telling me. I don't suppose it would help my chances at working there to mispronounce the owner's name."

Mr. Gould shrugged. "An honest mistake. On the other hand, there's no reason to announce the fact that you don't come from around here." The hotel was just ahead when he added, "I should probably warn

48

you about Fern. She can be mighty demand-
ing."

"I'm not afraid of hard work."

Mr. Gould smiled. "Then the two of you
just might get on."

When a local reverend asked to hire one of
Ira Gould's buggies for the day, Frank left
Emmet to finish mucking out stalls and
helped hitch up a bay gelding Luther re-
ferred to as "Dependable Old Dobbin."

As the reverend drove the hired rig away,
Frank glanced behind him to where Emmet
was busily cleaning out a stall. Lowering his
voice, he said, "About our wagon, Mr.
Mufsy —"

"Luther. Just call me Luther."

Frank nodded. "All right. Luther. Emmet
wants to sell it outright, but I'm thinking
there's plenty of work to be had down on
the levee, now the ice is breaking up and
freight's moving again on the river. Thought
maybe I could start a delivery business. I
can't pay you cash money for fixing that
axle, but —"

Luther interrupted him. "No reason to
worry about how to pay until we know if I
can fix it. I'll take a look after we get morning chores done." He paused, then asked if

Frank had a plan for "fixing" the aged mules.

"I can get a few more miles out of Bart and Bill," Frank said, sounding more confident than he felt. "I'm good with horses and mules." To prove the point, he reached for the lead rope hanging outside the closest box stall. "In fact, why don't I turn this guy out into the corral, then come back and muck out the stall. Maybe you could take a look at the wagon while I do that."

"Whoa!" Luther stayed his hand. "That's Outlaw, the meanest horse this side of a meat market. Kicks. Bites. I helped Ira's regular blacksmith shoe the son-of-a-gun last week, and you never saw the likes of it. We had to throw him on his side and lasso each foot separately to keep him from kicking the blacksmith all the way to Hades — which is where that horse was spawned, if you asked me."

Frank peered into the stall. "He talking about you?" When the black horse tossed its head and kicked the side of the stall, Frank forced a laugh. "Oh, yeah. I'm scared."

Emmet stepped up. "Look at the way he's standing. He's braced for a fight."

"I doubt the peppermint candy treatment would work," Frank said.

"Candy?" Luther snorted. "Not unless

you want to lose a finger."

Frank glanced over at Emmet with a grin. "Two bits says I can stay on longer than you."

Luther shook his head. "Even if I was a gambling man — which I am not — Outlaw's off limits. Unless, of course, you want to try him out later this morning when he's 'interviewing' Pony hopefuls."

Frank frowned. "What's a 'pony hopeful'?"

"Someone hoping to ride for the Pony Express. You know — the new mail run. St. Jo. to California in ten days." Luther paused. "You haven't heard of it?" When Frank and Emmet both shook their heads, Luther told them to stay put, then hurried into the livery owner's quarters. When he returned, he handed Frank a handbill.

PONY EXPRESS
St. Joseph, Missouri to California
in 10 days or less.
WANTED
YOUNG, SKINNY, WIRY FELLOWS
Not over eighteen.
Must be expert riders,
willing to risk death daily.
Orphans preferred.
Wages $25 per week.

Apply, GOULD LIVERY
St. Joseph, Missouri

"St. Joseph to San Francisco . . . in *ten days*?" Frank glanced over at Emmet. "How far is that? Has to be —"

Luther interrupted. "Nearly two thousand miles." He lowered his voice. "It hasn't been officially announced yet, but Mr. Gould said he has it on good authority that St. Jo.'s been selected as the jumping-off spot. Keep that to yourselves. It's supposed to be an all-fired secret." Frank and Emmet swore to keep the secret, and Luther continued. "First rider leaves April third. Fresh horses every ten or fifteen miles. Switching at Overland Stage stations wherever there is one, but they've had to add plenty of relay stations along the way. It's all about speed. I've seen the stock, and there's some fine animals lined up to make those runs. The Pony paid nearly two hundred dollars for some of 'em."

Frank whistled low.

"Like I said, some fine animals."

"And they're still hiring riders?"

"Yep. Outlaw's being treated like a king to keep him in shape for the 'interviews.'"

Frank pointed at the *$25.* "Is that real?"

"Real as spring rain on the prairie,"

52

Luther said. "I'd be trying for it myself if I was half a foot shorter, a hundred pounds lighter, and twenty years younger."

"With money like that —" Frank swallowed. "Shoot." He looked over at Emmet.

"It says 'not over eighteen.' " Emmet said. "We're both too old."

"Not by much," Frank said. He looked at Luther. "I'm nineteen. Emmet's twenty-four. But we're good riders. Better than most."

Luther shrugged. "I think the age is more of a guideline than a rule. And they aren't *all* orphans. I know that for a fact. Mostly they want fellers willing to ride like Old Scratch himself is after them. Night and day, rain or snow."

Frank grinned. Emmet nodded. Together, they asked, "When do we ride?"

CHAPTER 3

It was all Annie could do to keep from skipping alongside Mr. Gould when the time came to return to the livery. She couldn't wait to see Frank and Emmet. "I don't care what Frank said about her, I think we're going to get on just fine with Miss Stanton." She smiled up at Mr. Gould. "She seemed so stern when we talked to her last night. But she didn't hesitate to show me those two rooms just now — thanks to you. I don't quite know how to thank you for all you've done." In a rush of enthusiasm, she stood on tiptoe and planted a kiss on the old man's weathered cheek. If she had a grandfather, she'd want him to be kind, just like Mr. Gould.

"Well now," Mr. Gould blustered, "I'd say you just did. Don't give it another thought. And call me Ira, why don't you. I've known Ellie since the two of us were knee-high to a grasshopper. She's not to be trifled with, but she has a good heart. As for Fern up at the Patee House, just — be sure you keep her happy, or I'll never hear the end of it." He cleared his throat. "I, um, I squire Fern to church now and then."

"I won't let you down. You have my solemn promise." Annie smiled up at him. "You don't happen to need help at the livery do you? My brothers are just about the finest horsemen anywhere."

"Horsemen, you say." He sounded doubtful.

"I know what you're thinking," Annie said. "Bart and Bill aren't exactly a good advertisement for their abilities. But — have you heard of Hillsdale Farms?"

"Who hasn't? Mr. Hillsdale's sold dozens of mounts to the Pony Express."

Annie didn't know what a "pony express" was, but that wasn't the point. Mention of Mr. Hillsdale had made an impression, and so she continued that thread. "Frank was one of Mr. Hillsdale's jockeys for a while. Our pa was the head man over the broodmares before Mama died. Pa quit then. Said he needed to stay closer to home and that he'd take up farming. But then he started drinking and —" She broke off. It wouldn't do to make Ira think she was appealing to his sympathy. When it came to horsemanship, neither Frank nor Emmet needed anyone's sympathy. "Both Frank and Emmet spent a lot of time in those fancy Hillsdale barns."

Ira frowned. "Why aren't they working for Hillsdale instead of mucking out my livery to earn a night's keep?"

"Emmet's good with horses, but his heart's in farming. As for Frank, he and Mr. Hillsdale had a falling out." She hurried to explain. "Not because of anything Frank did wrong, mind you. It's just — well, I don't like to speak ill of a man, but when Frank was riding for him, if a horse won, Mr. Hillsdale took the credit. And if a horse lost —"

"— he blamed Frank?"

Annie grinned. "You really do know Mr. Hillsdale." Ira laughed, then broke off abruptly when a cheer rang out from a crowd gathered around the larger of the two corrals in the livery's back lot. Standing on tiptoe, she could just see a black horse pitching and fighting to escape the hold of several men. How had they managed to get a saddle on the crazed animal?

"You don't want to see that," Ira said. With Annie in tow, he led the way to the opposite side of the barn and the wide double doors that opened onto the street.

Annie glanced at a handbill nailed to the doorframe. "That wasn't there last night. We would have seen it when we drove in."

PONY EXPRESS. EXPERT RIDERS . . .

"I nailed it up myself this morning on my way back from the printer. Got a few boys hired to put 'em up around town today." He paused. "That horse in the corral? That's Outlaw. The Pony hired me to board him. Outlaw sorts the men from the boys when it comes to riding for the Pony."

The crowd whooped and hollered — and then fell quiet, as if taking a collective breath. A redheaded youth wearing a red shirt charged past the open stable doors. Shouting something about getting a doctor, he raced off up the street. Just as Annie's heart lurched, Emmet stepped through the single door they'd used when they returned to the livery last night.

Catching sight of Annie, Emmet called out, "It's not Frank." He hurried to where Annie stood, directing his next few words to Ira. "Jake Finney went for the doctor. Broken leg, most likely."

Annie tottered over to a rustic bench near the blacksmith's forge and sat down.

Emmet sat beside her. "Darned fool greenhorn had no business trying it. That horse is — evil. After he throws 'em, he wants to pound 'em into the dirt." He took his hat off and swiped his forehead with a dusty forearm. "You'd best stay here when we go. Won't be long, now."

"When you go . . . where?" Annie asked. Emmet reached into his shirt pocket and pulled out a copy of the same flyer Annie had just read. "I know about that." She snatched it away.

Emmet scratched the back of his neck, then raked his hand through his hair. "You can't expect us to turn down two hundred dollars *a month.*"

"You just said that horse is a killer." She crumpled the handbill. "And you said there's plenty of work *here.* In St. Joseph."

The redhead named Jake sprinted past again, this time with an older man in tow. "Hey, Emmet! You chickening out?" he called. Then he paused and turned to Ira as the doctor hurried on. "Doctor wants to use one of the wagons to haul the patient away."

The old man departed to help with the injured rider, and Annie latched onto Emmet's arm. "Don't do it," she begged. "Please. What would Luvina say?"

That made him hesitate. He seemed to mull it over, but then he shrugged. "Doesn't really matter. Earl Aiken will never give permission for us to get hitched unless I can provide for his daughter." Gently, he pried her hand off his arm. "This is my chance to do that *and* get you a little place — before Luvina forgets me."

"She won't forget," Annie said. Guilt flickered at the burden sharing her dream of a little house had placed on her brothers. She should have kept that to herself. She'd never meant it to weigh them down. "I don't expect you and Frank to do everything on your own. I got —" The words *a job and rooms* were drowned out by renewed shouting and hollering from the back lot.

Emmet stood up and put his hat back on. "You don't have to watch," he hollered. "It'll be over before you know it."

Emmet hurried back outside. Again, the horse screamed. The horrible sound sent a chill up Annie's spine. What if Frank or Emmet got hurt? *Or worse.* She couldn't bear to just sit here and wait. Nor could she bring herself to join the raucous crowd. If Emmet saw her, he'd probably order her back inside, anyway. She glanced up. *The loft.* No one would expect her to be up there. She'd be able to see into the back lot. She could watch in peace — or hide. At the moment she wasn't sure which it would be. At least she'd have a chance to collect herself before facing — whatever might happen.

Gathering her skirts, she scaled the ladder and made her way across to the open haymow door, ducking down behind a pile of fresh hay so the men below wouldn't see her. She could see a bit of what was going on if she peered over the top. Luther was in the corral helping three other men restrain the horse. Near the street, two men hoisted a makeshift litter and bore the injured man away.

When a boy she'd never seen before slid into the saddle, the animal screamed and lunged, but failed to break free. Annie ducked down, her heart pounding. When the crowd roared, she looked again. The hopeful rider signaled that he was ready and the men who'd been restraining the horse dove through the corral poles to safety. The creature reared. Coming down on all fours, it twisted and bucked. In seconds, the young rider went flying. He rolled beneath the bottom corral pole, barely ahead of the flashing hooves.

Frank was up next. *That horse is evil* Emmet had said. Annie gulped. She directed a *please* toward heaven just before Frank scaled the corral poles and settled into the saddle. The horse strained to be released.

Frank tugged at his hat to settle it firmly on his head. He shifted his weight in the saddle. The animal whinnied a protest. The second it was released, the creature reared up, pawing the air. Terrified, Annie ducked down, desperate for it to be over. Listening. Wishing she could pray better.

The second Frank slid into the saddle, he felt the horse collect himself, ready to explode with fury the moment the men holding him let go. Envisioning closing an iron vise about the horse's midsection with his legs, Frank gathered the reins to keep the animal in check. He nodded. The men let go and dove out of the way.

The shouts and sounds of the crowd faded. Frank was aware of nothing but the surging beast; its flying mane and flashing hooves; the tremendous power rippling beneath a gleaming black coat, all of it focused on freeing itself of the unwelcome weight on its back. When Outlaw arched his back and crow-hopped across the corral, Frank clenched his jaw and stayed put. The horse twisted and bounced, surged and fought. Every muscle in Frank's body screamed, every joint protested. He choked on dust, but still he hung on. Finally, after what felt like an eternity, a shot rang out, signaling the end of the longest three minutes of Frank's life. He flung himself out of the saddle, keenly aware of Outlaw charging to the far side of the corral. Taking a hasty bow, Frank trotted to safety. Men pounded him on the back. Congratulations rang out.

The redheaded kid who'd helped haul the injured rider away grabbed his hand and pumped it. "That was something! Best ride yet!"

This was better than winning a race for old man Hillsdale. Today, no one else would try to take the credit.

Annie hadn't wanted to watch, but in the end she hadn't been able to resist. She nearly cried with relief when Frank ducked out of the corral. Safe. Whole. The joy lasted only seconds, though, for Emmet would ride next — and Emmet wasn't quite as good as Frank. When he mounted, she closed her eyes. *Please don't let him get hurt. He talks to you all the time. Just — please.* She heard rather than saw what happened next. A loud crack, a collective *oh,* a thud, and horrible silence. With her hand clamped over her mouth to keep the scream in, she peered over the hay and down into the back lot. Emmet lay in the dust just outside the corral. Still.

Her heart in her throat, Annie spun about and charged toward the ladder, but before she reached it, a collective cry went up from the crowd. "He's okay!" She hurried back to the haymow door to see what was happening below. Frank was helping Emmet up. Talking. Nodding. Slapping him on the back.

"He wants to go again," Frank called out.

Anger replaced fear and dread. *Go again? Had they both lost their minds?* The crowd was silent for a moment, and then a tall man wearing a knee-length black coat and a broad-brimmed hat stepped forward. Emmet strode to where the stranger was standing and argued his case. He must have argued well. The man raised one hand and drew a circle in the air, as if preparing to throw a lasso. The crowd cheered. Luther Mufsy and the others took the black horse in hand.

Annie hunkered down again. Hiding. Closing her eyes, she waited, alternating between inwardly cursing the gol-durned horse and swearing at her dad-gummed brothers. And then she begged God to please forgive her bad thoughts and to keep Emmet from breaking his fool neck. *I'm not good at the words, but you know what I want. What we need. Please.*

It seemed to take an eternity, but when cheers finally rang out and Annie dared to look down, Emmet was — miraculously — safe. The black horse stood in the middle of the corral, head down. Four men moved in to subdue him, but the animal seemed done in. When he submitted to the removal of saddle and bridle without protest, someone shouted that the Paxton brothers had broken Outlaw. "Three cheers for the Paxtons! Three cheers for the Pony Express!"

Annie stayed seated, trembling with fear. The black-and-white cat emerged from a corner of the loft and minced toward her. Inviting itself to curl up in her lap, it began to purr as Annie stroked the soft fur absent-mindedly. It seemed a long time since she'd traipsed into St. Joseph with such a clear vision of what lay ahead. It hurt to face the stark truth that both her brothers had abandoned their plan — at the first opportunity. Without so much as talking to her about it. Without considering her feelings. *Without including her.* Apparently, neither Emmet nor Frank shared her vision of the future, after all.

CHAPTER 4

The crowd in the back lot had dispersed and Annie had calmed down before one of her brothers came looking for her. *You've always known they'd go their own way at some point. It's just happening sooner than you expected.* There was always a ray of light if a body looked hard enough. She would find it — although it might take a while. In the meantime she wasn't going to pretend to be happy about the way things were turning out.

At the first sound of someone climbing the ladder, the cat bolted. Annie sat with her hands folded in her lap. Waiting. The top of a head appeared. *Auburn hair.* Of course. Frank would be the one to talk to her first. Being twins, she and Frank had always been closer to one another than to Emmet. But that wasn't going to matter today. If Frank expected her to make this easy, he was going to be disappointed.

Instead of sitting down beside her, Frank leaned against the haymow doorframe, staring down into the back lot for a while. Saying nothing. Annie curled her arms about her knees and tucked her chin. Waiting. Staring off toward the opposite end of the loft.

Finally, Frank took a deep breath and said quietly, "Two hundred dollars a month, Annie. With both Emmet and me riding for the Pony, we'll be able to give you the home you want."

She didn't look at him. "Unless you break your neck on some midnight run aboard a half-wild horse. Or get shot by road agents. Or run over by stampeding buffalo. Or scalped by Indians."

Frank snorted. "We both just rode the worst they had to offer, and we broke him. Outlaw's no threat to anyone anymore. Shoot, I might even ask the Pony to let me ride him on my part of the trail. One thing that horse has is grit."

Annie shrugged. She could feel him looking at her, but she refused to look back.

"As to road agents, the Pony only carries mail — no money. There's nothing valuable to rob. And there's no Indians scalping people where we're going."

Where we're going. Not "where we might

66

go." *Where we're going.* That made her look at him. Frowning. "You've already agreed to it?"

He came to sit beside her. "The station's called Clearwater. Luther told us all about it. It started out as a trading post. Now it's also a regular stop for the Overland Stage. It sounds like a good place. Better than our old farm, for sure. Almost a village, spring through fall. There's a store inside the station, a big barn, and several corrals. *Two* wells with cold, clear water. Emmet and I will both ride out of there. I'll ride west and Emmet will bring the California mail back this way. A hundred miles each way and then back again, with Clearwater as home. Luther says there isn't any serious Indian trouble to worry about. It's less than a dozen miles to Fort Kearny, and they send out daily patrols." He paused, obviously waiting for Annie to say something.

All she could manage was, "It's not what we talked about."

Frank reached over to chuck her under the chin. "But it could be *better.*"

She shrugged. "I got the job at the Patee House. And rooms at Miss Stanton's. Ira — he said I should call him Ira — put in a good word for us."

"He told us. You did good, Annie. Real

good. But — Emmet says this is better. The answer to his prayers. I think he's right."

"When have you ever cared about Emmet's prayers?" She regretted the bitter tone, but she didn't apologize for it.

Frank nudged her shoulder. "Just because I don't talk to God doesn't mean I don't think he'd listen to a good man like Emmet and help him out." When Annie remained quiet, he said, "There's more to it than just making money. We'll be making *history.* Think of it, Annie. The president in Washington City telegraphs a letter, and ten days after it leaves St. Jo., the governor of California is reading it. Ten *days.* Not weeks. *Days.*" He paused. "Only about eighty men in the history of the world will ever be able to say they were good enough to be part of that first ride. Imagine it, Annie — carrying a letter written by the president's own hand. Emmet and I will be telling our grandchildren about it when we're old."

Grandchildren. It was the first time Frank had ever come close to talking about getting married and having children. She couldn't remember the last time she'd seen Frank this excited about anything.

He ducked his head and looked her in the eye. "We're supposed to report to the Pony office at that fancy hotel in a little while —

Emmet, Jake, and me. To take the rider's oath." Again, he nudged her shoulder. "You'll come and witness it — right?"

They're going. No matter what I say. It's done. Annie's throat constricted. Frank reached for her hand and gave it a squeeze. "Please. We came to St. Jo. for a fresh start. This is it. We'll earn enough money to get a little house here in town. Emmet will be able to get married. He'll have a hope of putting a down payment on some good land." He arched one eyebrow and adjusted the kerchief knotted about his neck as if it were a fancy cravat. "I'll be famous. Everybody wins." He winked at her.

Annie had never been able to stay angry with Frank for long. He was just too . . . charming. "It's a lot to take in. Especially when we didn't so much as talk about it before you both took the job." She cleared her throat to keep her voice from wavering. "I thought we'd stay together. Not always, of course, but — at least for a little while. I didn't think you'd both go off on your own all at once. So soon."

Frank frowned. "Wait a minute — you thought — you think Emmet and me — that we were leaving you here in St. Jo.? Alone?" Palms up, he waggled both hands back and forth. "No, no. That is *not* gonna happen.

69

Clearwater's more than just a stage stop. Like I said, it's a trading post. A blacksmith and a crew work the place, spring through fall. The station keeper needs a cook. We got you the job — and you'll stay as long as we ride for the Pony Express."

Speechless, Annie just stared at him.

Frank leaned close and nudged her shoulder. "You didn't think you'd get rid of us that easy, did you? You're going with us."

She twisted about so she could face him. "You got me a job. Cooking. At a place that's hundreds of miles from St. Jo. Without talking to me?"

The furrow between his brows deepened. "You were upset when you thought we were leaving without you. Now you're upset because we aren't?" He reached for both her hands and gave them a little shake. "It's only for a couple of years — at the most. We'll save our money, and when we all come back to St. Jo. — *together* — we won't need any sour-faced landlady's charity. Luvina's pa won't be able to stand in Emmet's way. We'll get you a little house and I'll paint the trim. By the way, is it still blue?" The black-and-white cat came into view. It sat, looking first at Annie and then at Frank. "New friend?" he asked. Letting go of her hands, he picked up a long piece of straw, and

70

enticed the animal to play.

At the sound of a distant steam whistle, Annie looked across the tops of the buildings toward the river just in time to see a puff of steam dissipate. Beyond the river, the rolling landscape was just beginning to turn green. With a sigh, she asked, "You said two years at most?"

"At most."

"And then we're coming back to St. Jo."

"Isn't that what I just said? '. . . when we all come back to St. Jo. *together.*' "

Slowly, Annie stood up. As she headed for the ladder, she called over her shoulder. "Yes. Blue trim. But before you paint the trim, I want those window boxes so I can plant flowers."

Annie had barely stepped off the last rung of the ladder when Emmet joined them, clearly bent on doing his part to prove that working for the Pony Express was a wonderful opportunity. "We'll use Pa's cash box. When the paymaster comes through, Frank and I will hand every penny over to you. You can keep the key on that ribbon around your neck." He looked over at Frank. "Did you tell her how much she's earning?" Frank shook his head, and Emmet said, "Twenty dollars a month. Between the three of us, in just two years we could have almost *five thousand dollars."*

Annie tried to envision someone handing her a twenty-dollar gold piece at the end of every month. She'd never had that much money in her life. And *thousands* of dollars? It was too much to take in.

"There's more," Frank said. "All the Pony Express riders stay and eat at the Patee House. And since you'll be working at Clearwater, so will you. Starting today and going until we leave."

"When's that?"

"Not for a few days at least. We're going out with Luther's outfit, and he has to wait for supplies to arrive from downriver. There's a dance in the ballroom tonight. Think you can remember how to waltz?"

What could a girl say to all of that? It was only for a couple of years. And the money. She'd seen the Pony Express flyer with her own eyes or she wouldn't have believed it. It wasn't as if Frank and Emmet had tricked her into swallowing a tadpole. Or tasting the frost on the pump handle. And when it came right down to it, she couldn't imagine life without her dad-blasted brothers.

"I, Franklin Emory Paxton, do hereby swear, before the Great and Living God,

72

that during my engagement, and while an employee of Russell, Majors, and Waddell, I will, under no circumstances, use profane language, that I will drink no intoxicating liquors, that I will not quarrel or fight with any other employee of the firm, and that in every respect I will conduct myself honestly, be faithful to my duties, and so direct my acts as to win the confidence of my employers, so help me God."

Even as he said them, the words gave Frank pause. First because he'd never taken an oath before and the solemnity of the moment carried weight. Second because it was obvious that the owners of the freighting company organizing the Pony Express — Russell, Majors, and Waddell — were darned serious about what they expected of the men who worked for them. Not that Frank intended to be anything but a trustworthy employee. Promising not to use profane language was all right — especially for Annie's sake. Not fighting with other employees only made sense. In-fighting among the jockeys during that short season he'd worked for Hiram Hillsdale had dragged everything down. The promise not to drink was problematic, though. After all, even educated men like doctors knew that whiskey had its benefits. Still, they were paying him $100 a month. He supposed they could make the rules.

After the oath, Superintendent Lewis shook each man's hand and presented him with a leather-bound Bible printed especially for the riders. Emmet expressed heartfelt thanks for his. Frank wondered how many would get "lost" as soon as the riders left town. Still, when he walked out of that office a Pony Express rider, Frank felt just a little taller.

Frank and Emmet returned to the livery to retrieve the three trunks stowed there, leaving Annie to sign them all in at the hotel desk. As if there was nothing to it. As if she was used to sashaying into a fancy hotel and signing the register as a matter of course. When an elegantly clad woman followed an equally well-dressed gentleman into the hotel and headed for the registration desk, Annie skittered toward a seating area in a far corner of the lobby, watching as the couple spoke with the clerk behind the desk.

Perhaps it was the way the clerk fussed with his silver-framed spectacles, but something about him reminded Annie of Mr. Hillsdale, who always seemed to look down his nose at the rest of the world. The clerk wore a crisp white shirt and a black cravat held in place by what appeared to be a diamond stickpin. Of course it probably wasn't a real diamond. Still, Annie was painfully aware of both her faded blue calico and her worn-out boots.

"Is there some difficulty, Miss Paxton?"

Mr. Lewis, the man who had hired them, stepped up. Careful to pull her feet back — darn her worn boots, anyway — Annie stuttered a reply. "Oh, no. N-not at all. I just — Frank and Emmet went after our things. They left me to sign the ledger. But then those other guests arrived and I thought I'd wait a moment. There's no rush."

Mr. Lewis's brows knit together for a fleeting second. He looked from Annie to the couple retreating up the sweeping staircase just beyond the front desk. After a brief hesitation, he looked back down at her, his frown replaced by a kind smile. He offered his arm. "Allow me to introduce you to Pierce. You'll find that behind that imposing exterior there's a softhearted grandfather."

When Mr. Lewis introduced Annie, Mr. Pierce smiled and tapped the ledger book. "It's an honor to serve the Pony Express," he said. "We're making history together."

"I assured Miss Paxton that you'd take good care of her," Mr. Lewis said. "She'll need two rooms. One for herself and one for her brothers." Wishing Annie a good evening, Mr. Lewis returned to the Pony Express office.

Mr. Pierce reached behind him and withdrew a key from a niche. He pointed out the dining room. "Dinner is served beginning at six o'clock p.m., although I believe most of the riders take it a little later." He winked. "They like to make a grand entrance."

Annie signed the ledger with a trembling hand, painfully aware of the fine script on the line just above hers. When Mr. Pierce asked if she'd like someone to escort her to her room, she said no thank you. "If that's all right." She didn't want an escort. She wanted to gawk at every detail of the splendid building. Then again, maybe they didn't allow just anyone to wander the halls.

Mr. Pierce said that of course it was all right and gave her a few directions. The stairs leading away from the lobby only accessed the first floor. "Once up there, you'll turn right. Midway down that hall, there's a winding staircase that will take you on up. Another right at the top of those stairs and you'll find Room 210. I'll send a chambermaid to check in with you before too long. If you need anything — anything at all — you let Molly know. She'll see to it."

Annie nodded, even though she could not imagine ordering a maid around. She paused at the top of the first flight of stairs and looked back down at the carpeted lobby, which gleamed from the light of two massive chandeliers. It was the finest, most beautiful room she'd ever seen. Behind her, the first floor hall opened onto a wide balcony looking down on an inner courtyard. At the center of the courtyard, flowers encircled a marble fountain with a rainbow of color. To the left and the right, two wings of rooms opened directly onto the balcony.

Behind Annie, a hallway running the length of the building and parallel to the street led to more rooms, but at the far end, large double doors inset with rows of small square windows beckoned. Curious, Annie went to those doors and peered in. *The ballroom.* Polished wood floors and more crystal chandeliers made Annie wish she had a gown worthy of Mama's lace mitts. She'd kept Mama's green silk gown, but parts of it were so delicate she feared it might fall apart if she so much as lifted the gown from the depths of the trunk. Had Ma and Pa once waltzed in a ballroom like this?

Laughter sounded from the courtyard below. Annie hurried away from the ballroom doors, toward the opposite side of the building, and up the winding stairs to the second floor. Once there, she passed a maid dressed all in black save for a starched white apron and cap. The girl didn't make eye contact. Instead, she turned aside to let Annie pass, offering a little curtsy and a *Good day, Miss* as Annie walked by.

Annie held up her key. "Would you mind pointing me to 210?"

"At the other end of the hall, Miss. I'll be happy to guide you."

When they reached the door, the girl held out her hand for the key. Annie handed it over, and the girl slipped it in the lock, opened the door just a fraction, and then stepped back as she returned the key. "Will there be anything else, Miss?"

"No, I — thank you." Another little curtsy, and the girl headed off up the hall.

Annie watched her go, wondering if someone gave the maids in a fancy hotel lessons in how to float. She'd never seen anyone move with such grace. Slowly, she pushed the door open and peered into the room. Gasping with surprise, she stepped inside, closed the door behind her, and leaned against it.

CHAPTER 5

The headboard on the massive bed positioned in the center of the wall to the left looked to be at least seven feet high. A matching marble-topped dresser and washstand graced another wall. The drapes at the two soaring windows matched the upholstery on two side chairs in the far corner. Those chairs flanked an oval table atop which sat a spectacular lamp with a painted shade. A room-size carpet covered all but the edges of the polished floor.

Annie crossed to the bed and ran her hand over the satin spread. When she pulled it back, the faint aroma of lemon wafted into the air from pristine white sheets and pillow covers. Picking up one of the pillows, she hugged it to herself as she perched on the edge of the bed. She thought about all the other people occupying other fine rooms like this one. People accustomed to luxury. It made her feel uncertain about dining here at the hotel dressed in faded blue calico. As for attending a ball . . . no. She wouldn't dare.

She started when someone knocked on the door in the corner — the door separating her room from her neighbor's. Relief coursed through her when Frank called out, "Delivery for Miss Paxton. Miss Ann E. Paxton." Annie hurried to open the door, and Frank and Emmet shuffled her trunk into the room and set it down.

Frank threw his arm across Emmet's shoulders and pointed to their identical red plaid shirts and denim pants. "Outfits provided by the Pony Express. What d'ya think?"

Annie smiled her approval. "Very handsome."

"I'd say so." Frank grinned. "We're all invited to the dance in the ballroom." He pointed to her trunk. "You should put on that green silk thing that was Ma's. Bet it fits just about right."

He couldn't be serious. "It's forty years out of style and so brittle in places it'd probably shatter in my hands." She knew what they were thinking. If it couldn't be worn, why was she keeping it? She didn't know why. Except that it was Ma's. Thankfully, they didn't ask. She forced a smile. "You both look dashing. I'll be content to lounge right here in the seat of luxury."

Frank looked her up and down and then tugged on a curl at the nape of her neck. "What you've got on isn't too bad. Maybe reconstitute your hair, though. Isn't that the word you used yesterday over at the livery?" He reached up and extracted a piece of hay. "Nothing a good brushing won't fix."

Horrified, Annie snatched it out of his hand. "I can't believe you two let me sashay through the lobby of the Patee House looking like I'd just come in from a barn."

Frank shrugged. "We *did* just come in from a barn. But we work for the Pony Express now, and we're the envy of just about everyone in St. Jo."

"You can decide about the ball later," Emmet said. "Right now, we're supposed to meet Jake Finney and the others in the lobby. Apparently the riders all parade into the dining room together."

She might not go to the ball, Annie decided, but she couldn't miss supper. She was too hungry. "Just give me a minute to 'reconstitute,' " she said and shoved them both toward the door, closing it behind them.

Slipping out of her blue calico, she washed up, all the while wishing she had an ensemble worthy of the hotel. She lifted her only other outfit out of the trunk. It, too, was calico, with small bouquets of bright pink and blue flowers scattered across a deep plum background. Not quite as faded as the blue, which had been her favorite for a long time.

She wove a bit of blue ribbon through her hair and then stared at herself in the mirror for a moment. A lace collar and cuffs would be a great improvement. Ah, well. Finally, she removed her boots, peeled off her red stockings, and pulled on the nicer ivory pair. Next, she retrieved Ma's old slippers from atop the silk gown. She didn't know if she'd have the courage to so much as step into the ballroom, but if she did, she wasn't about to clomp about with her feet clad in worn-out boots.

In spite of his reluctance to leave the dream world, Frank awoke. Opening his eyes, he lifted his head and peered into the darkness until finally, moonlight confirmed it. He and Emmet really were here at the Patee House. He closed his eyes, smiling at the memory of men cheering. Remembering how happy Annie had been as he waltzed her around and around a vast ballroom. The future really did look promising. With a low grunt of satisfaction, he stretched and yawned.

"What time is it?" Emmet muttered.

"Time for chores." He gave a low laugh. "Oh . . . wait. We don't have any today." With one hand, he reached over and gave Emmet a friendly nudge. "Time for bacon and eggs and ham and grits. All we can eat, courtesy of the Pony Express. Just the thought makes me hungry."

Emmet didn't move. "How can you possibly be hungry? We both ate as much last night as we usually get in a week."

"And I'm going to eat as much again today." Frank threw back the covers. "No 'making do,' no doing without. Ever again." He pulled his jeans on. "I'm going down to the livery to spend some time with Outlaw before breakfast. I'll catch up with you and Annie later."

"Outlaw? Why?"

Frank answered while pulling on his boots. "He lost his job because of you and me. But he's still not really broke, which makes him worth exactly nothing. No livery owner is going to keep a horse that can't be ridden. If I can gentle Outlaw so he's worth something, Ira might be grateful enough to agree to turn Bill and Bart out to pasture instead of — well, what we both know will probably happen to them."

"You going soft in your old age?"

Frank could hear the smile in his brother's voice. "Always have been soft when it comes to Annie, and she cares about those mules."

Emmet grunted. "Not that you aren't good with horses, but we aren't going to be in town long enough for you to turn Outlaw into a Sunday-go-to-meeting horse."

Frank shrugged into his shirt. "Then maybe I can turn him into a hell-bent-for-leather trail horse."

Emmet opened his eyes. "The truth comes out. You're hoping to ride the outlaw west." He lit the lamp on the table next to the bed and reached for the Bible he'd left out the previous night. "More power to ya. Think I'll read a bit. Maybe write Luvina. Then I'll rouse Annie and we'll walk down together. It's time to decide once and for all about the rig — and the mules. Maybe you could talk to Ira about your idea?"

"I will. See you later." Frank left the hotel alone. The streets were quiet, and instead of going straight to the livery, he decided this would be a good time to meander a bit. He spent most of his time on a street lined with shops selling everything from imported porcelain to top hats, finally locating what he wanted in a corner shop not far from Ira's livery.

Finally, Frank walked to the barn and put a halter on Outlaw. He led him out to the smaller corral in Ira's back lot, talking in low tones while he slid his hands down the horse's muscled neck, across his back, and down his haunches, and so on.

Sunlight had just begun to spill into the town when Emmet arrived — alone.

"No Annie?"

"I knocked on her door, but she didn't want to get up yet. Said she'd meet us in the lobby in a little while. We can have breakfast together."

"Good," Frank said, "because I haven't talked to Ira yet." He patted Outlaw's neck. "I wanted to see how things would go first."

Emmet nodded at the horse. "That hardly looks like the same animal. What happened to the hellfire and brimstone?"

Frank tugged on the horse's long black mane. "I reckon it'll show up the minute I try to ride him."

"You haven't tried yet?"

Frank shook his head. "Thought I'd try to convince him to trust me first. If I can do that, riding him will be easy."

Easy. Emmet shook his head. "You and your ideas."

"Speaking of ideas, I've got one that involves Annie." Frank grinned. "You'll like it."

Annie and her brothers lived in unimaginable luxury at the Patee House for nearly two weeks. They attended half a dozen balls, where Frank reveled in the attention afforded the Pony Express riders and Annie. Although she never quite felt like she fit in, she enjoyed being squired about the dance floor by a succession of gentlemen, both young and old.

Jake Finney — who claimed to be eighteen but who Annie suspected was probably three years younger — seemed to enjoy spending time with her, and together they often walked the city.

As the western terminus for many railroads, St. Jo. was a stopping place for thousands of immigrants headed west. The streets nearest the river were especially crowded, the levee lined with covered wagons and freighting outfits waiting to take steam-powered ferries across the river. Annie loved staring into shop windows, and she loved watching people. It seemed to her that half the world must be going west. As she and Jake talked, she learned that he'd walked to St. Jo. from somewhere in Kansas, spending his last few coins on the ferry across the Missouri. His willingness to speak of his past ended there.

Finally, one morning, the word that they would be departing came just as they were finishing breakfast. A courier came to the table with a message for "Mr. Emmet or Mr. Frank Paxton." Emmet read it quickly and summarized the contents. "The last of the freight's here. Luther wants us to take our trunks down to the livery this morning. We leave tomorrow."

"Yee-hah," Jake said quietly, his face beaming with joy.

Feeling like a stone had plummeted to the pit of her stomach, Annie folded her napkin and laid it beside her plate of half-eaten flapjacks. She wouldn't be able to swallow another bite. Excusing herself to pack, she left the men at the table and went up to her room. For a moment she stood by the window looking down on the street, trying to pray. *I don't want to go. I have to go. Help.* Taking a deep breath, she pressed against her midsection, willing the horrible tightness away. *Don't think. Just do the next thing. Make your bedroll.*

Opening her trunk, she took a last look at the treasures within: Ma's looking glass. The fragile silk gown. The remnants of the dancing slippers she'd worn out in the Patee House ballroom. The summer-weight unmentionables. The next time she'd open the trunk, she would be at Clearwater. *In the wilderness.* The knot in her stomach worsened.

She pulled the thin quilt she would use for a bedroll out of the trunk. Holding it against herself for a moment, she swept her palm over the surface, smiling at the haphazard arrangement of fabrics in dozens of colors and patterns. The variety reminded her of flowers blooming in a field, each one distinct and yet, when seen from a distance, blending into a beautiful whole.

A memory surfaced. Ma sitting in a rocking chair, stitching. When it threatened to fade, Annie held onto it. The blurred edges filled in a bit. A rocking chair *by the fireplace.* Ma humming. A different bit of patchwork, this one far more organized than the one in Annie's hands. Vibrant colors — orange and red and green against dark blue. What had happened to it?

Annie raised the quilt to her cheek and closed her eyes. A few deep breaths, and the knot in her stomach relaxed a bit. Perhaps breakfast would stay down after all. When she spread the faded quilt atop the elegant bed, she kept the patchwork side facing up. Only the blue striped backing fabric showed once she'd finished folding, rolling, and securing the resulting bedroll with rope.

She had just tucked her comb into her pocket and was about to lock her trunk when Emmet slipped into the room with a black metal box in hand. "You probably don't remember this, but Pa kept it beneath one of the floorboards in his room. You'll be the family banker for the next couple of years." He handed her the key, and she strung it onto the ribbon around her neck.

After Frank and Emmet left to transport their trunks and bedrolls to the livery, Annie took a last walk in the hotel courtyard to admire the blooming flowers. She sat on one of the marble benches and listened to the fountain. Finally, she climbed the stairs to the second floor and gazed into the ballroom, remembering the beautiful music she'd heard while dancing there. *You'll hear beautiful music again. This isn't the end. It's part of your new beginning.*

The next morning, Annie reveled in the luxury of lemon-scented sheets one last time until, finally, Frank called through the door. "Are Emmet and me gonna have to come in there and drag you out of bed?"

With a sigh, she threw back the covers. "I'll meet you downstairs in five minutes." One last turn of the magical water spigot. One last use of the dainty linen facecloth with the embroidered hotel monogram. One last morning peering out the window at the street below and pretending to be a princess.

She braided her thick hair, leaving the braid to trail down her back. Simple was best for what lay ahead. With a final look around the room, she grabbed the broad-brimmed hat she'd always worn on the farm — Pa had said it was a dragoon's cast-off — pulled the door closed behind her, and went downstairs. She'd just handed her room key to Mr. Pierce and bade him good-bye when Frank stepped up, looking annoyed.

"There you are. Finally."

Annie looked past him. "What are you upset about? I beat Emmet and Jake down."

"No, you didn't. They went on ahead." He nodded at Mr. Pierce, who turned around, took a box off a shelf behind him, and set it on the counter. Frank slid it toward Annie. "Emmet said I should do the honors. It was my idea, but it's from both of us."

The Paxtons were not a gift-giving family. Annie stared at the box. "What is it?"

"Open it."

Setting her hat on the counter, Annie untied the string and lifted the lid. Boots. *New* boots.

"Well now," Mr. Pierce said quietly. "That's as fine a pair of boots as I ever saw." He smiled at Annie. "You wear them in good health, Miss Paxton. And don't forget your friends at the Patee House."

"We didn't know what color," Frank said. "I personally thought red was the way to go, but you know Emmet. Always so conservative."

"They're perfect," Annie croaked. She'd never had a pair of new boots in her life. Every spring, Pa took a piece of paper and a pencil and drew around her foot. He carried the paper to town, usually managing to return with the right size, but always with a pair so worn Annie suspected he'd dug them out of the cobbler's patch pile. She quickly donned the boots and did a little two-step to show her delight before asking the inevitable question. How had they managed it? They had no money.

"We have money," Frank said. "A little. Ira bought Bill and Bart. And the rig."

"But he didn't want them."

"When Emmet and I told him what we'd do with the money, he changed his mind."

CHAPTER 6

Expecting to be assigned a nag ready to be turned out to pasture, Annie was thrilled when Ira led a paint mare out of the livery and said, "This is Shadow. She's as kind as she is pretty. The perfect lady to carry you west." He hitched the mare to a corral post as he talked. "You step on up and introduce yourself while I fetch the saddle and bridle." He hesitated. "Your brothers said not to bother with a side saddle. That right?"

Annie nodded.

Ira went back into the livery and Annie stepped up to the mare. Her head, neck, and chest were black, save for a wide white strip down her face. A hank of white at the base of the otherwise-black mane accented white withers. Her legs and tail were white, her powerful haunches splashed with more black. When Annie murmured, "You're a beauty," the mare lowered her head and nuzzled Annie's hand.

Ira returned and set a beat-up saddle and a striped blanket on the ground. Annie said, "I didn't expect anything this well broke."

"Just because she's not half-wild doesn't mean you should drop your guard," Ira warned. "She loves to run." He nodded toward the corral behind them. "If you've got things covered here, I'll help the boys. We've got to get those ponies sorted into three strings. Three ponies each for your brothers and Jake to lead west."

Annie said that was fine and in a few moments she had Shadow saddled and the stirrups adjusted. Leading the mare to the mounting block, she slid into the saddle and quickly tucked her skirt about her legs. She sat for a moment, patting the mare's neck and talking to her. It wasn't until she'd reined about to watch the boys working that she really paid attention to the three horses that had already been saddled. A bay, a buckskin, and — *Outlaw*? It looked like Outlaw, but this horse was waiting quietly instead of spitting fire.

Annie nudged Shadow closer to the corral where the men were working, taking care to leave a wide berth between herself and the black horse. When Frank looked her way, she nodded at Outlaw and called out, "You really think that's a good idea?"

"Nope," he called back. "I think it's a *great* idea." As if to prove his point, he strode up to the black horse and patted its neck.

Emmet spoke up. "I had doubts, too, but Frank's put a lot of time into that horse in the past couple of weeks. The two of them get along all right."

This was no time to cause trouble. Annie reached down and patted Shadow's neck again, then turned her attention to the action inside the corral. With Ira's help, each man singled out the lead pony for each string. Once that horse was haltered and hitched to a corral pole, the second in the string was caught and brought up. Next came an ingenious use of rope and tail. Each rider ran his hand along the back of his lead horse, across the haunches, and down the tail, stopping at the end of the tailbone. That located, they folded the tip of the tail over the lead rope attached to the second pony's halter. A few wraps about the tail, a half hitch, and the second horse was tied to the first's tail. The knots were secure, and yet they could be released with a quick yank on the right loop. After the final horse in each string was tied to the second in the same manner, Frank, Emmet, and Jake led their respective strings of three ponies out of the corral, mounted up, hitched the lead rope about the horn of their saddle, and were ready to go.

Frank sidled up to Annie and Shadow. "Outlaw's taken a shine to your horse. If you don't mind, we'll ride together."

"I don't mind — but I don't trust that black devil, either."

Ira stepped up and put a hand on Shadow's neck as he looked up at Annie. "Soon as you're back in St. Jo., Fern will put in a good word for you at the Patee House. If you still want it, that is."

"I will," Annie said. "Please thank her for me. Tell her not to forget me."

"That's not likely to happen."

"And thank you for your part in these." She took one foot out of the stirrup and wiggled her new boot.

"Glad to do it. Those mules have perked up a bit since they had a chance to rest." He smiled up at her. "If you was of a mind to brighten an old man's day now and again, I wouldn't mind hearing how you're getting on."

Annie promised to write. Bidding Ira good-bye, Frank nudged Outlaw forward. Annie followed his lead. As she reined Shadow to turn west at the corner, she took one last look back up the hill toward the Patee House.

Frank noticed. His voice was gentle as he said, "We'll be back before you know it. Blue trim and window boxes. Fruit trees and a blackberry bramble. And lots of flowers. I promise."

Annie nodded. She reached up to touch the place where two keys hung on a velvet ribbon. One key to preserve her past. The other to guard the future. *Two good things.*

When the steam-powered ferry transporting the Pony Express train across the Missouri had banged and whistled its way to the middle of the muddy river, Annie turned her back on St. Jo. and faced the opposite side, all the while murmuring comfort to Shadow. She wasn't sure whom the constant stream of conversation helped more, herself or the horse.

Shadow followed her off the ferry and onto dry land willingly, whickering and touching noses with Outlaw the minute the two were reunited. Frank helped Annie back into the saddle and mounted up himself. Luther would ride the taller of a pair of gray roans named Big Boy and Andy. The horses were the designated "wheelers," meaning they were positioned nearest the fully loaded freight wagon. Four mules would provide the power needed to haul the massive freight wagon along the trail.

As the sun burned away the last remnants of the early morning fog lingering in the dips and valleys, the Pony Express train wound its way through several miles of bottomland thick with trees, many of them festooned with the dried remnants of last season's wild vines and creepers. Annie and Shadow loped alongside Frank and Outlaw, with Emmet and Jake and their respective strings of ponies moving more slowly alongside the freight wagon. Several lighter immigrant wagons, each one pulled by only two teams of oxen, had made the river crossing just behind them. When Annie glanced back and saw the string of white wagon covers gleaming in the morning sun, she felt reassured.

Luther noticed the backward glance. "You already thinking about making a run for it?"

"Nope." Annie nodded toward the wagons. "I didn't realize we'd have company."

Luther looked behind them. "They won't keep up. But we still won't be alone. We'll catch up to another train before long, and if we pass them, there'll be another. You'll see."

By noon, they'd outstripped the wagon train behind them. In keeping with Luther's prediction, it wasn't long before more covered wagons appeared in the distance. He called Annie's attention to them. "Looks like sailboats gliding over a sea of grass, don't it?"

"You've seen the ocean?"

Luther winked. "Yes, Ma'am, I have. Seen it and sailed on it for a while. Grew up on a little finger of land that sticks out into a lake so big some folks thought it was another ocean when they first saw it. Of course it ain't nothin' compared to the Atlantic."

"And you came here," Annie said. "To this." She motioned toward the empty horizon.

"Yes, Ma'am, I did. Got sick and tired of fish and salty air. Decided to get as far away from it as I could. One day I tossed some things in a sack and started walking west. And here I am. Smack-dab in the middle of the continent, master of my own wheeled schooner, and happy as a big sunflower."

Annie looked toward the horizon. She couldn't imagine trading blue water and sailboats for a treeless, barren plain.

"Bet I know what you're thinking," Luther said. "You're looking out yonder" — he swept his hand across the expanse of blue sky — "and all you're seein' is what ain't there. Am I right?" When Annie didn't reply, he nodded. "I'm right. I've heard plenty of ladies camped on the trail, walking the trail, calling this a 'barren wasteland.' " He clucked to Big Boy, and the horse picked up the pace a bit. "Well it ain't barren at all. You give Mother Nature a few days with her paintbrush, and she'll give you more flowers than you can imagine. Grass as tall as a horse. Green so green and blue so blue you'll think you never saw those colors before. A little spring rain and everything will change, practically overnight. You'll see." He nodded toward a cloud hovering above the distant horizon. "In fact, from the looks of things, Mother Nature might just put a few swipes of color on her prairie canvas before the day's out."

Annie doubted that one little cloud would amount to rain, but she held her peace. Not long after they first spotted the cloud, a heavy layer of gray collected along the bottom edge. Luther called for everyone to don rain slickers. "There's a draw not too far ahead. If we make it before the rain hits, we'll hunker down until the storm's past."

Storm. Again, Annie wondered at the man's caution, but after the brief stop, the blue sky began to change color, fading first to a pale gray and then taking on the gray-green tones that had always made Pa send her to the fruit cellar. Out here in the open there was nowhere to go. Shadow began to dance a bit, tossing her head and snorting. Wagons up ahead pulled off the trail and circled. When sunlight streamed through a break in the clouds and reflected off a circle of canvas covers, Annie thought it looked like an immense halo hovering just above the surface of the dormant prairie.

Luther kept them moving. As they passed the circled wagons, Annie caught sight of two women peering out through the rear opening in the wagon cover. Both waved. Annie waved back. *What would it be like to travel the trail with another woman?* She hadn't said anything about it to Frank or Emmet, but one of the reasons she longed to settle in a city was an unvoiced longing for a friend. She'd planned to attend church regularly — maybe even join the choir. Eventually, she would meet another woman she could confide in. They would attend sewing bees and circle meetings together, trade recipes and gossip. She would never have to be lonely again.

Frank jolted her back to the moment, riding up and ordering her to "stay close to the freight wagon." The place where the sun had broken through had closed up. The clouds seemed lower — heavier, somehow. And angrier. Frank said that he and Emmet and Jake were going to ride away from her a bit. "We don't want you getting tangled up if the ponies try to bolt." Annie nodded, and Frank called to Luther. "How far to that draw you said we could shelter in?"

The wind had picked up. Luther had to raise his voice so Frank could hear the answer. "Not far, but it don't look like we'll make it before the storm hits." He glanced over at Annie. "Frank's right. You stick with me. My critters don't like storms, but they've been through plenty of 'em. They'll stay steady."

Shadow resisted staying behind while Outlaw moved away, but Annie held her back, doing her best to remain calm while Frank, Emmet, and Jake urged their horses to a lope. At the first sound of distant thunder, Shadow skittered sideways. Luther called out a warning. "Tighten up on those reins, now. Don't let her get away from you."

With the next crack of thunder, Shadow whinnied and reared. A blast of cold air nearly swept Annie's hat off her head. She reached up to grab it just as lightning flashed. The gesture gave Shadow a chance to take the bit. With the next crack of thunder, she bolted, and the clouds opened. Blinded by the downpour, all Annie could do was hunker down and hang on.

Frank and the others were little more than blurs as Shadow streaked past. Finally, the mare charged up a rise, and then the earth fell away. They were in the air, below them the rocky approach to a fast-running creek. Somehow, Shadow kept her footing when she landed. After only two steps, she lurched right to avoid the rushing water. Annie went flying into the creek. Soaked nearly to her waist with icy water, she fought to keep from being dragged under as Shadow disappeared into the distance.

The instant Shadow streaked past, Frank freed his string of ponies and spurred Outlaw into the storm, after Annie and the runaway paint. Through the pouring rain, he caught a glimpse of Shadow's white rump just before it fell out of sight. His stomach lurched. *The draw.* And Shadow had just dropped into it.

He barely managed to pull Outlaw to a skidding stop before the two of them pitched headlong down the steep creek bank. Down below, Annie was clawing her way out of the churning waters of a creek. With a shout of relief, Frank flung himself down from the saddle and slid down the bank to his drenched sister. Cursing Shadow, he grabbed Annie in a desperate hug. "You all right?"

Annie clung to him. "J-just c-c-cold."

The storm stopped as quickly as it had begun and the sun came out. Annie retrieved her hat and Frank helped her scramble back up to where, miraculously, Outlaw waited, his head down, his dark coat even darker where the rain had drenched him. "You're a wonder, you crazy horse," Frank said, patting the horse's neck before boosting Annie into the saddle and scrambling up behind her.

"C-can't believe he didn't run off," Annie chattered.

"He's got more sense than all the others put together," Frank replied, surprised by the affection that welled up inside of him for the same animal that had once seemed bent on killing him. The minute he reached around Annie and took the reins, Outlaw wheeled about and headed for the others. Emmet and Jake appeared in the distance, galloping toward them — without their strings of ponies.

"Thank God," Emmet cried out when he saw Annie. "You're all right?"

"Nothing hurt but her pride," Frank said before muttering to Annie, "an amazing bit of horsemanship, by the way."

Shivering with cold, she stuttered, "I w-would have landed that jump if sh-she hadn't jerked right so f-fast."

"Luther's making camp," Emmet called. "Jake and I can chase down your ponies. Can you track Shadow?"

Frank nodded. "Soon as I get Annie situated."

Back at camp, Annie used the wagon for cover while she changed out of her soaked clothes and wrapped up in a dry blanket. Frank spread her things on the wagon wheels to dry.

Luther was making coffee, and as soon as it was ready, Frank produced his flask and added a little whiskey to Annie's mug. "It'll warm you right up."

She frowned. "How's this fit with that oath I witnessed?"

"About as well as my swearing at the horse that nearly killed you."

"I — I'm sorry." Annie ducked her head. "I tried to hold her back. I just — couldn't."

Frank held out the tin mug. "I'm just trying to keep you from catching your death of cold. The last thing we need is for you to be too sick to do your job at Clearwater."

Annie drew the blanket close about her shoulders and sat down by the fire. Cupping the tin mug with her hands, she sipped the toddy. With a shudder, she inched closer to the campfire. She took another sip.

Frank spoke to Luther. "I'm riding back to the draw to pick up Shadow's trail. As for the other horses, I don't imagine they went far. Once the sun came out, they probably forgot why they were running and went to grazing."

Luther nodded. "It'd be good to make Valley Home before dark if we can. That's about ten miles on up the trail."

"We'll do our best," Frank said.

Once he'd put a little distance between himself and camp, he took a little sip of whiskey, grateful for the warmth it spread through his midsection.

He caught up with Shadow just before sundown. She met his approach — or, rather, Outlaw's approach — with a welcoming nicker.

CHAPTER 7

Early in the evening, a week into the ten-day journey to Clearwater, Annie and Shadow had just picked their way across a creek and come alongside Luther's wagon when the freighter pointed at a barely discernible gray dot on the horizon. "Hollenberg Station. One of the best-run places between here and Clearwater."

As they rode along, Luther spoke of Gerat and Sophia Hollenberg, the German couple who had, just three years previously, built a single-room log cabin at a prime spot on the California-Oregon trail. As their business grew, they added on. The single room eventually expanded to the current six-room building that, in addition to the family's quarters, housed a grocery and dry goods store, an unofficial post office, a meal-serving tavern, and a loft offering overnight lodging. "See that barn?" He pointed at the massive structure just past the station.

"Stalls for one hundred horses or mules." He waxed positively lyrical about Mrs. Hollenberg's cooking.

Dozens of immigrant camps dotted the landscape between the creek and the long, low building with the peaked, shingled roof. When Luther learned the barn was "full up," he pulled his freight wagon alongside a large corral. Everyone in their train worked together, unsaddling, unharnessing, and unhitching their nearly twenty animals and turning them into the corral. By the time the horses and mules were tended and the tack stored beneath the freight wagon, the evening star had come out.

Luther led the way up the hill to the clapboard building. Opening the main door, he waved Annie in ahead of him. She stepped into a large room with gleaming, whitewashed walls. An open door in the far wall revealed shelves laden with goods. A tidy woman dressed in an indigo calico dress and a spotless apron stood behind a counter to the left of that doorway, talking to a buckskin-clad customer. Nearby, a two-burner stove radiated warmth. Luther pointed to a door to their right, "The stairs to the loft — the 'hotel' part of the operation."

At the sound of Luther's voice, the woman

behind the counter looked up with a welcoming smile. "Luther Mufsy! You are in luck! Today we have dumplings." She handed a small cloth bag to her customer and stepped out from behind the counter. Without waiting for an introduction, she motioned for everyone to follow her as she led the way past the small stove and into the next room, where a large cookstove dominated the far wall and a rustic table and two benches provided seating for at least a dozen.

"I've been telling them they're in for a treat," Luther said, as everyone took a seat at the table. "Frank, Emmet, and Jake are the latest Pony Express riders. Jake's for Liberty Farm up in Nebraska. The Paxtons are going on to Clearwater. Annie's the new cook there."

Mrs. Hollenberg looked Annie up and down and, without comment, retrieved bowls from a corner shelf and began to ladle dumplings out of a massive stew pot on the stove. As she set Annie's bowl before her, she asked, "So. She is to be working" — she glanced over wire-rimmed spectacles at Luther — "for George Morgan?"

Luther nodded and clapped Frank on the back — a little too heartily, Annie thought. "Frank and Emmet weren't about to leave their sister alone in St. Jo."

Mrs. Hollenberg only grunted as she retrieved spoons from a drawer in the same cupboard housing stacked white dishes. She poured fresh buttermilk from a large white pitcher into tin mugs. Plunking the pitcher down on the table, she sat down across from Annie. "Is hard life, *Fräulein.*" She looked over at Luther. "Is too much for young girl."

Annoyed at being so quickly dismissed, Annie said, "I've been cooking for my family since I was nine years old."

Mrs. Hollenberg pursed her lips. "How many in this family?"

"Pa and Frank and Emmet and me."

Mrs. Hollenberg counted silently, tapping each tip of the fingers on her left hand. "Four."

Annie nodded.

Mrs. Hollenberg pushed herself to her feet. "Most days I am feeding many times that. I am having also Mr. Hollenberg's niece, Louisa, to help with cooking, cleaning, washing, tending chickens — and garden. She works very hard. I work very hard. Still, is not so easy to keep up." Again, she looked at Luther. "Is too much for one tiny woman." After the pronouncement, she rose and busied herself on the kitchen side of the room, rattling this and tasting that.

Annie defended herself — perhaps a little too loudly. She was young — she emphasized the word *young* perhaps a little too strenuously, but honestly Mrs. Hollenberg was, if not old, at least middle-aged. Definitely past her prime. Annie was young, healthy, and "perfectly capable of cooking for *fifty* people if the job demands it."

Mrs. Hollenberg said nothing.

When Annie opened her mouth to say more, Luther nudged her with his elbow and muttered, "Have a dumpling."

Annie scowled at him. Jake asked for more to eat. Mrs. Hollenberg served it, and then moved back to the stove and opened the oven door. When the aroma of fresh baked bread wafted into the room, Annie's mouth began to water. Her stomach growled. Mrs. Hollenberg served up thick slices of fresh bread, each one slathered with butter. Annie swallowed a spoonful of the broth in the bowl. She ate a dumpling. And another. She savored the tang of salted butter and the yeasty warmth of bread. The older woman might be outspoken to the point of rudeness, but there was no denying she was a wonderful cook. Annie dared a question. "Would you tell me how to make your dumplings before we leave in the morning?"

Mrs. Hollenberg turned around, a shocked

110

look on her face. "You don't know to make *dumplings*?"

Annie bristled. "*Anyone* can make dumplings. But I see flecks of green, and it doesn't taste like parsley. Sage, maybe?" *There.* At least the old woman knew she wasn't a complete idiot.

Mrs. Hollenberg studied her for a moment before responding. "Also bread crumbs fried in butter for stuffing. I can teach," she said, but then waved the idea way. "But there is no point. George Morgan don't keep chickens."

Annie looked over at Luther for confirmation. He shrugged. She looked back at Mrs. Hollenberg. "Maybe I'll make Clearwater famous for *buffalo* and dumplings."

Mrs. Hollenberg glanced over at Luther. Looked back at Annie. Finally, with a low laugh, she pointed at Annie's bowl. "Eat. Dumplings aren't so good cold." She spoke to the men. "Who wishes for more?" After serving thirds to Jake and seconds to everyone else, she went into the other room. When she returned a few moments later, she set a note on the table beside Annie.

Sophia's Dumplings
2 cups flour–4 teaspoons baking powder–1/2 teaspoon salt — sifted to-

111

gether. Add butter, cream, herbs for nice dough. Roll out. Cut in squares. Bread crumbs fried in butter into center of each square. Fold over. Pinch. Seal edge with cream. Boil in broth with meat of one whole hen. (Boil longer for buffalo to make tender.)

Annie suppressed a smile when she read the reminder regarding buffalo meat. The nonspecific word *herbs* was more than a little disappointing, but it paled in importance in light of Mrs. Hollenberg's pronouncement about chickens and George Morgan. He didn't keep chickens? She couldn't possibly do without eggs — not for two years.

As the party finished eating and rose to leave, Annie thanked Mrs. Hollenberg for the recipe and tucked it in her skirt pocket. Once outside, she followed the men down to their camp, her mind whirling with doubt. *No eggs.* She'd taken chickens for granted. If Clearwater didn't have a chicken coop . . . she hurried to catch up with Luther. "Do you know if there's a milk cow at Clearwater?"

"Could be one now, I suppose."

"But there wasn't the last time you were there."

Luther shook his head. "No, Ma'am. Not as of last October."

"And no chickens."

"It'd be a hard place to keep chickens. Hot, hot, summers. Cold, cold winters. Hawks in the air, varmints on the ground. Not to say it can't be done, mind you, but it'd take time and determination. I don't think Clearwater's ever had a cook with much of either. Most don't stay on through the winter. Far as I know, you'll be the first."

"But — how do I keep hungry men well fed without eggs — let alone without milk or butter?"

"Just keep it simple. Beans. Ham. Grits. Repeat." Luther busied himself building a small campfire to fight the chill of the early spring night.

Annie had hoped to take advantage of the "loft to let" over the Hollenberg's main rooms, but the men wanted to keep an eye on the animals. Pulling her bedroll out from beneath the wagon, she wrapped herself up in it. The mournful sound of a mouth harp floated up from someone's camp. She looked toward the other campfires glowing in the night. From the sounds of that music, someone over there felt the same way she did tonight. She was beginning to have her own doubts. And why had Mrs. Hollenberg spoken George Morgan's name in that tone of voice?

Annie woke long before dawn. The moment she saw golden light flickering in the kitchen window up at Hollenberg Station, she rose and made her way to the well pump to wash up. Frank must not have slept well, either, for when she returned to the wagon to roll up her bedroll, it had already been done for her.

"There's a light in the kitchen window up the hill," he said in a low voice. "Won't be long and there'll be coffee. Want to walk up with me?"

Emmet, Jake, and Luther joined Frank and Annie at breakfast, this meal served by Mrs. Hollenberg's niece, Louisa, who did not seem particularly happy to be doing it as she shuffled back and forth between the stove and the table with plates of Johnny cakes and fried ham. When Frank's attempts to flirt were met with blank stares, he gulped his meal and excused himself.

Luther must have thought they were taking too long at breakfast, because Emmet, Jake, and Frank were still sorting horses in the corral when he set off up the trail.

"Is Luther upset about something?" Annie asked, as she saddled Shadow.

Frank shrugged. "Didn't say much. Just headed out."

Annie decided to ride with Frank for a while, but just as she'd passed the station, someone called her name. When she looked back, Mrs. Hollenberg was standing at the back door of the gray building, waving a white handkerchief in the air to get her attention. As soon as Annie got close, the older woman held up a battered coffee tin filled with dirt — and a barely sprouted plant.

"Rosemary," she said as she handed it up. "For dumplings." She smiled. "Is to be our secret, *ja*? You keep inside for at least four weeks more. Too much cold and it will die."

Annie swallowed a lump in her throat. This was the kind of thing that could happen every day if only they lived in town. Neighbors sharing a cutting from the garden. Women giving each other advice. "Thank you. Very much."

Mrs. Hollenberg's voice was gentle when she said, "You will be all right, *Fräulein*. Is much hard work, but those brothers? They are good boys. I see they care for their sister."

Annie nodded. She peered into the woman's blue eyes. "You don't like Mr. Morgan. Why not?"

"*Ach,*" the old woman shook her head. "I don't know so much as that. Is most probably gossip. Don't be frightened." She smiled. "You make buffalo and Sophia's dumplings, yes? You will do well."

Annie blurted out the truth. "I never wanted to go west. I wanted to stay in St. Joseph. But" — she looked toward the trail — "I couldn't let them go without me. They're all I have."

The older woman nodded. "When I am young, I dream of nice little house in village. Many friends. Many children. God gives instead much work. No neighbors. No children." She smiled. "But also much blessing." She pulled an envelope from her apron pocket and tucked it into Annie's saddlebag. "Flower seeds from Sophia for to make you smile." She took a step back. "Now you must go. But also you must visit Sophia when you are coming back, yes?"

Annie nodded. "I will. I promise."

"Is *gut.* Maybe you are bringing me new herb you find in that Nebraska, *ja*? New secret ingredient." She nodded. "Go with *Gott, Fräulein.* For you I am praying."

Annie barely managed to say thank you. No one had ever promised to pray for her. She wondered what Mrs. Hollenberg would say in those prayers. Nudging Shadow into a lope, Annie rode up alongside Luther's wagon and held up the coffee tin. "A gift from Mrs. Hollenberg."

Luther nodded toward the back of the wagon. "I'll pull up and you can put the can inside the supply box. After you do that, you might want to take a gander at the off side of the wagon. Your brothers rustled up a little surprise, too."

As soon as Luther stopped, Annie nudged Shadow close to the box suspended at the back of the wagon, lifted the lid, and deposited the plant. Next, she urged the horse forward so that she could see the opposite side of the wagon. Someone had suspended a basket between the tall wheels. Sidling up to the basket, Annie lifted the lid. One, two, three, four . . . *twelve*. A dozen chicks. She glanced back toward Hollenberg Station.

"They're Rhode Island Reds," Luther said, after Annie closed the lid and rode up alongside the mules. "Your brothers wanted to buy a few chicks, but Sophia wouldn't take the money. You've got yourself a friend in Kansas, Miss Paxton."

By the time the Pony Express crew crossed into Nebraska Territory, Mother Nature had begun to do exactly what Luther had promised. Spring was beginning to transform the barren winter landscape. Buds on bushes and trees began to swell, and early blossoms dotted the greening hillsides. Once they were across the new toll bridge at Rock Creek Station, Annie looked back at the precipitous creek banks and wondered aloud how anyone could have gotten a wagon across the creek without the bridge.

"We used chains," Luther said. "Chains and horsepower to lower wagons down into the creek bed, and then more chains and more horse or mule power to haul them back up the other side. It could take hours — for just one wagon. I've known folks to be in camp for more than a week, just waiting their turn to cross. And come a spring storm to set the creek to running high?" He just shook his head. "There's folks who complain about the toll, but I'll never begrudge McCanles the money. He built a bridge, and I say God bless him for it."

After Rock Creek Station, trail conditions steadily degenerated. Luther ended up walking alongside his team, slapping his thigh with a quirt to encourage them as they struggled to pull the heavily loaded wagon through loose, sandy soil. Immigrant wagons struggled, too, often forced to double-team just to get things moving again.

When it came time, Annie hated leaving

Jake behind at Liberty Farm. She really had come to care for the boy. As she said good-bye, she appointed herself big sister for just long enough to kiss his cheek and murmur, "Good-bye, little brother."

"No need to say good-bye, Miss Annie. Won't be long, and I'll be tearing into Clearwater on a bolt of lightning and handing the mail off to Frank."

"I'll have a hot meal waiting," Annie said. "The best one possible." She looked back toward Liberty Farm more than once as she rode away. Every time, Jake was still standing exactly where they'd left him. Watching.

At Thirty-Two-Mile Creek, Annie met Mrs. Comstock, whose odd accent elicited questions about her homeland and the unexpected answer that she was from Vermont. She kept cozy clean rooms and a fine flock of plump, black-and-white chickens.

"Dominiquers," she said, when Annie asked after the breed. "They were good enough for the Puritans and they're good enough for me." She was not impressed with the Rhode Island Reds. When she offered the travelers canned peaches for dessert, Annie wondered aloud at the bounty. The older woman winked at her. "A pretty face like yours could lure lobster from the far seas, my dear. Be kind to the freighters and the soldiers, and they'll return the same in goods."

Soldiers? "I don't expect I'll see many soldiers. Fort Kearny is miles and miles beyond Clearwater."

"You're entering the Platte Valley, dear. Flat land for hundreds of miles to the west. Patrols from the fort can cover a lot of ground in a half day. Once word gets around that George Morgan's got a beautiful new cook working at Clearwater, you'll have your hands full keeping them at bay."

That night as they made camp, Luther said they'd easily cover the last fifteen miles to Clearwater by sunset the next day. While Emmet and the others picketed the horses, Annie asked him about what Mrs. Comstock had said about soldiers from Fort Kearny frequenting the station.

"*Flocking to* is more likely what will happen," Luther teased. "Once they get news of Miss Annie Paxton, I expect the boys in blue will be fighting over who gets to patrol down your way." When Annie didn't smile, he quickly reassured her. "Now, now, don't worry over it. Soldiers can be a rowdy bunch, but there's a gutter called Dobytown west of the fort for all that kind of thing. They won't be bringing it to Clearwater. George don't allow it."

120

Frank and Emmet returned, and Annie said nothing more. As the moon rose, she lay on her back staring up at the stars. It was a pleasant night. The horses were picketed close enough to the camp that she could hear them tearing off and munching grass as they grazed. In the glow of the dying campfire, she did her best to stop worrying and to think on good things. She was fairly certain the Good Book said something about that. *Think on these things.* She had rosemary to tend and flower seeds to plant and a dozen chicks. She had Sophia's recipe for dumplings. *And she promised to pray for me.* A woman who made a promise like that probably knew quite a lot about praying. There was comfort in the notion. Just as the Shepherd's Psalm promised, maybe goodness and mercy would follow her. All the way to Clearwater.

CHAPTER 8

The evening the company of riders approached Clearwater Station, a spectacular sunset provided a golden-red backdrop for the weathered buildings in the distance. Overhead, yellow-and-pink clouds glistened against an aqua sky that faded first to lavender and then to indigo on the eastern horizon.

When Annie exclaimed over it, Emmet, who was riding next to her, smiled. "God's painted a sky to welcome us."

Annie liked the idea, but thoughts of God were quickly dispelled by the hellish sounds pouring out the front door of the station as they approached. Shouts. Crashes. Thuds. Curses. A chair sailing out the open front door, followed by a man who, after slamming against the flagpole flying the Stars and Stripes, charged back inside.

When Shadow snorted a protest and skittered sideways, Emmet suggested that Annie "skedaddle on back to the barn and see to Shadow until things get sorted out up here."

With still more curses pouring out of the open station door, Annie was happy to obey. She'd heard plenty of bad language in her life — most notably back in the day when she hunkered in her room while the boys tried to get Pa to bed. But this was so vile it made her blush. Nudging Shadow, she hurried around the small sod portion of the long, low building constructed mainly of massive, square-cut logs. The station's front door faced the east-west trail. In the back lot to the south of the building, dozens of oxen and a few mules milled about in a series of corrals spanning the space between the station and a massive barn.

Dismounting and hitching Shadow just outside the open double barn doors, Annie stood, patting the horse's neck while she waited. The back side of the log station boasted two south-facing doors. A rustic arbor shaded the one opposite the front door and extended eastward, also shading a small window set in the sod wall. There was no door to the sod part of the building. The only other door, this one closer to the far west corner of the building, was closed. Next to it, a larger window admitted daylight into what must be a bedroom, for Annie could just see the outline of curtains through the glass. *Is that lace dangling from the edges of those curtains?*

Luther was leading the way for the others, driving his wagon past the main station building and pulling up alongside the only empty corral on the place. Emmet and Frank waited while he climbed down and opened the gate. Once inside the corral, Emmet dismounted, yanked on the rope wrapped around his saddle horn, and quickly freed his three ponies. Luther kept the gate open just wide enough for Frank to follow suit. It was all working quite well — until someone up at the station fired a shotgun. Outlaw screamed and reared straight up. Frank spurred him ahead and into the corral, but before Luther could get the gate closed, the three horses Emmet had just freed pushed through. The three men watched, helpless, as the ponies fled south.

In the melee, Shadow stepped sideways. A distracted Annie failed to get out of the way, and the mare stepped on her foot. With a yelp, she threw all her weight against the horse's flank. Shadow danced away. Annie pulled free just in time to see Emmet and Frank remount and tear off after the escaped ponies. She was grimacing and flexing her sore foot when she heard someone ask if she was all right. She looked about, trying to find the source of the voice.

"Up here. In the haymow." A handsome boy with raven-black hair and startlingly blue eyes motioned toward the open barn door. "Best to take cover in here until it's over. It probably won't be much longer. Once George gets the shotgun down, folks realize he means business."

The boy ducked out of sight. Glancing back at the station, Annie limped toward the open barn doors. She'd just ducked inside when the boy appeared at the far end of the row of stalls. He carried a small keg to where Annie was standing and set it beside her. "Have a seat. Not broken, I hope."

Annie flexed her foot again. Wiggled her toes. "Not broken."

The boy nodded. "I'm Billy. You with Luther?"

He wore heavy boots, gray work pants, and a checked flannel shirt. No beads. No feathers. Flawless bronze skin. Feeling self-conscious beneath the gaze of those blue eyes, Annie stammered her name. "A-Annie. Annie Paxton. My brothers are the Pony Express riders. Luther brought us out." She didn't want to stare, but she couldn't seem to stop. *Her first Indian.*

Someone up at the station yelled Billy's name. Annie looked that way just as a hulking figure staggered out the back door beneath the arbor and onto the rustic porch. When he stepped off the porch, Annie saw the blood. It streamed from somewhere along his hairline, down the side of his face, and into a thick beard. The giant managed only a few steps before falling to his knees.

As Billy hurried to the injured man's side, movement inside the station drew Annie's attention. She realized the front and back doors were aligned so that, when both doors were open as they were now, a person could see through the place. She saw two men flee through the front door. Seconds later, they were little more than blue smudges astride two horses galloping west. *Blue. Soldiers.*

The giant put a filthy paw to his face. Swiping at the blood, he stared down at his fingers with a frown. Just as Luther reached his side, he crashed to the earth. Together, Luther and Billy helped him to his feet and back inside.

Annie watched it all with a combination of fascination and horror. She glanced toward the south. Saw nothing but flat land and pink-tinged sky. To the west, the sun was sinking fast, and there was no sign of

Emmet. No sign of Frank. No sign of the lost ponies. She looked back toward the station.

Soldiers. A brawl. And the man who must be George Morgan. *Lord, have mercy.*

Clearwater grew quiet, save for the swishing of tails and the grunting of the oxen crowded into two corrals. With a slight wince, Annie hobbled over to the corral to free the three ponies who were still tied together. When one of the ponies nudged the empty water trough, Annie sighed. "All right, all right. I hear you." For the next few minutes she carried bucket after bucket of water from the well near the barn to the trough. At least the well had a pump. She wouldn't have had the strength to haul up a dozen buckets of water with a windlass. At least not this evening.

When there was enough water in the trough to keep the ponies from suffering, she carried water to Luther's team, one bucket for each of the six animals. Next, she turned her attention to Shadow, who was still hitched outside the barn. What was taking Frank and Emmet so long? How far could those ponies have gotten, anyway? She was not going anywhere near the disaster up at the station until they got back.

Leading Shadow inside the barn, she turned the mare into an empty stall. Once she had the saddle off, she went in search of a brush and hoof pick, finding both in a bucket sitting on the floor in a corner just beyond stalls. Apparently, this end of the barn was the western version of a tack room, with two rows of saddle racks mounted on the walls, hooks for bridles, halters, and lead ropes, and a row of grain bins lining the wall beneath the saddle racks.

After claiming a rack and a hook for Shadow's saddle and bridle, Annie stepped into the stall and brushed her down. At some point she realized her foot had stopped throbbing. Finally, she pumped one last bucket of water, hung it on a hook in the corner of Shadow's stall, and closed the door.

Just when she'd decided to return to the empty wooden keg and sit down, Billy trotted into the barn. "Luther's sewing him up. You should be able to go inside soon." He took a feed bag down from a hook just above the grain bins and scooped a measure of grain in. He looked up at her and with a mischievous grin said, "Luther tells me I'm your first Indian."

Embarrassed, she stammered, "I — um — not really. We saw plenty of Indians on the way here." *Exactly four.*

"*Kansas* tribes?" Billy snorted with derision. He changed the subject. "Luther also said something about chickens?"

The chicks! With a groan of dread, Annie spun about and hurried to the wagon. She lifted the basket lid and was relieved to see the chicks seemed all right. When she realized Billy had followed her, she motioned for him to look in. "A woman in Kansas gave them to me. Rhode Island Reds, she said."

"Mrs. Hollenberg?" When Annie nodded, he said, "Luther talks about her cooking. A lot." He reached into the basket and scooped up a chick, cradling it in the palm of his hand and stroking its downy head with the tip of one finger.

Annie pointed toward a nearby soddy. "Is it true they're cool in summer and warm in winter? That'd be good for chickens."

The boy sounded incredulous. "You might want to wait a few days before you ask George about turning his blacksmith's shop into a chicken coop."

After what she'd just seen of the man, Annie doubted she'd be asking George Morgan for anything. In fact, she'd be doing her best to avoid him. "Frank and Emmet could build one." They'd never worked with sod,

129

but surely they could figure something out — with Luther's help. Something small. "If I'm going to raise them, I won't want them freezing to death."

Billy put the chick down and began to untie the rope holding the basket in place. "You're staying the winter?"

"Of course. Why would you ask?"

"George's crew always goes east for the winter."

"We're not really part of George's crew. We work for the Pony Express, and in spite of your employer's antics, I don't plan on leaving until my brothers do."

Billy coiled the rope that had attached the basket to Luther's wagon and draped it over one of the wheel spokes. He picked up the basket. "*Antics.* I don't know that word."

"Fighting. Swearing. Shooting. Causing trouble." She followed Billy into the barn, where he set the basket down in a stall and opened the lid, laughing as the chicks tumbled into the clean straw.

"George didn't start the fight. And he doesn't swear."

Annie interrupted him. "I heard him with my own ears. It was . . . vile."

"*Vile.* Another word I don't know. But it sounds bad." He looked over at her. "That wasn't George."

130

If Billy didn't know words like *vile* and *antics,* he probably didn't know what *swearing* was, either. It was pointless to argue. She knew what she'd heard. And seen.

Billy returned to the topic of the chicks. "I'll scatter some grain for them and find something to hold water." He flashed a smile. "I hope you do stay. George is a terrible cook. Even Whiskey John's been complaining."

"Whiskey John?"

"One of the stage drivers. *Big* appetite. You'll meet him tomorrow when the stage rolls in."

Annie stood at the stall door watching the chicks. At the sound of horses approaching from the south, she hurried to the barn door. *Thank heaven.* Frank and Emmet with the runaways in tow. Billy hurried to open the corral gate for them. Moments later, Frank and Emmet led Outlaw and Emmet's bay into the barn.

Outlaw snorted and backed away when Billy approached. "Better give him a few days to get to know you first," Frank said.

"Or weeks," Emmet quipped.

"Instead of insulting Outlaw," Frank said, "how about you let me see to the horses and you check in with Luther and Morgan. See if Morgan's sobered up. I imagine An-

131

nie would appreciate it if she didn't have to spend another night in a barn loft."

Billy interrupted before Emmet could reply. "George doesn't drink. The fight was *about* drinking. Just not George's."

"Really?"

Billy nodded. "Two friends from George's trading days rode in earlier today. One white. One Cheyenne. George explained his 'no liquor to Indians' rule and offered to make coffee. They didn't like the rule and tried to make him change it. You saw how it ended." Billy backed away as Frank led Outlaw past him and into a stall. "That's a beautiful horse. Does sugar do anything to improve his opinion of strangers?"

Frank smiled. "It might."

Emmet left for the station. As he trotted up the dusty path leading past the half dozen pens and corrals, something wound tight inside Annie relaxed a little. The men she'd thought to be drunken soldiers racing back to Fort Kearny weren't soldiers, after all. And Emmet and Frank were obviously feeling protective of her.

After Emmet disappeared inside the station, and Frank had seen to the horses, Billy suggested they unhitch Luther's team. Darkness had fallen by the time Big Boy, Andy, and the four mules were contentedly munching hay alongside the Pony Express horses in the corral. And still, Emmet had not emerged from the station. When Billy lit a lantern and hung it in the barn, Annie busied herself brushing Shadow and combing through her long mane. Finally, Frank asked Billy about their sleeping in the barn "until things got settled."

Billy glanced above them. "All right. Just — let me get my bedroll down."

Frank looked toward the soddy. "I thought —"

Billy shook his head. "I sleep in the loft most nights. I like it better."

Annie spoke up. "Let's just get our saddlebags and bedrolls and go up to the station." It was time she met George Morgan.

The main room of the station was well lit, thanks to small mirrors reflecting the light of a dozen oil lamps nestled in wall brackets spaced at regular intervals around the room. Narrow stairs in the corner opposite the back door led up to a loft marked off by a short railing. A massive stone fireplace took up much of the wall to Annie's right. Beyond it and set into the same wall was a doorway that must lead into the sod room. To the left, a good-sized counter jutted out into the room a couple of feet and then made a ninety-degree turn toward the far wall. The counter was clear except for a lighted lantern and a large water cooler with a tin mug hanging from its spigot.

Behind the counter a door led into a storeroom. It was impossible to see much more than the shadowy outlines of goods lined up on the shelves. This main room was large enough to accommodate four square tables, each one apparently constructed from shipping cartons. The ones nearest Annie advertised Father John's Medicine and D. F. Stauffer Fancy Cakes and Biscuits. Upended crates and barrels sufficed for seating.

The room was rustic but spotlessly clean. No cobwebs hung from the bare rafters, no lampblack clung to the lamp chimneys. One end of a large stove was visible through the door centered on the far wall. To the left of that door, a sign advertised meals for fifty cents.

Annie and Frank had only been standing at the door for a moment when George Morgan, Luther, and Emmet filed through the doorway beyond the stove in the next room. Morgan still looked wild, but he seemed to have made some attempt to tame his unruly long hair.

Emmet broke the silence. "George was

showing me your room, Annie — and ours." He glanced over at Frank and then looked back at Annie. "You'll like it."

Luther cleared his throat. Placing his hand on Morgan's shoulder, he said, "Frank Paxton and Miss Annie Paxton, allow me to introduce Mr. George Morgan, the owner of Clearwater Road Ranch."

The bare wood floor creaked as Morgan crossed to where Annie and Frank stood. She hadn't realized how big the man was. It was as if a great brown bear loomed over her as he rumbled, "Sorry about earlier." He shook hands with Frank and then held out a massive paw to Annie. "Welcome to Clearwater." Her hand was completely swallowed up by his, although his grip was surprisingly gentle. He released her hand and looked over at Emmet. "You want to show the way?"

Emmet picked up the lighted lantern. Morgan retreated behind the counter and pulled out a checkerboard and a box of checkers. He didn't so much as look Annie's way as she and Frank followed Emmet past the counter and toward a doorway in the far wall that led to the kitchen.

As they passed through the kitchen, Emmet held the lantern high. "It's not the Patee House, but it's impressive."

"I'd say so," Frank agreed, pointing to a stove that looked every bit as nice as Mrs. Hollenberg's.

A faded quilt hung in another doorway just beyond the stove. Emmet pushed it aside, turned left, and led the way into a bedroom. When he set the lantern atop a dresser in the corner, Annie looked about with wonder. The light reflected by the dresser mirror revealed a tidy room with interior shutters closed across each of two windows, one facing west, one south. A white pitcher and bowl stood on a washstand across from the dresser. Above the washstand, a towel embroidered with a bouquet of flowers hung on a brass bar. Both the dresser and the washstand boasted pale gray marble tops. Frank gave a low whistle of appreciation. Annie crossed the bare wood floor and plopped down on the edge of the bed. "I don't know what to say."

Emmet smiled. "Told you you'd like it."

"But how — I mean — why wouldn't Mr. Morgan keep this for himself?"

"He stays in the soddy at the opposite end of the main room. That's the original Clearwater Road Ranch. Said it suits him just fine."

"Then — what's this all for?"

"The cook."

Annie just shook her head. It still didn't make sense. Why such a fancy room? That dresser was almost as nice as the one in the room at the Patee House. And she'd been right about the curtains. The edges dripped with lace.

Emmet gestured about them. "Maybe this will make the next couple of years a little easier to bear." He pointed toward the heavy plank door. "Frank and I bunk just through there. You turn left out of the kitchen, we go right. Need anything before we turn in?" Annie shook her head. "Sleep as late as you want tomorrow," he said. "Morgan's managed without a cook for this long, he can go another day."

"And I'll see to your chicks," Frank said. He draped her saddlebags across the foot of the bed and left.

Before Emmet left, he kissed her cheek. His mustache tickled. Annie put her hand to the spot, surprised by the unexpected show of affection from her quiet older brother.

"I told you we'd be all right, didn't I?"

Annie nodded. As soon as he'd closed the door behind him, she rose and doused the lamp, undressing in the dark and leaving everything where it fell. When she pulled back the bedcovering and lay down, the mattress crinkled. The aroma that wafted into the air wasn't the scent of lemons, but it told her the straw bedding was fresh.

CHAPTER 9

Cold. When had it gotten so cold? Content to remain suspended between sleep and wakefulness, Annie burrowed into her pillow and dozed for a few more minutes. Finally, she opened her eyes. *Light . . . sunlight pouring through shutters.* What time was it?

Slipping out of bed, she tiptoed to the south-facing window and unlatched the shutters. *Snow . . .* collecting on the ground, piling up against fence posts and the walls of buildings, frosting the backs of the animals in the corrals. And it was cold. *So cold.* On April 3. What had happened to spring? The Pony Express mail was supposed to leave St. Joseph at five o'clock this evening. They would probably hear Jake Finney's approach here at Clearwater at midday tomorrow. A couple of days after that, it would be Emmet's turn to carry the

California mail eastward. *And it was snow-ing.*

Annie shivered. She hadn't given much thought to Frank and Emmet's riding the trail in the dead of winter. She'd comforted herself with the idea that by the time snow covered all but the most prominent landmarks, riders and horses alike would have memorized the trail. All her brothers would have to do by then was to hang on. *And hope not to freeze to death.*

She would need to get busy knitting socks for them all. Maybe she'd knit some for Jake Finney, too. She wondered about the other riders she'd meet in the coming days. As a home station, Clearwater would be at the center of a long relay race, with riders shuttling mail in both directions in all kinds of weather. *A hundred miles in a snowstorm.* She would need a lot of yarn. She'd ask Luther to bring some with him on his next supply run. How long would it take to get it? There was so much she didn't know about living in this place.

After shaking out the clothing she'd dropped on the floor the previous night and smoothing it as best she could, Annie dressed. There was water in the pitcher on the washstand. Who'd brought it in? She poured some into the bowl, rinsed her hands, patted her cheeks, and then looked about for an alternative to the embroidered hand towel, which seemed too pretty to use. Finally, she relented.

As she left the room, she noticed a board leaning against the wall beside the door. Two L-shaped iron brackets on the door-frame would hold that board in place. It would be an effective lock, but Annie wasn't quite sure whether it made her feel safe or afraid. What looming danger made it necessary?

Frank heard the creak of the door hinges and realized Annie was coming. He barely had a chance to tuck his flask out of sight and stand up before she appeared in the doorway of his room. "How'd you sleep?"

She looked about the room. "Like the dead."

"Can you believe the snow? George said that with the sun out, it'll probably be melted before noon. Like your room?" He barely took a breath before adding, "When the snow started, Billy put the chicks back in the basket and took them up to the loft. Half-buried the basket in hay. They're fine."

"How do you know all that?"

"We've all been up since before dawn."

She reached over and swept a hand over

the foot of Emmet's cot. "Those blankets look awfully thin. How'd you keep from freezing in the night? And — where do you wash up?"

"I almost did freeze. What was the other question? Oh — we wash up down at the pump with the rest of the crew."

"Did you haul water up and in for me, then?"

"Not *up* — just *in.* There's another well just out back."

Annie gestured around the room. "This is awful."

"It's fine. Once we unload our trunks, there'll be more blankets for the cots. We aren't going to be here much, anyway." He paused. "By the way, before you think to wonder and worry, George said the plan is for Pony Express riders who don't happen to be your brothers to bunk either upstairs in the station loft or out in the blacksmith's soddy where the rest of this season's crew will stay. In other words, you don't have to worry about your privacy." Morgan hadn't been quite so clever as to say that bit about "riders who don't happen to be your brothers." That was Frank's way of trying to cheer her up — and she looked like she needed cheering up this morning.

"Where's Emmet?"

"Helping Luther hitch the team. I wanted to check on you." It wasn't exactly a lie. It had been Emmet's idea to see how Annie was doing this morning, and Frank had offered to do the checking. When he'd seen she was still sound asleep, he'd decided to get a little something to combat the cold.

"Luther's leaving? We just got here."

"He's in the business of moving freight — as much as possible as quickly as possible. There's half a ton to be unloaded before he can pull out, and he's in an all-fired hurry to get it done and get back on the trail."

"But — he just got here."

She must really be tired to be repeating herself that way. Frank gentled his voice. He gave her a one-armed hug. "Don't be sad. He'll be back through before you know it."

"I just — it's all happening so fast." She rubbed her forehead with the back of one hand. "I'm sorry. I feel . . . foggy. And sore."

"It was a long ride. Let's get you some coffee." Frank led her into the kitchen.

As it turned out, Annie didn't need the coffee to wake up. Her first real look at the kitchen did that.

She'd been too tired to pay attention to the kitchen the night before, when Emmet had led her through by lantern light, but she'd been right about the stove. It was every bit as nice as Mrs. Hollenberg's. An impressive array of cooking utensils and tools hung from iron hooks on the wall just above a worktable opposite the stove. And there was a window in the north wall — a window surrounded by shelves.

She walked over to peer out the window and toward the trail. There weren't any covered wagons in view at the moment, but she could hear the crack of the whip as a bullwhacker drove his oxen along. Taking a step back, she surveyed the crocks and jars lining the shelves on the wall around the window. It would be an adventure discovering their contents.

Frank had been leaning against a wall, watching as she looked about the kitchen. When someone pounded on a door, he said, "That'll be Emmet and Luther," and stepped into the room off the kitchen. Annie hadn't even noticed it last night. "You've never had a storeroom like this," he called back. "Come and take a look."

He opened the door set into the far wall. Luther's freight wagon was just outside, sidled up to the building, the cover already off, the tailgate down. Morning light streamed into the storeroom. Sacks lined the floor beneath half-empty shelves. Still, there were cracker boxes, dried fruit and more — a pure wonderment of goods.

"Your trunk's coming off first," Emmet called from the back of the wagon. "Where do you want it?"

"Beneath the south window," Annie said. To get out of the men's way, she retreated into the kitchen and stirred up the fire to reheat the coffee. She'd just begun to investigate the crocks on the shelves by the window — dried apples! Raisins! — when a bell clanged and George Morgan hollered through the back door out in the main room. The stage was coming.

For a moment, Annie panicked. She was supposed to feed whoever was on that stage. What was it Billy had said about the driver? He had a big appetite. She could scramble some eggs and — no. No eggs. *Beans. Ham. Grits. Repeat.* Luther had said that. Or something like that. There wasn't any ham, and beans needed to cook the better part of a day. She rushed to the doorway of the storeroom just as Emmet and Frank hauled in one of their trunks. Frank asked what was wrong.

"The stage. I'm supposed to feed them. I don't know where anything is. How many there'll be." Her cocky response to Mrs.

Hollenberg's concerns about "one little girl" handling things came back to haunt her. She looked down at the bags lined up on the floor. Flour. Flour. Beans. Cornmeal. *Grits.* Thank goodness. "Grits," she said aloud.

"Sounds good," Frank called over his shoulder as he and Emmet hauled her trunk past.

There was a bean pot on a kitchen shelf. Setting it on the stove, Annie grabbed a crockery pitcher and hurried out into the main room. It nearly emptied the cooler, but after two trips she thought she had enough to make grits for . . . ten? She didn't really know how many she'd have to feed. She went into the storeroom to measure out the grits. There was guesswork involved when it came to the amount of water. She'd just have to hope for the best. *Think three times what you'd make for you and Frank and Emmet. Maybe four times.* In time, she'd learn. At least it'd be a hot meal. On a cold day, a bowl of warm grits tasted mighty good *with cream and butter.* Except she had neither.

She glanced over at the crocks of dried apples and raisins. But she didn't want to use all of that the first day. Fruit was something to be treasured. Kept back for

146

pies and such. *Molasses.* There had to be molasses. Except she couldn't find any in the storeroom. She did, however, find coffee beans. At least she could make more coffee. As soon as she roasted the beans.

If only there was tea. Perhaps there was, but she didn't have time to look for it. She could hear the stage clattering toward the station. Thundering hooves, a cracking whip, and a shout from the driver. What was it she'd heard about him? *Whiskey John. Big appetite.*

The water was finally hot enough to add the grits. She still hadn't found the molasses, but she could stir the grits and keep an eye on the roasting coffee beans at the same time, and so that's what she did. When Frank set a big sack of something down in the storeroom with a thud, she called out for him to see if he could find a bucket of molasses on the storeroom shelves. He rummaged about there. She scanned the shelves in the kitchen for the coffee grinder. She saw it, but it was obvious Morgan had been the one to put it away. She was going to need to step up on something to reach it. Frank wouldn't be able to reach that top shelf, either.

The grits were cooking nicely. Slapping a lid on the pot and moving it off the heat a little, she concentrated on the coffee beans. They'd be ready in a few minutes. People would just have to wait. She was doing the best she could. Frank was still rummaging about in the storeroom. She went to the door. "Any luck?"

"Depends on what you call luck," he said. When he turned around, he was holding a dead rat by the tail. "You'll want to set some traps."

Of all the varmints it could have been . . . it had to be a rat. When she was little, Frank and Emmet had done their share of hiding toads in her bedding and garter snakes in her sewing basket. When it didn't earn them a screech, they stopped, somewhat amazed that their sister seemed immune to that kind of prank. She could sweep a mouse out the door with her broom without comment. But rats? That was another thing entirely. Rats made her feel sick.

Backing away from the storeroom, she motioned toward the outside. "Just — get it out of here."

When Frank stepped outside, Annie heard Emmet call for him. Something about the stage. He looked back at her and she waved him away. "Go. I'll figure something out."

Frank left. Annie peered out the kitchen window, expecting to see a beautiful Concord Stage just outside. It wasn't there. Crossing to the storeroom door, she saw it. For some reason, the driver had gone on down to the barn. No . . . actually, he'd pulled up near the soddy. If he needed a blacksmith, he was going to be disappointed. But at least she would have a little time before everyone stomped into the main room expecting a hot meal.

Hurrying out there, she grabbed one of the empty crates Morgan used for seating and brought it back into the kitchen. Climbing up on the crate, she retrieved the coffee grinder, just in time to keep from scorching *all* the coffee beans. Hopefully, no one would notice. *If I had cream they could put in their coffee to mellow the flavor, they probably wouldn't.*

While the beans cooled, she took the empty crate into the storeroom. Intent on finding a bucket of molasses somewhere, she began to move things on the shelves. Out of the corner of her eye she saw something move. Thinking *rat,* she screeched and took a step back. Off the crate. Into the air. Against the opposite wall. And . . . thud. Atop the flour and meal sacks lined up on the floor.

CHAPTER 10

Somewhere between the curse words, Annie was fairly certain she heard the stage driver inquire as to whether or not she was all right. At some point she realized the man was concerned for her well-being, but it took her a moment to suck in enough air to be able to answer. By then, Mr. Morgan was standing behind the driver. She could hear Frank and Emmet, too, although they were too short for her to actually see them past the driver and hulking George Morgan.

Finally, she managed to spit out the words *I'm. All. Right.* Each word forced out individually, with a little intake of air between. Whiskey John moved to help her up. "More embarrassed than hurt," she finally said, waving him off.

"You're sure?"

She tapped the crate. "Stepped on this looking for molasses. For the grits."

Morgan pushed past the stage driver and

reached for a bucket on the uppermost shelf. "Guess I'll have to bring a ladder in."

He sounded upset. Because of her needing a ladder? Annie reached for the bucket. "No need. The crate's fine. I didn't expect the stage, and I haven't had time to —" *Stop making excuses.* She looked over at the stage driver, who had at least seemed concerned that she might be hurt. "I'll have a lunch ready in a few minutes."

He winked. "You take all the time you need, little lady. Problems with the thoroughbrace a few miles up the trail. Might have to lay over. I've only got the two passengers and they're chasing down your two brothers, all confibulated about the chance to write home about meeting 'two real Pony Express riders.' Guess them back-East papers been talking it up more than we realized." He tugged on the brim of his black hat. "We'll just wait to hear the dinner bell." He turned to Frank and Emmet. "You boys have a minute to talk to the greenhorns I brung on the stage?"

The three men left, but Morgan stayed, making Annie feel even more self-conscious.

She had no idea what a *thoroughbrace* was, nor had she ever heard the word *confibulated.* She wasn't certain it *was* a word. It didn't matter. She carried the molasses into the kitchen and set the can on the small table opposite the stove, then looked back at Morgan. "I heard a bell earlier. Where is it?"

He pointed toward the main room. "Just outside the back door off that room. Three rings for the stage. More when the food's ready."

Annie nodded. *All right.* She could relax a little. The stage was going to be delayed for reasons that had nothing to do with her. She took a deep breath to calm herself as she lifted the lid on the bean pot full of grits. *Oh no.* The "simple meal" had turned into a lump of grainy, white glue.

Morgan stepped up and peered over her shoulder. "Not enough water. Too much cooking time."

Did he think she didn't know that?

"Is that all you were going to serve?"

Annie pulled the pot off the burner. "I thought eggs, but there aren't any. Then I thought biscuits, but I didn't know where to find the saleratus. And there wasn't time, anyway. Beans take too long, too. That left grits." She looked up at him. "We always had butter and cream with ours. But there's none of that. Which left molasses." When Morgan was silent, she nodded toward the storeroom. "Frank found a dead rat in there."

"He take care of it?"

"Yes." She barely managed to stifle a shudder.

Morgan reached under the worktable and pulled out a copper boiler with a towel stretched across the top. "The crock out in the main room is drinking water. Here's your cooking water. There should be enough to fill the bean pot again for a second try. Once you get the ruined grits scoured out." Stepping into the storeroom, he reached above him, and took something down from the rafters. Bringing it back into the kitchen, he plopped it down on the worktable, then took down the largest of three knives hanging in a row above it. "Maybe slice up some ham. Be careful you don't cut yourself. I just sharpened the knives yesterday." After reminding her to ring the bell when the meal was ready, he left.

She hadn't even noticed a ham hanging up high. Morgan hadn't told her where to dump the ruined grits. He hadn't really told her much of anything — except for pointing out the fact that she'd used the wrong water for the cooking. Why did that even matter? Didn't it all come from the same place? He didn't seem to think that rats in the storeroom were all that much of a problem. And apparently he didn't think she could be trusted with sharp knives without a warning to be careful. For a moment, she stood staring out the window toward the trail. Half a dozen wagon covers gleamed in the sun. Remembering Luther's mention of sailboats made her wish she could sail away.

Just get through today. That'll be one less day standing between you and the life you want. Taking a deep breath, she grabbed the now-cooled pot of ruined grits and headed outside to dump them.

Late on the night of her first-day fiasco, Annie was hunkered in bed when someone knocked on the door. She pulled her pillow over her head, gave a shuddering sob, and was quiet. Except for an occasional sniff, which surely the pillow would muffle.

"Open the door, Annie. I'm not going away."

Emmet. At least it wasn't Frank. Teasing and jokes worked for some things, but she just couldn't take teasing tonight. Who ruined *grits,* anyway? She never had. Until today. And then there was the ham. How was she supposed to know she shouldn't fry up the whole thing? Morgan told her to cook it. Billy said Whiskey John had a big appetite. How was she supposed to know it was the last ham until the next freighter arrived? And how could she have known that mattered to George Morgan? He told her to fry the ham. *And be careful not to cut yourself.* That little bit of unnecessary advice still bothered her.

She'd scorched the coffee beans, not once, but twice. That wonderful stove got hotter faster and stayed hot longer than the little two-burner she'd always used. Which was why her attempt at dried apple cobbler for the evening meal had failed so miserably. All she had to show for that was the aroma of cinnamon and baked apples. The apples had baked until there wasn't anything left of them. They hadn't burned, but she'd still had to scrape more ruined food atop the pile of gluey grits out back. At this rate, she'd be wanting to use some of her first month's pay to buy a pig just so she'd have a way to hide the evidence of her failures. Mrs. Comstock had said she'd probably be able to charm the freighters to bring things "from the far seas." Would Luther haul a pig?

She'd never been the kind of girl who cried at the drop of a hat. She'd always tried to be like Ma, trusting the Good Shepherd and finding good things to cherish. Tonight, though, she was too tired to look for "good things." She hadn't even bothered to undress before climbing under the covers. She'd squeezed her eyes shut and waited to fall asleep. But then some tears leaked out and once the dam broke there was a flood. The flood was over now, but apparently her brothers had heard the rushing waters.

Emmet knocked again.

Annie called softly, "I'll be all right. I just need to sleep."

"Of course you'll be all right. I still want to talk to you, though."

With a sigh, she threw back the covers and padded across to the door and opened it. The moon was bright, and she hadn't bothered to close the shutters over her windows. She could see that Emmet was carrying something. A book.

The only book Emmet owned besides the Bible that had been Ma's was the one given to each of the riders as part of the oathtaking ceremony. Frank had joked about the piety that inspired the custom. It was a nice-enough gesture, he said, but Mr. Majors must know that most of the leather-bound Bibles would be "misplaced" rather than cherished and read. Emmet had said something about how it would do Frank good to keep the book handy and take a look at it sometime. Frank said it would do Emmet good to keep his sermonizing to himself. But Annie had never minded Emmet's reading to her.

Emmet set the new Bible on her washstand while he lighted the oil lamp on the dresser. "You can get back under those covers, if you like. I won't be here long."

When Annie complied, Emmet perched on the edge of her trunk and flipped through the pages of the Bible. Presently, he read aloud, " 'Be strong and of a good courage; be not afraid, neither be thou dismayed: for the Lord thy God is with thee whithersoever thou goest.' " He looked up at her. " 'Whithersoever thou goest,' includes a kitchen where things aren't going your way. And a storeroom housing a rat."

Annie nodded. "I know." She did know — at least in her head. After all, the Shepherd's Psalm said that God would "follow me all the days of my life." It was hard to believe it, though, after a day like this one.

Emmet was quiet for a few long moments after that. He took a deep breath. "We just want to make things better for you. And it'll happen — if you can stick with us through this." Again, he paused. "I just couldn't see any other way to make it happen. For you. For Luvina and me." He grimaced. "Guess

I was thinking more of Luvina and me, though. I'll admit that." He looked down at the book in his hands and muttered, "I'm sorry."

Emmet was the strong one. Always had been strong in a way that neither she nor Frank were. Frank was rebellious and quick to strike out. Quick to defend himself and everyone he loved. Anger lurked very near the surface of his personality. Emmet, on the other hand, took things with a steady calm that had created a haven for Annie in the midst of Pa's decline. If Emmet had doubts, he never let them show. It was almost frightening to think he was just like everyone else. "Don't apologize," Annie croaked. "You've done nothing wrong."

After a moment, Emmet said, "Just one more. 'Peace I leave with you, My peace I give unto you: not as the world giveth, give I unto you. Let not your heart be troubled, neither let it be afraid.' " He closed the Bible. "I read those when I'm discouraged. Or afraid. I thought they might bring you some comfort, too."

Emmet? Afraid? Annie blurted out the question, even though she wasn't sure she wanted to hear the answer. "When have you ever been afraid of anything?"

He looked surprised. "The first time Pa

got drunk. And the next. And the next — until I decided to be angry instead. Most days since I realized there was no way for me to save the farm. At least once a day since we left St. Joseph. Most recently, when Shadow ran off with you into that storm —"

She'd never suspected. Wanting to put his mind at ease if she could, Annie said, "I'm not really afraid. I'm just — miserable. Frustrated. Ashamed, I suppose. The way I sassed Mrs. Hollenberg about how I could manage out here, and then I made a mess of everything. *Every. Single. Thing.* On the first day."

"It was just one day. You need time to find your way. Anybody would."

"I don't have *time* to 'find my way.' It's my job to feed people every day. There's another stage coming through in a few days, and I can't figure that stove out."

"Of course you can. Have a little faith in yourself."

Annie shrugged. "George Morgan doesn't like me."

"Why would you think such a thing?"

"Did you hear what he said about the ham?" She mimicked his deep voice. " 'The whole thing? You used up the whole thing? It was the last one.' Was I supposed to know that? And he was upset about my needing something to help me reach the shelves in the storeroom. He muttered about my needing a ladder. As if a ladder cost a hundred dollars."

"He just wants to make sure you don't fall again."

"He doesn't think I can keep up — or cook well enough." *And he might be right.*

"Did he say that?"

"He didn't have to. I could tell. And who could blame him after today? All a body has to know to cook grits is how to boil water."

"You'll figure it out. You have to, because I'm counting on you to cook up some buffalo and dumplings one of these days."

He was trying to joke, but he wasn't very good at it. Annie harrumphed softly. "Think I'll ever figure out George Morgan? He hardly said three words today."

Emmet was quiet for a moment. Finally, he said, "Morgan's not what any of us expected, I'll give you that. He's a man of few words, but he's not profane and he doesn't drink. He's obviously hardworking or he'd never have built this place up the way he has. Billy's been here since the beginning. I talked to him a little while ago. Morgan started with nothing but that one sod room at the far end of the building.

160

When he decided to dig a well, the clear water convinced him he'd chosen a good spot. He decided the effort to drag logs in was worth it. He and Billy built the main room and put up one corral. Next came the barn and the blacksmith's soddy. More corrals. A kitchen instead of a lean-to. Finally, Morgan added the rooms we're using and raised the roof to add the loft. You've got to admire what he's done."

With Billy's help. "Billy's been here the whole time?"

Emmet nodded. "He was living with his people, the Pawnee, when he met George Morgan. He didn't really say why he left with Morgan and came here to Clearwater, but I hear respect and admiration in the boy's voice when he talks about George. I'd say there's a lot more to Morgan than meets the eye."

Billy was nice. He'd been around George Morgan for a long time. If both he and Luther trusted George Morgan, that meant something.

Emmet cleared his throat. "You know that neither Frank nor I would ever leave you in a place where we didn't think you were safe. Right?"

Annie did know, but it was nice to hear the words. She nodded.

Emmet held up the Bible. "How about I mark some verses and leave this one with you? Then, if you ever want to read them for yourself, you'll be able to find them."

"Thank you." Whether she read the book or not, it would be a comfort to have something with her that meant a lot to Emmet.

Bible in hand, Emmet got up to leave. He put out the light and then, for the second time since they'd arrived at Clearwater, he kissed Annie on the cheek.

After he left, Annie lay awake, thinking how lucky she was to have two brothers who cared about her.

CHAPTER 11

When he turned in on the night of April 3, a mixture of nerves and excitement kept Frank on the edge of sleep. If things had gone as planned, the train bringing mail from the East had arrived in St. Jo. about the time he and Emmet were trying to think of something good to say about the singed ham and the dried-out biscuits Annie had served for supper. That meant Jake Finney would likely ride in around noon the next day — maybe early afternoon. There was no reason not to sleep. None at all. Lying on the narrow cot in the room he shared with Emmet, Frank closed his eyes. Listened to Emmet's even breathing. And could not sleep. It was still dark when he finally rose and, boots in hand, padded through the kitchen and the main room and out onto the front porch — which wasn't really a typical porch, but rather a shaded spot created by the roof's extending about three feet beyond the station's log wall and out over the dirt.

Mindful of the glow of campfires near the trail, Frank stared off toward the horizon. Finally, he dropped into the rocking chair sitting just outside the front door and pulled on his boots. As the sky began to change from pale blue to gold, he rose and stepped out from beneath the overhang. Hands on hips, he studied the horizon.

Emmet appeared in the doorway. "You know it'll be at least noon," he said. "Likely later than that, given that it's everybody's first time at handling the exchange. And that assumes everything went according to plan in St. Jo. — and that no one will have trouble with a horse throwing a shoe — or a rider."

Frank shrugged.

"Come on in. Annie's about got breakfast ready." He chuckled softly. "And I don't think anything's scorched this morning."

"Don't think I can eat," Frank said. "Too many knots in my gut."

"You need to try," Emmet reasoned.

With one last look eastward, Frank followed Emmet back inside. He was grateful for the coffee, but one spoonful of grits and he realized he didn't dare try to eat. Excusing himself, he marched down to the barn.

■ ■ ■ ■

A repeat of grits and molasses had to suffice for breakfast on Annie's second full day at Clearwater. They were all preoccupied with thoughts of the first mail exchange, and Frank was too keyed up to eat much, but Annie counted it a small victory that she managed not to burn anything — except herself. A slight scorch on the index finger of her left hand, and it didn't even need wrapping. Thank goodness it didn't blister. Thank goodness no one noticed.

After breakfast, she put the ham bone in a pot with beans and set them on the stove to cook. Needing to keep an eye on the stove, she decided to stay close. She'd take the day to learn what was in all the crocks and boxes in the kitchen and storeroom. And she'd clean as she sorted and rearranged, using the empty crate to step up on the table. Donning the apron hanging on a nail just outside the storeroom door, she began by climbing from crate to tabletop so she could reach the shelf above the window. She had the first crock in hand and had bent to set it on the tabletop when George Morgan walked in, two rat traps in hand.

"Get down," he said brusquely. "I'll reach

those for you."

Annie obeyed, albeit rather awkwardly, since Morgan didn't offer his hand. Once she was back on solid ground, she reached for the traps, all the while doing her best to camouflage her revulsion. "Thank you."

He didn't hand them over. "Your brothers say you hate rats."

"Doesn't everyone? What do you use for bait?"

"I'll see to it." Setting the traps down, he moved past her and pulled everything off the top shelf, plunking it all on the table. He pulled an amber bottle out of his pocket. The word *poison* dominated the red and white label.

"By the way," Annie said, "it was just a mouse up on that storeroom shelf yesterday. I saw it again just now." *And I neither screeched nor fell.*

He grunted. "I've got mouse traps in the store." He put the poison back in his pocket, set the rat traps down, then hesitated. "Did I explain the store?"

You haven't explained much of anything. Annie shook her head.

"Goods can move from the store I sell out of," he pointed toward the main room, "to your storeroom here off the kitchen. Never the other way. When something's gone from

166

out there, we're out of it, plain and simple. That way the cook doesn't make plans only to find out I sold something she was counting on."

"That's thoughtful."

"Not really. The last cook taught me to respect her kingdom. She needed cornmeal for something, and I'd invaded her storeroom and sold it the day before. She launched a plate at my head."

Annie didn't know whether to smile or frown. She couldn't exactly tell if Morgan was telling an amusing anecdote or not. "I'm not prone to throwing fits like that."

"Good," Morgan said. He pointed into the storage area off the kitchen and repeated the word. *"Storeroom.* Follow me and we'll talk about the *store."* In the main room he produced a ledger book from beneath the counter. "You can take anything out of the store you need. Just make sure you write down what you take." He paused. "You can write?"

"Of course." It came out a bit more snappish than she intended, but really, he thought she couldn't read and write?

He frowned. "No offense intended. Some folks passing through Clearwater never had a chance to learn."

Feeling a bit less defensive, Annie said, "I

had to quit school to keep house when our ma died, but I'd made it through the third reader."

Morgan opened the ledger and turned it about so Annie could read the headings. "Find the right page and write what you take or sell."

He pointed to a line on the page marked FLOUR 200# AT 20¢.

Surprised by the fineness of the handwriting, Annie studied the line. "Where do I write how much folks paid?"

"They don't always pay cash." Morgan retreated around the corner into the storeroom, returning with a black metal box not all that different from the one Emmet had given her to keep their money in. He opened it. This one had a tray in the top for loose change. "This stays on the shelf just the other side of the doorway. The ledger keeps track of what goes out so I know when to put in an order. That's the most important thing, since it takes nearly a month to get something delivered. As to cash money, most folks barter." He reached below and brought up a small balance scale. "Once in a while, a miner headed east wants to pay in gold dust. Doesn't happen as often as it used to, but if it comes up, just ring the bell by the back door. I'll take care of that."

"When you've a mind to," Morgan continued, "take a look-see in the store so you know what's what. Might be the ladies would appreciate a lady behind the counter. If you're willing. Then again, you've probably got enough to think about, just keeping up with the cooking. I'll get those traps." He left abruptly, retrieved the rat traps, and went to work in the storeroom setting traps.

Goodness, but the man's mind did work in curious ways. He'd wandered from an apology to an explanation of how he ran his store to a suggestion about her working the counter to withdrawing the idea and then back to setting mouse traps. And somewhere in there was the hint that he had his doubts about Annie's ability to keep up with the cooking.

Annie closed the ledger and returned to the kitchen. She began unloading the rest of the shelves to ready them for scrubbing. When Morgan was finished setting traps, he called for her to come and see where they were.

"Wouldn't want you to get any more surprises and fall off that box again. Next time Luther comes through, I'll order a ladder — if we haven't traded for one by then. Best get myself down to the barn and see to things." He tugged on the brim of his hat and left by way of the storeroom door. He initially pulled it closed behind him, but then opened it again. "That shelf over the window. Leave it be. I'll get it moved down one of these days." Again, he closed the door. Again he opened it. "You want this open or closed? If you raise the window, you'll get a nice breeze through. Have a better chance of hearing the Pony Express arrive, too. But maybe it's too cool." He looked behind him. "Gets a bit dusty if the cattle get to milling around. Last year's cook said she liked the fresh air. Suit yourself."

He departed, heading toward the barn, before Annie had a chance to say a word. The door was open and she left it that way, enjoying the sounds of the lowing cattle and the occasional sound of voices as the men worked. Morgan had them hauling everything out of the soddy today and doing a general clean-up. Apparently he was expecting a blacksmith to arrive soon. Another big appetite. Which reminded her to check the stove.

The fire had gone out.

Frank spent the morning in the barn helping Billy muck out stalls. That work done, he retrieved a curry comb and headed for Outlaw's stall. George meandered in, pausing to peer over a stall door at Annie's chicks.

When Frank walked by, Morgan said, "Too early to be saddling up."

"I know," Frank said. "Thought I'd give him a good brushing." He stepped into the black horse's stall.

"This is a hard place to keep chickens," Morgan said. "Don't believe I know anyone who's tried it with much success."

"Luther said the same thing." While he brushed Outlaw, Frank told Morgan about Mrs. Hollenberg's saying the work was just too hard for "one tiny girl." "That made Annie mad." He looked over at Morgan. "She was already headed someplace she didn't want to be and then Mrs. Hollenberg was telling her it was going to be too hard. Anyway, the next thing I knew, Mrs. Hollenberg's niece was fetching me so the old lady could arrange a little surprise. Maybe she felt bad about what she'd said. Annie didn't even know we had the chickens until we were back on the trail. The old lady sent some kind of plant, too. Some special ingredient for chicken and dumplings."

"Rosemary," Morgan said and smiled. "Sophia does make a good pot of chicken and dumplings."

"You know about that?"

171

"Did some freighting before I landed here at Clearwater. Always looked forward to Sophia's cooking." He paused. "It's too early to set out a plant. You should tell your sister."

"I think she knows. She set it on the trunk in her room. Said it would get good light there."

Morgan returned to the subject of chickens. "They either die of the heat or freeze to death come winter. Or get carried off by a hawk or eaten by some other varmint."

"Like I said, Luther warned her about all of that." Frank looked toward the stall where the chicks scrabbled about and muttered, "She's only here because Emmet and I signed her up. We didn't ask her. We just did it. Told her it was a faster way to get what she wanted."

"What's that?"

"A little house in town. White, with blue trim and window boxes. There's more to it than that, but you get the idea."

"Luther says she was young when her ma died."

Frank nodded. "We were both nine. Emmet was fourteen."

Morgan gazed toward the station. "Billy was nine when his ma died." He glanced over at Frank. "That's when he hitched a

172

ride with me." He shrugged. "It's not the same with a girl and her ma, though. That'd be harder, I guess."

"It wouldn't have been so bad if Pa — well, Pa might as well have died, too, for all the good he was after that. Emmet and I took on the farming and Annie took on the house. We managed. When Pa died the banker let us know he'd gambled the place right out of our hands. We had to leave. I don't think Annie minded. She had an idea that moving to town would make her happy. Emmet and I mean to see her happy. In the meantime, she's going to be all alone out here — again — just like she was on the farm. So if you could see your way clear to helping us build some kind of chicken coop, we'd be mighty grateful."

Morgan stared toward the station. "Maybe off the arbor that shades the back door."

"She won't care where it is. But she wants those chickens to thrive. It doesn't seem a lot to ask. You already said you like chicken and dumplings. And Annie's not a half-bad cook — if only she could have eggs to work with." He led Outlaw outside and hitched him to a corral post, then came back and began to fork hay into the stalls. Billy climbed down from the loft. Together, he and George began to haul water.

After he'd hung the last bucket of water in the last stall, Morgan came alongside Frank, who was standing near Outlaw staring east, keeping watch for Jake Finney. "Little thing like her, she'd never make it through the drifts we get in the winter. It should be close up to the station."

"Luther said sod was the way to go," Frank said.

Morgan shook his head. "Can't spare the time to cut sod. I've got some scrap lumber piled behind the soddy. That'll have to do for now. Might be in the fall I could have the crew cut sod after all the haying's done."

The morning dragged by. Annie served lunch and again, Frank could barely manage to swallow. He was pacing out front, barely taking his eyes off the eastern horizon when, finally, he caught sight of a horse and rider. *Jake!* His heart pounding, Frank charged around to the back and clanged away at the bell mounted by the back door. Billy raced out of the barn, unhitched Outlaw, and hurried up to help with the exchange. Annie handed Frank a sugar sack. She'd worked twine in and out around the mouth of the sack to form a loop he could hang over the saddle horn.

"Ham and crackers," she said. "You've barely eaten."

Frank barely had time to thank her before a gray pony streaked past the wagons trundling up the trail. Horse and rider arrived in a cloud of dust. In what seemed like one fluid motion, Jake Finney hauled back on the reins, dropped to the earth, and snatched off the mochila. He took a step toward Outlaw. The black horse danced away. They'd nearly made a complete circle when Frank motioned for George to step up and take the black horse's head. "Let me try," he said and reached for the mochila.

Jake stepped away, talking all the while. A courier had missed a connection on the train somewhere to the east. "We were three hours late before we even got started," he said. "They got a special train and one heck of an engineer to make it up. Reckon we'll read all about it. The *Gazette* is putting out a special edition."

While Jake chattered away about this horse and that swing station, Frank held the mochila up so that Outlaw could take a good look. "Nothing to be afraid of, you big galoot," he said, allowing Outlaw to snuffle the leather. "See? Can I put it on now so we can go for a run? You like to run. Remember?" Outlaw snorted, but he let Frank slip the mochila over the saddle horn and cantle. "That's my boy," Frank said, and patted the horse's neck.

Taking the reins from Billy, he leaped into the saddle. Outlaw took off as if shot from a cannon. Settling the horse into an easy lope, Frank glanced behind him. Annie and the others were still standing outside the station. He raised one hand to signal goodbye. And realized that his stomach had come unknotted. He'd never felt so happy.

CHAPTER 12

Not long after leaving Clearwater, Frank realized that literally everyone looked his way as he and Outlaw loped past wagon after wagon after wagon. "See that?" he said to the horse, grinning when a black ear turned back. "That's right. You listen to Frank. We make a good team."

When the first "bonnet" raised a hand to wave at him, Frank acknowledged the attention with a dignified raising of one hand, just to let her know he'd seen her. *Not wishing to ignore you, Ma'am, but as you can see, I'm about serious business, here.* With all the publicity about the Pony in the newspapers, most of the folks on the trail would have heard of the Pony Express. A few bored souls might just be waving because of the red shirt and the fast horse. No matter the reason, Frank loved the attention.

When two boys straggling along behind a wagon took their hats off and cheered,

Frank added a little tug on the brim of his hat. The boys saluted. When he raised his hat off his head and waved back at the next "bonnet," she clasped her hands before her and jumped up and down with glee. When he got back to Clearwater, he'd ask Annie to stitch red stars to the backs of his gloves. Red, to match the red shirt. Maybe he'd see about getting gauntlets like the ones Whiskey John wore. White ones. With fringe and a red star on the cuff. People would really notice that, and why not give them something to remember. He'd probably meet Luther on the trail, for once the freighter delivered the rest of his load to Fort Kearny, he'd be turning around and heading back to St. Jo. Maybe he'd slow down just long enough to holler and ask the freighter to bring him a pair of gauntlets on his next trip.

By the time Frank and Outlaw reached the first relay station, the black horse's shoulders were crusted with white, his nostrils flaring wide to suck in air. As Frank dismounted and pulled the mochila off, he asked the station keeper to take good care of the horse. "He's special," Frank said.

The station keeper grunted something noncommittal.

"I mean it. I might try to buy him when

the paymaster comes through." He hadn't really thought about doing so, but once he'd said the words, he decided it was a good idea.

"Think he'll last that long?"

Frank hadn't thought about that, and it gave him pause. There was no way to tell how the other riders would treat their animals, no way to know when or if he'd be aboard Outlaw again. It surprised him how much that bothered him. He would try to find out about buying him.

The rangy dun he mounted next almost left before Frank was in the saddle. He blushed with embarrassment as he scrambled to find his seat. The mare's choppy gait made for a miserable ride, and Frank was more than a little happy to catch sight of the flag flying over the parade ground at Fort Kearny. He was supposed to stop and check for mail at the fort post office, but he was distracted by gawking at the military buildings, and when the mare fought him, he almost got dumped. She was still feeling her oats when it was time to leave — much to the amusement of a couple of soldiers lounging in front of a store. They hooted and hollered while Frank tried to remount. By the time he managed to get back in the saddle, his face was burning with embarrassment.

Luther had warned him about the next place — Dobytown, just off the ten-mile-square military reservation to the west. Dobytown had twice as many saloons as it did residents. When Frank raced past, a few garishly clad women lounging against one of the buildings behaved in a distinctly unladylike manner. Maybe he should have ignored them, but he didn't. Instead, he stood up in the stirrups and made a show of tipping his hat to them all. White gauntlets were definitely called for.

After Dobytown, the road deteriorated. The sobering possibility that if he didn't keep watch his horse might drop into a chuckhole and break a leg ended all the waving and saluting for quite a while. By sunset, Frank had managed five flawless exchanges. His legs were beginning to feel it, but he'd expected that. Overall, he was feeling great about everything — and then he met his nemesis.

"Keep your eye on this one," the station keeper warned. "I been callin' her Jezebel. She bites. Hard. I wouldn't put it past her to try to reach back and get a piece of your leg if you don't keep her moving."

Frank nodded. "I'll watch her." The station keeper let go of the mare's head and

Frank nudged her to move out. Instead, the mare gave a little buck and then, quick as a flash, bared her teeth and went for Frank's right leg. "Whoa, there!" he hollered, yanking on the bit with all his might. The mare missed, but it was close. She started to rear. Frank dug in the spurs and the mare took off.

Darkness fell. The battle with the horse raged. Without warning, the mare would whip left or right in a perfect imitation of the move that had unseated Annie on the way out. The difference was that Shadow had been fleeing out of fear. Jezebel was acting out of sheer malice for her rider, and as he ground out the final leg of the 100-mile ride, Frank began to feel every stride the cantankerous beast took. Muscles he didn't even know he had hurt. Just when he thought the mare was too tired to cause more trouble, she'd try something new. He nearly shouted *hallelujah* when he finally caught sight of the lights glowing in the windows at Willow Island.

As the station keeper brought a fresh horse up, Frank called out a warning.

"She's the devil in disguise," he hollered. "She bites and bucks. I imagine she kicks, too."

The station keeper was ready. The second

181

the mare bared her teeth, he slapped her hard with one hand and grabbed her bridle with the other. "I'll work on curing her of that while she's here."

"I won't be the only one who thanks you."

As Frank switched to the new mount — he thought this one was a bay, although it was too dark to be sure — the station keeper said, "She's a sweetheart named Rachel. Be good to her, now."

Frank promised, and it was an easy promise to keep. The mare's gait was so smooth and he was so worn out that he might have fallen asleep in the saddle — if he hadn't needed to keep his eye on the tall weeds that marked the edge of the trail just to keep from getting lost. Thankful for the full moon, he raced on through the night, catching snatches of sound as he passed campfires and circled wagons. Coyotes in the distance, a bit of accordion music once. A crying baby. Once, a scream. Or was it a wail? Either way, his first instinct at the sound of human misery was to stop and see if someone needed help. Of course he couldn't. The mail had to go through, no matter what. Still, the sound haunted him all through the long night ride and into the next day when finally, as dawn was just beginning to light the sky, he reached Midway Station.

Frank slapped the mochila in place and stood back so the fresh rider could mount up. As he charged up the trail, Frank pulled the dust-caked kerchief away from his face and followed the wrangler leading his weary horse past the fence keeping someone's garden safe from roaming cattle.

"Well, now," he said, taking his hat off and staring up at a windmill over the well in place of a windlass. "That's an improvement." His horse drank deeply from the stock tank while Frank rinsed his hands beneath the trickle of water being pumped out of the earth and into the round stock tank. Next, Frank cupped his hand beneath the flow and sucked down the cool water.

"Yeah," the wrangler said to his comment about the windmill. "Pa's always up for improving the place. Even if it means risking his neck climbing halfway to the moon to rig up a piece of machinery."

There was something odd about the wrangler's voice. Weak. The poor fellah probably got teased a lot about it. It just didn't sound manly. Wait a minute. What was it he'd heard about — "Hey!" he snatched his hat off his head. She turned around. She had a square jaw and tan skin. Freckles sprinkled across her nose. Two long dark braids that reached almost to her waist. Amber eyes and an expression that said *If you want trouble, you'll get it.* She spoke to the horse. "That's enough, now. Let's get you cooled down and then I'll bring you back." She led the horse away.

"No, wait." Frank trotted to catch up with her. Wow. She was tall. "I didn't mean it the way it sounded. I'm sorry I didn't greet you proper. That's all. I mean. I didn't expect — you. A girl. I meant — a l-lady. You didn't look like a lady."

The woman stopped. She looked down at him, one eyebrow arched, emotion flickering in her amber eyes. She looked over at the horse and then back at Frank. "If you aren't going inside, you might as well help." She traded the bridle for a halter and handed him the bridle, then tied the lead rope to the top corral pole with an expert hitch. While Frank stood there holding the bridle and feeling foolish, the girl loosened the girth on the saddle. About that time, the horse decided to protest the entire routine and lashed out with a hind foot. Frank sidestepped just fast enough that the worst of the blow missed. But it was close.

The girl grabbed the halter and gave it a shake. "You settle down or you and I are gonna have a problem. I'll have you hobbled and hog tied in about two minutes if you try that again."

The horse rolled its eyes and snorted. "Aw, now, just give it up. One way or the other, you're gonna have to let me do my job." She reached up to touch the animal's head. When the horse flinched visibly, she swore softly. "Who's been beating up on you, anyway?" She glared at Frank.

Frank held his hands up. "Don't look at me."

The girl pursed her lips. Slowly, ever so slowly, she laid her palm on the horse's cheek. The mare did not relax, but she stayed put. "That's better. Now." She ran her hand across the cheek, to the throat, and then along the neck. Gradually, the mare relaxed, and the girl looked over at Frank. "If you're responsible for her being afraid of a man's hand, you and I are gonna have words. Later. I've got work to do right now. Mama's got a meal in the oven, keeping it warm for whenever you showed up."

Frank hadn't mistreated the horse, but he didn't defend himself right then. He was looking forward to "having words" with the prettiest ranch hand he'd ever seen.

A few days after Frank departed astride Outlaw, Emmet left carrying the Eastbound mail coming from California. Annie stood out front watching him ride away until he was little more than a pinprick on the horizon, fighting the tightness in her throat. For the first time in her nineteen years, she was absolutely and truly alone. Frank and Emmet weren't just out in the field plowing or planting. They hadn't just gone to find Pa and drag him home. They were a hundred miles away. *A hundred miles.* It might as well be a thousand.

"You going to feed me or not?"

Brought back to the moment by the gruff question, Annie looked over at the exhausted rider mopping his face with a filthy bandanna. "Right away," she said, and scurried inside to fry a bit of salt pork and dish up a plate of beans.

As she set the plate before the rider, she introduced herself. He grunted something unintelligible and scooped beans.

"Frank's my brother," she said. "Frank?"

He took a gulp of coffee.

"He would have been at Midway Station."

The rider shrugged. "Don't know anything about any Frank." He shoved the empty plate across the table at her. "Load me up again."

Just as Annie took the plate and headed for the kitchen, George Morgan stepped out of the store. Reaching beneath the counter,

186

he pulled out the ledger book and opened it. After she was back in the kitchen, she heard Morgan say something to the rider, although she couldn't quite make out the words.

When she set the second helping of beans and bread before him, the rider thanked her. "Sorry I can't tell you more about your brother. Didn't hear any news of any trouble, so I reckon he's all right. He was probably just resting up in the bunkhouse."

Annie nodded. "You're probably right. By the way, you didn't tell me your name."

"Reynolds."

"Well, Mr. Reynolds, welcome to Clearwater. How about a slice of bread to go with that refill?"

"I would be much obliged, Ma'am. Thank you."

Back in the kitchen, Annie decided she would want Frank and Emmet treated well by whoever was feeding them, and so she reached for a treasured jar of preserves and put an extra-large dollop atop the slice of bread. *If only I had butter, too.* When she set the plate in front of Reynolds, he took a huge bite of the bread, clearly savoring the preserves.

He looked up at Annie. "I know I act like I was hatched under a rock, but I weren't.

My ma used to make some mighty good preserves." He held out his mug and Annie poured more coffee. "Thank you, Ma'am."

"You're welcome. And if that doesn't fill you up, there's more. Just holler and I'll serve it up."

George Morgan lingered over his ledger while Reynolds ate and then Morgan offered to show him to the soddy. Annie thought that rather odd. After all, the soddy was right there in plain sight. Oh well. In the short time since she'd met him, Annie'd realized that understanding a man who barely said three words at a time probably wasn't going to be possible. She resumed her cleaning and sorting. She intended to scrub every square inch of the kitchen and the storeroom including the walls and floors. She would even scrub the shelf George Morgan had ordered her not to use. She'd just discovered a bag of raisins tucked into a crock she'd expected to be empty and thought *raisin molasses pie* when Jake Finney came in the back door.

"Came to check the traps for you," he said. "George was going to do it, but I told him I would. He's got his hands full right now with some wagon master that wants to trade for fresh oxen."

Annie stepped to the door and looked

toward the barn. She'd been so busy scrubbing and cleaning she hadn't even heard a wagon roll in. But there was no wagon. "Where's the wagon? Are the oxen so bad they can't even make it to the barn?"

"Oh, no. The wagon master had them stay up on the trail."

"But — why?"

"Billy said something about knowing him from last year. He headed up a bigger group headed for Oregon. Seems to fancy himself something of a legend-in-the-making. Prides himself on making hard bargains 'for his people.' " Jake smirked. "He actually calls them that. 'His people.' Anyway, he wants George to go to the oxen, not the other way around. In case he decides George won't deal. Hey. That Reynolds isn't much of a talker, is he?"

"He was tired," Annie said. "He seemed to appreciate the preserves I put on his bread."

"Said he was a cowhand down Salina way when he heard about the Express. Doesn't play checkers. Didn't seem interested in much of anything but getting some sleep."

"Salina's in Kansas, isn't it?"

"It is."

"How about that," Annie said, smiling.

"Another Kansan riding for the Pony Express."

Jake was crouched down resetting a trap. Obviously there were more rats. Smart ones. Annie tried not to think about it.

"I don't claim Kansas anymore. I'm liking Nebraska just fine."

"You won't go back then, someday?"

"Nothing to go back to," Jake said.

"No family?"

"None I want to claim, that's for darned sure." He reached for the copper boiler beneath the table and left — abruptly — to haul in water.

Annie had just measured out flour and lard to make a piecrust for her raisin molasses pie when she heard someone come in the front door. Wiping her hands, she moved toward the main room just as a woman bent down to speak to a child. A towheaded little boy Annie guessed to be about four years old. "Hello," she called out. "Welcome to Clearwater. How can I help you?"

The woman glanced behind her. Back toward the trail. The little boy began to cough. Annie hurried to the water cooler, filled the mug with water and took it to where the woman was kneeling beside the child.

"Thankee," she said, and urged the child

190

to drink. "I was hopin' — while we was stopped — we got a team that ain't gonna make it over the mountains. I told Norbert they was ailin' but he wouldn't listen. Now Reuben here's taken a fever and —" The child coughed harder.

Annie crouched down beside them, more as a show of sympathy than anything else. The little boy ducked away from her and against his mother and turned his head away, but not before Annie saw the shadows beneath his eyes and the scarlet blush of his cheeks. "Bring him over to the counter," she said. "I'll get a cloth and you can cool his forehead with a compress."

The woman lifted the child and did as Annie instructed. She filled a crockery bowl with water from the cooler, set it beside the child, and handed the woman the cloth.

"I was hoping you'd have some Wistar's? In the store?"

"I'm afraid I don't know what that is."

"You ain't never heard of Wistar's? Balsam of Wild Cherry. Best thing they is for the croup. And cough. And consumption — although Arnold here ain't got consumption. It's the dust out on the trail. He can't abide it. Starts every day bright eyed and bushy tailed and by noonin' he's feelin' poorly." As if on cue, the little boy began to cough yet again. His mother helped him sit up. He began to cry.

"Let me look and see," Annie said and scooted into the storeroom. She should have come in here sooner. So she'd know what was what. She'd just about decided to run down to the barn and ask George Morgan about cough syrup when she heard an angry voice out in the main room.

"I told you to stay with the wagon!"

Annie stepped to the doorway just as a lanky, dark-haired man marched across the room and grabbed the woman by the elbow.

"We got no money for medicine. I told you that."

The woman pulled away. "I got the butter," she said. She looked at Annie. "Ain't checked on it since I milked the cow this mornin', but it's likely nigh on to churned." She paused. "I hang the bucket on the back and the wagon does the churnin', ya know."

Annie didn't know, but she nodded as if she did. "If I've got what you need for the little one, I'll be happy to trade for butter."

"And we'll just go without, I suppose," the man said.

The woman held her ground. "It won't hurt us to go a day without butter if it'll give little Arnold a rest from that cough."

The man looked at Annie. "Well? You got

what she wants or not?"

"I'm sure we have something. Just give me a minute." She paused. "In the meantime, could I interest you in a . . . drink?"

The man looked doubtful. "Drink of what?"

"Coffee."

"You expect I'd pay you for coffee?"

"Of course not. There'd be no charge."

The man strode to the back door and stared off toward the barn. He shook his head. "Can't see why it's takin' so long to strike a deal for a couple of cows. It's not like there ain't plenty of 'em just waitin' to be yoked up and driven off."

"Well, now," the woman said. "Mr. Longwood's just tryin' to see that we aren't taken advantage of." She looked quickly at Annie. "Not to say the station keeper would do that."

Her husband whipped his head about. "You mind your tongue, woman." He pointed at Annie. "I'll take that coffee."

Annie hurried to pour coffee, served it, encouraged the man to take a seat "out back under the shelter where you can enjoy the spring breeze," and then returned to the store. Finally, on a high shelf — *Must things always be on a high shelf?* — she saw a few dusty bottles of what looked like medicine.

But she couldn't read the labels. Again she needed a ladder. She'd just retrieved the crate and reached the three bottles when she heard someone clear his throat. She looked over just as George Morgan appeared at the end of the row of shelves.

"Didn't want to startle you," he said. "Guess I'll need two ladders."

"Only if you insist on putting things as high as possible," Annie said. She looked down at the three bottles in her hand. The child started coughing again. "The woman asked for something called Wishter's something-or-other."

"Wistar's," Morgan said.

"Yes. That's it. But I don't think you have any." She looked about her. "At least I couldn't find it." She held up the three bottles. "Will any of these work? She offered to trade butter for the Wistar's."

Morgan stepped closer. He took the middle blue bottle. "This will help. If anything will." He shook his head. "That child needs a doctor, not some home remedy." He took the bottle back out to the main room and handed it to the woman. "This is the best I've got. It'll help some. Until you see the doctor at Fort Kearny."

"Doctor?" The man had stepped inside and called out from just inside the back door. "We got no money for a doctor." He glanced at the boy. "He'll be fine. Folks come west when they've got bad lungs, ain't that right? The farther west we get, the better he'll be." He looked over at the woman. "You just see if he don't get better. He don't need no doctor."

Seated on the counter, leaning against his mother, the little boy had fallen asleep. The man strode over and gave him a little shake. "Time you was gettin' back to the wagon train, boy. Look sharp, now, ain't nobody goin' to carry you."

"I'll carry him," George said, and glanced at the woman. "Then I can bring back the butter you were going to trade." He looked over at the man. "Longwood's out by the corral. Maybe you'll want to talk to him about the cattle."

The woman took the bottle of medicine and tucked it in her pocket. "You'd best let me carry him. He don't take to strangers."

Morgan put his massive hand to the child's back, and the little boy stirred and opened his eyes. He leaned down. "I'm just George," he said. "All right if I carry you for your mama?" He picked the boy up. The child put his head on his shoulder.

"Well don't that beat all," the woman said.

After George Morgan and the woman left,

Annie looked around the store, so she'd know what was where. Morgan didn't return for a long while. When he finally did, he was driving a couple of pathetically thin oxen. Thinking she would save him the trip in with the butter, Annie walked down to the corral, but Morgan had no butter. It had "slipped his mind."

CHAPTER 13

Is too much for one tiny woman. Mrs. Hollenberg's warning sounded often in Annie's mind during her first weeks at Clearwater. Truth be told, it was more of a haunting. How she regretted the saucy tone of voice she'd first used with the older woman. *Anyone can make dumplings.* What a fool she'd been. How naïve to think that cooking for Emmet and Frank and Pa had prepared her for life at a busy road ranch. At home she'd had time for things like gardening and tending chickens and their only cow. In fact, those things had been welcome distractions from the loneliness hovering over every day without Ma. Annie had thought life was hard then. She'd had no idea.

At Clearwater, Annie's life revolved around the kitchen. She rose before dawn to make coffee and bake bread. Lunch had to be started the moment breakfast was finished. Once she'd served lunch, she had to plan for supper — unless, of course, she was serving beans, in which case she had to start supper while making breakfast. Work wasn't even finished with the washing of the last supper dish, for if she intended to serve hot bread for breakfast, she had to mix the dough and set it to rise overnight. And, whether she ground them or not ahead of time, it paid to roast the next day's supply of coffee beans before turning in. The days went by in a blur of mixing, grinding, kneading, roasting, scrubbing, sweeping, cooking, and cleaning.

As April gave way to May, the trail west grew busier, with dozens of outfits passing by every day. There was no way to predict when immigrants might stop at Clearwater or what they might need or want — including a fifty-cent "home-cooked meal." Annie rarely left the station except to check in with her Rhode Island Reds. She was thankful for Billy's watchful eye over the chicks. Most nights, she fell exhausted into bed and was asleep almost before her head hit the pillow.

On the rare night when she didn't fall instantly asleep, Annie inevitably thought back to Mrs. Hollenberg's warning. More often than not, she was tempted to think the old woman's prediction had been right. The work was too much. The first visit from the paymaster helped strengthen her resolve to succeed or die trying — metaphorically speaking. After the man left, Annie sat in her room staring down at the open cash box in wonder. Two hundred dollars. And a gold coin. A coin she'd earned. Just feeling it in the palm of her hand made it easier to face the next day.

She often thought about the women plodding along the trail in the distance, their calico hems trailing in the dust, their bonnets tied snugly to keep the sun off their faces. Would they find what they were seeking out there in the Far West? Would their dreams come true? She wondered about the woman who'd come seeking medicine for her sick child. What would become of those two, living with an angry man unmoved by his own son's illness? Inevitably, she remembered George Morgan holding the little boy close as he carried him for the weary, worried woman. She hoped the child was sleeping soundly at night.

By the end of the first week of May, the rest of George Morgan's crew had arrived — a blacksmith named Hitch, half a dozen wranglers responsible for driving the cattle out on the prairie to graze, and another trio charged with cutting firewood and fence posts in distant cedar canyons. They would alternate between that and cutting and stacking hay, all of it in preparation for winter. As for the fence posts, Morgan sold those to ranchers in the region.

After his first full circle with the mail, Frank returned to Clearwater happier than Annie had ever seen him. Emmet, on the other hand, was worried. He'd expected at least one letter from Luvina to be waiting for him at the end of his first circuit. When Annie told him no letter had arrived, disappointment dropped over him like a shroud. When she turned in that night, she peered into her brothers' room. Emmet was sitting on the edge of his cot, his Bible open across his knees. He didn't look her way. Right before she fell asleep, Annie offered a pathetic prayer on his behalf. *Oh Lord, Emmet's shepherd . . . have mercy.*

The next morning, pewter-colored clouds obscured the blue sky. Over the next several days, a steady drizzle transformed the earth into a kind of mud George Morgan called gumbo and travelers called a variety of colorful terms that made Annie alternately blush and wonder at mankind's creativity when it came to profanity.

The "field crew," as George Morgan called them, had brought their own cook. They stayed mostly to themselves, but with the advent of rainy weather, they took shelter in the station every night, playing checkers and cards to while away the time. Annie learned that George Morgan was something of a legend when it came to checkers. He inevitably won, even if he played with only two checkers. She also learned that Frank liked to play cards, something that would have concerned her except for the fact that George Morgan wouldn't allow gambling at Clearwater — not even when Hitch promised they'd bet navy beans instead of pennies.

The mud and rain made travel difficult, but it didn't keep the stage from delivering the three newspapers Morgan subscribed to — the *Nebraska City News*, the *St. Joseph Gazette*, and the *Philadelphia Leader*. When he wasn't playing checkers, the station keeper spent rainy evenings standing behind the store counter, a newspaper spread before him. One evening when Annie was making the rounds to serve fresh coffee to the men, she paused near the counter and asked Morgan why he subscribed to a Philadelphia paper.

He didn't even look up. "It's home. Or was. A long time ago."

"Really? I'm surprised to hear it."

He took a sip of coffee, peering at her over

the rim of the cup. Finally, he said, "I can see that. Why?"

She was sorry she'd said anything. "I just — I don't know." She did know, but she wasn't about to tell George Morgan. People from big cities were refined, and their speech showed it. Both the Patee House dining room and the ballroom had buzzed with conversation. People even talked while they were dancing. George Morgan's interchanges with people could barely be called conversations. He was abrupt to the point of rudeness. Annie could not imagine him fitting into any kind of life in a big city. He didn't bother to trim his beard, and it had clearly been a very long time since he'd cut his hair. Of course she could never tell him that, and so she apologized. "I didn't mean anything by it. Luther said you'd been a trader before you built Clearwater. Billy said you'd spent some time with the Pawnee. I thought you were from out here."

Morgan set the coffee mug down. "The only people 'from out here' are Pawnee. Cheyenne. Sioux."

Well, of course she knew that. She also knew the expression on his face all too well. She saw it every time she did or said something George Morgan thought ignorant.

Now he actually scowled down at the

backs of his hands as he asked, "You think I look Indian?"

So much for trying to have a conversation about something beyond rats in the pantry or troublesome chickens Morgan labeled "doomed to die." Annie shook her head. "Of course not. Then again, the only Indian I know happens to have blue eyes. I don't suppose most people would think Billy 'looks Indian' — whatever that means." *There.* That wiped the frown off his face. She turned to go.

"Wait. I — I'm sorry. I didn't mean —"

Annie whirled back around. "Didn't mean what, Mr. Morgan? To make me feel even more ignorant?"

He just stared at her for a moment. Finally, he swept a hand across the surface of the newspaper. "I recognize an occasional name. There's an odd comfort in that. I don't know why. And you're not ignorant."

Well. That was something. He didn't think her ignorant — and he liked reading about home. Just like Annie, who enjoyed the *St. Joseph Gazette.* Not that St. Joseph was home — yet. But it would be. "Perhaps you miss Philadelphia."

"Don't miss it. Never regretted leaving."

Then why do you find comfort in reading that newspaper?

Morgan must have seen doubt on her face. "Leaving meant I didn't have to listen to my father's favorite lecture anymore — the one about the son who repeatedly failed to measure up. By the time I left, I'd titled it." He held up both hands to create quotations marks in the air as he said, " 'Destined to Disappoint.' "

How awful. "Our pa used to say things like that to Frank. Mostly that he'd never amount to anything."

Morgan grunted softly. "Well — your pa was wrong about Frank."

"Yes. And your father was wrong about you." Annie motioned about them. "Look what you've built."

"This place you never wanted to come to and can't wait to leave?"

Annie protested. "Just because I —"

Morgan interrupted her. "There's another reason I like to read a back-East newspaper. There's war in the wind, and I like reading a back-East perspective on the situation. Lately, the *Gazette* is little more than rattling sabers. You'd think shots had already been fired."

Annie nodded. St. Joseph hadn't been the most peaceful place back in March. North-versus-South sentiments had been evident even then, both in newspapers and on the streets.

Morgan pointed to a headline in the *Leader.* "Here's news that'll interest you. The telegraph is expected to reach Fort Kearny by fall. I expect the Pony will add another official stop so riders can pick up the latest news."

Not long after the brief conversation, Annie returned to the kitchen and began preparations for the next day's meals. As she worked, she mulled over the things she'd learned this evening. Morgan had grown up in the East. When he thought about his father, he remembered disapproval and the awful words *destined to disappoint.* Pa's last years had been awful, but if she chose to, Annie could reach beyond those years and call up good memories. She wondered if George Morgan could do the same — if he tried. She hoped so.

One thing from the conversation stood out more than anything else, though. *He doesn't think I'm ignorant.* It was good to know it. Very good.

When the gray canopy obscuring blue sky finally gave way to sunshine, the world around Clearwater was transformed. Green prairie stretched away from the station like an emerald carpet, and wildflowers began to bloom. Luther had been right about Mother Nature's paintbrush.

One day, Annie stole away to gather a bouquet. Back in the kitchen, she laid the flowers on her worktable and retreated to her room to retrieve the damaged lavender and white teapot she'd often used as a vase. The finish was crackled, the spout chipped, and there was no lid, but none of that mattered. It had been Ma's, and that made it precious. The delicate design — a drawing of a well-dressed couple standing on a path leading to a castle in the distance — contrasted sharply with Clearwater's rustic crockery and plain white dishes. As she arranged the flowers, Annie smiled, envisioning the day when she'd be able to order an entire set of dishes reminiscent of Ma's teapot.

She had just set the finished bouquet on her worktable when George Morgan opened the exterior door that led into her kitchen storeroom and asked her to come outside. After gathering up the leaves and stems she'd trimmed away while arranging her bouquet, Annie complied. Morgan indicated a pile of weathered boards in the back of a nearby wagon before pointing to the space between the open storeroom door and the arbor shading the back entrance to the main room.

"I thought you'd want it close."

Annie stared at him, uncomprehending.

"Billy has more important things to do than tending chickens." He pointed at the space again. "So. Is this all right?

Oh. He's going to build a chicken coop. "I — yes," Annie stammered.

"It shouldn't take long."

"Thank you."

"Don't thank me. I could have rented that stall more than once last week if it wasn't housing a hen party. So I'll build your coop. But I still don't think they'll last. They're too scrawny to thrive out here." He began to unload the lumber.

Annie went back inside. Grabbing the broom, she began sweeping, muttering to herself as she worked. Just when the man seemed to be doing something nice, he buried it beneath a thick layer of *don'ts*. *Don't* thank him. *Don't* expect the chickens to live. And for goodness sake, *don't* expect Billy to tend them. As if she'd asked Billy to do that. She'd actually told him not to pay them any mind. She'd told him she'd see to them. Was it her fault if Billy seemed to *like* tending chickens?

Huh. Cobbling together a chicken coop

207

from scraps of half-rotten lumber was more about George Morgan's getting free of a nuisance in his barn than being kind to his cook. He was sure they'd drop dead before laying any eggs. Well. She'd show George Morgan a thing or two. The sweeping finished, Annie put the broom away. Come heck or high water, she would serve that man chicken and dumplings before the year was out or die trying. She scowled at the storeroom door. "And for your information, George Morgan, not a single one of those birds is *scrawny.*"

Neither Emmet nor Frank was at Clearwater when Whiskey John brought news of trouble in Nevada. Paiute Indians had raided a Pony Express Station and killed five men. "They had a bad winter out that way," the stage driver said, "and things were already warming up for trouble this spring. Heard about one chief fasting for peace, but no one's listening to him. Now the settlers are arming themselves. They even called up a Texas Ranger to help 'em fight a war."

When Frank arrived a few days later with the last of the mail from California, the deep furrow between his brows was back. As he watched Jake Finney charge eastward, he swore softly. "That's the last of it until things get sorted out with the Paiutes."

"I'm so glad you're safe," Annie said.

"Why wouldn't I be safe? There's no Indian trouble anywhere near Clearwater."

All right. Change the subject. "The paymaster came through," Annie said. "We've got a good start on the future. Want to see it for yourself?"

Frank just grunted. "Make sure you hold on to it. If this trouble lasts, the Pony Express will go dead broke. We might not see another penny."

There wasn't much point in trying to talk him out of his mood. Frank would have to wallow a bit. Later tonight, she'd show him the gauntlets Luther had delivered a few days ago. Maybe she'd convince him to draw the pattern for the red star he wanted her to stitch to each one. For now, though, Annie changed the subject to the chickens. "George Morgan built a chicken coop. He said you talked him into it. Want to see it?"

Frank followed her around to the back of the station, but he wasn't impressed with the ramshackle assembly of weathered boards. He grabbed one and gave it a wiggle, impervious to the protests from the Rhode Island Reds inside.

"They're a little skittish," Annie said.

Frank went to the divided door and peered over the closed lower half and into the gloom. "No nesting boxes?"

"That'll come. Morgan didn't have the time — and they're too little to need them, anyway."

Frank grunted. "One thing I'll have now is time. I'll see what I can do." The furrow smoothed out a bit as he turned to her and said, "I'm not angry at you, ya know."

"Of course I know."

He nodded and then looked toward the covered wagon down by the blacksmith's soddy. "Looks like Hitch is doing a good business."

"I'd say so. That forge is going sunup to sundown. I had no idea Clearwater would be such a busy place."

"One of the riders up the trail said they counted the traffic coming by Fort Kearny one day last summer." He paused to take the bandanna from about his neck. Walking over to the near well pump, he soaked the bandanna and mopped his face before asking, "Want to guess how many wagons rolled past?"

Annie considered. With a little shrug she said, "A hundred?"

"Hard to believe, but it was *five* hundred. Guess you'll be serving plenty of meals whether the Pony's running or not." He nodded toward the kitchen. "You make peace with the black iron beast yet?"

"More or less. I'm truly thankful the extra crew brought their own cook along. There's plenty to do without cooking for them, too."

Frank nodded. "Fall off any crates lately?"

Finally. A glimmer of humor in his dark eyes. Annie nudged him. "You fall off any horses lately?"

"Almost. There's this one mare named Jezebel . . ."

Frank talked all the while Annie poured fresh water for the chicks. He was still talking when he followed her inside so she could make him something to eat. By the time he'd eaten, Annie had learned about more than just Jezebel.

Frank had asked the station keepers along the way to handle Outlaw with a gentle hand. He described the various stations and the men who ran them — and a girl who worked the ranch built up around Midway Station. A girl her father called Pete because "she's his right-hand man."

Something in the way Frank talked about her made Annie suspect that Pete was more woman than girl.

CHAPTER 14

The Paiute War raged on in the West all through May and into June. A restless Frank rode out on any excuse he could find. Emmet was more content to stay at Clearwater, happily performing whatever task George Morgan assigned. When he finally heard from Luvina, she mentioned her hope chest and a wedding quilt. Emmet's spirits soared.

Thankfully, the Pony Express continued to pay its employees.

"Your employers are determined to see the effort succeed," the paymaster said, "and they've got the financial backing to do it. The Pony is too important to fail just because of a little rebellion in the West."

For several nights in a row after the paymaster left in early June, Annie opened the black cash box and recounted the stack of bills. She palmed the three gold coins she'd earned and wondered at the miracle of Annie Paxton having the key to a cash box containing over $600. And she worried. What if this was all the money they would earn? The paymaster's assessment of the "little rebellion in the West" did little to assuage her fears, especially when news arrived of yet another death at yet another Pony Express Station.

Still, Annie tried to be thankful. At least they'd been assigned to a peaceful station. At least the trouble was far away. Until, one morning, war cries and gunfire sounded, and a mounted war party charged in from the North and surrounded the station.

Paralyzed by fear, Annie saw little more than a flash of color outside the kitchen window before Emmet charged into the room, grabbed her, and propelled her beneath the worktable. He crouched down, placing himself between her and the doorway. Annie didn't know when he'd snatched up a knife, but at the sound of footsteps pounding through the main room toward the kitchen, Emmet shielded her with one arm while he brandished the weapon.

An unarmed George Morgan bolted into the room. Why hadn't he grabbed the shotgun mounted just inside the door leading into the storeroom? But it was too late for that, because the attackers were here now. Inside the station.

A painted face loomed in the doorway behind Morgan. He whirled about and roared, "Are you out of your *mind*?" Then he charged the Indian, pushing him backward and bellowing words Annie didn't understand.

Expecting to hear a desperate fight, she cowered behind Emmet. But there was no fight. As quickly as the melee had begun, it ended. Everything grew quiet.

Finally, George Morgan stepped back into the kitchen. "It's all right," he said. "You can put the knife down, Emmet. It's just Badger and his friends having a little fun. He's gone now."

Emmet sprang to his feet. "Wh-what did you just say?" He held on to the knife.

Morgan leaned down and spoke directly to Annie. "Come out. It's safe."

Annie crept out from beneath the table, trembling so violently she kept one hand on the table to steady herself.

Morgan scratched his beard. He looked away for a moment. "I'm sorry. I didn't expect them for at least another week."

Emmet put the knife down.

Morgan explained further. "They stop by every year, right before the spring buffalo hunt."

Annie pointed out the window and stammered, "Th-that is *not* 'stopping by.' "

"I know. And one of these years, someone who doesn't know what's going on is going to start shooting back and all he — heck will break loose." He shrugged. "There's not much I can do about it. It's their way. They'll only be here for a few days."

Annie sputtered, "A few *days*?"

"Yes. To celebrate spring. And the hunt. Feasting and talk around the campfire. I hang a side of beef in the soddy. Age it. Save it for spring. We feast. Later, we trade."

"Trade what?" Emmet asked.

"Buffalo robes. Dried tongue. I pay a dollar a hide for the robes and a quarter a dozen for tongue. By fall, I'll have a stack of hides — and pelts — to send east. Last year, I made three dollars apiece profit on the hides alone. I sell the dried tongue to folks on the trail."

As he talked, Morgan was standing with his back to the main room. Annie was the first one to notice when the same Indian he'd forced out of the kitchen moments ago stepped in the back door. Half of his face was painted white, the other half red. A wide black stripe accented each cheek. His two braids were wrapped with some kind of fur, his muscular neck adorned with a necklace made of what looked like giant claws — or bones. He wore fringed buckskin leggings and carried a huge knife thrust into a wine-colored sash wound about his waist. When he saw Annie, he stopped. She took a step toward Emmet. Morgan glanced behind him. "That's Badger," he said. "He's Billy's uncle." He raised his voice and spoke to the Indian, then turned back to Annie and Emmet. "I'll introduce you."

Annie hesitated, but Emmet nodded and together they followed Morgan into the main room. While Morgan talked, the Indian studied her, his eyes roving from the top of her head, downward, and then back up again. When the Indian looked away from her and over at Emmet, Annie relaxed a bit. Whatever was going on behind those dark eyes, she didn't think the man intended harm. Finally, he spoke to Mr. Morgan and then, laughing, turned to go. Annie couldn't help but smile at the way he swaggered as he retreated toward the barn where a half-dozen other Indians waited.

"You said he's Billy's uncle?" Annie asked.

Morgan nodded. "The last of that family, as far as I know."

"How so?"

"Small pox."

Annie flinched at mention of the dreaded

disease. "I can't imagine how horrible that must have been."

"Hell on earth," Morgan rumbled.

"You were there?"

"I was." He grunted. "And finally, being a doctor's son did me some good. I was vaccinated. So I carried water and did what I could."

Annie gazed toward the barn. "So Billy and Badger owe you their lives."

Bitterness dripped from every word as Morgan said, "They owe me nothing. I did the same thing for every single person in the band. Everyone died — except Billy and Badger. You'll see the scars when Badger isn't painted. Billy didn't scar as much. I don't know why." He shook his head. "I don't know why any of it had to happen."

Not an hour after the Pawnee made camp, another ruckus erupted outside. This time it was the army — a double column of mounted men, charging this way. Annie hurried out the front door. The soldiers were just a short distance away when they pulled up abruptly, sending a cloud of dust into the air. George Morgan trudged into view and hurried out to meet them. The man at the head of the column dismounted and together, he and Morgan walked toward the station. The rest of the column remained in the saddle.

Annie could hear every word. "Really, Morgan, you've got to talk to Badger. He's going to get someone killed. Everyone between here and Fort Kearny thought the Paiute War had spread to Nebraska. The poor civilian who saw them charging toward Clearwater had nearly lost his voice by the time he stormed up the stairs to the captain's office. He'd been yelling warnings the whole —" He noticed Annie for the first time and stopped, midsentence. Tugging on the brim of his hat he greeted her. "Ma'am."

"This is Annie Paxton," Morgan said. "Cook for the Pony Express. Her brothers ride out of here."

The soldier swept his hat off his head. "Lieutenant Wade Hart, Ma'am. I've heard about you. I'm pleased to finally make your acquaintance." He looked back at George Morgan, speaking sternly. "You're lucky I caught sight of Badger's camp before we came in with guns blazing."

"I know it. I warn them every year."

"Well warn them louder," the soldier said, and gestured toward the column of mounted men. "A dozen men missed chow because of some infernal wild-goose chase."

Annie spoke up. "I don't mind cooking if

they don't mind waiting." She glanced up at George Morgan, a question in her eyes.

He nodded and looked back over at the lieutenant. "How's that, Hart? Unless you think it's a bad idea to have your boys out front while my friends are camped out back."

"I'll order them to hitch their horses right here — and to mind their manners. Then you and I can try to talk some sense into Badger about his penchant for dramatics. Does that suit?"

Annie could not take her eyes off the man. He was almost as tall as George Morgan, but any resemblance ended there. Morgan had dark hair and gray-blue eyes. Lieutenant Hart was blond-haired, with china blue eyes. Shaggy, lumbering George Morgan reminded Annie of a barely tamed bear. Clean-shaven, dark-eyed Lieutenant Wade Hart was the most beautiful man Annie had ever seen.

News of the Pawnee encampment at Clearwater traveled all up and down the trail, and a steady stream of the curious found its way to Badger's camp. Many visitors stayed either to buy something from the Clearwater store or to eat a meal. Annie expected the Pawnee to resent being intruded upon.

Instead, they extended hospitality, sharing meals around their campfire. When Annie expressed surprise, George Morgan explained that Pawnee culture revolved around a notion of hospitality foreign to whites.

"White people think of 'home' as a place they withdraw to," he said. "They share, but only on their terms. The Pawnee see welcoming guests as a point of honor. Sharing is expected. In fact, the man who gives most is respected most."

The explanation gave Annie a lot to think about. It also helped her understand why it was so important to Morgan's business that Badger and the other hunters feel welcome at Clearwater. Her own part in showing hospitality was an odd one. She was an almost-constant object of fascination — a fascination that led Badger's men to gather just outside the kitchen window and watch her work.

The first time she looked up from kneading dough and saw Badger and another young brave watching her, Annie yelped. Badger's expression transformed and he spoke a rapid apology. Annie didn't understand the words, but the tone was clear. His intent was friendly, if unnerving. Remembering what Morgan had said about Pawnee ways, Annie snatched up a basket of leftover biscuits and held it out. The men scooped them up with obvious appreciation. Later that evening, George Morgan thanked her.

"It was just leftover biscuits," Annie said. "I was embarrassed. Do you think they'd appreciate a delivery of fresh bread in the morning?"

"You don't have to do that."

"But if I *wanted* to bake a couple extra loaves of bread, you wouldn't object?"

"Of course not."

"Then I'll double the batch for tomorrow morning."

The next morning, satisfied that her four loaves of bread would turn out nicely, Annie stepped outside to tend her Rhode Island Reds. She paused for just a moment, turning her face to the sky and reveling in the fresh breeze and the warmth of the sun on her face. She gazed toward the prairie, mindful of the wildflowers bobbing and dancing in the breeze. For just that brief moment, she understood what might draw people west. And then she peered over the half door and into the chicken coop.

"No-no-no-no!" Yelling at the top of her lungs, she unlatched the door. She didn't even think before snatching up the huge snake coiled about three terrified chicks and flinging it out the door with all her might. The snake flew through the air, landed a few feet away, and was still. Annie dropped to her knees. Holding the two corners of her apron together, she counted as she dropped the cheeping chicks into the resulting pouch. *Ten.* Only ten. It wasn't until she'd given up the search that she sensed someone standing behind her. Emmet, George Morgan, and Badger. Blushing, she staggered to her feet. "D-darned snake got two of my chicks. Somebody needs to kill it."

"Somebody already did," Morgan said, as Badger held up the dead snake. The hideous thing was long enough to span the space from his outstretched hand to the earth.

Annie looked up at Morgan. "Please thank him for me. Darned bull snake."

Emmet's voice sounded odd. "It's not a bull snake."

"It is, too. It's brown and mottled just like . . ."

Badger snatched up the snake's tail and gave it a shake. One, two, three, four . . . five rattles.

Annie took a step back. She gulped. "Well. It's dead now." Trembling, she turned back around, releasing the surviving chicks and closing the coop door.

"Guess we'd better be patching the holes in the walls," Morgan said.

Badger walked a few feet away, took the knife out of the sash at his waist, and cut the rattles off the snake. He cast the carcass aside and presented the rattles to Annie as he said something that made George Morgan smile.

Annie tucked her hands beneath her apron, hoping Badger would take the hint. She didn't want the rattles from the hideous thing. "What?" she asked. "What now?"

"He's going to call you Rattlesnake Woman." Morgan laughed softly. "How about that? Less than three months in the West and you've already earned yourself a Pawnee name. Not many Missouri girls can claim that honor. Then again, I doubt many Missouri girls have killed a rattler with their bare hands."

"I just wanted to get it away from my chickens. I don't even know how the thing died. And I thought it was a bull snake."

"Well, it wasn't. And it's dead. As far as Badger's concerned, you are not a woman to be trifled with. He'll be telling that story for the rest of hunting season. Maybe for the rest of his life."

CHAPTER 15

Not long after Badger and the hunters went on their way, a freighter named Jim Willard rolled in with three loaded wagons pulled by six pairs of oxen. Annie heard both his bellowing and his bullwhip long before he arrived. Unloading the supplies intended for Clearwater took the better part of two days, but by the time it was done, every shelf in both the store and the storeroom groaned with ammunition, canned goods, barrels of whiskey, pork, ham, coffee, salt, pepper, vinegar, soda, flour, corn, dried apples, peaches, oysters in tins, and, wonder of wonders, eggs, the last nestled in a barrel of sawdust.

Having fewer failures in the kitchen nowadays gave Annie the courage to bring up the subject of milk and butter early one morning when George Morgan was tending the rat traps. "If anyone mentions wanting to trade for a milk cow, I'd be very pleased if you'd take them up on it."

Morgan looked at her as if she wanted to fly to the moon. "Seems to me you have enough to do just keeping those chickens alive. And anyway, I've never been offered a cow."

"Think about all the business it would bring if word got out that folks could buy butter at Clearwater. And milk. Anyone traveling with children would want to stop."

He shook his head. "You're asking for more work than you realize."

"I'm not," Annie insisted. "We had a cow when my mother died. I was nine years old. I managed." It wasn't a lie. She had managed — eventually. "Without milk and butter, there's only so much a cook can do."

Morgan seemed to be considering the point. But then he said, "Nobody's complained about the food. It ain't broke. No need to fix it."

Frank lay on his side staring at the wall. *Four weeks.* It had been four weeks and nobody knew when — or if, for that matter — the Pony Express would get off the ground again. He thought about the white gauntlets Luther had delivered. He might not even get to wear them. And Annie had sewed the red stars on the cuffs. What a waste.

Emmet was sleeping soundly just across the room. Waiting patiently. Rereading Luvina's letters as if they contained the secret of life. He didn't seem one bit worried about the Pony. He wasn't unhappy, either. Emmet found a million things to do around the station. Of course there was always plenty to do, and that was all well and good, but Frank wanted to . . . run. He wanted to see Pete again. He wanted to be on the move. If he could at least go out with the wranglers and herd cattle or go cut wood with that crew, it wouldn't be so bad. But riders weren't supposed to go farther from the station than four hundred yards. They had to be ready to go the minute the Pony started up again. *If that ever happened.*

Frank closed his eyes. He turned over. Yanked on his blanket. Tried to settle. But it was no good. He wasn't going to sleep and there was no reason to keep trying. Slowly, he dressed. Quietly, he left the station, pausing for a moment to look up at the moon and the stars. He'd ignored the lure of Dobytown for an entire month of long days and longer nights. There couldn't be any harm in a moonlight ride. He'd be back at Clearwater before anyone so much as knew he was gone.

The minute Frank stepped into a stall to slip the bridle on Rachel, the sweet bay mare he'd ridden in, Billy called from up above. "That you, Frank?"

"Going to take a little moonlight ride. Be back before sunup." Billy said nothing, and before long, Frank was headed away from Clearwater, riding at an easy pace, getting the feel of the trail and thinking about having a little fun tonight. All night, maybe. Two hours there, a good long rest for Rachel while he tried his luck with a hand or two of poker, and then two hours back. He'd learned a thing or two about poker when he was riding for old man Hillsdale. Who knew but what he could add a little unexpected cash to the family till. Maybe, just maybe, if Good Luck rode with him tonight, Frank could once-and-for-all destroy Rotten Luck, the red-eyed shadow that had dogged the Paxtons since the day Ma died.

RL poured drinks for an old man with one foot in the grave and scattered weeds on poor soil. It shrieked with joy when a banker evicted a good family and, just when things looked like they might be turning around, RL stirred up Indian trouble in the West and brought the Pony Express to a screeching halt.

Frank spoke to the horse. "Tonight's going to be different, ain't it Rachel?" When the mare whickered and tossed her head, Frank looked up at the night sky and called out, "Hear that, RL? Tonight's the night I kick you out of our lives for good." Rachel snorted, and Frank laughed. He'd have a few drinks and a little fun with one of them pretty little gals who'd waved when he rode past Dobytown the last time. He'd tell a few stories and win a few dollars and be back in bed at Clearwater before sunrise, with nothing but good memories.

He heard Dobytown long before seeing its light in the distance. A rambling piano. Laughter. And the report of gunfire, which made Rachel pull up. "Go along, there," Frank said, touching her sides with his spurs. As he closed in on the place, the golden light spilling out over a dozen different saloon doors and half as many windows beckoned. Raucous laughter helped him decide which one to visit first. The place looked and sounded much more inviting at night than it had by day.

Frank had just dismounted and was wrapping Rachel's reins around the hitching post, when the general noise inside the saloon quieted. A lone voice called out, "I tell you, unless you repent, you shall all likewise perish." Frank frowned, wondering at the level of drunkenness required to inspire a saloon customer to shout religion. The smudged outline of a black-clad form with one arm raised appeared just inside the filthy window to the left of the door. Again, a voice rang out. "You know not the hour when the Lord may come. Today is the day of salvation."

The only response was more laughter, accompanied by a taunt or two in regards to what the folks inside the saloon did and did not know. But the preacher wasn't giving up. "Brethren. I preach unto you the gospel by which ye must be saved. For since by man came death, by man came also the resurrection of the dead. For as in Adam all die, even so in Christ shall all be made alive. Repent, and be baptized every one of you in the name of Jesus Christ for the remission of sins, and ye shall —"

The sermon ended with an unintelligible squawk as someone grabbed the preacher. In the next moment, he came flying out the door and landed in the dirt at Frank's feet. Rachel snorted and danced away. "Whoa, there, girl. Whoa, now." Frank settled the horse before looking down at the man in the dirt. "This is no place for a preacher."

The man sat up. Blood trickled from his lower lip. He swiped at it with the back of his hand. "That's where you're wrong, son. This is exactly the right place for a preacher." He waved a hand toward the saloon. "Where is the saving power of Christ more needed than in a den of iniquity such as that?" He grabbed Frank's sleeve. "Don't go in there, son. If you haven't gone in yet, I beg of you. Don't. Get back on your horse and return from whence you came."

With a groan, the preacher got up. Pulling a handkerchief out of his pocket, he dabbed at his split lip. Presently, he put the handkerchief away and headed back inside. This time, he didn't get a chance to open his mouth. Frank didn't see what happened, but the result was the preacher's being propelled backward through the door with such force that when he landed on his backside in the dirt, it was more than a minute before he could get his breath.

When he finally sucked in air, Frank helped him up. "You're going to get yourself killed. Haven't you heard of Dobytown?"

"Of course I have," the man said. "That's why I came. They all said I was insane. But God said, 'Go.' "

They were right — whoever they were. "You telling me you hear God's voice?" He really was crazy.

The preacher reached inside his coat, pulled out a small book, and held it up. "He speaks to all who read His Word. Matthew twenty-eight, verses nineteen and twenty. 'Go ye therefore, and teach all nations, baptizing them in the name of the Father, and of the Son, and of the Holy Ghost: Teaching them to observe all things whatsoever I have commanded you: and, lo, I am with you always, even unto the end of the world. Amen.' "

Frank waved a hand up and down the row of saloons. "And you think this is a good place to do that?"

"The Lord himself went to the poor and lowly."

"And from what I hear, they thought *He* was crazy, too." Frank dusted off the back of the guy's dark coat. "Come on, now, Parson. How about you ride back with me to Clearwater? Have a little breakfast. If preaching's what you want to do, you can preach there. At least you won't get yourself killed."

The parson seemed to consider it. "You'd do that? Call people to a service?"

It was about as far as you could get from what Frank had in mind, but Annie would like it. Going to church was probably one of

231

the things she was looking forward to about living in St. Jo. "There's already enough people at Clearwater to give you a good hearing. Besides that, the stage is due in tomorrow. What with them and the rest of us, I'd say you'd have a congregation of nigh onto thirty people." He was exaggerating, but if the stage was full, not by much. "And they'll be polite."

"I'll think on it. But first —"

The old guy could move, that was for sure. Like a flash, he darted back into the saloon. And just as quick as a flash, he was pushed back outside. This time when he got up he was rubbing his jaw. Blood dropped from a new cut over his left eye. He bent to retrieve the small Bible, groaning with the effort of standing upright. Surveying the row of saloons, he muttered, "Maybe I should try another door. One will open. I'm certain of it."

Frank just shook his head. This was a strange kind of rotten luck, but it was old RL all over again. Try to steal away for a little drink and some harmless fun, and who lands in the way but a parson with no sense to know when to quit. It would be funny if it wasn't so darned annoying. "*I'm* opening a door. At Clearwater."

"Clearwater." The parson said the word as

if he'd never heard of the place.

"First road ranch east of Fort Kearny," Frank said. "You must have come past it on your way out here."

"No, son, I've come from California by way of Fort Laramie."

"There's a war on out that way," Frank said. "How'd you get through?"

"By the full and merciful grace of the almighty God."

Or dumb luck. "Where's your horse?"

The preacher waved a hand toward the far end of the row of saloons where the ugliest mule Frank had ever seen waited at a hitching post. "I am currently being refined in the matter of transportation," he said. "Her name's Cordelia."

"Well, mount up. I need to get back before anyone misses me."

The old guy peered at Frank for a moment. "Deeds of darkness and deception are not worthy of a fine young man such as yourself. Perhaps our meeting was foreordained by the Almighty to keep you out of trouble."

"Or to keep you from getting yourself killed?"

The old guy chuckled. "A secondary benefit." He began to limp down the row of saloons toward the mule. As they passed first one door and then the next, he hesitated, muttering and mumbling. By the third doorway, Frank realized the preacher was praying. Thank goodness, though, he didn't dart into any more doorways.

The mule wasn't just the ugliest Frank had ever seen. She was also probably the oldest. When the parson fumbled to stow his Bible in a battered saddlebag and she turned her head to watch, Frank noticed white hairs about her eyes. Her muzzle was white, too. She brayed a protest when the parson mounted up. "Cordelia is as crotchety and recalcitrant as they come," he said, "but she is sure-footed and for that, I praise the good Lord Who made her."

"You know," Frank said as they plodded toward Clearwater, "you'd have ended up with more than a sore jaw and a black eye if I hadn't come along. Nice coincidence, eh?"

The old man chuckled. "Think what you will, young man, but there are no coincidences in God's economy."

Frank just shook his head. The parson might not be the kind of crazy that landed people in an asylum, but he wasn't normal, either.

It was barely past dawn, but Annie had the coffee made and the biscuits baked before she stepped outside to tend her chickens. Movement down at the barn drew her attention. Frank. And another rider. What on earth? Where had Frank been? She glanced east, and her heart sank. *Please. Not Dobytown.* She'd been more than a little worried about Frank for a while now. Whereas Emmet could manage most things with patient acceptance, Frank fidgeted and fumed. Annie didn't like thinking it, but there were times when her twin brother reminded her of the worst things about Pa.

Ah, well. Wherever Frank had been and whoever that was astride the mule, they'd both expect breakfast. Scattering the last bit of grain held in her apron–turned–feed bag, she filled a bucket with well water at the pump and then went back inside. When Emmet stumbled into the kitchen a few minutes later, Annie asked, "Did you hear Frank leave?"

Emmet shook his head. "Why?"

"Because he just came back. On that bay mare named Rachel. With someone else riding a mule."

Emmet's expression went from surprise to doubt to annoyance. "I'll take care of it," he said. "Don't worry."

Annie nodded. But she did worry. She couldn't help it.

CHAPTER 16

The parson was like no preacher or reverend or missionary Frank had ever heard of. Not that Frank was all that up on the subject, but a person just grew up with a certain impression of what a preacher was, and Charlie Pender wasn't it. First of all, he insisted they call him "just plain old Charlie." "Never cared much for fancy titles," he said. Second of all, he told George Morgan over breakfast that he'd appreciate the chance to stay at Clearwater while he healed up — his eye was swollen almost closed and from the looks of it would be turning several different shades of blue and purple over the next day or two — but he did not accept handouts and he could only stay if George let him "earn his keep."

"I'm a terrible shot, so I'm no good at hunting, but I can wield a hammer or a saw. I've been a wrangler and a bronc buster and a gold miner, and if I were even a decade younger I'd have wanted to be riding right along with these rambunctious Pony Express boys. So put me to work. Or I can't stay."

Morgan considered for a moment. "How are you with chicken coops?"

Annie looked up. She seemed surprised, and Frank winked at her.

Morgan nodded and then spoke to Frank. "You mind helping the parson?"

Frank was glad for the assignment — for a lot of reasons, not the least of which was a chance to understand what was really behind Charlie Pender's odd behavior. Whoever heard of a preacher choosing to go to a place like Dobytown? Beyond his curiosity about Charlie, Frank hoped that helping the parson with Annie's chicken coop would keep him from having to listen to Emmet go on and on about Frank and Dobytown. The last thing Frank needed was a lecture on that subject. Fixing up the chicken coop would also show Annie how sorry he was for causing her worry. It wasn't enough, though. He needed to apologize.

While the parson looked over the project, Frank stepped inside. Annie was standing at her worktable, measuring ingredients into a bowl. Frank spoke from the doorway. "I was wrong to go over to Dobytown. I'm sorry."

Annie glanced up. "Okay."

Oh no. She was trying to hide it, but that was definitely a tear leaking out of one eye. With a sigh, Frank crossed to where she was standing. As he approached, she began putting more energy than usual into the process of pinching flour, lard, and cold water together to make piecrust.

"Raisin molasses," she said.

"How about that parson," Frank said. "He told me he doesn't believe in coincidence. Said he and I had a 'heavenly appointment' over there at Dobytown. I don't know what to think, but if he's right, I guess that's one of those 'good things' you like me to notice." When she didn't respond, he changed the subject. "It's nice George asked him to spend some time on that chicken coop. A strong wind would blow that thing to kingdom come."

Annie shrugged. "He thinks they'll all die in the heat. Or another snake will gobble them up. Or a badger. Or something. Anyway, he doesn't want to be bothered putting up a proper chicken coop. Just like he doesn't want to trade for a cow."

"You asked him for a cow?"

Annie scattered flour on the tabletop, plopped the pie dough in the middle of the spot, and began to roll it out. "I asked him to consider taking the trade if one was offered. Told him I was willing to take on the milking and such." She settled the piecrust into the waiting pie plate. "Did you know he traded for all that fancy furniture in my room? Billy told me about it." She snorted. "He trades for things he doesn't even need. But he doesn't want to try for a cow. And I know why. He's not happy with the job I'm doing, and he's not about to give me something else to take care of."

"He was probably thinking ahead to winter. He knows how hard it is to get out and care for livestock when it's blowing a blizzard. Billy says they sometimes winter as many as two hundred oxen. And from what I hear, the winters out here make Missouri's feel like spring."

Annie reached for the bowl of pie filling and began to pour it into the waiting pan. She glanced over at Frank. "You can't be running off to that place." Her voice wavered.

"You're right." He grunted softly. "I just needed — I don't know. I can't explain it. Something just — builds up inside me."

"What if the Westbound mail had come through last night?"

"Emmet would have taken it. And I'd have

gone east for him. It would have worked out."

"And what if it didn't?"

"Nothing bad happened. Except for Charlie getting beat up. And I saved him from worse. Like I said, isn't that one of those 'good things' you're always telling me to notice?"

Annie took a minute before saying quietly, "Promise me you won't go there again."

"I promise."

"And you'll keep that promise?"

"Would I have made it if I didn't mean to keep it?"

She sighed. "I hope not. But — sometimes I wonder."

If she'd slapped him it wouldn't have hurt as much as hearing the doubt in her voice. Frank was about to march away when Annie did the strangest thing. She touched the place just above her nose. It left a floury smudge. "I worry about that crease between your eyebrows. It gets deeper when you're upset about something, and — I wish you didn't have it. I wish you were happy."

Frank grabbed a towel and wiped the smudge away. "Know what will make me happy, Ann E.?"

He said the name slowly, with a break between her first name and the second initial — which was where *Annie* had come from in the first place. Ann Elizabeth. Ann. E. She shook her head.

"Seeing *you* happy. Hanging your window boxes and painting the trim on your cottage. To finally, once and for all know that you have the home you deserve. That you don't have to wonder how to stretch a cup of grits into a meal for four or hope the neighbors share something from their garden so we don't all go hungry. That will make me happy." Another tear leaked out of the corner of her eye. He handed her the towel. "I won't go back to Dobytown. I promise."

A few days after the parson arrived at Clearwater, Annie had just taken two pies out of the oven when she heard the now familiar rattle-rock-creak-clatter of the approaching stage. Setting the pies to cool on her worktable, she hurried through the main room and stepped onto the back porch just as Whiskey John hauled back on the reins. He dropped to the earth the moment the stage rolled to a stop, moving quickly to open the Concord coach's bright red door.

The first passenger to exit was a ramrod-straight, elegantly dressed woman who moved with all the bearing of a queen. Her shining dark hair made the blue of her gown and hat seem even more brilliant. She wore black leather gloves and carried a black parasol, which she did not bother to open as she paused to look around.

Two of the three men who clambered down behind the lady seemed bent on vying for the privilege of escorting her into the station, but she shooed them away. "Thank you, gentlemen, but I'd like to enjoy the fresh air here on the porch for a while."

Annie welcomed the passengers, promised a meal soon, and retreated inside. *Four passengers, Whiskey John, Billy, George Morgan, Emmet, Frank, the parson, and me.* Thank goodness she'd made two pies. She'd crossed the main room and reached the door leading into the kitchen when one of the men called after her.

"See here, girl. Don't scurry away until you've taken care of your customers. I've a craw full of road dust, and I require something a good deal stronger than water to clear it out."

Annie turned back around, taking note of the man's tailored suit. When he pretended to brush dust off his coat, he "just happened" to reveal a holster and a glimpse of what was probably a pearl-handled gun. "I

242

can have coffee ready in just a few minutes," Annie said.

"I asked for whiskey," the man snapped.

The lady passenger cleared her throat. Her blue hoopskirt swept the floor as she marched across the room, firmly planting the tip of her closed parasol with every step. When she'd reached the water cooler, she filled the tin mug that always hung on the spigot and held it out to the willful dandy. "It won't kill you to drink a cup of water."

With a smirk, the man with the gun took the cup, emptied it, and slammed it down on the counter.

"There now, was that so bad?"

The man slipped around the counter and helped himself to the bottle of whiskey on the shelf below. And a glass. "No, but this is better." He looked over at Annie. "And it's what I asked for in the first place."

The lady leaned her parasol against the wall and removed her gloves as she spoke to Annie. "Please tell me Fort Kearny isn't much farther. I don't think I can take much more of these three." She added in a stage whisper, "And I suspect the feeling is mutual."

The man with the gun spoke again. "Madam. No *gentleman* would dream of being so crass as to admit such a thing.

We've enjoyed your company immensely. It is a rare thing to make the acquaintance of a woman who speaks her mind so eloquently — and so often."

The lady rolled her eyes. "As you can see, Mr. Valentine is capable of gallantry." She sighed. "If only gallantry and truth-telling resided in the same neighborhood."

Hoping to lower the level of tension in the room, Annie said that Fort Kearny was less than a dozen miles away. "You should be there a little after dark."

"If only *that* were true," moaned one of the other men.

Annie glanced past the lady and into the main room again. The speaker was sitting across from the drinker. He'd removed his bowler hat and was mopping his bald pate with a handkerchief as he spoke. "The coach encountered some trouble a few miles from here. Something about a thorough-brace, I believe. And a thrown shoe or a bruised foot or some such. The driver says we'll be staying the night while repairs are made."

Ah. That explained George Morgan's absence. He was helping with whatever was going on with the stagecoach. "I'm sorry you'll be delayed," Annie said, "but I think you'll find the accommodations comfortable." She stepped back into the main room and indicated the stairs to the loft. "There's a window tucked under the eaves at the west end. The air circulates nicely. Feel free to get settled in. I'll ring the dinner bell when everything's ready." She excused herself to see to supper and had just lifted the lid on the pot of stew simmering on the stove when she realized the lady had followed her into the kitchen. "You'll be more comfortable out in the public room, Ma'am," she said. "As you can see, there's no place to sit here in the kitchen."

"Please don't banish me," the lady said, leaning forward as she whispered, "The one in the bowler has nauseatingly bad breath. The second pontificates on every subject that comes up. And the dandy — well, I wouldn't be surprised to learn that Mr. Valentine is running from the law."

Annie glanced into the other room. The man with the gun had lit a cigar. He'd dragged the rocking chair in off the back porch — another of George Morgan's pointless trades, as far as Annie was concerned — and was leaning back as if he owned Clearwater. She could not blame the lady for not wanting to keep his company. She retrieved the crate she was still using for a stepladder and set it on end. "That's as good as I can offer."

"Having just exited that dreadful Concord coach — Do *not* believe the ads about those things, by the way. If I knew who was responsible and if my father had allowed me to read law, I'd be intent on taking someone to court for fraud. At any rate, the last thing I need is a place to sit down." She stepped forward and extended a hand. "Miss Lydia Hart. On my way to Fort Kearny to visit my brother."

Hart. "Lieutenant Hart?" To hide the fact that she was blushing, Annie turned away, making a show of tasting the stew, adding a bit of salt, and checking the bread in the oven.

"Yes. You've met him?"

Annie nodded. "He was at the head of a patrol sent out from Fort Kearny a few weeks ago. Someone reported Indians raiding the station."

"A false report, I assume, from the way you just said that."

"Yes, although no one could be blamed for misinterpreting what they saw."

"What did they see?"

"A Pawnee named Badger at the head of a hunting party. They camp here at Clearwater every year before going on the spring buffalo hunt, and they make quite a show of their arrival — painted ponies and all."

"And you were here when it happened?"

Annie nodded. She described hiding under the table while Emmet brandished a knife. "And then George Morgan came in to tell us what was happening. And Badger followed him." Annie held a hand up to one side of her face. "This side painted red." She moved her hand over. "This side painted white. He looked quite terrifying."

"And Wade came charging to the rescue," the lady said.

Annie smiled. "There was no one in need of rescuing. I think he was quite put out about that."

Miss Hart nodded. "I can imagine. Wade's always fancied himself the hero in every story." She sighed. "I don't suppose he can be blamed for that, though, handsome devil that he is." She changed the subject abruptly, waving a hand about the kitchen. "You seem awfully young to be in charge of a place such as this."

"I'm not in charge of anything. I'm just the cook."

"That's not a 'just,' Missus — ?"

"Annie."

"Very well," the lady said. "Then you must call me Lydia. As I was saying, put *me* in here with a few sacks of something and a pot of whatever and we'd starve before I managed to build a fire and boil water." She paused. "Still, you and your husband seem to have quite a growing concern, what with all the corrals and that massive barn. And I noticed the store as I came through the main room. It looks quite well stocked."

She thinks I'm married to George Morgan? Annie hurried to correct the misunderstanding. "I don't live here. I mean . . . not really. I'm here because of my two brothers." She allowed a tinge of pride in her voice. "Frank and Emmet ride for the Pony Express."

Miss Hart clasped her hands together. "I was in St. Joseph for the inaugural ride. It was *thrilling.* Will your brothers dine with us this evening? Do you think I could meet them? An editor friend of mine back home is having parts of my letters published as 'Travel Notes from a Lady in the West.' I've already written about the inaugural ride. I visited the Pony Express stables while I was in St. Joseph and spoke with a Mr. Lewis about the organization. Clearwater is what they call a home station, correct?"

Annie nodded.

"Most excellent. Now that things are off and running, I'd love to speak with a rider about his experiences on the trail."

"You know the mail run's been suspended, right?"

"Yes." The woman gave a little shudder. "That awful trouble in Nevada. Still, there is nothing more Western than the Pony Express." She paused. "Unless, of course, you have an Indian or two hidden somewhere."

Annie laughed softly. "I imagine Emmet and Frank will be happy to talk to you once the day winds down. As for Indians, we do have Billy. Billy Gray Owl. He works for Mr. Morgan, who owns Clearwater. I imagine Billy's seeing to Whiskey John's team at the moment."

A rumbling voice sounded from just inside the back door. *George Morgan.* The drinker who wore a gun beneath his coat wouldn't be able to cause any more trouble now.

CHAPTER 17

Annie was washing dishes on a rickety table just outside the storeroom door when Lieutenant Hart's sister sought her out. "I hope you don't mind," she said and held up a coffee cup. "I helped myself."

"Not at all."

"And I won't be in the way if I ask you a few questions?" She brandished the small notebook she held in her free hand.

"It's nice to have the company. Did you get what you were hoping to from Frank and Emmet?"

"Oh, my goodness, yes," Miss Hart said. "Emmet made me work a little harder to draw him out, but Frank —" She smiled. "He is a charmer, isn't he?"

Annie chuckled and nodded.

"Now I'm curious about you. How did you feel about their taking on the job? I saw the flyers in St. Joseph. They made it sound like it's dangerous."

"I didn't want anything to do with it, and I told them so."

Miss Hart seemed surprised by the answer. "And yet, here you are."

"They're my brothers. I couldn't let them down. You'd do the same."

Miss Hart didn't answer right away. "I'd like to think so, but I haven't seen Wade in a very long time, and the truth is we've never been close." She paused. "I doubt he'd ever have invited me to visit, except for one thing. A cad named Blair Bohling left me literally standing at the altar last month. Wade's invitation is his way of helping me escape the humiliation of coming face-to-face with my former fiancé and the woman he left me for at some social function."

Annie looked up, shocked. "I'm very sorry that happened to you."

"Thank you." Miss Hart took another sip of coffee. "Ironically enough, from the vantage point of hindsight, I'm not sure I am. Blair is thirty years old, and he's never set foot outside Philadelphia. He converses like a world traveler, but it's all a ruse. He's well read but not at all well traveled, and travel is something I am determined to do. Perhaps for the rest of my life. Suffice it to say, I am far from brokenhearted." She paused. "To return to the topic at hand, though, did you try to talk your brothers out of it? I heard stories while I was in St. Joseph. A lot of men were badly injured just trying out. Until someone 'busted the bronc.' I think that's the term."

Annie let pride sound in her voice as she said, "My brothers did that. Frank went the distance, and then Emmet followed. Together, they broke Outlaw. In fact, Frank rode him out here."

"He didn't say a word about that," Miss Hart said. And then she smiled. "I need to learn to ask better questions. I shall have to speak with your handsome brother again."

Five weeks into what newspapers were calling the Paiute War, Frank spent an afternoon working alongside Charlie in bottomland about two hours from Clearwater. George had sent them out to cut enough sod to lay around and over the top of the chicken coop to provide insulation against both the intense heat sure to arrive with summer and the frigid cold that would come with winter.

Charlie worked the specially designed plow, laying the earth open in three-foot-wide swaths and curling it over, the latter accomplished by the curve of the plow itself. Frank walked behind, cutting the sod into strips to be laid up like bricks once they were back at Clearwater.

As the men worked, Charlie began to sing. A hymn, of course. When he called back to Frank to join in, Frank just shook his head, "Can't. Don't know it."

"Tell me one you do know, and we can sing that instead. It makes the work go easier."

"Don't know any hymns," Frank said, grunting as he cut through a swath of sod.

"Not a single one?" Astonishment sounded in the parson's voice.

"Not a one."

"Surely you know 'Amazing Grace.' Everybody does."

Frank rolled the strip of sod up and hefted it onto the sled — a low, sideless wagon they would use to transport the sod back to Clearwater. The exertion cleared some of the anger out so he could answer without swearing. "*Everybody* doesn't. I don't." While he hacked at another swath of earth, he told Charlie the short version of what he called his "heathen" past. It wasn't until he'd finished cutting all the way through the strip of sod that Frank realized the plow wasn't moving. He looked up at Charlie.

"I am sorry you had to go through that, son. Very sorry."

The pure sympathy and kindness in the man's voice made it hard to answer. Frank gulped. Finally, he croaked, "No need to be sorry. It's done."

"If only that were true," the parson said and went back to plowing.

Frank called after him. "You go right ahead and sing, though. I don't mind it."

Charlie sang out in a rich tenor Frank thought just might carry all the way back to Clearwater. Maybe even to Dobytown. He sang about amazing grace "that saved a wretch like me. I once was lost but now am found, was blind but now I see." The words touched a place deep inside. Like someone had reached in and started digging around. When Charlie sang about grace teaching his heart to fear and then relieving those fears, Frank wondered what that meant. He rolled more sod and carried it to the sled. They probably had enough, but Frank didn't want Charlie to quit singing, and so he didn't say anything. Not until Charlie got to the end of the song. Of course Frank didn't know for sure it was the end until the singing stopped, although he thought he could feel it coming with the mention of ten thousand years in heaven. The idea that time wouldn't run out on people in heaven was downright hopeful.

Frank had just set another roll of sod on the sled when Charlie chirruped to the mule they were using to plow and guided the animal to loop back around so they could head back toward the sled. He looked at the stacked sod and then at Frank. "Why didn't you tell me to stop?"

Too embarrassed to admit the real reason, Frank shrugged. "Wasn't sure we had enough yet."

Charlie smiled. "Son, there's enough sod on that sled to build three chicken coops." He shrugged out of the traces and mopped his brow. "But that's all right. Time's never wasted when we're praising the Lord's amazing grace. On the other hand, I'm glad to be heading back. Your sister said she was planning to try a peach cobbler in that oven, and I've faith enough to expect it's going to turn out just right."

Frank smiled. "You pray over the stove so it'd behave?"

"Well now, I suppose I could have, but it didn't come to mind. I just asked the Lord to bless and guide Miss Annie. She needs to see how much good she does every day. How important she is, not only to the crew but also to the good people passing by on the trail. A kind word can go a long way to easing a troubled soul, and from what little

255

I've seen of how things work at Clearwater, your sister speaks more than her share every day."

After improving Annie's chicken coop, the parson sorted cattle and stacked lumber. He also conducted Sabbath services beneath the arbor extending off the south side of the blacksmith's soddy. The messages were short and to the point — and somewhat repetitive, to Annie's way of thinking. All men were sinners, and sin carved a canyon between man and God. The wages of sin was death. But God so loved the world that He gave his only Son to pay those wages. So Jesus came to earth and lived perfect. When He died on the cross, He could pay everyone else's death wages, because He didn't owe any of His own. The parson said a man couldn't ever do enough good to deserve eternal life, but that was okay because he didn't have to earn it. He just had to ask God to take Jesus' death as payment for those death-wages. Because of Jesus, God could hand out forgiveness and eternal life as a free gift. *Free.*

When Annie commented on the simplicity of the parson's sermons — and the brevity — Emmet agreed that it wasn't what people generally expected from a circuit rider. He also said that almost every word Charlie spoke was in the Bible. He'd show her the verses, he said — if she was interested. Annie was, and Emmet spent an entire evening underlining passages in the Pony Express Bible so she could read them for herself.

As time went on, she wondered at the idea that Frank, who never wanted to hear Emmet "sermonize," seemed drawn to the parson. She hoped it meant the something deep inside Frank that seemed to keep him from being happy would eventually be dug out and tossed aside. Maybe Charlie would help Frank see the Lord as his shepherd. Maybe that would erase the deep line between Frank's eyebrows once and for all. That would be something.

News of the end of the Paiute War arrived in late July. The Pony Express would resume mail service on July 29. Frank rode west. A week later, Emmet rode east, and the next morning the parson ate a hearty breakfast, thanked George Morgan for "giving him a place to land for a while," and said he'd be leaving.

"Hate to see you go," Morgan said.

"Not as much as I hate going. I could be as happy as a flea in a pack of dogs here at Clearwater. Which is why it's time to go.

The Lord's calling upon my life does not include settling down. At least not for now."

"Then I'll see to getting Cordelia saddled," Morgan said and left.

Instead of following the station keeper down to the barn right away, the parson helped Annie clear the breakfast table, talking while he worked. "I've sowed some good seed here at Clearwater, and I'm praying the Lord of the harvest will work His will. I will pray to that end, for all my friends at Clearwater."

"I'll miss you," Annie said as she piled dirty dishes into the pan out back and then retrieved the wash water she'd been heating on the stove. While she worked, the parson said some very nice things about Annie's kindness to travelers and how he thought she had a gift for hospitality. Annie shook her head. "A gift for burning supper is more like it."

"Folks hanker for kindness and a smile a lot more than they do a perfect meal," the parson said. He went on to say he hoped Annie would spend some time with the Good Book. "It contains words of life. Everybody ought to read 'em." When Annie nodded, he raised one hand like he was taking a vow and said, "The good Lord bless you and keep you, Miss Annie. The Lord

258

make His face to shine upon you and be gracious to you. The Lord lift up His countenance upon you and give you peace."

Embarrassed that tears had sprung up, Annie murmured a thank-you without looking up from her work. She'd finished the dishes and carried them back inside when she heard a mule bray. Peering through the kitchen window, she watched as Cordelia carried the parson westward.

August ushered in the kind of heat that sometimes made it hard to breathe. A permanent cloud of dust hung over the corrals and the trail. It blew in the open doors and sifted over everything inside. A short time after Annie dusted a counter, swept the floor, or scrubbed a shelf, it returned to its former state — dust, dirt, and grit. The endless battle to keep things clean occasionally reduced Annie to weary tears over the uselessness of it all.

As the sun blazed away without mercy, the rosemary plant from Mrs. Hollenberg began to wilt, and in spite of the sod Frank and the parson had stacked up and around the chicken coop, a young hen died. Annie took to keeping a damp cloth in a bowl of water so she could mop the back of her neck in a vain effort to keep cool. Every time she opened the oven door, she barely managed to resist the urge to stagger backward.

The crew rose before dawn and tried to get as much work as possible accomplished as early as possible. In the heat of the day they took a long break, lounging beneath the arbor down by Hitch's soddy until evening and then working until dark.

Annie knew it would be best to follow their example and do her baking at night, but by the time the sun went down she was so spent she simply could not manage it. Summers at home had been hot, but summer out here on the prairie was punishment. By noon every day she was drenched with sweat. The best part of the day was when she could slip away to the pump and draw up cold water from the depths. One afternoon, she hauled a bucket of well water into her room, closed the door, took her boots off, and reveled in the sensation of cool water bathing her feet.

With creeks drying up and the sandy Platte River running slow and filled with silt, the artisian well down by the barn became a regular "watering hole" for patrols from Fort Kearny. The idea of rowdy soldiers frequenting the station had originally made Annie feel apprehensive, but after the first few visits, she began to look forward to seeing a column of dusty, thirsty men riding toward Clearwater. Especially when Miss Hart's handsome brother rode at the head of the column.

One day when Annie said something to Frank about how the "brave soldiers" appreciated the cool, clear water, he smirked. "Yeah. That's it. That's the attraction, all right. That's why they congregate around the pump instead of drifting up to the station. Oh . . . wait . . . they *do* spend time up at the station." He shrugged. "Can't imagine why. Surely can't have anything to do with your pretty face."

Annie felt a blush creeping up the back of her neck. "I'm sure I don't know what you mean."

"And I'm sure I hope you're telling the truth," Frank retorted. "You just stay focused on your St. Jo. dreams. You don't like the West, remember? If any of those soldiers takes a notion to flirt, you let me know. I'll see they mind their manners. And if I'm gone, tell George. He'll set 'em straight."

Annie waved a dismissive hand in the air. "You have nothing to worry about. Lieutenant Hart's men have been polite to the point of gallantry."

"And you don't think George had anything to do with that?" Frank didn't wait for a reply. "Who do you think saw to it that Harris Reynolds changed so quickly. You remember Reynolds, don't you?"

Of course Annie remembered. Harris Reynolds had been rude at first, but he'd responded to kindness — so why was Frank bringing him up? "Who told you about Harris Reynolds, anyway? As I remember it, he said he didn't know you."

"Never met the man," Frank said, "and he's long since ridden off into the unknown. Doesn't work for the Pony anymore. But thanks to him, the word is out up and down the line. 'Don't mistreat the cook at Clearwater unless you're ready to take on a riled-up George Morgan.' So when you pass out the credit for those soldiers' behaving themselves, don't pour it all in the direction of the golden-haired Lieutenant Hart. Everyone in these parts knows they'll answer to George if they cause you any trouble." He paused. "And now that I've told you, don't you tell George I said anything. I don't think he'd appreciate me jawin' about it."

Annie agreed to keep the conversation to herself. To be honest, she thought Frank might have exaggerated things a bit when it came to George Morgan's watching over her. She was growing used to the idea of looking out for herself now that Emmet and Frank were gone so much. She wasn't sure she liked the idea of someone else stepping into their role unbidden. After all, she'd held her own against Harris Reynolds and an entire host of other riders and visitors to Clearwater. Including Badger — and a rattlesnake.

At midday one particularly hot August day, Annie had just pumped a stream of cold well water over a kerchief and was tying it about her neck when a patrol rode in. After dismounting down by the barn, Lieutenant Hart handed the reins of his horse to another soldier and strode toward the station. As he approached, the lieutenant unbuttoned his uniform jacket and reached inside, withdrawing an envelope.

He held it out to Annie. "A note from Lydia. And a copy of the article she wrote about your brothers."

"Please thank her for me. I hope she's enjoying her stay at Fort Kearny."

The lieutenant chuckled. "She is. Although the rest of the ladies probably feel a bit like they've been blown off center. Lydia does have a way of taking charge. In fact, she's convinced the captain that it would be good for 'military-civilian relations' for the ladies to host a social at the end of October and to invite everyone from surrounding ranches. She campaigned for September, but I was able to convince her she'd get a better turnout if she waited until hay-cutting season was mostly over with." He pointed at the letter. "I'm sure she's told you all about it. And I do hope you'll come. Lydia's calling it a 'grand cotillion.' "

Annie didn't know what to say. Her time wasn't really her own — was it? The idea of an entire day away from Clearwater was likely impossible. But an evening of dancing would be wonderful. Especially if the lieutenant — well. Best not to daydream about that. She probably wouldn't be able to go, anyway. "Thank you. I don't know what to say beyond that."

Hart glanced behind them and toward the barn, then asked, "If I spoke to George Morgan about it — if he didn't object to your being gone for an evening — would you come? I'd be honored to be your escort."

Annie stammered yes and thank you.

"Lydia will be delighted. As am I. I hope the heat hasn't been too hard on you. I can't imagine being trapped in a room with a hot stove on a day like today."

"And I can't imagine riding through clouds of dust for hours on end."

Hart smiled. "One of the advantages of rank is leading the way. I eat less dust than the average soldier." He nodded toward the chicken coop. "How are your ladies faring?"

"I lost one to the heat and another disappeared without a trace. Carried off by some varmint or another, I suppose." Annie looked over at the coop and shook her head. "Not much I can do about it — at least about the heat, anyway."

Hart nodded and looked eastward. "This is the time of year our mother always took Lydia and me out of the city to escape the heat." He untied his bandanna and pumped water as he talked, mopping the back of his neck before tying the wet bandanna back on and tucking it inside his shirt collar. "I have wonderful memories of the little cottage we stayed in. Flowers spilling out of window boxes. Fruit trees in the back. And a little skiff Lydia and I could row out into the lake. The Meadows wasn't nearly as big as the places where some of our friends spent their summers, but we loved it."

The Meadows. A cottage with window boxes. Fruit trees. "It sounds delightful."

"It was. I haven't thought about it in a long while." He smiled down at her. "But I'm certain you'd love it there."

Annie's heart thumped. For a fleeting few

265

seconds, the heat didn't matter. But then a blast of hot air swept up from the corrals and the pungent smell of manure erased the magic. Hart glanced toward the barn again. "With your permission, I'll deal with any objections Morgan has to your attending the cotillion."

"Y-yes. All right."

With a quick tug on the brim of his hat, he took his leave. Annie watched as he strode away. When George Morgan emerged from the barn and the lieutenant went to talk with him, she skittered back inside. It wouldn't do for either man to know just how much she cared about the outcome of their conversation.

CHAPTER 18

Annie didn't read Lydia's note right away. Tucking it into her apron pocket, she carried it with her through the rest of the day, ever mindful of its presence, ever thankful for the promise it represented. *Lydia Hart wrote. To me. Lieutenant Hart and I had a real conversation about his family. He told me about the Meadows. He wants to escort me to the cotillion.* Annie frowned. *And I have nothing to wear but cotton calico.* It might not have mattered at the Patee House when everyone was in the throes of enthusiasm for the Pony Express, but it would surely matter when she was on Lieutenant Hart's arm. What had she been thinking, saying yes to his invitation? *You weren't thinking. Who could, looking into those blue eyes?*

Late that evening, after Emmet and Frank had had a chance to read Lydia's article, Annie lit the lamp in her room and perched at the foot of her bed to read both the article and the accompanying note.

I thought Frank would especially love to see that he is now known in the East for his daring accomplishments for the Pony Express. With Wade's help, I have written about the Paiute War, although that article will not appear for some weeks yet. I am still collecting firsthand accounts from Eastbound travelers who have passed through the country and seen the depradations firsthand.

After many weeks in residence here, I have learned to recognize the various bugle calls that order the men's lives. They look very fine when they assemble on the parade ground for inspection. It makes me glad that I have come here, if for no other reason than to see my brother in his element and to feel the same kind of pride I heard in your voice when you first spoke of Emmet and Frank.

The ladies and I are planning a social for the last Saturday in October, and I hope you will attend. I often wish that you could "come calling," but I realize that life in the West necessitates the forgoing of many of the niceties practiced by others. I do hope to see you again soon, and I have reason to believe my brother would welcome your visit as well. You do realize, I hope, that there is more to the military patrols' frequent stops at Clearwater than the artesian well down by the barn.

A circuit rider named Charlie Pender has caused quite a stir here in recent days. He is one of the most unusual men I have ever encountered. He mentioned you with the highest regard. I close now, in hopes of seeing you soon.

I remain your friend,
Lydia Hart

Annie wondered if Charlie would return to Dobytown. *Lord, you are his Shepherd. Please protect him.* She smiled when she read "Travel Notes from a Lady in the West." "Daring Frank Paxton, the moonlight messenger" of the Pony Express featured strongly in Lydia's article. How Frank loved the romantic moniker *moonlight messenger.* Perhaps there was something to his prediction that he would one day be famous.

Annie read and reread Lydia's note, thrilled by what she said about her brother's visits to Clearwater. She also treasured Lydia's closing words. *I remain your friend.* How strange that hundreds of miles from

269

where Annie had planned to make friends, a woman from even farther away, both in social station and in distance, had used that wonderful word.

Friend.

Dawn had tinged the eastern sky pink on the September morning when, just after Annie set the coffeepot on the stove, George Morgan opened the storeroom door and called for "Rattlesnake Woman" to come and check on her Rhode Island Reds. "I heard a ruckus just now."

Annie's heart lurched. *Rattlesnake! Not again.* Steeling herself against what she was about to see, she brushed past Morgan and into the chicken coop. It took a moment for her eyes to adjust to the dim light. When they did, she didn't see anything amiss. "They seem fine."

"I didn't say there was anything *wrong.* I said I heard a ruckus. Check under the one with the black tail feathers."

Frank had kept his word to build nesting boxes, and the hen Morgan was talking about had claimed the one on the far right. Gently, ever so gently, Annie slid her hand beneath the hen. *Yes! At last. An egg.* She quickly checked the other boxes. Only the one, but it was a beginning. In due time, she'd have a proper flock. Eggs enough to cook. *And chicken and dumplings. Perhaps for Christmas dinner.* She stepped back outside and held up the egg, beaming with joy. "How did you know?"

"Been keeping an eye out. Hoping they'd finally start to earn their keep. After all the trouble they've been."

"It's going to be worth it," Annie said. "You'll see. How do you like your eggs, Mr. Morgan?"

"It's a little early for that, don't ya think?" He changed the subject. "Got a long day of plowing ahead. Best be getting to it."

"Plowing? But — why?"

"Prairie's drying out. We need a fire guard."

Annie looked past him to the horizon. *Fire.* She'd learned not to worry too much about Frank and Emmet chasing across the prairie alone, but — *fire.* And the wind. A terrifying combination.

Morgan seemed to read her mind. "They can set a backfire." He explained the practice of putting out one fire with another, the second set purposely to consume a wide swath of dried grass. "First fire goes out for lack of fuel."

"And the second?"

"The second stays under control at the

hand of whoever set it," Morgan said. "I'll make sure they carry matches. They'll be all right. And so will you."

"Who — why would anyone start a fire in the first place?"

"They do it in the spring to renew the prairie. This time of year it's generally an accident. A spark from a campfire some fool doesn't take time to douse. Or lightning." Morgan's voice gentled a bit. "We'd see it long before it got here. Smell it, too."

With those few words, he left. Annie returned the egg to its nest, praising the hen she'd named Lucille and encouraging a repeat performance.

That night she opened the Pony Express Bible, seeking the comfort of a verse she remembered Emmet reading to her. Thankfully, he'd written page numbers on the inside cover, and Annie quickly found the verse about fear in chapter forty-one of the book of Isaiah. "Fear thou not; for I am with thee: be not dismayed; for I am thy God: I will strengthen thee; yea, I will help thee; yea, I will uphold thee with the right hand of my righteousness." It was a good message, but it didn't comfort Annie as much as she'd hoped, largely because of the four words *I am thy God.*

Annie lay in bed a long time thinking

about those four words. Was God *hers*? She didn't like admitting it, but she didn't think He was. At least not in the same way He was Emmet's God. How could she make sure she could claim the promises about God's strengthening and helping her — in the same ways He strengthened and helped Emmet and the parson? She wished she'd listened to Charlie's sermons better.

The Lord is my Shepherd. I shall not want. Funny that she hadn't really pondered the little word *my* in the Shepherd's Psalm, either. She frowned and tossed a question into the night. Was the Lord *her* Shepherd? Was God *her* God? Was He, really?

Much to Annie's great relief, as September faded into October, all she or her brothers experienced of prairie fires was a distant red glow along the far horizon. Nights grew cool enough that George Morgan occasionally built a fire in the fireplace on the eastern wall of the main room. Annie spent a few minutes each evening sitting in the rocking chair he'd dragged in from the porch, knitting socks and mittens as fast as she could. She was inclined to doubt Morgan's prediction they might see snow by the end of October. Still, she would do what she could to see her brothers properly outfitted.

When Fort Kearny patrols were sent out to help ranchers beat back the flames of distant prairie fires, Annie saw little of Lieutenant Hart, but she thrilled at the personal note he scrawled at the bottom of one of Lydia's letters.

We are sent to wage war on flames seeking to destroy all the settlers have battled to create. Thoughts of Clearwater remind me that you are safe inside a swath of plowed earth, and I am thankful. The cotillion looms bright on my horizon.

Respectfully,

W.H.

She consulted the almanac George Morgan kept in the store and began to count the days until the last Saturday in the month. There'd be a full moon two days after the cotillion. As she knitted, she daydreamed about dancing in the moonlight with a handsome blond-haired lieutenant.

The second week of October, the Overland Stage delivered a letter for Emmet. Annie smiled as she carried it into her brother's room and laid it on his cot. When Emmet rode in a few days later, dismay and sadness swept over her when she saw his horse. In fact, she barely paid attention to the handoff between Emmet and a rider named Bill Garrett, so intent was she on Shadow.

"Hey, girl," she said, and patted the paint mare's neck. Shadow whickered and nuzzled her hand. "How about that," she said. "She remembers me." She glanced over at Emmet. "You go on in and get something to eat. There's a pot of beans on the stove and fresh bread in a basket on the table. I'll see to Shadow."

Emmet nodded. "The Pony hasn't been kind to her." He paused. "What's this I hear about a social over at the fort?"

"Who told you about that?"

"The rider — Bill Garrett. Didn't you hear him just now? He was lamenting that he might not be back this way before some co-tillun, whatever that is."

"Cotillion," Annie said. "It's just a fancy word for a dance." She smiled. "Lydia sent a note inviting me, and Mr. Morgan said I can go." It was probably best not to mention Lieutenant Hart's part in the invitation — at least not yet. "In fact, he promised to ride over with me."

Even in the fading light, she could see Emmet frown. "George Morgan is squiring you to a dance?"

"No. No . . . it's not . . . no." Annie shook

her head. "The ladies at the fort are inviting everyone in the region. All the ranchers and station owners. No one's squiring anyone. I'm going to see Lydia. And speaking of notes, there's a letter waiting for you. From Luvina."

Thankfully, in the wake of that news, Emmet forgot all about the matter of who was squiring who — or not — to a cotillion at Fort Kearny. With a "hallelujah," he handed Shadow over and hurried inside. Annie led the mare away, pained to see how thin she'd become. How she moved, head down, shuffling wearily along. She led the mare toward the barn with a heavy heart.

George Morgan came in while she was brushing Shadow down. "Reminds me of that flashy paint you rode into Clearwater."

"This is her," Annie said. "Only — it's not." Her voice wavered.

Morgan reached over the stall door and stroked the white strip running down the mare's face. "Poor little gal." Moments later, he was handing a feed bag over the stall door. "Mixed up a little treat."

Just as Annie strapped the feed bag in place, Emmet stumbled into the barn, letter in hand. He held it up and croaked, "Luvina."

Oh, no. Had her suspicions been right all

along? Had Luvina broken it off? Annie put her hand on his arm. "Tell me."

"Remember that bull I warned her father about?"

A chill washed over her. "You always said he was dangerous."

"I must have warned him a hundred times about that da— darned beast."

"You did. You *swore* about that creature." As he almost had just now. And Emmet just did not swear.

"It tore through a fence. Gored the old man and — he's dead. Earl Aiken is dead."

"Oh, no!" Annie's hand went to her heart.

"Luvina was out in the garden. After goring Earl, the bull —" Another deep breath. He pointed at the letter. "It says she'll mend, but she's hurt bad."

Morgan spoke up. "You'll want to go to her. You can take my horse."

Emmet blinked. "Banner? You can't mean that." The flashy chestnut was the best horse on the place.

Morgan nodded. "I do mean it. He'll take you through without any trouble. Just remember it's a loan, not a gift."

Emmet looked over at Annie. "Maybe you should come with me."

"And lose my wages? Not on your life." She stepped out of Shadow's stall and tugged on Emmet's sleeve. "Come on. I'll get you something to eat while you pack."

"And I'll saddle Banner," Morgan said.

Back at the station, Annie assembled a hodgepodge of a meal from leftover ham, half a loaf of bread, and some dried fruit. Shoving it into an empty flour sack, she hurried into the store. Retrieving a treasured wheel of cheese, she cut off a wedge and added it to the sack. If they tied it to the saddle horn, Emmet would be able to eat without stopping. She and Emmet trotted back to the barn, where George Morgan waited, the tall gelding with the four white socks at his side.

Emmet took the reins, but he didn't mount up. "You're sure about this?"

"I'm sure," Morgan said.

Tying the sack of food to the saddle horn, Emmet scrambled aboard. "You'll get him back. I'll see to it."

"Just take good care of him." Morgan reached up to shake Emmet's hand.

"I'm trusting you to take care of my sister."

"I will. You have my word."

Feeling desperate to say something — anything that would comfort Emmet, Annie promised to pray for Luvina.

He nodded. "Remember: 'What time I am

afraid, I will trust in thee.' "

Annie wondered if he was saying the words for her or himself. "I'll remember."

Emmet thanked George, then spoke to Annie. "I love you, Ann E." He spurred Banner to action. Annie stared after him. *The Lord is your Shepherd, Emmet. Don't forget.*

"He said your name different."

Annie started and looked up at Morgan. "What? Oh — that. Mama named me Ann Elizabeth. Hence, Ann-initial-E. Ann E. Annie."

Morgan began to douse the lanterns hanging in the barn, but when Annie moved to leave, he called after her. "That hen you lost last month. Not the one that died in the heat. The other one. The one that just disappeared."

He wants to talk about chickens — now? She turned back. "What about her?"

He snuffed the last of the lanterns and walked up beside her. "Don't know that it would have saved her, but you'll have a proper chicken yard around the coop before much longer. Luther's delivering a roll of wire with his last load of supplies."

Last load. A reminder that winter would soon be upon them. Unlike the freighters contracted by the government to supply the military, Luther didn't haul supplies in winter. When he departed after this next delivery, Annie would not see him again until spring.

"Emmet will be all right," Morgan said quietly. "Banner's a good horse."

"I know. And Banner will be all right, too. Emmet won't abuse him."

"I'm glad you said *no* to leaving just now. And I don't mind the chickens."

The man could not keep a singular stream of conversation going. "The last time you said anything about my Reds, it was to grumble about how much trouble they've been." She looked up at the vast night sky, folding her arms across her body and hugging herself to stave off a shiver.

"I don't remember grumbling."

"The morning you found that first egg, your exact words were that you hoped they'd start to earn their keep, 'after all the trouble they've been.' "

"That was — teasing."

"Were you teasing when I asked how you like your eggs and you groused about it being too early to have that conversation?"

"I don't remember — did I really say that?"

"Yes. Right before you said you had to plow a firebreak, so we wouldn't all die."

She felt rather than saw him looking down at her. "I said *that*? About dying?"

"Not exactly. But it was implied."

After a long silence, Morgan apologized. "Never meant to frighten you." His voice gentled. "Scrambled. I like my eggs scrambled."

Annie nodded. "I'll remember."

"Is it true Sophia gave you her recipe for chicken and dumplings?"

"She did. I'm hoping to make use of it for Christmas dinner."

"She didn't happen to share one for peach cobbler?"

"No. Why?"

"Best I ever ate. Except for my sister's."

Annie looked up at him, wishing she could see his expression better. But the moon wasn't bright this evening. "You have a sister?"

"*Had.* Rose passed on right before I left home."

"I'm so sorry, Mr. Morgan."

He was quiet again. Finally, he said, "About that *Mr. Morgan.* It makes me feel old. Think you could see your way to just *George*?" He made a leap to a new subject before Annie could reply. "You got thrown into the deep part of the pond here. A pond you never wanted to wade in, let alone swim. At least according to your brothers."

"I suppose that's a good way to put it." *And I can't swim.* "But I'm not as miserable as I expected to be."

"Still, you are . . . miserable?"

Was that disappointment in his voice? Or hurt? Annie looked out over the corrals and toward the station, thinking about the years of hard work Morgan had poured into the place. "I don't mean to take anything away from what you've accomplished here. But it is true that I'm here because Frank and Emmet forced my hand." She paused. "And things didn't exactly get off to a successful start."

"Like I said," he rumbled, "deep part of the pond."

"At least I'm fairly reliable when it comes to making grits instead of glue now. And it only took six months."

"More like two weeks," Morgan said. "For the grits, anyway." He paused. "Billy and I have been here at Clearwater for five years. Haven't had a cook stay the winter yet."

Annie understood why a woman wouldn't want to spend a winter here. But with Emmet gone, her pay was even more important for the future. Besides that, she had nowhere to go. The Aikens would take her in because of Emmet, but that prospect made living at Clearwater almost attractive. At least here she was in charge of her own kitchen. She had a clear purpose, and she got paid to fulfill it. She cleared her throat. "Well, *I'm* staying."

After another brief silence, Morgan said, "That wire'll help keep the hawks away and discourage bigger varmints. Best turn in now. I'll see you safe inside."

"You don't have to do that. It's not that dark. I can find my way."

"Emmet's a man of his word. So am I. He said he'd take care of Banner. I said I'd take care of you." He led the way past the corrals and to the station. When they reached the storeroom door, he said quietly, "This life isn't easy for a woman. I didn't think you could do it."

Annie snorted. "That was obvious."

"It was? How? I mean — why?" He huffed. A frustrated sound. "What made it obvious?"

"For one thing, you hardly said two words to me for what felt like weeks. It probably wasn't really that long, but it felt like it."

"But that — that's just — that's me."

"I know that now. You're a 'man of few words.' And the few words you do speak are sometimes — abrupt. But that was hard to get used to — especially when I was making such a mess of everything."

"You learned. Quick."

"It didn't feel quick. You said I got dropped into the deep part of a pond? I felt like I was drowning. But then Badger gave me that ridiculous name. I didn't let on, but it made me feel good. To have impressed him."

Morgan was quiet for a moment. When he finally spoke up, Annie listened in amazement. "W-when I w-was a b-b-boy I t-talked l-l-l-like thi-this. R-rose helped me with it. Fewer words. Fewer stumbles."

He stuttered? "I wish I'd known that. It would have made things easier."

"What things?"

She was about to tell him. To list the ways he'd made her feel awkward or stupid. But what he'd just said put all of that in a different light. And so Annie just shook her head and said, "It doesn't matter. I'm just glad to know that your — *blunt* ways aren't because you don't like me."

He sighed. Shook his head. "Never. I — you're — good. For Clearwater. I —" He broke off. Again. "We got off to a bad start. That first day. Those men — the fight. I was embarrassed. And then you were so . . . young. So . . . miserable. I didn't know what I should do. What I could do."

"This," Annie said, motioning from herself to him and back again. "You can do this. Just — talk to me."

He nodded. "I'll try."

CHAPTER 19

Frank sucked in a deep breath. Opened his eyes. *Dark. No moon.* He shivered. Where was he? What had happened? It felt like his head was in a vise. He reached up. His left hand encountered something sticky. *Ouch.* He moved to get up, but when he lifted his head, the pounding nearly made him retch.

He lay still for a moment, thinking. Trying to remember. One minute he was tucked into the saddle, making good time on his way back to Clearwater. The next he was — here. *Where's here?* He looked about, willing his eyes to make sense of the darkness, wondering what had happened to his horse. The worst horse yet. A spotted mare born and bred from Hades. So many bad habits he'd have a hard time naming them all. Especially now, when it hurt to think.

Slowly, he managed to sit up. The world spun. He rested his head in his hands. He'd been so busy fighting the mare to keep her moving ahead — she must have stepped in a hole. How long ago, he didn't know, except that he'd mounted the mare just before sunset back at the relay station, and now it was dark. He was off the trail. The mare had been constantly shying away from things like wagon covers and odd sounds. She'd gone crazy over a boy banging a drum as he walked along with a little girl. Frank had nearly been thrown then, distracted by the oddity of a family group traveling west this late in the year. He sure hoped they had plans to lay up somewhere before getting too much farther west. At any rate, he'd decided to ride off the trail for a bit and see if he couldn't settle the mare. *Bad idea.*

Wincing, he reached up to feel his head again. Most of the blood was dried, but it had trickled down from his hairline to his jaw. Even dribbled down his neck some. Slowly, he untied the kerchief knotted about his neck and used it to bandage his head. He felt about him for his hat. Nothing but rocks and dirt at first, but finally, a stroke of luck. His hat had landed within arm's reach. He pulled it on over the bandage, wincing when the band connected with the cut and the egg-sized lump beneath it. One good thing about the lump, he supposed, was that it made the hat tight enough to stop any more bleeding.

Standing up made him sick to his stomach. But at least he *could* stand up. Nothing seemed broken. Except his head. He concentrated on staying upright. Resting his hand on the grip of his pistol, he listened carefully for any sound, hoping for the clink of a bit or the swishing of a hoof through grass as the mare grazed. The only thing he heard was a far-off howl. *Far-off, thank goodness.*

He took a few steps, each one more difficult, and finally sat back down, breathing heavily, wondering why he felt so all-fired sick. A knock to the head shouldn't do that — should it? He peered off to the north. You'd think he'd at least see a campfire, but there was nothing. Just darkness.

He tilted his head. Struggled to stand up again and took a few steps. His foot struck a shape he first took for a mound of sand. We swore softly as he reached down and swept his palm across the mare's side. A fine crust adhered to her flanks. She was breathing, but barely. His heart sank. He murmured comfort as he felt his way along, trying to understand what was wrong. Suspecting the worst, he found it. A broken leg. She would have struggled mightily to get up, but the fight was gone out of her now. There was nothing he could do for her but to end her suffering.

Frank sat back. She'd been an ornery cuss, but he still hated thinking of the pain she must have endured. *You need to end it,* he thought, remembering that distant howl. Taking a deep breath, he pulled the gun out of its holster. Muttering "I'm sorry, girl," he pulled the trigger. He felt his way to the saddle. Carefully, he pulled the mochila off. It took some doing to free the side tucked beneath the mare. He fumbled to loosen the girth and get the saddle, too, but had to give up. Every time he bent down his head pounded and his stomach roiled. At least he could get the bridle.

He had to rest again before he could face walking. Had to rest every little while, in fact. Dawn would be here soon — he hoped. He didn't really know what time it was. Daylight would help him find water. The Platte was over there somewhere, but he didn't really know how far. He couldn't think straight. For a moment, he thought maybe he should turn around and go back to Plum Creek. Maybe that was closer? *No. Keep the mail moving. Just. Keep. Walking.*

The morning after Emmet left for Missouri, Annie awoke refreshed and looking forward

289

to the day. She'd had only a few hours' sleep, but she wasn't nearly as tired as she'd expected to be. In fact, the first thing she felt as she faced the new day was a surge of hope. Just about everything she'd assumed about George Morgan — about *George* — had been wrong. His few words weren't because of anything she'd done — or undone. His few words had been a way to overcome a stutter, and the habit stuck. Who could blame him for that? Living at a place like Clearwater didn't exactly inspire orations. Even the parson had kept his sermons short and to the point.

Thinking about Charlie Pender reminded Annie of something he'd said the day he left Clearwater. "In a world full of sadness and travail, kindness is not to be underestimated. You have a chance to do a great deal of good, my dear, just by showing kindness to those the trail brings your way. Whatever you do, do your work heartily, not as unto men but as unto God. He will take notice and He will be pleased."

After feeding her chickens and finding two more eggs, Annie retreated inside, leaving the storeroom door open and enjoying the cool promise of fall. While she cooked, she thought of Emmet and poor Luvina. Even though Emmet would take care not to push

Banner beyond the breaking point, he might reach St. Joseph in as little as a week. He would undoubtedly report in to Mr. Lewis at the Pony Express office so a replacement rider could be assigned to Clearwater. Riding from St. Joseph to the Aikens' would take the better part of a day. All told, it would be at least a couple of weeks before Annie knew anything about how Luvina was faring. *Poor Luvina.* Bereft of her father as the result of a tragic accident.

She felt a tinge of guilt at the way she'd judged Luvina Aiken, just because the girl didn't show her emotions. Maybe she simply was not good with words — like George. Emmet loved her. That was what mattered. Luvina's quiet ways were well suited to a man like Emmet. They would probably be very happy together, in their own sweet, dispassionate way.

Passion. The very word made Annie blush. Of course it didn't always refer to romance. A person could be passionate about life, too. Frank was that way. In his case, passion sometimes got him into trouble. On the other hand, it would help him succeed as a Pony Express rider. It might even make him famous. Annie smiled, thinking of the white gauntlets with the red stars.

She'd just stepped outside to ring the

breakfast bell when she heard an approaching rider. A lone rider. Coming fast. She hadn't been expecting the mail for at least another day. Still, she clanged the bell furiously before hurrying to the front of the station to tell the rider to be patient. A fresh horse would be here directly. But it wasn't a Pony rider at all. It was Lieutenant Hart. When he caught sight of Annie, he brought his horse to a skidding stop and leaped out of the saddle.

"You're not to worry," he said, "but Frank's in the post hospital. The stage found him stumbling along the trail." Her palm to her mouth, Annie staggered back. The lieutenant caught her, just as Billy trotted up with a fresh horse. "It's not the mail," Hart said. "Frank Paxton's been hurt. He'll be all right, but I knew Annie would want to know."

"I'll get George," Billy said, leading both the Pony Express horse and the lieutenant's away with him.

"Let's get you inside," Hart said. "I'll get you a drink of water. Then I'll tell you everything."

Moments later, Annie was seated at a table in the main room, with George on one side and Lieutenant Hart on the other, listening as the soldier repeated what little was known about Frank's accident. "He's had a bad blow to the head." Hart drew an imaginary line across his forehead and down one side of his face. "Twelve stitches. A lot of swelling."

"How'd it happen?"

"No one knows exactly. He passed out after the stage picked him up and still hasn't regained consciousness."

George stood up. "You'll want to go," he said to Annie. "I'll get a horse saddled."

Annie didn't move. "But — I — you — what about the cooking? The chickens?" *And now I'm the one babbling about chickens in the midst of a crisis.*

"Stay until you know Frank's going to be all right," George said. "In fact, stay until you can bring him back with you." He looked over at Lieutenant Hart. "If she needs anything, you get word to me and I'll see that she gets it the same day."

In a fog of worry, Annie hurried to pack. When she grabbed her comb off the dresser, she caught sight of Emmet's Pony Express Bible. *Fear thou not. The Lord is my Shepherd.* She still hadn't settled the issue of that word *my,* but absent Emmet or the parson's advice, something about having the book with her seemed like a good idea. She wrapped the Bible inside her only other

293

outfit and stuffed everything into her saddlebags.

By the time Annie stepped outside, George
and Billy were waiting, Billy with the lieutenant's horse in hand and George with the
buckskin gelding he'd been riding since
lending Banner to Emmet. When Annie was
ready to mount up, George simply picked
her up and set her in the saddle. He briefly
covered one of her hands with his and gave
it a little squeeze. "Hart says Frank's all
right. You remember that. Buck here's pretty
reliable, but he's still a horse — and he's
not used to you. He'll —"

"I know," Annie said, tucking her skirts
about her legs and settling in for a long ride.
"He'll test me. And I'll win."

"I don't doubt it for a minute," George
said and stepped back.

Over the first mile or so, Annie had to
fight the horse through several bouts of
crow-hopping and mild bucking until,
finally, Buck gave up and settled into a
steady if choppy lope. The lieutenant
seemed to sense that Annie was in no mood
to talk, and so they covered the miles in
silence. After what felt like an eternity, he
pointed into the distance and said, "It won't
be long now."

Annie peered ahead. Was that a flag? The

indistinct shapes on the horizon melded into a collection of buildings gathered around an open space.

"The parade ground," the lieutenant said, when Annie asked about it.

"No walls?" Who'd ever heard of a fort without defensive walls?

"Many of the Western forts are built this way," Hart explained. "Fort Kearny sprawls atop a low table that affords a good view of the area. We don't have walls, but that doesn't mean we're without defenses. We've a couple of mountain howitzers and plenty of other pieces at the ready." He broke off, adding quickly, "And no expectation they'll be needed. Things are peaceful in this part of Nebraska Territory." He led the way to the north of the grounds, past a corral and the post stables, past adobe buildings and, finally, to the post hospital in the southeast quadrant of the fort. Annie slid to the earth just as Lydia stepped through the hospital door.

"He's awake," she called, "and he'll be glad to see you."

Relief washed over Annie as she handed Buck to Lieutenant Hart and hurried up the wood stairs. "You waited with him?"

"Of course." Taking Annie's hand, Lydia led her inside, past a desk where a soldier was looking through a mountain of paper and then into a long room with cots arranged in two rows on either side of a wide aisle. She pointed toward the far right. "Just past that last curtain."

Frank's head was swathed in bandages, one eye swollen shut, the visible part of his face a riot of purples and blues. He was lying on his back, his eyes closed, both hands visible above the sheet. His lip was split. Beneath the bruising, he was frighteningly pale. Sinking to her knees beside the cot, Annie reached for his hand. "Frank? Frank, it's me. Annie."

It seemed to take forever for him to open his eyes. When he did, he looked at her for a long while before saying anything. Finally, he managed a weak smile. "What you doin' here?"

Resisting the urge to cry with relief, Annie produced a mock frown to accompany an affectionate scolding. "I thought you said you 'broke the best' when you broke Outlaw." She tapped her own head where his was bandaged. "Looks to me like 'the best' was out here in Nebraska — and the best broke you."

Wincing, he reached up and touched the bandage. "Aw . . . I'm aw-right. It's jus' a bump." He started to sit up, winced, and

296

lay back down. "Got a headache's all." He grimaced. "A bad one. Don't remember much. Dark night. That mare — straight outta Hades. She stepped in a hole. I woke up feeling like someone with a hammer used my head for a nail." He touched the bandage. "Twelve stitches."

"I heard. And the stage brought you here."

"Yep. Prolly thought I was drunk, layin' there in the grass. Sure glad they stopped." He shrugged. "I didn't lose the mail, though. Still got my job. Soon as I can do it again. I'm not quittin'. Don't you worry."

"I'm not worried about that," Annie said — although she had thought about it. A little. On the ride over. "I'm sticking around to make sure you don't do anything foolish."

He frowned. "What about your job?"

"George said to stay until I can take you back with me." She forced a smile. "So be forewarned. If I have to, I'll tie you to the bedpost to ensure you follow doctor's orders."

"Hunh. Like to see you try that."

"It wouldn't be hard today."

Frank closed his eyes. "Got that right."

A middle-aged man with a stern face and kind gray eyes stepped into the cubicle. "I'm Dr. Fields. You must be the sister. Annie, I believe Frank said?" He held out his hand and Annie shook it. "As long as he doesn't go back to riding too soon, he's going to be fine. But it's going to take some time. And he's going to have to be patient."

Annie tapped the back of Frank's hand. "You heard that, right?" She turned to the doctor. "Patience is not one of my brother's virtues."

"I suspected as much," the doctor said. "But he's going to have to develop some if he wants complete healing. We don't understand all that much about the brain and I'm not particularly well informed regarding the latest research. What I do know indicates that rest is the most important part of recovery from something like this."

Again, Annie looked down at Frank, but it seemed he'd fallen asleep. "Can I take him back to Clearwater?"

"I'd like to keep an eye on him for at least a few days," the doctor said.

Lydia spoke up. "Wade and I already discussed that. You'll stay with me." She smiled at Frank. "Until the famous 'moonlight messenger' is ready to ride."

Without opening his eyes, Frank muttered, "Lydia's got it all worked out."

"*We've* got it worked out," Lydia said, smiling at Annie. "He's agreed to be good so he'll be ready for the cotillion by the end of the month. He's promised me the first dance."

Frank gave a weak salute.

Dr. Fields asked for a moment "with my patient." Annie kissed Frank on the cheek and followed Lydia outside. This was no time to talk about Emmet's leaving. That could wait until Frank was feeling better. Lieutenant Hart was waiting on the hospital porch, having already taken the horses to the stables. As he led the two ladies toward his quarters, he identified each of the buildings facing the parade ground. "Commander's quarters, adjutant's office, quartermaster store, commissary store." He paused. "Those three across the way are soldier's quarters. I've been staying in the middle building since Lydia arrived."

Lydia chuckled. "He's hoping to use my presence to land a larger apartment the minute someone transfers out. If I stay, he can make the case for needing it."

They stopped outside a north-facing, two-story building with a sweeping front porch. "We're on the ground floor on the right," Lydia said and led the way up the stairs and through the door.

The apartment was a row of small rooms with a walkway running straight through to the back door. The simply furnished parlor boasted a small writing desk in front of the single window looking out onto the porch. The lieutenant had deposited Annie's saddlebags on a chair in this room. "We'll get a cot set up in here today."

The next room, a tiny bedroom, was crowded with two large trunks and an assortment of bandboxes and traveling cases that obviously belonged to Lydia. The modest kitchen was outfitted with a small cookstove, a table by the window, two chairs, and a small worktable. Open shelving served as both cupboard and pantry. Annie could see why the lieutenant was hoping for something bigger. Her room at Clearwater was more comfortably furnished — and larger — than these. As for the kitchen, there was no comparison.

Someone knocked on the front door. Lieutenant Hart leaned out and looked down the hall. He grunted softly. "I thought she might at least give you time to freshen up."

"She who?" Lydia asked.

The lieutenant didn't answer directly. Instead, he looked over at Annie. "The ladies of Fort Kearny are very meticulous about making calls. And that is my cue to take my leave."

Lydia leaned close and said, "He means he'll be hiding out until Miss Collingsworth and her mother have departed. The young lady has had her eye on my brother since arriving with her parents a few weeks ago."

The lieutenant sputtered something about the young lady in question being a "mere child" and scooted out the back door. Lydia looped her arm through Annie's and drew her to the front of the apartment to meet the two ladies waiting on the porch.

CHAPTER 20

Annie was already awake when a bugle sounded in the night. Throwing her blanket aside, she snatched up her skirt and dropped it over her head. Next came the blouse, which she buttoned with trembling hands, stuffing it into her skirt as she rushed to the front window to peer outside.

Lydia spoke from the doorway to the bedroom. "First call," she groaned. "Were you up already?"

"Just awake. But — I thought it meant something bad, so I hurried to dress."

"I thought I wrote you about it. Life here is ruled by that infernal bugle. You'll learn to ignore it." She paused. "No, that's not quite right. You'll adjust. Like someone with a clock that gongs and chimes its way through the day. You still hear it, but you don't consciously react."

"How often does it go off?"

Lydia tapped the tips of the fingers on her

left hand as she counted off more than a dozen different calls, from First Call to Reveille and, finally, Taps.

"And you recognize them all?"

"It becomes second nature. You'll see — if you're here for more than a few days." She waved Annie toward the back of the apartment, joking that they would have their own "mess call" in a few minutes. Annie watched while Lydia donned an apron. "I'm very sorry for the reason you're here at Fort Kearny," she said, "but I won't pretend not to be delighted to have company." She pointed to one of the two chairs at the kitchen table. "Sit. We'll walk over to the hospital as soon as we've had breakfast."

Annie sat, but by the time the lady slid what she called a Johnny cake onto her plate, Annie was gripping the edge of the table to keep herself from getting up and taking over. Poor Lydia. In all the weeks she'd been at Fort Kearny, she hadn't learned much when it came to cooking on a two-burner stove. If the raging fire she started was any indication of the way she usually worked, it was a wonder she hadn't set fire to the building by now. As far as the Johnny cakes went, Annie was grateful there was coffee. Even bitter coffee was useful when it came to washing down what amounted to a disk of scorched cornmeal.

When Lydia slid another disk onto her plate, Annie protested. "I've had plenty." She dabbed at her mouth with a napkin. "It feels too strange for someone to be cooking for me." She glanced toward the front of the apartment. "And it's past time I was at the hospital with Frank."

Lydia set the iron skillet aside and sank onto her chair. "They're really awful, aren't they?" She stabbed the cake on her plate with a fork. Finally, she picked it up, went to the door, and tossed it outside. "Abominable. You were very kind to choke even one down."

"The coffee's good," Annie said, and took another sip to prove the point.

"Barely drinkable."

"I've had to grind up toasted grain and call it coffee." Annie lifted the mug as if to toast her friend. "This is good by comparison."

Lydia grimaced. "We should just hire a cook. The officers' wives all have them — hired from the ranks of the enlisted men's wives working over on laundress row." She drank down the rest of her own coffee and set the mug down firmly. "But I'm stubborn. I don't want to admit defeat."

"If you really want to learn, I can show

you a few things."

"Would you? You wouldn't mind? Do you think I could master that pie you served at Clearwater the day I arrived on the stage?" Lydia pointed at the stove. "And how to build a proper fire?"

"I grew up cooking on one of those little stoves," Annie said. "It's the big beast at Clearwater that gives me fits. At least it did for the first few weeks. I think I've finally got that figured out."

Lydia jumped to her feet. "Let's get started. I mean — let me get dressed and we'll go see Frank and then when he needs a nap we can come back here and — thank you. You have no idea how much this means to me." She smiled. "I can write an article about it. 'The Lady in the West Learns to Cook.' "

While she waited for Lydia to dress, Annie stepped out the front door and onto the porch. She truly liked Lydia, but it was strange to be friends with someone for whom cooking was fodder for rich Easterners reading "Travel Notes from a Lady in the West" — people sitting before fires they hadn't built in homes they didn't clean. She thought back to the maid serving the family in the mansion she'd passed on her way into St. Joseph, Frank's reaction to her fascination, and her own thoughts about how it would be all right to serve others for the privilege of handling fine things. The Patee House seemed very far away.

Midmorning of Annie's third day at Fort Kearny, she was sitting in the chair beside Frank's cot watching him sleep when he opened his eyes and looked over at her. "You should get back to Clearwater before George Morgan complains to the Pony Express and we've both lost our jobs. There's no reason for you to waste time watching me sleep."

"First of all," Annie said, "I've only been here an hour or so. And second of all, George would never do something like that."

Frank arched an eyebrow. "It's *George* now?"

"It is." Annie shot him a piercing look. "And I don't care to be teased about it."

"O-o-o-kaaaaay," Frank drawled. "The *George* notwithstanding, Emmet will worry more than he should if you're still over here when he next rides in. If anything changes with me, Lieutenant Hart can bring the news. I don't imagine he'd mind an excuse to pay you a visit."

Emmet. Annie took a deep breath. "About

306

Emmet . . ." As she talked, the deep crease reappeared between Frank's eyebrows. And deepened.

"Of all the rotten luck," he muttered, swearing softly. "Two hundred dollars a month down the well."

"Don't think about that," Annie said. "Just get better. Once you're back in the saddle, we'll start saving again. We won't have as much as we planned, but — just don't worry about it. Please." She leaned close and lowered her voice. "And don't tell anyone, but I'm rather enjoying it here. I've finally found time to write Ira. And I'm giving Lydia cooking lessons."

"*Cooking* lessons?" Frank barked a laugh. His hand went to his bandaged head. "Ouch. Don't make me laugh."

"She's going to write an article about it. 'The Lady in the West Learns to Cook.' I can't possibly abandon her until she's flipped an edible Johnny cake."

Frank studied her for a moment. "Lydia's nice, isn't she?"

"You sound surprised."

He shrugged. "She'd fit right in with all those dandies who were looking down on us the night we walked into St. Jo. Except she doesn't 'look down' on us in that way." He paused. "You think she really meant it

— about the dance? My name at the top of her dance card and all that?"

Annie sighed and shook her head. "I hate to admit it, but she's probably just saving you the humiliation of being ignored. Surely you remember how all the ladies at the Patee House acted. How they avoided you. Why, if I hadn't been there, you probably wouldn't have had more than three dozen dance partners, you poor thing."

"Only three dozen? I thought sure it was four. Guess hitting my head made me forget the particulars."

Annie laughed. "If you're feeling well enough to rewrite the past to aggrandize your charm, I do believe you'll be ready to leave the hospital in no time." She bent to kiss him on the cheek. "Rest. I'll be back this afternoon."

After exiting the hospital, Annie made her way past the young trees lining the parade ground. According to Lydia, a former post commander had ordered them transplanted from the banks of the nearby Platte River. How hard would it be to keep a tree alive over at Clearwater? Just one tree by the chicken coop would make such a difference. She could already imagine how nice it would be to step into a shady spot just outside the back door. The well wasn't far away. It would be easy to keep a tree watered. She could do that at the same time she watered the rosemary plant. Assuming the rosemary lived through winter. She would need to get it dug up and brought inside the moment she returned to the station. She glanced up at the blue sky. *Please. No killing frost until I get back.*

Her musing about transplanting trees was interrupted when Lieutenant Hart strode up from the direction of the post office. "How's the patient this morning?"

"On the mend but not ready to leave the hospital yet."

"The captain's wife is hosting her weekly quilting bee over in the officer's quarters. Lydia's already there. May I walk you over?" He offered his arm.

A servant answered the lieutenant's knock and then backed away from the door to admit him and Annie. Although the parlor was easily three times the size of Lydia's, it was still crowded to the point of overflowing because of the quilting frame dominating the center of the room.

"Ladies," Lieutenant Hart said, "I present Miss Ann Paxton."

From the opposite corner of the room, Miss Collingsworth called out, "Why, if it's not the lovely *cook* from Clearwater road ranch."

Lydia asked for a report "on the patient." Once Annie delivered it, she invited her brother to "run along."

"Unless you'd care for a glass of lemonade," Miss Collingsworth offered.

"Thank you," the lieutenant said, "but duty calls." He turned to go.

Miss Collingsworth protested. "Please, Lieutenant Hart, we are in need of advice." She glanced around the quilt. "I've been put in charge of the refreshments for the cotillion, and a problem has presented itself just now." She held both hands up as if tossing things from one to the other as she said, "Pumpkin or sweet potato pie? Bread stuffing or cornbread? Turkey or ham?" She looked pointedly at the women seated around the quilt. "Some of us feel that with the election looming in only a few weeks, we should show our support for the Union and serve only *Northern* dishes. Others insist that we give equal attention to Southern favorites."

"And some of us," a woman with a distinct Southern accent retorted, "believe that the political situation has been carried entirely too far by our Northern 'sisters.'" She rose from her chair. "Cinda. If you are determined to politicize your position as chair of the refreshment committee, then — do what you will with your little 'grand cotillion.' I'll stay home." She dropped the thimble into the bag at her wrist. "I declare, if I hear one more word about that homely rail splitter from Illinois —" She broke off. Gulped. And turned to Annie. "Miss Paxton. I do apologize to you. But I cannot and I will not sit here and be insulted because the self-righteous among us seem to think Abraham Lincoln should be anointed for sainthood and my beloved South remanded to Hades."

As the lady in question charged for the door, Lieutenant Hart moved aside to let her pass before following her outside. Lydia broke the uncomfortable silence. "Well, then. I'd say you have your answer, Cinda. Both pumpkin *and* sweet potato." As a nervous titter sounded in the room, Lydia looped her arm through Annie's and drew her to the quilt. "Annie's staying with me while her brother mends." She pointed to the recently vacated chair on the far side of the quilt. "Sit there, dear. Ladies — I think it best to table the topic of refreshments and move on to decorations. Mrs. May had a lovely idea for creating swags from native grasses — hopefully we can all agree that will neither celebrate nor excoriate any particular political party. And I suggest we stick with harvest colors when it comes to ribbons and such."

Annie didn't know what *excoriate* meant, but more nervous laughter relieved the tension in the room. She looked down at the quilt. The lady who had just stormed out wasn't a particularly good stitcher. Annie picked up where she'd left off, listening as the ladies talked. It sounded like the cotillion would be a wonderful event.

At one point, Miss Collinsgworth called out to Annie. "I do hope your employer will allow you to come." The words were sincere. The tone was not.

"Of course she'll attend," Lydia said. "I happen to know she's already been invited. As my brother's guest."

Miss Collingsworth's false smile disappeared. She glared at Annie.

She's jealous. And you're enjoying it far too much. Annie hurried to correct Lydia. "Your brother has been very kind, but I'll be riding over with George Morgan."

Miss Collingsworth shuddered. "I don't know how you endure working for that man. He's absolutely terrifying. And so ill-kempt."

"To be precise," Lydia enjoined, "Annie

works for the Pony Express. As for Mr. Morgan, I think he's fascinating."

"You would," Miss Collingsworth sniffed.

An older women in the far corner chuckled. "I'll allow he doesn't quite look civilized, but I think it's oddly attractive."

"Annabelle Greeley," another woman scolded.

But Mrs. Greeley didn't back down. "Just because I'm not fishing anymore doesn't mean I can't admire the view from the banks of the stream."

"Did you know he lived with the Pawnee? Mr. Smith says he arrived at Clearwater with that boy in tow. What's his name? You know, the Indian."

"Billy Gray Owl," Annie said.

Mrs. Smith shuddered. "I wouldn't be able to sleep at night with an Indian lurking in the barn."

Miss Collingsworth asked, "Are you really staying the winter in that place?"

"Of course. The mail must go through, and that means the men must be fed."

"Won't you die of boredom?"

Annie forced a smile and tried a little joke. "I hope not, for the riders' sake. Billy says George is a terrible cook." *And yes. I know Billy and I call George "George," and I don't like you, either, Miss Nose-in-the-air. I wonder if there's a Pawnee name for that.* She would ask Billy. Annie concentrated on the line of stitching at hand while conversation and gossip circled around her. She said very little, but she learned a lot — especially about Miss Nose-in-the-air, who spoke of "Lydia's brother" with an undertone of ownership and expectation that obviously annoyed Lydia. When someone wondered aloud if the post commander would still be on duty in the spring, Annie learned more about how the political situation in the East was taking a toll here at Fort Kearny.

Mrs. Greeley spoke to the post commander's political leanings. "If Lincoln wins the election, our commander will resign and don a different uniform." She smiled at Lydia. "And your brother is the likely candidate to be promoted to his position."

Talk continued about the horrible possibility of a war between the states. Finally, Annie excused herself to check on Frank. Lieutenant Hart intercepted her on the way to the hospital. "I owe you an apology."

"For what?"

"Throwing you to the she-wolves."

Annie smiled. "I survived." After a moment she added, "I didn't realize the North-South tensions were quite so strong among the ladies." She glanced up at him. "You never did answer Miss Collinsgworth as to your personal preference in the matter of pie. Which is it, pumpkin or sweet potato?"

"Neither," he said. "I'm partial to the raisin molasses pie served at a road ranch a little to the east of here. Perhaps you know it?"

Say something, you idiot. He's flirting with you. She could think of nothing to say.

"As your escort, I'm speaking for the first two dances at the cotillion. If you don't object."

Object? Of course she didn't object. She'd dream of it every night. She nodded.

"You do object?"

"No. I mean — yes." She took a deep breath. "I don't object. I will give you the first two dances." *And the third, if you want.*

"I shall hold you to it," he said, "and count the days." He nodded toward the hospital door. "I hope Frank mends quickly. And while I'm sorry that an injury was the cause for it, I'm very glad you've spent some time here at Fort Kearny. I was running out of excuses for leading patrols past Clearwater."

CHAPTER 21

The day after Annie met the ladies of Fort
Kearny at the quilting bee, she was dusting
the furniture in the apartment's parlor when
Lieutenant Hart stepped in the door. "Do I
dare hope that's raisin molasses pie I smell?"

"It is," Annie replied, "but not mine.
Lydia's."

The lieutenant grimaced.

"I saw that," Lydia called from the doorway leading back to the kitchen. "It's just
now ready. Annie was going to get the first
taste, but seeing that look on your face just
now, I think you should do the honors." She
waved him toward the kitchen. "Come
along."

The lieutenant obeyed. When he joked
about being punished for honesty, Lydia
smacked him — playfully. He put his hand
to his cheek. "Ouch. That hurt."

"Just sit down," Lydia said, and pointed
to the chair by the door. She served up a

piece of pie and handed him a fork.

"Can I at least have something to wash it down with? A cup of coffee, perhaps?"

"I'll make coffee in a moment. It remains to be seen if I'll be serving it to *you.*"

Taking a deep breath, Hart tasted the pie. He closed his eyes for a moment. Frowned. Opened one eye and looked at his sister. Took another bite. Finally, he spoke to Annie. "Tell the truth. She didn't make this. You did."

"I had nothing to do with it."

"Not true," Lydia enjoined. "She's been a most patient instructor in recent days. In fact, she's suffered through three miserable failures."

The lieutenant took another bite. "Well, there's nothing miserable about this. It's delectable."

"Really?" Lydia stared at him in disbelief.

"Really."

With a shout of joy, she grabbed Annie and gave her a hug. She looked over at her brother. "Wait until you taste my Johnny cakes. And grits. And — next I'm going to master jumbles. Do you remember Grandmother's jumbles?"

Lieutenant Hart looked over at Annie. "What wonders have you wrought, dear girl? And in only one week. Lydia Morton Hart in the kitchen? Willingly? *Joyfully?*"

"She's writing an article," Annie said. " 'The Lady Cooks Western Fare.' "

"And I'm going to share the pie recipe," Lydia said. She looked over at Annie. "I wish Frank nothing but a speedy recovery, but from a selfish standpoint I'm going to hate to see you leave."

"I second that," the lieutenant said.

After Hart left and while coffee brewed, Lydia asked Annie to follow her into the next room. Opening the largest of her trunks, she set a few things aside on the floor and then pulled a blue silk gown from the depths. "It's not the latest style, but if you think you'd like it, we could remake it to fit you. For the cotillion."

Annie caught her breath.

"Well? What do you think?" Lydia waggled the dress.

"I couldn't. It's too elegant. Too fine." *It's gorgeous.*

"Oh come now. It's just a dress. And an old one at that." She held the gown up to Annie, folding it at the bodice and inspecting the waistline. "If we add a sash, we can draw it in." She pulled a length of ivory silk out of the trunk. "Happily," she said, "I'm not that much taller than you, so the sleeves will work as they are. We have plenty of time to hem it up." She looked over at Annie. "I'm actually quite handy with a needle. I can easily have it ready by the twenty-seventh. You'll need to arrive a few hours early, just in case we have to adjust something at the last minute."

What could it hurt to try it on? Annie stepped out of her calico and into the silk. The gown rustled as she walked to the front of the apartment to peer into the mirror by the front door. What she saw made her gasp with delight.

Lydia reached around from the back and tied the ivory sash in place. "There. It almost looks like an original part of the gown." She stood back. Tilted her head. "If I can find some matching silk — or something complementary — I'll add an accent to the hem." She rushed back to her room and returned with a nosegay of pale ribbon flowers. Turning Annie back to look in the mirror, she tucked the flowers into the twist at the nape of her neck. "That'll look nice. I wish I had blue ones, though. They'd look so nice with your eyes. And — one more thing." Again, she retreated to her room, this time returning with a velvet box.

When she opened the lid, Annie gasped at the stunning array of sparkling blue and silver. She had no idea what the stones were, but from the look of the box, they were incredibly valuable. She pushed it away. "I can't. It's too much."

Lydia insisted. "It's not 'too much.' It's just right. All the officer's wives will be showing off their best. Why shouldn't we? Besides, it isn't even my best. I'm keeping that for myself." She draped the jewels about Annie's neck. "This is simple and tasteful." She leaned sideways and looked at Annie in the mirror. "I'm wearing rubies and a claret gown. We'll look like fire and ice. It'll be fun. Wade will think he's dancing with a princess."

Annie touched the necklace. The only thing missing was a pair of glass slippers.

The morning after Lydia's success with raisin molasses pie, something clicking against the parlor window accompanied First Call. Pulling her patchwork comforter about her for warmth, Annie rose and padded across the floor to peer out the front window. Sleet had transformed the world into a silver wonderland — at least for those with nothing to do but peer at it from the warmth of their apartments. It would be a treacherous day for everyone else. The stage might be forced to lay over. The thought sent a pang of guilt through Annie, as she thought of George, alone at Clearwater — alone save for Billy and the two or three members of the summer crew who were staying over to try their hand at trapping this winter.

Annie's concerns grew when, after breakfast with Lydia, she stepped outside and had to navigate the stairs. She made her way to the hospital with careful steps, nearly slipping and falling more than once, until Lieutenant Hart called out for her to wait for him to help her. But when he tried to hurry to her side, he fell on his backside.

"Are you all right?"

"Nothing hurt but my dignity," he laughed as he righted himself. "Just — wait."

Annie waited and together they slipped and slid their way to the hospital, laughing so hard by the time they got there they were both out of breath.

"Thank God for bannisters," the lieutenant said as he handed her off to the railing leading up to the hospital's front door. "That's far more dependable than I am at the moment. I hope you get good news inside."

Frank sensed rather than saw Annie sitting beside his cot. He didn't open his eyes at first, but rather lay quietly, listening to the clicking of her knitting needles. When he finally did open his eyes, however, he was surprised that the chair beside his bed was empty. So what was clicking? A glance in the direction of the window answered the question. *Sleet.*

Annie peeked around the curtain separating Frank's cubicle from the rest of the ward.

"Thought you'd still be asleep," she said.

He nodded toward the window. "I thought you'd borrowed someone's knitting needles."

"It's letting up some," Annie said, shivering and drawing her shawl close as she settled on the chair next to his cot. "Too bad I didn't borrow knitting needles. I could have gotten a lot done by now."

"Check over at the commissary. From what I heard, they have just about anything anyone could want, and they sell to civilians."

"There's no point in spending money when I have what I need back at Clearwater."

"If we ever get back there," Frank groused.

Dr. Fields stepped into view from just beyond the curtain. "You really don't like the accommodations here at Fort Kearny, do you?"

"Don't take it personally," Frank said.

"Let's see how you're doing." The doctor extended his index finger and ordered Frank to follow with his eyes as he moved his hand back and forth, up and down. Next, he checked beneath the bandage. Looking over at Annie he said, "If you think you can handle removing the stitches in a few days, I'd be open to letting your brother go today — assuming the weather lets up later this morning."

"Of course she can do it."

"I believe the doctor was talking to *me*," Annie snapped.

Whoa. Since when did she mind his answering for her? "You killed a rattlesnake with your bare hands. Compared to that, what's snipping a stitch or two?"

"It's *twelve* stitches," Annie said, and then looked at the doctor. "But of course I can do it. As long as the weather improves."

The doctor nodded. "Take the ride to Clearwater at a nice, steady walk." He looked over at Frank. "By the time you get there, you'll probably feel like you just set a hundred-mile speed record for the Pony Express. I'm telling you that so when it happens, you won't be discouraged. It's going to take some time for that hard head of yours to return to normal."

Frank reached for the shirt draped over the back of the chair Annie had been using when she visited.

"You just settle back," she said firmly. "We're not running out of here this morning."

"Well, of course we are. We're just not running. I heard the doc about that — but — we are leaving. You said you rode Morgan's buckskin here, right? I'll just ride" — he glanced at Dr. Fields — "I mean I'll *walk* Buck to the Pony Express relay station down the road and bring another horse back. Shouldn't take long at all."

Annie shook her head. "*I'll* ride to the relay station and bring back an extra horse. *You'll* wait here until I have things sorted out. And we aren't going anywhere if the weather doesn't improve." She thanked the doctor for all he'd done and left to see about the horses.

Moving slowly, Frank finished dressing, surprised at how much effort it took and pondering how bossy Annie had become in recent days. By midmorning, though, he and Annie — along with Lieutenant Hart, who insisted on escorting them — were on their way back to Clearwater.

Fort Kearny had disappeared from view when Frank reached behind him to grasp the cantle, hoping it looked as though he were slouched comfortably in the saddle. The truth was, his head had started to pound. A jackrabbit sprang from behind a bunch of grass. Outlaw snorted and stepped out. Frank had to grab the saddle horn to keep his balance.

Annie looked over, frowning. "When I saw him in the corral at the relay station, I knew you'd want Outlaw, but — I hope he isn't too much for you."

"I said I'm fine," Frank sputtered. If only the world would stop quaking. If only his stomach would settle once and for all. Outlaw's ears twitched forward. With an instinctive "Whoa, there," Frank peered at a moving smudge in the distance. Finally, the smudge resolved into a lone horse and rider headed toward them.

Annie had better vision than either of the men. "It's George!" As soon as he was within earshot, Annie called a hello.

With little more than a nod by way of greeting, Morgan reached inside his coat and withdrew a wrinkled envelope. "News from Emmet."

When Frank reached for the letter, Annie asked him to read it right away. "At least find out if it's good news." She thanked Morgan for making the effort to deliver it.

"You could have sent it by stage."

He shrugged. "Didn't think you should have to wait."

As Frank scanned the letter, he smiled. Rotten Luck hadn't followed Emmet back to Missouri, after all. "They're doing all right," he said, flipping the single piece of paper over; squinting and blinking when the handwriting blurred. Finally, he deciphered the most important part of the letter and looked up at Annie. "They're *married.*"

"Married? But — I thought they'd wait."

"What for?"

"For us to be there. To witness it."

Frank shook his head. "There's no telling when we could do that. I'm glad they went ahead. They deserve to be happy."

Annie brushed something out of her eyes. "You're right." She offered a weak smile.

Morgan nudged his horse alongside Buck as he said to Hart, "You'll want to be getting back. I'll see them home from here." He smiled at Annie. "Lucille's not the only hen with chicks now. Three of Henrietta's had hatched before I left this morning."

"Lucille?" Confused, Hart looked to Annie for an explanation.

She seemed embarrassed. "I know it's silly, but I've named them." She looked over at Morgan, surprised he'd listened enough to know which one was which. "And I sure hope they don't all freeze in this weather."

"Not likely," he said. "I brought them into the storeroom before I left. Henrietta, Lucille, Clifford — the whole bunch of them. Billy's keeping an eye on them."

Hart spoke to Annie. "Guess I'll be getting back. Don't forget, now. You promised me the first two dances at least." And with that, he rode away.

CHAPTER 22

October 27 dawned crisp and cold. Neither stage nor mail run were expected at Clearwater, and Annie decided to indulge in the nearest thing to a bath she could manage. First, she dragged a copper boiler into her room and slowly filled it with water she'd pumped, hauled in, and heated on the stove. By the time she had enough, her "bath" was barely lukewarm, but it would do.

Barring the door to her room, she disrobed and knelt to wash her hair. That done, she scrubbed herself, reveling in the sensation of being clean before donning the blue calico she'd laundered the day before. Back in the kitchen, she stirred up the fire in the stove and opened the oven door, perching on an upended crate and combing through her waist-length hair as it dried.

Frank sauntered in. "Fort Kearny's going to think an angel flew down for the cotillion."

Happy to see her brother wearing his Pony Express shirt and jeans, Annie grinned. "I could say the same to you. You look right fine. Impressive scar and all. You sure you're ready for a long ride?"

"Not at a dead run I'm not, but I should be all right if we keep an easy pace. I promised Lydia Hart a dance, and I aim to keep that promise." He tied his yellow bandanna in place as they talked.

It was good to see Frank smile. Good to see him looking forward to something. They chatted about the pile of buffalo robes stacked beneath the stairs to the loft in the main room and how, when they had arrived at Clearwater back in March, neither of them had known a thing about what was involved in running a road ranch. When Annie said she was looking forward to seeing Luther again, Frank grinned.

"Which is it you're really excited about — seeing Luther or getting that wire so George can build your chicken yard?"

"Both," Annie said, reaching back to comb through her thick hair with her fingers.

Frank talked about the various station masters he'd met up the line to the west and inevitably touched on the topic of the girl named Pete.

"Will she be at the cotillion? I'd like to

meet her." Annie studied her brother carefully while she waited for the answer.

"I don't think Pete's the type to care much for dancing." He'd been leaning against the doorframe leading into his room while they talked. Now, he looked past Annie toward the main room. "Speaking of folks you wouldn't expect to dress for a dance — you look vaguely familiar. Have we met?"

Annie spun about. Her jaw dropped. George Morgan had trimmed both his beard and his long hair. Sporting a long black coat over blue denim pants and a white shirt, he looked . . . *handsome.*

"Billy's bringing up the horses," he said to Annie. "We can leave whenever you're ready." He raked one hand through his hair and donned a black hat. "If you're up to it," he said to Frank, "you could help me roll up a buffalo pelt for each one of us to take along. It'll be cold when we ride back, and one of these days we're going to get some snow. Best be prepared."

While Frank helped George, Annie retreated to her room and tied up her hair, all the while thinking of the gown and jewels waiting at Lydia's. Once her hair was done, she gathered extra socks, mittens, and a scarf. Stuffing them into her saddlebags, she grabbed the campaign hat she always wore outside and tied a shawl about her. With a patchwork comforter draped over one arm, she headed for the door.

The day was cool, but the shawl and comforter did their job, and she was only slightly chilled when at last she caught sight of the flag flying over the Fort Kearny parade ground. "I'm supposed to meet up with Lydia," she called to the men. "We'll see you at the cotillion." Without waiting for a reply, she nudged Shadow ahead, turning off the trail to head straight for Lydia's back door. Sliding to the earth, she hitched Shadow and hurried inside. Lydia was standing in the parlor inspecting herself in the mirror. Tucking an errant curl into place, she turned to greet Annie.

How long had it taken to iron all that ruching? Yards of it formed a scrolling pattern of ruffles across the surface of the wine-colored skirt. More ruching accented the V from Lydia's shoulders to her waist. Deep red jewels dripped from her necklace. Annie stammered, "Y-You look gorgeous."

Lydia curtseyed. "Thank you. I had help, of course. Annabelle Greeley really is a dear." She reached for Annie's saddlebags and set them aside. "Let's get you dressed. We've only a short while before the band starts to play. I can't wait to see the look on

Wade's face when he arrives. We ladies have outdone ourselves, even if I do say so myself."

Annie had dreamed of candlelight and music, of gallant men and laughter, of beautiful women and trembling fans, but even her most outlandish dreams of the cotillion itself paled by comparison to seeing Lieutenant Hart's expression when Lydia opened the door to admit him to the apartment. For the longest moment, he simply stared at Annie — until, finally, Lydia cleared her throat and brandished a blank dance card and a pencil.

"As I recall, you wanted the first dance with our guest."

The lieutenant didn't look away from Annie as he held out his hand and accepted both card and pencil. "I'd rather command the first two — if you'll still allow it?"

Annie felt her cheeks warm beneath his gaze. She nodded. "Of course. If you're certain."

As the lieutenant scribbled his name on the first two lines, he murmured, "I've never been more sure of anything."

While Annie tucked the dance card into the silk bag at her wrist, Lydia reached for the two shawls draped across the back of a nearby chair. Taking one for herself, she handed the other to Annie and together they stepped out onto the porch. The lieutenant offered each lady an arm and together they descended the stairs and set out for the mess hall. The interior of the hall glowed in the light of at least two dozen lamps and what seemed to be hundreds of candles. Nearby tables groaned with ham and turkey, pumpkin and sweet potato pie, pickles and jams, cakes and punch.

The band was just taking its place when Frank stepped up. Making a show of inspecting Annie from head to toe, he said, "You remind me of my sister."

Annie leaned close and muttered, "She's still in here. Feeling like a weed pushing its way into a flower bed."

Frank whispered back. "You're no weed, Ann E. You're the prize-winning rose. Try to enjoy it." He turned to Lydia. "I hope you meant it when you promised me the first dance."

"Dear boy," Lydia said, and reached out to adjust the bandanna knotted about Frank's neck. "I always mean what I say and say what I mean." She handed Frank her own dance card. As soon as he'd signed it, she looped her arm through his. "I hope you don't mind, but I promised to introduce you. The ladies all want to meet the intrepid Pony Express rider they've read so much about."

"I thought that article was for the back-East news," Frank said.

Lydia made a show of tucking a dark curl behind her ear with a gloved forefinger. "I might have left a copy or twelve lying about at this quilting bee or that afternoon tea." She batted her eyes at Wade. "Will you be all right without Frank and me for a few moments?"

"We'll manage," the lieutenant said. He asked Annie to produce her dance card. "Do you mind if I monopolize you?"

"I can't say. Are there rules?"

"None that rank can't overcome."

Annie stayed his hand. "I'd like to dance with my brother a time or two."

"Of course." He wrote his name on several more lines before handing back the card.

Annie glanced down. He'd left the bottom line blank. One dance for Frank, and that was all. She caught sight of George, standing with a group of other ranchers gathered just inside the door. He was staring at her as if she'd grown an extra head.

Frank was standing at the refreshment table sipping punch and waiting for his head to stop spinning when Annie put her hand on his arm. "Are you all right?"

"Don't I look all right?"

"You look very handsome."

"Don't I always? And stop worrying. I just got a little dizzy. I'll be fine. Although I fear I may have to disappoint a few of the ladies this evening. Hate to admit it, but I'm plum tuckered out." He nodded toward the dance floor. "Happily, George can take up where I've left off." He grimaced. "*There's* something I never expected to say. Not that I've been keeping track, mind you, but I think he's danced with every woman in the room. Even the uppity one who's spent most of the night staring daggers at you."

"That's Cinda Collinsgworth," Annie said. "And I don't know why, but she doesn't like me."

"You really don't know?" He sounded doubtful.

"Not for certain. I suppose it might have something to do with Lieutenant Hart."

Frank raised his glass. "How observant of you. Hart only has eyes for you, and she only has eyes for him." He looked about the room. "Speaking of the golden-haired wonder, where is he?"

"Why don't you like Wade?"

She was calling him Wade, now? *Blast it.*

"Tonight? Because he's rude and selfish. Monopolizing your dance card. Shutting all the other men who'd like to dance with you out. Just because he can."

"It's one night out of an entire year of socials," Annie said. "They'll soon forget all about me. The clock will strike midnight soon, all this finery will go back into Lydia's trunk, and I'll go back to being the calico-clad cook at Clearwater road ranch."

Frank chuckled. "Say that three times if you can. And if I'm not mistaken, that particular fairy tale had a very nice ending."

Annie reached for his cup of punch and drank it down. "Dance with me."

"What will your lieutenant say?"

"He's not *my* lieutenant, and he won't say anything. You're my brother. He wouldn't dare try to pull rank on you."

CHAPTER 23

A week to the day after the Fort Kearny cotillion, Frank stumbled into the kitchen at Clearwater and, with a groan, sank onto the upturned biscuit box that served as a sometimes perch. "I'm not getting better."

"Of course you are," Annie insisted, as she stirred the giant pot of oatmeal cooking on the stove. "You've helped Billy with chores every morning this week."

"And had to take a nap every afternoon. Right when Luther was here and George could have used help with that chicken yard."

"Luther didn't mind. We were his last delivery before he turned back toward St. Jo., and he didn't seem in any particular hurry to leave."

"Doesn't matter. It's taking too long for me to get back in the saddle."

"Dr. Fields said that if you hurry it, you could do permanent damage. And you're already damaged enough, dear brother of mine." Frank didn't laugh at her joke. He didn't even smile. Annie set the spoon down on the stovetop and gently moved his hair out of the way to inspect the cut. "No swelling. The bruise is entirely faded away. And I did an excellent job taking the stitches out. You'll have a very impressive scar. Boys like scars, don't they?"

Frank pulled away and smoothed his hair into place. "Sure. They make us look tough. Which impresses the ladies."

"You *are* tough. You could barely stand upright, but you didn't lose the mail. Last week, you impressed plenty of ladies at Fort Kearny — including Lydia Hart, who does not impress easily."

"My head still pounds when I move fast."

Annie only knew to repeat what the doctor had said, and Frank didn't want to hear *It takes time.* She dished up some oatmeal. "Molasses or sugar?"

"Sugar. And butter?"

Annie hesitated. She had one precious bit of butter left, and she was saving it. Two of the chicks were roosters, and Clifford was entirely rooster enough for her little flock. Chicken and dumplings was on the menu for Christmas Day, along with biscuits served with butter and chokecherry jelly.

"I'm still wounded," Frank pleaded. "Spoil me. Just a dollop."

Annie complied, handing the bowl back with a blob of butter melting into the cooked oats. She even sprinkled a bit of cinnamon on top.

Frank savored the oatmeal before saying, "We need a cow."

"Talk to Mr. Morgan about that. I'm done trying to convince him."

Frank studied her as he finished his oatmeal. "Mr. Morgan? You and George on the outs?"

"Why would you think that?" Annie grabbed a mug off a shelf and poured herself a cup of coffee.

Frank shrugged.

"Has George — Mr. Morgan — said something to you?" Annie asked.

"Well . . . sure. We talk all the time."

"That's not what I mean." Annie stared out the window toward the trail. The only traffic these days amounted to freighters, the weekly stage — with few passengers compared to this past spring and summer — and the Pony Express. In the span of a few weeks, Clearwater had begun to feel exactly the way she'd always expected it to feel. Lonely. And George Morgan was back to barely talking. What had happened? Annie turned around and leaned against her worktable, coffee mug in hand. "He's barely said two words to me since the cotillion."

Frank shrugged. "He's been busy sorting cattle. Stacking hay near the corrals and firewood by the back door. Building your chicken yard. Trying to get things done before it snows. Not to mention beating Luther at checkers every game they played while he was here."

"He didn't dance with me. Not once."

Frank snorted surprise. "That been simmering for a whole week?"

"Simmering?"

He mimicked her voice. " 'He didn't dance with me. Not once.' You sound like a little girl who didn't get invited to a birthday party."

"How would you know about that? Whoever had a birthday party when we were growing up?" Annie huffed frustration. "Sorry I said anything."

"What you should be sorry about," Frank blustered, "is letting Wade Hart take over what should have been one of the best nights of your life. But it wasn't, was it? I could tell that when you stole my punch at the end of the night."

"It was wonderful," Annie said. *Not perfect, though.*

"It could have been better, if only you'd stood up to Hart."

Annie set her coffee mug down and pretended to inspect the rosemary plant she'd brought inside and set near the window. " 'Stood up to him'? How? What are you talking about?"

"The same thing I was talking about the night of the dance." He paused. "It would have made a lot of lonely boys happy to waltz with the prettiest girl in the room. Maybe you didn't know that, but the great and glorious Lieutenant Wade Hart definitely did. And he didn't care. He used you to make a point about his power over the men under his command."

"Used me?" Annie raised her voice. "Are you saying he only pretended to want to dance with me?"

"Of course not. But he didn't have to write his name on every single line but one. That's the part I'm talking about, and I stand by what I said. He's rude and selfish."

"Well, I am sorry you don't approve of Lieutenant Hart," Annie retorted. "But that doesn't fix whatever's bothering George Morgan, does it?"

"Neither does your talking to *me* about it. If you wanted to dance with George, why'd you let Hart take over?"

"Mr. Morgan said he was going to talk to the other ranchers about the election. He never mentioned dancing. I didn't know he *could* dance."

Frank shook his head. "For a smart little gal, Ann E., you can be awful stupid sometimes. You really think George trimmed his beard and polished his boots for a meeting with a bunch of ranchers?" He reached for a mug and poured himself a cup of coffee. After taking a sip, he added, "He did that for *you*. And then you ignored him."

Annie frowned. George dressed up for her? Could that be right? She let regret sound in her voice as she said, "Before the cotillion, we'd started talking. We were getting along. I'd finally gotten over being afraid of him."

"You were afraid of George?"

"A little."

"Well, you ought to be over that, especially now that you know the only times he's ever done violence was in defense of people he cares about. And you, Ann E., are one he happens to care about."

"I miss him." She'd blurted out the words without thinking. And of course, what would happen but George Morgan stepping up to the doorway between the kitchen and the main room. He'd probably heard every word. Setting her coffee mug down, Annie reached for a bowl. Time to make something. Anything. Just to give her an excuse to avoid those gray-blue eyes.

"And he misses you," George said.

Annie wheeled about. "You were listening. That's called eavesdropping." She glanced over at Frank. "And it's rude."

"I was working in the store. And you were talking kinda loud. And by the time you were into it and I realized you wouldn't want me to hear, it was too late to sneak out. Although now that I think on it, I suppose I could have lifted the trap door and gone down into the root cellar. Glad I didn't."

Frank snorted a barely disguised laugh. Annie glared at him. He ducked his head and concentrated on the coffee. Looking up at George Morgan, she blurted out a question. "Where'd you learn to dance like that?"

"Lessons when I was a boy. Hated every minute of it."

"Well, you learned it very well."

"So I'm told."

"I should have saved you a dance."

"I should have asked." Morgan hesitated a moment, then held out his hand.

"There's no music."

"We can hum. You have a favorite?"

"I . . . no."

"I do." He began to hum. Off key.

Annie took his hand and followed him into the main room, where George waltzed her past the counter, around the tables, and back again, with all the skill of a dance master. A very tall dance master with a booming laugh.

Frank was forking hay down from the barn loft early in November, when the clanging of the bell up at the station announced the approach of the eastbound Pony Express. Hurrying down the ladder, he helped Billy saddle a fresh pony, then grabbed the reins, insisting that he'd take the horse up and help with the exchange. Running through the snow with the fresh pony in tow left him gasping for breath.

Jake Finney had already dismounted and was waiting, stamping his feet to keep the blood flowing. He handed over the reins of his spent mount and slapped the mochila in place while he talked. "Telegraph just carried the biggest news since it reached Fort Kearny," he said, as he jumped into the saddle. "It's *President* Lincoln now. Telegraph operator said the westward riders are going all out to set a record. Five days to California." He spurred his horse and was gone before Frank could manage a reply.

Five days. How many horses will die to make that happen? Sucking in a deep breath, Frank watched as Jake disappeared eastward. He started when Annie called from the doorway. "Did I hear right? It's Lincoln?"

Frank nodded. Without a word, he led the horse away. Bitter regret accompanied him to the barn and throughout the rest of the day. The biggest news of his lifetime, and he could barely manage a run from the barn to the station. Some "moonlight messenger" he was. He spent the remainder of the day in the barn, brushing down horses, fiddling with tack, doing anything to avoid talking — especially to Annie, who would know how he felt about not being part of the historic mail run and try to cheer him up.

When it came time for supper, he told Billy he was worried about the horse Jake had ridden in and was going to stay in the barn and keep an eye on him. "I'll see to evening chores here in the barn," he said. With a nod, Billy headed for the station. Later, Annie trudged through the snow to bring down a ham sandwich. Frank called down from the loft and asked her to just leave the sack hanging on a hook and he'd get it in a minute. He waited to eat until she'd retreated and then waited again until the moon had risen and she was likely in bed before making his way back to the station. Shivering with cold, he dove beneath the pile of covers on his cot and waited to fall asleep.

But Annie just couldn't let him be. He was almost asleep when she stepped into his room and said quietly, "If you think it would help, you could see Dr. Fields again."

He was facing the wall, and he didn't turn over. "I might do that. Right now, though, I'm going to sleep."

"You could take the stage. We have enough money. It wouldn't cost much."

"Leave me be, Annie. Please. Just let me sleep."

"I just want to help. I'm worried about you."

He barely managed to swallow a torrent of angry, bitter words. "I just told you how to help. Let me be." For a long moment, he could sense her presence as she lingered in the doorway, staring across the room. Finally, she did what he'd asked. He heard her pad across to her own room. The door creaked as she closed it.

■ ■ ■ ■

With the first serious snowfall in late November, George carried a small trunk into the main room and set it on the counter. Opening the lid, he took a muslin-wrapped package out and unwrapped it. He ran his palm over the dark surface of a leather-bound book, smiling as if looking down at an old friend. Curious, Annie went to see what he was up to.

George brandished the book. "The secret to surviving winter at Clearwater." By the time he was finished unwrapping the package, over a dozen books stood on the counter, a small crock at either end holding them upright. Picking one up, he recited, " 'It was the best of times, it was the worst of times, it was the age of wisdom, it was the age of foolishness, it was the epoch of belief, it was the epoch of incredulity, it was the season of Light, it was the season of Darkness, it was the spring of hope, it was the winter of despair, we had everything before us, we had nothing before us, we were all going direct to Heaven, we were all going direct the other way . . .' " He paused. "Magnificent, isn't it? And strangely applicable to the recent election news."

Annie's heart lurched. "You think there's going to be a war?"

George set the book down. "I wish I could believe that cooler heads will prevail and a solution be found. But to be honest, it's probably too late for that."

Annie rubbed her arms to dispel the goose bumps. She remembered the woman storming out of the quilting bee at Fort Kearny a few weeks ago and the prediction regarding the post commander should Lincoln become president.

"What's it mean for us — I mean, for people in the West?"

"Much of the regular army will likely be called east. The rest of the ranchers and I talked about that at the cotillion. We'll form a volunteer militia to take their place." His voice gentled. "It's good to remember a verse in the Psalms at times like these. I can't quote it exactly, but the general idea is that when 'the nations are in an uproar,' God is still on His throne. Remembering that can get a man through many a 'winter of despair' and on to the 'spring of hope.'"

Annie reached over and opened the book George had laid on the counter. *Oliver Twist; or, The Parish Boy's Progress* by Charles Dickens. "I'm impressed you liked this well enough to memorize it."

"Oh, that's not the one I quoted. I don't have that book yet. It's Dickens, just a different story. Newer. I read the opening in a magazine a stage passenger left here while you were at Fort Kearny. Captivating language. The story's set during the French Revolution. It was published in pieces last year — a serial in *Harper's*. I'd like to own a copy, though. Rose loved Dickens."

Annie set the book down. "Tell me about Rose. A favorite memory."

"That's easy." George chuckled. "We stole a peck of apples from the neighbor's orchard. *Green* apples. And ate nearly the whole thing."

"That makes my stomach hurt just to hear about it."

"Mine, too, even after all these years." He shook his head. "That girl got me into more trouble."

"Poor George, an innocent child, dragged into trouble against his will."

"Absolutely. I was always the good one. Rose was the troublemaker." His tone denied the words, and they shared a laugh. "All right. I caused my share of trouble, too, but probably more than I would have on my own. Rose was never one to stay still for long. She was like Frank in that way." He looked over at the books. "After the accident, she said literature saved her. She didn't know it would save me, too. All those hours reading to her after she got hurt cured my stutter, once and for all." He sighed. "Did I ever tell you what happened to her?"

Annie shook her head. "Only that she passed on before you left home."

George looked toward the fire blazing in the fireplace across the room as he talked. "She sneaked off with our father's best rig and challenged a boy she liked to a race. She would have won, too — except she rounded a corner too fast and the carriage overturned. She never walked again." For a moment, he was silent. Brooding. But then he looked at Annie and said, "I haven't thought about that green-apple episode in a long while. I should think more on the fun we had and less on the accident." He pointed at the row of books. "She taught me to cherish a well-told story."

Annie wondered if reading might help Frank. She glanced toward his room.

George read her mind. He pulled another book from the row and handed it over. "This might appeal to his adventurous side."

The Iliad. What a strange word. "I can't even pronounce this," Annie said and started to hand it back.

George stayed her hand. "Trust me. It'll

appeal to Frank. War and sieges and calamity galore. It'll get his mind off things here at Clearwater."

Nineteen winters on a poor Missouri farm taught a girl how to cope with a lot of things — including winter. Annie knew what it was to battle deep drifts and to spend long days shivering beside a tiny stove in a futile attempt to keep warm. There was nothing to be done but to endure it, knowing that spring would come again. But neither Annie nor Frank had ever endured weather like what Mother Nature threw at Clearwater in the winter of 1860 to 1861.

All through December, a succession of fierce storms piled snow in ever-deepening drifts. News filtered in from stage drivers about horses slipping or enduring injuries so profound they had to be shot. One such incident resulted in the death of a Pony Express rider who, after shooting a horse with a broken leg, grabbed the mochila and tried to walk to the next station. He perished when yet another storm blew through. The resemblance to Frank's accident made Annie shudder.

George and Billy ran ropes from the station to the corrals, from the corrals to the barn, from the barn to the well, and so on.

George warned Annie and Frank against thinking they could find their way without those ropes. "Men have been lost within a few feet of home when the wind came up and turned the world white. If that happens when you're out doing chores, you keep hold of that rope, no matter what."

The notion of getting lost in a storm plagued Annie as she thought about the men riding for the Pony Express. How could any of them survive? When she asked the question, George said, "By trusting their horses to know the way home. Those ponies know the trail better than their riders by now. A man gets lost in a storm, best thing he can do is to just wrap the reins around the saddle horn, hang on, and trust the horse."

Night after night, howling winds rattled the shutters locked across Annie's windows. As the thermometer plummeted, she added successive layers to her bed until she huddled beneath two buffalo pelts, several blankets, and the patchwork comforter she'd brought from home. Some nights, she slept fully clothed. And still, she shivered.

She'd just dozed off one night when she heard someone moving about out in the kitchen. Reaching from beneath the covers, she retrieved her boots and put them on without getting out of bed. Drawing a buffalo hide about her shoulders, she padded into the kitchen. George Morgan was sitting cross-legged on the floor, a wooden crate crowded with live chickens on either side of him. Presently, Billy — who'd been sleeping up in the station loft since the onslaught of winter began — came inside accompanied by Luke Graber, a new Pony rider. Both men had a hen tucked beneath each arm. Shivering, they set the hens in the crate and hunkered down next to the stove.

Graber muttered, "It's so cold the thermometer froze."

"At least forty below," George said. He pointed at the chickens. "Can't do much about the cattle or the horses, but there's no reason to let Christmas dinner freeze to death."

As the night wore on, the men carried feather beds down from the loft to cover the kitchen floor while George nailed blankets over the doors and windows. They scattered loose hay in the storeroom and released the chickens, blocking the doorway with stacked crates to keep them contained. Finally, the birds turned in, cocooned in the kitchen. Annie's last thoughts before drifting off to sleep were of the riders on the trail. *Lord, have mercy on them. Please.*

CHAPTER 24

In spite of the snow, the stage ran with surprising regularity. Passengers were rare, but newspapers and regular mail got through. An island in a world of white, Clearwater was not entirely cut off from the rest of the world. Emmet wrote every week. Lydia stayed in touch, writing frequent notes laced with humor and goodwill. As expected, the election news had precipitated the departure of several men from Fort Kearny — the post commander among them. The resulting shift in housing netted a larger apartment for the Harts, and Lydia was now ensconced in her own room. *They call it a room,* she wrote, *although it's only slightly larger than the chicken coop outside your storeroom door.* One letter included a warmly worded invitation from Lieutenant Hart to attend the Christmas gala at Fort Kearny. *I have missed you. Please do all you can to join the festivities planned for Christmas*

Day. Annie carried the letter in her apron pocket for a couple of days before broaching the topic with George.

He just shook his head. "You'd be taking your life into your own hands." He paused. "Unless — I suppose if there's a break in the weather when the next stage comes through, you and Frank could take it over. But if a blizzard blows in, you could both be at Fort Kearny for a good long while."

"You wouldn't mind, though? If we did that — if we took the stage?" Annie mentioned Frank's seeing the doctor again.

"You work for the Pony Express, not for me. It's not my business to order you about."

Frank said no. They couldn't risk not being able to get back. Annie's twenty dollars a month wasn't much, but they needed it. Annie knew he was right, but she still held out hope that unseasonably warm weather would make it possible for the two of them to ride to the fort and return early in the morning after the Christmas Ball. But the weekend before Christmas, yet another storm blew in. As drifting snow buried Annie's kitchen window beneath a mountain of white, her dream of once again donning the blue ball gown and Lydia's jewels faded.

In spite of her disappointment, Annie did

her part to see that the humans huddled inside Clearwater Station marked the holiday happily. When she set a steaming bowl of chicken and dumplings before him, George smiled. He looked about the table at Luke Graber and Jake Finney, Billy and Frank, and referenced a Charles Dickens story he'd read aloud to everyone over the past few evenings. " 'God bless us every one.' " He took a bite.

"Mrs. Hollenberg uses butter for the dumplings," Annie said. "I didn't have any, because I wanted what little was left for the biscuits and jelly."

George nodded. He took another bite.

"She didn't indicate how much rosemary to use, either. I had to guess."

"Mmm-hhm."

Annie glowered at him. "Could you kindly do more than grunt? Is it good or just passable?"

"When a man can't stop eating long enough to say anything, seems a cook would know the food's good."

Annie folded her arms. "I'd still appreciate actual words, Mr. Morgan. I sacrificed two of my Reds for that food you're gobbling down without so much as a *thank-you*."

Humor twinkled in the man's gray-blue

eyes. "You mean those two roosters you didn't want fighting with Clifford? Seems their demise was already decided the day they hatched." He held up a hand. "But all right, all right. If it's words you want, then it's words you'll have." He paused. "The not-so-subtle reference to the absence of a milk cow is noted. As is the fact that we're about to use the last of the butter." He cupped the bowl of dumplings with both hands as he said, "As to the chicken and dumplings. With or without butter, they're delicious. You used exactly the right amount of rosemary, although I personally lean toward a little more salt. All told, even Sophia would be impressed." He set the bowl back down. "How's that, Miss Paxton? Enough words to earn me the right to eat some more?"

Annie smiled and batted her eyelashes at him. "Quite. Just save room for pie."

Right after Christmas, the stage delivered news that sent a different kind of chill through the inhabitants of Clearwater Road Ranch. South Carolina had seceded from the Union five days before Christmas. By the end of January, Mississippi, Florida. Alabama, Georgia, and Louisiana had followed suit. When George's newspapers reported that secessionist mobs had torn down United States flags in St. Jo., Annie worried for Ira Gould and Luther. Initially glad Emmet was "safe" in Missouri instead of riding into blinding snow and life-threatening cold, Annie now began to worry about him for a different reason. As a slave state, would Missouri secede from the Union? Would Emmet volunteer to fight?

Occasional bouts of dizziness continued to send Frank wobbling back to bed. Sometimes, after he helped with chores, he slept for twelve or sixteen hours. Although she did her best not to let it show, Annie was worried. She was also fairly certain Frank was stealing a drink now and then from George's medicinal stores.

In February, the newspapers reported the burning of stage stations along the southern mail route in Texas "with the stated purpose of interrupting enemy communications." When railroad bridges along the southern route west of St. Louis were also burned, the central line became the main overland mail system. On hearing it, Frank let out a string of profanity.

"The Pony's needed more than ever, and what am I doing about it?" He looked over at Annie and bopped himself on the head. "Waiting for my brains to unscramble." He stormed outside.

On February 18, Jefferson Davis was inaugurated president of the Confederate States of America. Luke Graber brought the news with him from Fort Kearny as part of his Eastbound mail run. The next morning, when she skittered into a cold, dark kitchen to stir up the fire and cook breakfast, Annie found a scrawled note. Six words.

Gone to see doctor. Don't worry.

Wincing from the pain of what felt like the thousandth headache since he'd been thrown by that cursed horse, Frank leaned into the wind. At least the sun was shining today. If it kept up, the temperature might actually get above freezing. Annie meant well, but he was sick and tired of hearing her talk about how he should rest and wait. She was right about one thing, though. He needed to get away from Clearwater. He was tired of hearing about Jake Finney's adventures in the snow. Tired of hearing Luke Graber talk, period. The blond-haired, blue-eyed rider had mentioned Pete just one time too many. Frank had "rested" long enough.

What if being dizzy and having his head feel like it was caught in a vise was the way things were going to be for the rest of his life? The only thing that helped was whiskey, and he was pretty sure Annie knew he'd been hitting George's medicinal stash. He could read the worry in her eyes. And he didn't want to see it anymore. Now he wouldn't — at least for a few days. Once he'd decided to leave for a while, he was packed and ready quicker than Outlaw could throw a greenhorn.

Outlaw. He'd never have a chance to buy him now. The Pony Express might have paid them while the Paiutes were raiding, but they weren't paying Frank now. With Emmet and his money gone back to Missouri, Annie's dream-come-true was looking more and more impossible by the day. And all she could say was *Wait. Be patient. Rest.*

Well, he was done with all that. He was going to see the doc at Fort Kearny and if the doc had nothing to offer . . . well, if he was going to have a headache all the time, it might as well be one he'd earned having a little fun.

The moon was a mere sliver in the night sky and Annie had just stretched out on her bed when someone pounded on the front door. *Frank!* She'd barely slept, hoping he'd return as soon as he saw the doctor. Rising quickly and using the patchwork comforter for a shawl, Annie hurried into the main room just as George stumbled out of the soddy at the opposite end of the station and unbarred the door. A dark-haired, buckskin-clad stranger staggered across the threshold and went down like a felled tree.

By the time Annie got to his side, George had knelt and turned him onto his back.

"Badger, old friend," he muttered. "What's happened to you?" He shouted for Billy.

"I'll get water," Annie said.

"Light some lamps first. And — stay in the kitchen until I call for you. I need to look him over."

Annie shoved four tables together and spread a buffalo hide atop them. "Put him up here," she said. "You'll be able to see better."

"Good. That's good." George spoke to Billy. "Help me move him."

Annie hurried to light the lamps around the room while the two men lifted Badger and placed him on the makeshift examination table. Lastly, she lit the lamp on the store counter and carried it to George.

He thanked her as he took it. "Hot water," he said. "I'll call for you when we're ready."

Annie hurried into the kitchen. While she worked, she tried to pray. For Badger and for Frank. When George didn't call for her right away, she slipped into her room and dressed, leaving her braid to trail down her back as she rushed back into the kitchen. George was standing at her worktable, rummaging through a hide box she'd never seen before.

"I need to make a poultice," he said. "Can you gather up some rags or towels? As long as they're clean, it doesn't really matter."

A few moments later, he was stirring a stinking concoction on one burner while Annie brewed strong tea from a handful of dried herbs that had come from the medicine box.

"Do you know what happened?" she asked.

"He's been shot. The bullet went clean through his shoulder, but it happened a while ago and now it's pouring green pus." He stopped short and looked over at her. "You squeamish?"

Annie shook her head. She looked around the kitchen. "What if we move Emmet's cot in here? Wouldn't it make it easier to tend him?"

"The cot's a good idea, but we'll set it up in my room where I can keep a better eye on him. He's burning with fever. There might be something more going on than just the wound."

It was three days before Badger opened his eyes, and during those three days Annie barely had time to think, let alone worry about Frank. Without consulting George, she killed one of her hens to make broth.

When the aroma finally wafted through the station, George came to the kitchen door. "Is that what I think it is?"

"Chicken broth," Annie said. "Best thing I know to help a body heal."

"You didn't have to —" He broke off. Smiled at her. "Thank you."

Either George or Billy stayed by Badger's side day and night, changing the poultice, pouring tea down his throat, and praying. When delirium transported the Indian to other places to fight battles, George choked out the words, "I've done everything I know. All we can do now is pray."

Knowing her friend was reliving those horrible days fighting small pox drove Annie to the Pony Express Bible, looking for better prayers than the ones she knew. Some of the verses Emmet had written on the inside cover took her to Psalms. Realizing many of them were ancient prayers, Annie ended up reading them aloud, surprised when her mind wandered from Badger to

George, and then on to Emmet and Frank. Surely Bible words would reach God, wouldn't they? *Oh, Lord, please save Badger. And Frank. Where are you, Frank?*

Folks said a lot of bad things about Dobytown, but to Frank's way of thinking, they just didn't have the right attitude about the place. He'd been having a right good time making his way from saloon to saloon the past few days. As a Pony Express rider, he was something of a favorite. After all, he was one of a select few. Or had been. Folks didn't need to know about the knock on the head that might have ended that. They never seemed to tire of hearing how he'd broken Outlaw or how he'd ridden two hundred miles through a pouring rain just to get the mail through.

Only one thing was bothering him at the moment. The pretty little redheaded gal who'd welcomed him when he first arrived had deserted him. Guess she wasn't much of a friend after all. He thought about finding a new gal, but the smoke was thick in the saloon and he was in the midst of a game with a couple of fellows he'd just met. He was feeling a little off. Headache coming again, most likely. Nothing he could do, the doc had said. Frank had to be patient.

It felt good to rest his head on the table until it was his turn again. The table vibrated a little when the piano man hit certain chords. Interesting. Not something he'd care to drink to, but interesting, anyway. He'd be all right. He'd bounce back. Or not. What difference did it make, anyway?

Someone grabbed the back of his shirt and jerked him upright. "Hey!" Frank shouted. "What-d-ya think yer doin'?" He took a swing at whoever it was. Missed.

Rotten Luck not only wreaked havoc in a man's life; he was a killjoy. Tonight — or was it morning, Frank had lost track of time — anyway, right now, Rotten Luck looked suspiciously like golden boy Lieutenant Wade Hart. Who was not supposed to be anywhere near Dobytown and yet here he was, looking down at Frank with a disgusted expression that reminded Frank of Pa. *You'll never amount to anything. Couldn't even ride Hiram Hillsdale's best horse to a win.* Never mind that the horse in question had a bowed tendon and had been drugged to run in spite of the pain. Pa didn't know anything about that, he said. That horse was a ringer to win, Pa insisted. Frank was just making excuses. Well, Frank had learned to ignore Pa, just like he was ignoring Hart right now, pretending he hadn't heard the suggestion that he get up and come outside.

Holding onto the hand he'd been dealt, he tossed his last poker chip into the pile in the center of the table. Hart repeated the "invitation" to follow him outside. Frank squinted up at him. "Does Captain Whoever know his prize officer is off the military reservation?"

Hart rested his gauntleted hand on the butt of his sidearm. "I'm here on army business. Rounding up a few wanderers before they get themselves into worse trouble."

Frank nodded. "Good to know." He held up his drink by way of a toast while waving his cards in Hart's face with the other. "As long as this hand isn't going to be interrupted, you may carry on." Emptying the glass, he set it down with a thump and peered at the cards. *Straight flush. You see this, RL? Old Frank's about to add some money to the family till, after all.*

Hart leaned over. "Come on, now, Paxton. Think of your sister."

Frank narrowed his gaze. Thinking of his sister had gotten him into this mess. If it weren't for Annie, he probably wouldn't have stayed home after Ma died. Not for long, anyway. Might never have heard of the Pony Express or come west or fallen off that blasted horse. *Think of your sister.* Who did

Hart think he was, anyway? Frank spat out the words. "What I'm *thinking* about is none of your gol-durned business."

Hart motioned for the soldier standing by the door. "Get on the other side of him so we can haul him out of here." He reached for the cards.

Frank jerked his arm away.

The barkeep called out, "Now hold on, there," and stepped out from behind the bar. He strode toward Hart, shoving the chairs in his path out of the way as he walked. The piano music stopped. The barkeep turned around and made a circular motion in the air. "No need to stop the party. I'm just gonna have a little talk with the lieutenant." He pointed to a balding string bean of a man who'd been leaning against the bar. "Set 'em up, Jed. One round on the house."

The music started up. The barkeep came to stand behind Frank. "I don't want any trouble, Lieutenant. But the fact of the matter is, you don't have any authority over the civilians in this place. If Frank wants to stay, then you need to round up the boys you came for and leave. Now, if you don't want to do that, you can stir up a hornet's nest and ruin the night for some of my customers. But I guarantee you that after I have a

368

little talk with your captain, you'll wish you hadn't."

"Yeah," Frank said. "You tell him, Harley."

"The name's Marley," the barkeep snapped, "with an *M.*" He spoke to Hart again. "So, what's it going to be, Lieutenant? Are we going to have a problem?"

Frank thought Hart might just break his jaw, he was gritting his teeth so hard. Or have an attack of apoplexy if his face got any redder. Finally, he looked down at Frank. "I'm not letting this go."

Frank burped and managed a sloppy salute. Hart left. And that was that. Except for the relentless pounding of the words *think of your sister.* He hadn't thought about much else ever since he'd cracked his head open. All he wanted to do was keep riding so he could add to the family till. Take care of Annie. Now he couldn't even do that.

Guilt was a hard thing to get away from, but Frank was determined to do his best to outrun it. He was no good to anybody — especially now, when he'd broken the only promise Annie really cared about. He was back at Dobytown.

This time, there was no parson to rescue him. Wherever Charlie Pender was spending the winter, it wasn't in these parts. Lydia Hart had said something about Charlie making another run at Dobytown and then heading west. Good old Charlie. He meant well, but he'd been wrong about something. Frank Paxton wasn't a candidate for "God's amazing grace." *I once was lost . . . and won't be found.*

He took another drink. He'd wagered his horse to stay in the game. Not *his* horse, exactly, but that was okay, because he was about to make up for everything. Annie might not forgive him for coming back to Dobytown, but she'd take the money he was about to win. With a flourish, he spread the straight flush on the table before him. And then, Rotten Luck landed the best knock-out punch of Frank's lifetime. With a last puff on his cigar, the stranger across the table showed his hand. *A royal flush.*

What were the chances of that? For a moment, Frank thought his eyes were fooling him. He looked again. Nope. Clear as a bell. Shoulders back, head up, he looked across the table at the flinty-eyed, red-faced personification of Rotten Luck. If it took his last breath, he would not let anyone see the truth about how he felt just now. He finished his drink and set the glass down with a flourish. Next, he settled his hat back on his head at a jaunty angle.

"It would appear," he said to the gambler

across from him, "that you have just won yourself a horse." Placing both palms on the poker table, he pushed himself upright. "Congratulations."

The stranger took another drag on the monstrous cigar and then blew a stream of smoke across the table in Frank's direction. Frank made a show of brushing first one sleeve and then the other, as if to rid himself of the stench of the smoke. His chin held high, he exited the saloon.

The stranger followed to where the bay Pony Express mare waited, hitched with only a halter and a lead rope. Rotten Luck had already seen to it that Frank had lost the saddle, the bridle, and the saddle blanket. The straight flush was supposed to have redeemed it all. The gambler unhitched the bay mare and his own horse and mounted up. "Nice horse," he said and rode away, laughing.

Frank stood outside for a long moment, watching horse and rider disappear into the night. He shuddered. Bracing himself with one hand, he doubled over and vomited. Backing away from the saloon door, he scooped up a handful of fresh snow and swiped at his face. For a few minutes, he stood in the dim light shining through the saloon window, wondering what to do. The moon had gone behind some clouds. The wind had picked up.

The redhead Frank had spent much of the day drinking with appeared in the doorway to the saloon. "Hey honey," she called. "You're gonna freeze to death out here. Whyn't you come back inside? Marley's closing up. He won't mind if you sleep it off in a corner."

"I'm aw' right," Frank said. He was surprisingly clearheaded. Clearheaded enough to realize he'd had his fill of painted women and poker, at least for a while. He looked about him at the expanse of snow stretching away to the horizon in all directions. How far was it to Fort Kearny, anyway? He could catch the stage — if he had money, which he didn't. Although if Whiskey John happened to be the driver, he could probably hitch a ride without paying the fare. Then again, the last thing he wanted right now was to run into Hart. He looked past Fort Kearny and a little north. That was it. He'd trek over to the Pony Express station just off the military reservation. What was the station keeper's name, anyway? Conroy, he thought. He'd offer to work in exchange for a meal. And think. He needed to think.

Back inside, Frank retrieved his saddlebags from the floor beneath the poker table.

Slinging them over his shoulder, he called to the barkeep. "I appreciate what you did for me when that army boy wanted to haul me outta here."

Marley nodded. When Frank turned to go, he called after him. "You'd best do what Shirley says and sleep here. It hasn't snowed much in the last few days. We're due. Not a good night to be walking anywhere."

"I'm much obliged," Frank said, "but I'm not going far. Just up to the relay station. Can't be more'n a couple miles. I'll be all right."

The barkeep shrugged. "Suit yourself." He grabbed a broom and began to sweep.

"Don't do it," the girl pleaded.

Frank noticed the dark smudges beneath her eyes. Her bad breath. The foul smells in the place. The filth on the floor. His head swam. He was going to be sick if he didn't get out of here. "Like I said, I'm not going far."

The girl skittered through the door behind the bar and returned with a frayed blanket. "At least take this."

Frank recoiled from the stink of cheap perfume, but the girl persisted and so he took it. Muttering an insincere *Thanks,* he stumbled into the night, suddenly eager to leave Dobytown behind. *Take that, Rotten Luck.*

CHAPTER 25

At last, on a gray morning a week after he'd staggered through the front door at Clearwater, Badger was well enough to sit up. For a few days he tottered about the station, his thin frame housed in one of George's shirts and a pair of pants held up with a piece of rope for a belt. Annie realized that small pox had ravaged a face that had once been quite handsome, and she wondered anew at the miracle of Badger's and Billy's survival.

And then he disappeared.

"He'll be back in the spring," George said with a slow smile. "And this time, you'll be ready. Thank you for everything you did for him." He took a deep breath. "And now I'm going to try to do something for you." He reached for the coat and hat hanging on a peg by the door. "Billy will see to the livestock. The stage isn't due for a couple of days, and there shouldn't be any riders coming through, either. I want you to bar the doors and stay put until I get back. It'll probably be sometime tomorrow."

"Where are you going?"

"After Frank."

Finally. Wrapped in the stinking blanket he'd almost rejected, Frank saw it. The faintest glimmer of light. The relay station. It had started to snow a little while ago. No more than an occasional flake. Still, he'd made a giant triangle of the blanket and draped it over his head, grateful for a way to keep the wind off his neck. When a blast of cold air pierced the blanket, he stopped long enough to adjust his bandanna, pulling it up over his mouth — just as he had when he was still a Pony Express rider. It helped some, but he was quickly losing feeling in his feet. That light in the distance was a good thing.

A good thing. The phrase sent a pang of regret through him. Aside from the fact that he wasn't going to freeze to death — assuming a blizzard didn't come up in the next few minutes — there wasn't much good in the world. Except, of course, Annie. She was good. So was Emmet. Goodness had skipped right over Frank. He'd spent a lot of time at Dobytown proving it.

Unbidden, Charlie Pender's voice

sounded in his head. Not a sermon, for Frank hadn't paid all that much attention to those. What Frank "heard" was the song Charlie seemed to think everyone should know. "Amazing Grace." He remembered taking issue with the words and the idea of a holy God letting "just anyone" ask for grace.

Charlie had just laughed. "That's good, son. Frank Paxton telling the Almighty God how to arrange His universe. Just be forewarned that if He listens, He'll want you to rewrite the Bible for Him, too. If it isn't a 'gift of God' there's a passage in Ephesians that will have to go." Charlie had paused. "Romans will be problematic, too. And you'll need to rework a lot of what Jesus taught. He was big on the word *whosoever*."

"That's not what I mean," Frank said. " 'God so loved the world' you said the other day. All right. He loves the world. But shouldn't folks have to make up for all the bad they've done before God hands out ten thousand years in heaven?"

"A fair exchange, you mean?"

"Something like that."

"All right. Let's say that's the way it works. Who decides what's fair? How does a person know when he's made up for what he did?"

377

Frank frowned. "What d'ya mean?"

"Let's say I stole something. I walk into the mercantile and I see something I like and I take it. Is it enough to take it back and say I'm sorry?"

Frank nodded. "That'd probably do it. Maybe offer to pay for it."

"What if I broke it?"

"Then you'd *have* to pay for it."

"All right. Say I killed somebody. How do I pay for that?"

"You can't."

"So I can earn grace — and heaven with it — if I only sin a little, but if I sin big, I'm outta luck. I've sinned bigger than God can forgive. Is that what you're saying?"

Frank huffed frustration. "I'm saying it shouldn't be free."

"Well we agree on that, son, because it wasn't free. It cost more than any of us will ever be able to appreciate. It took the sinless, guiltless Son of God's life — poured out after He was declared guilty in a Roman court, nailed to a cross outside the city, and left to die." Charlie's voice wavered. "That's what it took to make God's amazing grace free to the likes of Charlie Pender and Frank Paxton."

Frank stumbled. It was snowing harder. His fingers were numb. He drew the blanket

378

tighter and walked on. *Amazing grace. How sweet the sound. That saved a wretch like me.* At least he had the *wretch* part right. *I once was lost but now am found.* He was lost, too. In just about every way a man could be. He peered into the night, relieved to see the light still shining in the distance. Not that far away now. *Good thing.*

He stared at the expanse of white separating him from the light and went back to thinking about the song as he walked. *Through many dangers, toils and snares I have already come, 'tis grace that brought me safe thus far, and grace will lead me home.* A blast of frigid air picked up the snow and swirled it around him. Frank stumbled again, but avoided falling and trudged on. It wasn't far now. He imagined the light shining through a window from a room where he could thaw out. It would feel good to be warm again.

When swirling snow erased the light from view, he was tempted to panic. *I once was lost but now am found.* Was it possible for someone like him to find the kind of hope that had sounded in Charlie's voice when he sang those words? Ten thousand years in heaven sounded good, but what about the rest of life here on earth? Would Annie ever forgive him for what he'd done? Would

God? *I'm lost. I need help.*

Pulling the bandanna away from his mouth, Frank yelled into the storm. "Hello! Can anybody hear me? Hello at the station!"

He trudged on. Now that he couldn't see the light, he wasn't certain he was headed the right way. If he didn't get there soon, he was going to find out if Charlie Pender was right about a lot of things. The notion terrified him. He called out again. "Hello! Can anybody hear me? Hello at the station!" *I'm lost. I need help. If Charlie's right . . . if grace is free . . . I need some.*

As if in answer to the unspoken prayer, the storm picked up. Frank grimaced. So this was it. Frank Paxton, the "famous" Pony Express rider, was about to die in the middle of a Nebraska storm. He opened his mouth to holler for help, but the words were knocked back when he slammed into something solid and floundered in a drift deep enough to get him out of the wind. *Hunh.* It felt warmer down here, wherever he was. Hadn't Billy said something about the Indians digging into deep snow to survive a storm? He sure hoped that was right, because he couldn't feel his feet anymore and he had no idea which way to walk. He was exhausted. He'd just close his eyes for a

380

minute. Just a minute. *I'm lost. Help.*

With a start, Frank opened his eyes. It was still snowing, but there must have been a break in the clouds, because moonlight was shining off the snow and . . . the creature that had bounded across his lap had awakened him. Or maybe he hadn't really fallen asleep. Except it had to be a dream. Rabbits did not emerge from snowdrifts and hop across human laps. Unless — Frank blinked a few times and peered at the animal sitting a few feet away, poised to make a quick getaway.

He felt behind him. Dried earth, laid up like bricks. He'd slammed into a sod wall.

Clutching at the blanket, Frank staggered to his feet. The rabbit bounded away, but not before Frank got a good look. He inched along the sod wall until it ended. He peered around the corner. *At a corral.* And the relay station, a short distance away to his right. He gazed up at the sliver of moon shining through a break in the clouds. *Was that You?* He didn't hear a voice, but Frank knew the answer, just as surely as he knew that everything Charlie Pender had ever said about amazing grace was true.

Annie sat bolt upright in bed and peered into the dark, listening as the wind rattled her bedroom window. Unbarring the shutter with a trembling hand, she stared into the night, hoping against hope for moonlight to illuminate the landscape. Sitting back, she closed her eyes. *Please. George is out there looking for Frank. It can't storm. Not tonight.* The wind whistled as if to reply, *It can. It is.*

There was no point in huddling here in bed. She wasn't going to sleep. She dressed in the dark, unbarred her bedroom door, and went into the kitchen, lighting the lamp on her worktable and then moving on into the main room. The quiet in the station had never frightened her . . . until now. A creak overhead made her jump. She set the lamp on a table near the one window looking out on the back lot. Unbarring the back door, she opened it just enough to peer out into the dark. Billy was down there in the soddy, but all Annie could see was swirling snow. It was as if the soddy and the barn, the corrals and the creatures huddled together inside them did not exist.

Closing the door, Annie left the lamp on the table near the window and grabbed another to carry back into the kitchen. She hoped Billy would see it. Hoped he'd bring reassurance that George was not out in the gathering storm. That he had undoubtedly

382

reached Fort Kearny before the storm hit.

She set water on to boil, and wished for dawn so she could tend the chickens. So she could see the horizon and *Please, God,* blue sky. Retrieving her knitting basket from where she'd left it on the store counter the night before, she set it on the worktable in the kitchen while she made coffee. Because of the cold, the bread she'd set to rise before retiring was still little more than a lump of dough. Still, she formed loaves and put it in the oven, moving through her morning routine, all the while listening. Mindful of the wind. Watching for dawn through the north-facing window. Reciting the Isaiah verse about fear, which by now had become almost as dear as the Shepherd's Psalm.

At last, the back door opened and Billy stepped inside. "Coffee's on," she called.

"Smells good," Billy said as he crossed to the kitchen. "You're up early."

"The wind," Annie said and waited for reassurance that did not come.

"Do you want me to help bring the chickens in?"

She glanced toward the window. "You think it's going to be that bad a storm?"

"Impossible to know."

"I'll do it," Annie said. "With George gone, you have so much more to handle."

"Doesn't mean I can't help you."

Annie shook her head. "No, I — I need to keep busy. I was just waiting for dawn." Her voice wavered. "Hoping for blue sky on the horizon."

"That's a good hope," Billy said. "Hold on to it." He headed back outside, but then turned back around. "He'll know what to do."

Annie cleared her throat. "I know. I just — I wish there was a way to notify Lieutenant Hart at Fort Kearny. To send out a search party."

Billy gave a low, barking laugh. "George doesn't need help from any blue coats. He's forgotten more about living out here than they'll ever know."

The stagecoach had just left the Pony Express relay station near Fort Kearny when it lurched dangerously. Frank barely managed to stay in the seat next to Whiskey John. The driver swore cheerfully and hauled on the reins. "Got off the trail a bit there. Happens from time to time." He glanced over at Frank. "Sure you don't want to ride inside?"

Frank shook his head. "Thanks, but I like it up here." He did, too. He marveled at the skill demonstrated as Whiskey John managed six sets of reins as deftly as Frank had ever handled a single horse. Besides that, now that the sun was shining, the view from atop the Concord coach was something he didn't want to miss. He looked back toward the relay station, little more than a dot on the prairie. It was a pure miracle that he'd ever found it in that storm. And the rabbit? He didn't know if he'd ever tell anyone about that. Who'd ever believe it — well, besides Charlie Pender.

When the coach pulled up to the telegraph office at Fort Kearny, Frank stayed put. From his perch, he scanned the grounds, smiling at the memory of dancing with Lydia Hart and wondering how she was faring through her first long, hard winter in the West. When he caught a glimpse of a soldier who might be Wade Hart, he ducked his head and pulled the bandanna up. He'd have to face the lieutenant sooner or later and probably even thank him for trying to drag him out of Dobytown. But he wasn't ready.

When Whiskey John climbed back up beside Frank, he brought all kinds of news. William Russell of the freighting company that had founded the Pony Express had been in all kinds of trouble since the first of the year. Congress had agreed to spend

$800,000 to keep the Pony Express going. They'd also decreed that the Union would not pay any company on a mail contract that would take the route through a state that had seceded from the Union.

Whiskey John looked over at Frank with a smile and a wink. "You know what that means? Means those of us chasing across Nebraska Territory are more important than ever." He shouted at the team before relating how Pony Bob Haslam out in Nevada had been attacked by Indians and wounded while carrying President Lincoln's inaugural address westward. "Still finished the hundred and twenty miles, though," the driver said. "Set a record, too. Eight hours and twenty minutes." And then he added a profanity-laced, albeit kind word to Frank. "Don't you worry, son. You'll be back in the saddle before long."

Frank smiled and nodded. He believed Whiskey John was right. He was feeling better than he had in weeks. But then the driver reported news that struck a somber note and sent Frank's thoughts spinning eastward and off into the unknown.

"You won't believe what them Southern boys gone and done. They're calling themselves the Confederate States of America — acting like they're their own gol-durned country." He leaned over and spat tobacco before adding, "Things is about to get a might more testy. The boys back at Fort Kearny talked like they's expecting to mount up and ride east any day."

Frank's heartbeat ratcheted up when Clearwater came into view. He knew what he was going to say, but he had no idea what would happen after that. And so, as the stagecoach lurched to a stop down at the barn and he climbed down, Frank hesitated. Whiskey John whistled to catch his attention and tossed his saddlebags down to him, just about the time Billy trotted up to switch teams. When he saw Frank, he stopped in his tracks.

"Where's my team?" Whiskey John sputtered. "It's hard enough making up the time lost because of that last storm."

"I'm running a little late," Billy said. "George isn't here."

"Well where in tarnation is he?"

"Looking for Frank," Billy said, and glanced Frank's way as he added, "He rode out a couple of days ago."

Whiskey John swore through a sentence that essentially meant that George should know better than to do something like that.

"It wasn't snowing when he left," Billy

said, and began to work the harness. "The storm came up after." He looked past Frank toward the station. "Your sister's seen you."

Frank turned around, just in time to see Annie step off the back porch and come running. Breathless, she threw herself at him, laughing and hugging him close. "Thank God! You have no idea how I've worried!" She let him go then and looked about. "But — where's George?"

Frank cleared his throat. Shook his head. "I haven't seen him."

"But — he came for you. First to the doctor. And then — Dobytown?" She said it as a question.

"I was there. For nearly a week. I was walking to the relay station north of Fort Kearny when that last storm hit."

Annie's hand went to her heart. "You were *walking*? But — why?"

Frank swallowed. "Because I lost — no, wait. I didn't *lose* the horse. I gambled it away. And the bridle. And the saddle. And the blanket. I gambled it all away, except for my saddlebags." He waited, fully expecting to see the smile fade. Which it did. Fully expecting to see anger or spite or something like that take its place. It did not. What replaced the smile was a trembling hand over her mouth as Annie looked over at Billy.

"But George came to find you," she croaked. "Badger came to us and we took care of him and then as soon as Badger left, George went after you. He was going to trace your steps. He was going to bring you home." Tears spilled down her cheeks.

And in that moment, Frank wished that all he had to face was Annie's anger.

"I put a pot of beans on this morning," Annie said to Whiskey John. "I'll make coffee and there's fresh bread. Be sure you come up and eat before you leave." Frank said that he would stay down at the barn to help with the horses, and so Annie was left alone to retrace her steps back to the station and to set places at the table for the men. But not for George. *Don't think about that right now. Do the next thing. Make coffee.*

She strode past the counter and toward the kitchen. When she caught sight of George's books, she looked away. Taking an apron off a hook in the storeroom, she measured out coffee beans and began to roast them. All the while she worked, she prayed for more movement out on the trail. Listened for muffled hoofbeats. And swallowed back the tears that would do no one any good at all.

There was work to be done. She would do it. She would serve up the beans she'd flavored with roasted buffalo hump and set the last jar of chokecherry jelly out and pour coffee and she would smile if it killed her. And that's what she did, although none of them had anything much to say as they ate.

Frank thanked Whiskey John for the ride and promised to repay the favor, and then the stage rattled on its way. Billy excused himself to feed the livestock, and Frank went to help him. Annie cleared the table and washed the dishes. She went out to scatter feed for the chicks and checked the traps in the storeroom, relieved when there were no dead rats to deal with. She made another pie and had just slid it into the oven when the storeroom door opened. Her heart lurched and she wheeled about.

"It's just me," Frank said. He closed the door behind him and took his mittens off. "I am so sorry, Annie."

"It's not your fault."

"Of course it is. Will you let me tell you what happened?"

"I know what happened." She let the disappointment sound in her voice. "You broke your promise."

"Yes. I did. Again." He took a deep breath.

Let it out. "Can you ever forgive me?"

"I want to. But I don't — I just don't know. I can't think about it right now. Not with George — not until he's back. We can talk then."

"All right. That's fair, I suppose." Frank pulled his mittens back on.

"Should you be doing that?"

"Doing what?"

"Working so hard. Dr. Fields said —"

Frank interrupted her. "I'm better. The headaches are almost gone. I should be able to ride again soon. I'll tell you all about it when the time's right." He paused. "I tried to talk Billy into coming with me to look for George."

"I wanted to ask Lieutenant Hart to send out a search party." Annie shrugged. "Billy said George has forgotten more than the 'blue coats' will ever know about living out here." Her voice trembled. "Do you think that's right?"

"Billy knows him better than either of us."

Annie was quiet. She wanted to be glad that Frank was feeling better. She supposed she did feel glad, but it felt wrong to talk about good things right now. She motioned toward the stove. "I should see to supper."

Frank nodded. "I understand."

Once he'd closed the storeroom door, Annie sat down, abruptly, on the upturned crate. *The Lord is my shepherd; I shall not want. He maketh me to lie down . . .* She closed her eyes. *Nothing's changed. I still want. I hope You're my shepherd, but right now, more than that, I want George to come home. I'm sorry. I don't know how any of this works, but — I just really need You to bring George back.*

Annie was amazed the next day, when God did exactly what she'd asked.

CHAPTER 26

Frank had just forked a mountain of hay out of the loft when Billy charged into the barn and shouted, "George is back!" He raced back outside.

Intending to run tell Annie, Frank hurried down the ladder, but Billy had already gone up to the station with the news, and so Frank waited at the barn, smiling a welcome — until George got closer. The look in the man's eyes made his mouth go dry.

George dismounted slowly. He led his horse into the barn and put it in a stall. Next, he pulled his mittens off and stuffed them inside his hat. With his free hand, he raked through his wild hair. Finally, he said, "I've been following your trail. From here to Fort Kearny. Then to every single saloon in Dobytown."

"I'm sorry," Frank stammered. "I —"

George's hand went up. He said no more for a time.

When the station keeper finally spoke, his voice was so quiet, Frank had to strain to hear the words. Something about that was worse than if George had yelled. "I just don't understand why you'd cause so much grief for one of the best women that ever walked this earth. Why can't you at least try to be the man Annie sees when she looks at you?"

"I *am* going to try."

George looked doubtful. "I've had a good long while to ponder what I'd say next time I saw you, Frank. If there's anything in this world I know, it's that if a man is bent on ruination, there's no human with the power to stop him. You can be the man Annie and Charlie Pender and I know you can be. Or you can ride to perdition. Only you can make that choice. But I can make a choice, too, and I have." He paused. "Here it is. The day you choose to set foot in that hellhole again is the last day you sleep under my roof."

Frank nodded. "I'm grateful. I don't deserve another chance. But I aim to prove it wasn't a mistake for you to give me one." It was hard to tell if the look on Morgan's face was surprise or disbelief. Frank didn't suppose it really mattered. In time, George would see the change and know it was real.

"Mind if I ask you something?" he asked.

"Guess not." Frank steeled himself against the worst.

"The storm. You *walked* into it. How'd you manage to survive?"

Frank shrugged. "I didn't manage anything. I walked into a wall." He told the whole story and did not spare himself at all as he described brushing Wade Hart off and gambling away a horse that wasn't even his. When he came to the sod wall and the rabbit, he almost choked up. "I know it probably sounds crazy, but there's more to what happened that night than a sod wall and a rabbit. I think I've finally begun to understand what Charlie Pender meant when he talked about 'the full and merciful grace of the Almighty God.' "

For a moment, George said nothing. Then he chuckled. "Saved by a bunny. You'll have to tell that one to Lydia Hart so she can write it up for the folks back East." He looked toward the station. "Well, I reckon we've given your sister enough to worry about for a while. I hope she's in a forgiving mood."

For at least the tenth time, Annie looked toward the barn, longing to get a glimpse of George. *He wants to talk to Frank,* Billy had said. *He asked for you to wait for him to come up to the station.* And so Annie waited. While she waited, she cooked. The usual meal didn't seem quite enough tonight — not when George and Frank had both come home safe.

First, she descended to the cellar beneath the store and took down the last ham hanging from the rafters. Back in the kitchen she sliced it all. While the ham fried, she put dried green beans on to simmer, adding bits of ham to the water for flavor. She boiled potatoes and made biscuits. Out in the main room, she drew the tables together, then cut a few sprigs of rosemary and arranged them in her mother's cracked teapot for a centerpiece.

She'd just set the last plate on the table when, at last, George stepped in the back door.

Joy surged through her. She barely managed to keep from running to him. "You're back! I'm so glad —"

For a moment, he just stood there. Looking. From her to the table. From the table to the kitchen. And back again, an odd expression in the gray-blue eyes that Annie could not quite discern. She motioned at the table. "I thought we should celebrate."

"Celebrate . . . what?"

"Frank," Annie said abruptly. "And you. I was worried."

He removed his hat and hung it on the peg by the door. "I don't think you'll need to worry about Frank anymore. There's something — different with him."

She nodded. "I was worried about you, too."

He shrugged out of his heavy coat. "Nothing to worry about. I've weathered worse."

"Billy said as much. I still worried."

He looked past her toward the kitchen. "Is that the last ham I smell cooking?"

Now she felt silly for going to all this trouble. Apparently she was the only one who thought the safe return of two men she cared about merited a celebration. And he didn't seem all that pleased about her frying up the last ham. She called back over her shoulder as she retreated toward the kitchen. "I can serve leftovers for breakfast — ham and fried potatoes. There's probably enough for several days. The ham bone can flavor soup. I'll put a pot on after breakfast tomorrow. The stage passengers will love it."

He followed her to the kitchen, lingering in the doorway as she worked. "It's a little early for us to see much in the way of stage passengers yet." He motioned toward the table where she'd set a pie to cool. "I didn't know we had any kind of fruit left."

"It's a *celebration.* Is there something wrong with that?"

He shrugged. "No. It's just — it's a lot of food, and there's no more coming until the weather breaks. You knew that — right?"

Of all the rude, ungrateful — Annie had gone from confusion to hurt. Why would he object to anything she'd done? Didn't he appreciate being appreciated? "Have I misremembered your telling me to make this kitchen my own?"

"No. Why?"

She motioned about her. "*This* is what my kitchen looks like right before I feed a bunch of hungry men — men I care about. Men I've spent sleepless nights worrying about."

"You didn't need to be worrying about me," he repeated. "Like Billy said, I've forgotten more about living out here than your Lieutenant Hart will ever know."

"My Lieutenant Hart?" Where did that come from?

"I'll get a fire going. That's some story Frank told. About the rabbit." He didn't wait for Annie to respond, just pointed at the pie and the pots on the stove and said something about Annie being able to man-

age "well enough" until Luther brought supplies.

He was doing that thing where he jumped
from one subject to the next, never landing
on one thing long enough for them to have
a conversation and inevitably saying something that came out like thinly veiled criti-
cism. On a whim, Annie dished up a piece
of pie and shoved it at him. "Here. I didn't
have Sophia's recipe, so you probably won't
approve of this, either, but maybe it'll
improve your mood. Or your manners. And
you might as well know there's a raisin
molasses pie in the oven. That's Frank's
favorite. And if you think that's a waste of
your precious groceries, I don't want to hear
about it." She waved him toward the main
room. "Go. Build a fire. Light the lamps.
Polish something. Just — stop grumbling."

Pie plate in hand, Morgan retreated. He
built the fire and, when it was roaring, asked
her to come out to the store counter. He
pointed at the sign advertising meals for fifty
cents. "Think you'd be able to make a pie
or two every day once Luther brings more
supplies?"

"I thought you just said you don't want
me cooking so much."

George frowned. "No, I said I hope we
don't run out before — never mind. About

the pie. What d'ya think? Could we offer pie as part of the meals? Folks would like it. We'd get more business."

Business. He wanted to talk business. There was no *we* in George Morgan's business. He'd made that clear just now, complaining about her using up a ham. How glad she was that she'd resisted the urge to throw her arms about his neck when he first stepped in the door. "If *you* think it's a good idea, I'm happy to give it a try." She paused. "And if you're really looking to make improvements around here, get a cow." *And stop complaining about my cooking.*

Later that evening, as Annie went about cleaning up the meal — which everyone had enjoyed, after all — she realized that George had hung the sign advertising meals back up. He'd increased the price from fifty to seventy-five cents. She'd just wiped the last dish and set it back on the shelf when George appeared in the doorway.

"Saw you looking at the sign. Figured if you'd agreed to baking pie every day, we could charge more. What d'ya think?"

Not yet quite recovered from the jumbled feelings that had accompanied his safe return, Annie merely shrugged. "You're the boss."

He grunted softly and shook his head.

"No, Ma'am. Truth be told, when it comes to the kitchen and such, I don't believe I am." He smiled. "But I don't believe I mind."

Soon after George's return, Frank took off on his first mail run since his injury. Annie's heart swelled with joy as she watched him speed past the first wagon train of the season. Looking up at the brilliant blue sky and the countless geese honking on their way northward, Annie whispered *Thank you.*

On the next Sunday, Lydia and Wade paid a surprise visit to Clearwater to extend an invitation to a spring cotillion planned for the middle of May. When George said the busy season was just beginning and he doubted he'd be able to take the time away, Lydia shushed him. "I refuse to take *no* for an answer. In fact, I've already put your name at the top of my dance card." She glanced over at Annie. "Assuming, of course, your handsome brother is off on his Pony Express adventure at the time. If not, Mr. Morgan will have to be second."

One day early in April, Annie had left the storeroom door open to take advantage of the spring breeze while she cleaned shelves when she heard a clunk just outside the door. She peered out just as George jammed a posthole digger into the earth. A brown-and-white-spotted cow was picketed nearby, snuffling at the greening prairie.

Annie screeched with delight. "I could hug your neck."

George barely glanced up from his work. "You might not feel that way this time tomorrow. She kicks. Supposed to be able to handle hard winters, though. And the owner promised nearly a gallon of milk a day. Ayrshire. You ever heard of the breed?"

Annie shook her head. "No, but she's beautiful. I'll need a churn."

"Look to the left. And I milked her before I picketed her over there."

A butter churn sat on the earth next to the rosemary Annie had just set out the previous day. Annie lifted the lid to the churn. *Glory be.* At least a gallon. Maybe two. "Did you already drink some, or can I bring you a glass?"

"I don't really care much for milk."

And she'd once argued the case for a cow with the idea of cold buttermilk on a hot summer day. "At least you know you can look forward to all the butter you want on your grits and cornbread. Mind telling me what you had to trade for her?"

He jammed the digger into the earth and brought up another pile of dirt. "Didn't trade. Paid cash money." He peered into the hole. Repeated the process. Paused. "You want me to move that churn into the kitchen?" When Annie said that'd be nice, he swiped his hands on his pants, hoisted the churn, and took it inside, setting it in the corner by the worktable.

"Custard for lunch and sweet rolls for supper," Annie said. "Peaches and cream and so much more. All because of that beautiful cow. You won't regret buying her. And I'll cure her of kicking."

"Any chance of testing out the peaches and cream later today?" He grimaced. "Never mind. I forgot you used the last of the peaches for that pie a couple of weeks ago. But I don't mind. I'm content to wait. It's your kitchen, and I'm the one who put you in charge of it. I haven't forgotten."

Annie laughed as he bowed and backed his way toward the door. "You're putting her close to the station, then?"

"Thought I would. Unless you don't think it's a good idea."

"No, it's fine."

"But?" He held a hand out, encouraging her to keep talking.

"Trees," Annie said.

"Trees?"

"You know. Tall plants with green things

on them. We call them leaves. They create this wonderful thing called shade." She paused. "Shade would be nice. For the cow. And the chicken coop. I was thinking maybe I could transplant one or two from the river? Lydia said that's where the trees around the Fort Kearny parade ground came from. I could keep it watered. The well's right there."

"Sunday," George said. "We'll take a ride and see what we can find."

"You don't mind?"

He shook his head. "Might be I could ask the cook to rustle up a picnic lunch. If I catch her in a good mood."

Being back on the trail again was more than Frank had dared to hope for. Still, after being in the saddle for over twelve hours, his legs screamed for relief. In fact, just about every part of his body complained at one level or another. It was all normal fatigue, and in that way he could be grateful and even think of the pain as a "good thing," but as he pulled up at Midway Station and dropped to the earth, all he wanted was to stretch out and sleep. In fact, he kind of hoped that Pete was off somewhere tending to whatever a rancher did in the spring, because he was just too tired to try to make a good impression — and too tired to explain whatever she might have heard about him from other riders. The telegraph might not have gotten past Fort Kearny yet, but news and gossip still traveled westward along the trail.

Relief surged through him as Pete's pa trotted up with a fresh horse. It died when the old guy delivered the worst news possible. There was no rider to take Frank's place. "I don't know what to tell ya. He disappeared without a trace. The missus went to tell him chow was ready last night, and he was just gone." He shrugged. "Hightailed it for home, I reckon. He was of the Southern persuasion, if you get my drift."

If God and George Morgan and everybody else in his life was giving him a second chance, Frank wasn't about to fail at the Pony Express. Not if he could help it. His arms trembled as he lifted the mochila onto the fresh horse. There would be no gallant springing into the saddle today. If he tried that, he'd land on his backside in the dirt. He was looking around for something to use for a mounting block when the Pete's ma hurried out the door of the station with a bag in hand.

She gave Frank an odd look and exclaimed, "Why, you're the young man Pete mentioned. We thought maybe you'd quit the Pony Express."

"No, Ma'am." Frank took his hat off and swept his hand back to show her his scar.

"Oh, you poor thing." Her voice was kind and her smile genuine as she handed him the sack of food. "There's some chunks of ham and a couple boiled eggs in there. Two slices of white bread — lots of butter holding them together." She held out a quart jar filled with water. "You drink as much as you can, son. And try to get more water at every stop. That'll help more than anything."

Frank gulped the water, swiped his mouth, and scrabbled back into the saddle. The few people on the trail still waved as he streaked past wagon camps in the morning light, but he didn't have the energy to respond. It was taking everything in him just to hold on, on to Gilman's Station and then up the Platte Valley and across the prairie where trees grew along the river and bluffs rose in the distance.

For all his misery, he could think of plenty of good things as he pounded west — not the least of which was the story he'd have to tell when he finally got back to Clearwater. And to Lydia Hart, if she was interested. He might not be setting any records like Pony Bob Haslam, and he sure didn't care to get attacked and wounded by Indians, but riding nearly two hundred miles was nothing to shake a stick at. Especially after being thrown and knocked out and stitched up and nearly frozen to death.

As daylight spread across the landscape, Frank clung to the saddle, determined not to give up. Determined never to be like Pa — or the old Frank Paxton who'd let Rotten Luck win too many battles. At midday, he rode out of Cottonwood Springs, around lagoons sprouting water rushes, and on to the next relay station, where towering clay buttes to the south glowed red in the sunlight.

By the time Buffalo Ranch came into view in the afternoon, Frank was slumped over the saddle horn, clutching handfuls of black mane just to stay in the saddle. He nearly fell to the earth when the horse stopped. Didn't even remember pulling up. Didn't remember much of anything until, after stumbling into a bunkhouse and falling onto a narrow cot, he woke up hours later to the sound of a rooster crowing. He'd made it.

Amazing grace. How sweet the sound.

CHAPTER 27

It was mid-April, and to Annie's way of thinking Luther Mufsy was long overdue when at last she heard a wagon approaching from the north. She hurried out front. The eastern sky was a fabulous shade of orange, and for a while the approaching wagon and the team pulling it were little more than a black silhouette. It wasn't Luther, but the closer the wagon got, the more it piqued Annie's curiosity.

The team were smaller than any draft horses she'd ever seen. Their full, pale manes shone against deep golden coats. Red tassels dangled from their bridles. The brightly painted wagon was about the same size as Luther's, but this one was enclosed. The driver wore a stovepipe hat and a black, dusty coat with long tails — the latter evident only after he'd pulled his team up and jumped down.

"Good morning, My Lady," he said, as he

swept his hat off his head and bowed low.

He held the hat over his heart as he introduced himself — with a poem.

Finnegan O'Day, here to supply all your
   needs,
Be it buttons or bows, hankies or clothes.
If it's needles you need, take your pick, if
   you please.
And thimbles? Why sure, I've the best one
   can procure.
Now, a lady such as thee — let think, let
   me see . . .

He undid a latch on the side of the wagon but held the door shut until he finished his poem.

"You've a wish? Take a look!" He opened the door. "O'Day sells the best in books."

At least a dozen books were lined up on a shelf. George would be thrilled.

The peddler hurried to open the other doors, revealing an impressive array of goods stashed into every nook and cranny. "Now, Madam, if I may introduce my two ladies." O'Day walked to the head of the team. "This one" — he patted the flank of the near horse — "is my Dinah." He leaned over and spoke to the horse. "Dinah, say hello to the lady." The horse bowed. He pointed to the off horse. "And the naughty one over there, that's Delilah." He raised his voice just a little and called out, "Be a love, now, won't you, Delilah, and say hello to the lady?" Delilah lifted her upper lip in a more-than-acceptable imitation of a smile.

Annie burst out laughing. "Pleased to meet you, ladies. Welcome to Clearwater. And how may we serve you, Mr. O'Day?"

"Well, Ma'am, I find myself in a bit of a pickle. Short on cash. Hearing more than one traveler on the trail mention the bustling little settlement called Clearwater, I've come to hope that someone at this fine establishment would have need of a bit of tailoring. A new suit of clothes, perhaps? I've all manner of cloth stored on the off side of the wagon. And a machine. I could set up camp right here, if you please. Perhaps do a bit of business with passersby, pedaling away with my ladies picketed just past the flagpole, perhaps? And I'd be most obliged to take payment for my work in grain for the girls and a wee bit o' breakfast for myself."

He waited for a reply, mopping his brow with a red kerchief he pulled out of his rear pants pocket. When Annie didn't answer right away, he tucked the kerchief away. "Or perhaps the lady has a hankering for a new dress?" He rushed around the wagon and out of sight and returned with a bolt of blue calico. "Nothing better than the newest Prussian blues to set those blue eyes to sparkling. I bet the mister would like to see it, eh?"

"It's 'Miss,' " Annie said, "and I've got to get to the making of breakfast. You're most welcome to join us. You can speak with Mr. Morgan about your wares. It'd be up to him to buy or trade. If you'd care to drive around back, you're welcome to water your team. There's a pump up by the station and another down at the barn."

The little man bowed. "Thank you, My Lady. Water for my girls, then." Quickly, he returned the bolt of blue cloth to its place, latched the doors, and climbed back up to the wagon seat. He whistled as he turned the team and drove them around back.

Annie poured hot water over the lunch plates she'd just settled in the wash tub on the table outside the storeroom door and left them to soak. The crew had gathered around O'Day's wagon down by the barn. George had said that he was sure they could make a trade for at least one meal and grain for "the girls," and Annie supposed that was what was going on now.

Hoping she wouldn't be interrupted, she slipped into her room and closed and barred the door. Quickly, she unbuttoned her shirtwaist and slipped the ribbon that held her keys up and over her head. She unlocked the trunk. Taking the black cash box in both hands, she retreated to her bed and sat down with it on her lap. The money inside was precious little compared to what they'd all hoped for when first they came west. And yet, of the $1,640 in the cash box, $240 was Annie's, represented by twelve gold coins. She picked up one, caressing the surface and studying the impression of the eagle. It was a beautiful thing. She'd likely never in her life own as many again. Surely it would be all right to spend part of one. A dress would require at least ten yards of the Prussian blue. It might be as much as twenty cents a yard. She'd need buttons, too. And thread.

As the list grew, so did her nervousness about the transaction. She put the gold coin back in the box. No. She did not need a new dress. The two she had might be a little worn, perhaps more than a little faded, but they were perfectly adequate. She looked down at the money. Oh, but it would be wonderful to wear something new to the spring cotillion at Fort Kearny. Something that was just hers. She wondered if O'Day had dancing shoes tucked away somewhere in that incredible wagon.

It wouldn't hurt to take a look. Slipping a single gold coin into her pocket, Annie locked the cash box and returned it to its place in her trunk. She pulled the ribbon back over her head, buttoned up, and unbarred the door. *Prussian* blue. It sounded so exotic.

Annie waited until the sun was setting before she walked down to where the beautifully painted wagon stood by the barn. She hoped that the newly arrived summer crew would be otherwise occupied at that time of day, thereby giving her a chance to indulge herself in a bit of feminine fantasizing without an audience. No one would likely understand what a momentous occasion this was for a woman who'd never had her own money, never purchased anything for herself.

Frank and Emmet had always seen that Annie had what she needed, right down to the new boots they'd given her in St. Jo. After Mama died, things just magically appeared in her room. A skirt and petticoat just when she'd outgrown the old ones. Winter drawers right when it was time for the first cold snap. On the rare occasions when she accompanied her brothers into town and to a general store, she knew better than to ask for things. A piece of candy was a pure miracle. The few times she'd received one, she'd kept it for days before finally indulging. Even then, she'd put a peppermint in her mouth just long enough to get the taste and then quickly take it out, wrap it, and hide it under her pillow.

Even when Annie accompanied her brothers to town, she never saw money exchange hands. There was an account at the store and Mr. Burton wrote down what they bought. It was a long time before she realized that someone at some point had to actually pay for the things listed in that book. Finally, the Paxtons had owed so much they'd had to give up the farm. Owing money was a terrible thing.

As she walked down to the barn, Annie kept her hand in her pocket, feeling the gold coin. Delilah and Dinah stood, nose to tail, in a nearby corral. For a moment, Annie thought Mr. O'Day must be over at the soddy playing checkers with Hitch. But O'Day was sitting just inside the barn, taking advantage of the shade, no doubt.

He closed up the little knife he'd been whittling with, rose, and tucked it in his pocket. "And here's the pretty colleen I was hoping to see before nightfall. What'll it be, now? The books or the pins and needles?" He flipped a couple of latches and lowered a door that ran the entire length of the lower half of the wagon, forming a display shelf. "Here, now," O'Day said and pulled out a shallow box crammed full of twists of yarn in a rainbow of colors. Annie touched the red. Frank would like a red scarf. There was nothing wrong with planning for the fall. "How much is this one?"

"That's a lovely color. It'll cost you . . . oh . . . let's see . . . an extra piece of pie?" O'Day smiled. "Now, Miss, I can tell you think I'm not serious. But I am, and that's a true fact. I'd rather have food than cash. And you know why? Because a highwayman can steal a money box, but there's no taking the pie that's in my belly or the memory of its sweetness."

The dark green of one of the books drew Annie's eye. It was a beautiful thing, but she didn't touch it before asking, "And the books?"

"A wee bag of sugar so I can treat my girls." The peddler leaned close. "Delilah's especially partial to peppermint candy. You don't happen to have any of that?"

"Mr. Morgan keeps candy in the store,

but I've no right to barter the store goods away." She hastened to explain that he'd given her full rein over the kitchen, so she could be a bit freer when it came to the food she cooked and the things in her own larder.

"Well, then." O'Day made a great show of considering this new information. "I'm to linger a day or two — I've some things to make up for the blacksmith in exchange for fresh shoes for the girls — and let us say two meals for your choice of the books." When Annie reached for the dark green one, O'Day nodded approval. "You can't go wrong with Dickens, Miss."

Annie looked at the spine, thrilled when she read the title. *A Tale of Two Cities.* "Is it all here? I mean — Mr. Morgan said it wasn't being published all in one."

"And so it was at first Miss. But what you have there is the first edition of the entire book, newly printed in these United States."

Annie set the book down. She quickly selected a few more twists of yarn, and gathered up her purchases with joy, pleased with the notion that she hadn't had to produce the gold piece, after all. She hesitated. Looking didn't cost a thing, and Mr. O'Day wouldn't mind. But when she asked about the blue cloth, O'Day sighed.

"Oh, my dear, I am so very sorry. Your

employer took the entire bolt up to the station."

Of course. Ladies traveling west would delight in that gorgeous color. It would sell at a nice profit. George was nothing if not a wise trader. Annie made her way back to the station, well supplied, excited to show George the book. *It was the best of times.* She returned her gold coin to the cash box before going to look for George and was horrified to find him out back, milking the cow she'd promised he'd never have to tend.

"I'm so sorry. I — I was down at the peddler's cart."

"I saw." He didn't look up. "What did you buy?"

"We bartered. Traded. A piece of pie for this, a lunch for that."

"Smart." He glanced up. "And what thises and thats caught your eye?"

"Nothing very exciting," she said, and then smiled. "Except for one thing. Wait right there. I'll show you." She hurried inside and returned with the book. "Take it," she said. "And let me take over with the milking."

George reached for the book without getting up, laughing when he read the title. "You beat me to it. I was going to get it in the morning."

"Let me finish the milking," Annie insisted. "I really am sorry."

He patted the cow. "No need to apologize. Neither Elizabeth nor I begrudges you a little enjoyment."

"Elizabeth?"

"We decided it was high time she had a name. I told her I considered *Elizabeth* a bit high and mighty, but she would hear of nothing else." He sat back. "There. Finished." The cow lifted one hind leg. George patted that flank. "Now, now, Elizabeth. You promised that if I gave you a dignified name, you'd behave in kind. Remember?" Amazingly, the cow lowered the hoof. George pointed to the pail of milk. "Churn?"

Annie shook her head. "Mr. O'Day said he's fond of fresh milk. He'll be up for it in a little while." She smiled. "And that last piece of pie."

George slapped his palm to his heart. "I had my name on that." With a deep sigh, he set the pail inside the storeroom door.

Annie covered it with an empty flour sack. "You made a good choice, by the way, buying the blue calico for the store. The ladies will love it."

"You think so?"

"I know so. I nearly bought it myself when

Mr. O'Day showed it to me on his arrival. But I resisted."

"You'll be happy to hear you no longer need to resist. It's not for the store. It's for you."

Speechless for a moment, Annie finally managed to stammer her thanks.

"You're welcome. I'm very grateful you didn't run off into the night after the horrendous scene that greeted you when you first rode in. Grateful you've stayed. Grateful for . . . everything." He paused. Shrugged. "I have great difficulty these days imagining Clearwater without you, Annie." He brushed her cheek with the back of his hand. Gently. And then he took a step back and muttered something about needing to do something and hurried off, leaving Annie just standing there feeling . . . happy.

After only a few days at Clearwater, Finnegan O'Day was lured away by Wade Hart's promise — after seeing O'Day's fine blue wool — that he could make a good profit tailoring uniforms for the officers at Fort Kearny. That he would, in fact, sell every yard of the blue wool he had on hand.

O'Day had proven to be a master storyteller, and Annie watched him go with a sense of loss mitigated only by Frank's return and his own story of riding past Midway Station because a rider had deserted. He arrived back at Clearwater in the middle of a soaking spring rain, happy and talking about how the Almighty had pulled him through. He then launched into a lyrical few minutes of Pete this and Pete that, eating his way through a dozen scrambled eggs and nearly half a loaf of bread as he talked. When Annie poured the second glass of milk, he stopped abruptly.

"You have milk."

Annie laughed. "Good of you to notice. Elizabeth arrived while you were gone. That's the cow George bought."

"He bought you a cow?"

"He bought *Clearwater* a cow. I should probably warn you that he's talked about asking you to help build another shelter. And string wire to keep her safe this winter. She seems content to be picketed on the prairie to the west for the present."

The rain had stopped by the time Frank woke later that day. When Annie led him outside to "meet Elizabeth," he stopped just outside the storeroom door to remark about the trees.

"Lydia told me some earlier commanding officer had the trees around the parade ground at the fort transplanted from the banks of the river. I made a good case for following suit to shade the chicken coop and the cow shed. George said fine. We took a Sunday afternoon ride. They're cottonwoods. George said they grow fast. Maybe as tall as a hundred feet in time."

Frank pointed to the strip of freshly plowed earth west of the station. "And that?"

"The peddler had garden seeds. We'll sell what I can't get canned or dried. Same as with the milk and butter — which, by the way, has already begun to make George a tidy sum." She smiled. "He's almost enthusiastic about the garden — even if he did grumble about plowing." Frank was quiet for so long that Annie wondered what might be wrong. "What are you thinking?"

"Nothing." Frank nodded toward the barn. "I'll just see if Billy needs help with anything."

Annie put her hand on his arm. "It's not nothing. What is it?"

"I'm just surprised, that's all."

"By?"

"A cow. A garden. You're planting trees. If I didn't know better, I'd think you were settling in."

"Don't be silly," Annie said quickly. "I'm just doing my part." Whatever she had planned to say beyond that was interrupted when a lone rider galloped past, yelling at the top of his lungs about news telegraphed to Fort Kearny. In faraway South Carolina, a Union garrison had been driven out of a place called Fort Sumter.

Frank paled.

"What's it mean?" Annie asked.

"Apart from a miracle of God, it means the United States and the Confederate States are going to war. May the Lord have mercy on us all."

CHAPTER 28

Luther Mufsy's supply train arrived within days of the attack on Fort Sumter. Along with tons of supplies to stock the shelves of the Clearwater store and Annie's storeroom, he brought news of President Lincoln's declaring a "state of insurrection."

"He's called for seventy-five thousand troops to serve in a ninety-day militia," Luther said. "You remember Johnny Fry — the first rider out of St. Jo. last year? He's talking about quitting the Pony and joining up as a courier. And he's not the only one. I counted at least three riders missing from the stations between here and St. Jo. on my way out. Just up and left to sign on with the militia." He paused. "Speaking of . . . shouldn't there be a couple riders right here at Clearwater?"

"Frank's probably resting up at Midway, ready to come back this way," Annie said. "Luke Graber's due in any minute now, and we can always count on Jake Finney."

"I hope you're right," Luther said, shaking his head. "There's a real fever among those youngsters to put on a uniform and 'teach Johnny Reb a lesson.' I'm glad you weren't in St. Jo. to see the things I've seen. There's such an uproar, they've had to close the schools."

Annie asked about Ira Gould. Luther reassured her. "Business is booming for anyone handling horses and wagons. It's manpower that's going to be in short supply now."

Annie could not imagine the trouble back East having much effect on the men of the Pony Express. They were a hardy, daring lot who reveled in their unique place in history. They wouldn't just abandon their posts. At least the ones Annie knew wouldn't. She had faith in them.

Until, that is, Luke Graber disappeared.

"It'll be all right," George said. "We'll send word about Graber and there'll be a replacement before you know it. Frank rode an extra route not long ago. Jake can do the same. Just put some food in a sack so he can eat while he rides. He'll be fine. In fact, when all is said and done, he'll probably love having a story as good as Frank's. Who knows, maybe Lydia Hart will feature them

424

both in that column of hers."

George had gone down to the barn to keep watch over a mare expected to foal at any moment. Though it was April, the weather had turned cold again. Annie made sure there was plenty of wood by the fire for when George finally came in. She was just turning in when she heard Jake ride in. She stepped out on the back porch to ring the bell, but Billy had heard the approach and was already bringing the horse up. Annie smiled, thinking of Jake's future boasting about the endurance run he was about to take. *A hundred miles at full speed? Bah. That's nothing. I did over two hundred once. Let me tell you about it . . .*

As the horse approached, Annie's heart sank. Poor Jake was already so tired he'd fallen asleep in the saddle. But Jake wasn't asleep. When the horse came to a stop, he groaned.

"Thank God. Never thought I'd make it." He slipped to the earth. "Sick." He shuddered. "So . . . sick." He staggered toward the station, but he didn't make it to the door before leaning over and retching, then collapsing on the porch, his head in his hands.

"But — you have to keep going, Jake," Annie said. "Graber's disappeared. Frank isn't back yet. There's no one else." Jake groaned and shook his head. Annie put her hand to his forehead. He was burning with fever.

The nation was at war. The Union depended on the Pony Express, now more than ever. Annie spoke to Billy. "I'm going to help Jake inside. Can you switch the mochila?"

Billy protested. "I can't go on any Pony Express run. I can't ride worth anything."

"You aren't doing it. I am."

Billy took a step back. "You can't."

"There's no one else. Think of all the men who've risked their lives. Who've died to see it through. Who knows what's in those locked mail pouches? There could be another letter from the president."

Billy shook his head. "George will kill me. And then Frank will kill me again when he finds out."

"I ride better than Emmet. Frank's said that himself."

"You think that's going to matter to George?"

"He'll be angry, but he'll realize I can do it. Especially if you tell him what I just said about Emmet. When Frank gets here, he'll tell you the same thing." She helped Jake to his feet. "Let's get you to bed."

Jake fell into bed and promptly leaned over and vomited into the chamber pot. Annie rummaged about for one of Frank's shirts. A pair of jeans. Gloves. Back in her room, she changed with lightning speed, pulling on wool socks and flannel drawers before stepping into Frank's clothes. Thinking of all the stories she'd heard about late spring blizzards in the West, she grabbed a scarf. At the last minute, she went back into Frank's room for the horn he'd been issued. He'd stopped carrying it in favor of the gun, but she wasn't much good with a gun, anyway. Lord willing, she wouldn't need it.

Billy protested again the moment she set foot outside. "I can't let you do this."

She slung the loop attached to the horn over the saddle horn and pulled her mittens on. Next, she tied the scarf about her neck. "You aren't 'letting me' do anything. It's my decision. If it makes you feel any better, I'll tell George you tried to lock me in the station, but I escaped. Just — give me a boost."

The second she was in the saddle, she kicked the chestnut mare into a lope. The trail stretched out before her, and as Clearwater receded in the distance, fear set in. The moon hung low in the sky. She was alone in the world. The next few hours would be nothing like the ride west last spring. There would be few campfires glowing on the trail — no children watching her ride by, no women waving hello. The only sound was the muffled beat of the mare's hooves. If she fell . . . if anything happened . . .

Just keep the river on your right. That's all you have to know. Tucking her chin into her scarf, Annie peered into the night. *The Lord is my shepherd. The Lord is mine. He leadeth me in the path . . . for His name's sake. I will fear no evil, for Thou art with me. Oh, Lord. Be my shepherd.*

At Fort Kearny, Annie glanced across the parade ground toward the Hart's quarters and thought of Lydia and Wade, sleeping soundly. Safe. Warm. She slowed when a sentry called out, relieved when he waved her on. A light glowed in the window over at the hospital, and she wondered about who Dr. Fields was tending tonight. The thought of military hospitals brought the reminder of war. She pushed it away. *Keep your wits about you.*

At the fort telegraph office, a sleepy soldier stumbled out to stuff a few bits of paper in the one unlocked mail pocket. Annie didn't even have to dismount. At the relay station near the fort, her numb fingers fumbled when she tried to pull the horn off the saddle to switch the mochila.

"You new?" the station keeper groused. "Nobody's carrying those horns anymore. We can hear you coming a mile away, ya know."

Annie nodded. "Yeah. New." She patted her horse's neck, muttered "Good girl," and climbed aboard the next horse with renewed energy and determination. *I can do this. I can.* It was a beautiful, clear night. By the light of the nearly full moon, the landscape didn't seem quite so threatening. If she was careful, it would be all right.

The wind had picked up. Clouds were building in the sky. What was it George had said about being caught in a storm? A rider could generally trust their horse to take them home. Maybe that would apply to-night, too, alone in the dark, with just her and the horse chasing across the snow-dusted prairie. *Fear not. Do not anxiously look about you. Trust the horse. Trust in the Lord. He leadeth me beside the still waters.*

After she'd switched at Platte Station, the station keeper handed up a sack of food. "Give me the horn," he said. "You don't need it. Just take the food."

"I'll take both," Annie said, as gruffly as she could. She couldn't get at the food without taking off her gloves. It took every bit of concentration to manage that and to keep moving. She almost lost a glove. But she didn't. Her fingers nearly froze before she'd gotten so much as a few bites of bread and cheese down. The food helped settle her stomach. But it tightened up again as she approached each relay station. *What if they figure it out? What will they do?*

By dawn, she was approaching Craig's. Thankfully, the horses she'd drawn tonight weren't the ornery beasts she'd heard riders talk about — although Emmet hadn't really complained about his mounts. She'd just assumed that was because Emmet didn't complain about things. Maybe it was because Jake and the others exaggerated. Either way, if things kept going this well, she'd be all right.

The Craig's station master barely looked at her as she switched the mochila over and mounted up. At first she thought she'd drawn Outlaw, but this was just another black horse. She wondered where Outlaw was now. Wondered if he'd returned to his ornery ways without Frank to keep him in hand.

Annie was many miles beyond Craig's when she first heard the eerie howls of a pack of wolves. They were far enough away that she didn't think it would be a problem, but soon she realized she'd been wrong.

They kept coming closer. The horse got nervous. Annie spurred it on. Moonlight revealed a flash of gray just off to the right. In desperation, she grabbed the horn and blew it for all she was worth. It seemed to work. But only for a moment.

Again, they came at her. Bolder, this time. Running with her, just at the edge of the trail. A pack of six. At least that's how many she could see. What if there were more? What if the horse reared? What if — *The Lord is my Shepherd. Lord, have mercy. What time I am afraid I will trust in Thee.* Again, she blasted away on the horn. The wolves veered off the trail. Annie imagined them looking at each other, wondering at the noise. She hoped they were terrified. That they could not smell her fear. That the strange sound would be enough to keep them away.

But the beasts continued to give chase. And so it went, with the wolves gaining and Annie blowing the horn. Through an eternity of moments stretching all the way to Plum Creek. When the station came in sight, Annie nearly cried with joy. She hurt all over. Whether it was from the cold or fear or a combination of both, she didn't know.

"W-wolves," she stuttered, when the station master asked why she'd blown the horn so many times.

He looked past her into the night. "Why didn't you shoot at 'em?"

"No gun."

"You darned fool desperadoes. What d'ya mean no gun?" He didn't wait for her to answer. "Yeah, yeah, I know. 'The more I carry the slower I go. It's easier on the horse.' " He snorted angrily. "How easy will it be to get brought down by a pack of wolves, huh? And they could do it, too. Don't you think they can't. You wait here." He trotted away with the spent horse, muttering all the way. When he returned, he was armed with a shotgun. "Ride on," he said. "I'll get rid of the beasts once and for all. They won't bother you again tonight. But you listen to reason, young man. You carry that pistol and if the Pony Express don't like it you tell 'em where they can put their mo-chee-lah."

Annie heard the report of the shotgun after she'd ridden a short distance away. *Let it work. Keep them away. Lord, have mercy.* She couldn't stop trembling. Her feet were numb with the cold. She'd stopped being able to feel her toes a long time ago. She might have bragged to Billy about being "better than Emmet," but adapting to a new

432

horse every couple of hours meant adjusting to a new pace while at the same time figuring out which gait would help both the animal and her go the distance as quickly as possible but with the least risk. Most horses would give a rider what they asked — even if it literally meant a killing pace. Last November's election announcement had traveled from St. Joseph to California in record time by killing several horses. *A killing pace.* Snarling wolves lent a new and terrifying meaning to the term. If anything happened to her horse — *The Lord is my Shepherd.*

She began to recite every phrase, every song, every tiny bit of anything she had ever memorized. By the time she was on her way to Willow Island, the last relay before she found "home," Annie was reciting Sophia Hollenberg's recipe for chicken and dumplings.

Willow Island brought a new kind of trouble. The sun had risen, and when Annie pulled her scarf down to take a drink, the station keeper looked. Looked again. And protested. "Hey — you can't — What d'ya think yer doin', Sis?"

"What's it look like?" she growled back. She didn't want to ask for help, but she was simply too exhausted to leap into the saddle.

She yanked the reins out of the station keeper's hands. "You gonna give me a leg up or not?"

"Not." The man stood back.

"What's Superintendent Slade gonna say when he finds out you refused to help get the mail through?" Slade was the Division II superintendent, and while Annie had never met him, she'd heard stories. The man had a reputation for violence of just about every kind.

"He don't know about this," the man said, gesturing the length of Annie's body. "He'd never allow it."

"You sure of that?" She looked about for something — anything — she could use as a mounting block. *Please. God.* Finally, the man relented and boosted her into the saddle.

"I'm gonna talk to Slade next time I see him," the old codger groused. "Ask him if he knows there's a gal hiding out among the riders."

"You do that," she snapped. "And I'm not hiding. I'm filling in in an emergency. My name's Ann. Ann E. Paxton. And if Mr. Slade wants to talk to me, tell him to come on over. I'll be cooking at Clearwater as soon as I finish this run."

"Don't think I won't."

"Don't think I care whether you do or not," Annie retorted, and she was off.

The minute the station was out of sight, her energy drained away. Trembling, she pulled the horse to a brisk walk while she tried to collect her scattered nerve. She wished she could remember more Bible verses. *It was the best of times, it was the worst of times.* Boy if that wasn't the truth about today.

She urged the horse back to a lope, grateful that the trail here was a wide, welcoming expanse of what seemed to be level earth beneath a skiff of snow where the wind had blown it off. Soon, she'd be able to rest. Soon. *Just a little farther.*

Finally, she caught sight of a flag flapping in the wind at the top of a flagpole in the distance. Had to be Midway. Every part of her body ached. How did Frank and Jake and the others endure this over and over again? Thanks be to God, she could see the next rider waiting alongside a flashy sorrel. She slid to the ground and stepped back. The new rider didn't really even look at her.

"Yer late," he groused. Then he slapped the mochila on and was gone.

Annie pulled her gloves off. "Sure would appreciate a drink of water," she said. She took her hat off to swipe her brow, and felt some of her hair fall about her shoulders.

The station keeper finally looked at her. His jaw dropped. He motioned toward a well a short distance away. With a nod, she started to march away.

"Hold on there," the station keep said. "I'll get it. Miss — ?"

"Paxton. Frank's my brother."

She leaned against the well while the station keeper handed her the dipper. Never had water tasted so wonderful. She drank two dippersful and swiped her mouth with the back of her hand. "Thank you."

"Thought you *were* Frank at first."

Annie nodded. "My twin brother."

"Couldn't let him outshine ya, hunh?"

"I'm the cook at the home station down at Clearwater. A couple of riders have disappeared — probably joined up with the army. We thought the other rider could just keep going, but he was too sick. Practically fell off his horse when he rode in." She shrugged. "Had to do something." She forced a weak smile. "The mail must go through and all that."

The man looked her up and down. Finally, he gave a low laugh. "Well, ain't that something. You come on inside and meet the missus."

Annie took a step. Staggered.

"Here now, little miss." The man put a strong arm about her. Somehow, she managed to wobble up to the house and inside.

The station keeper called out for Maude, and a middle-aged woman stepped into the room. One look at Annie, and she clucked and fussed and practically carried her to the cot that occupied the corner of a lean-to. She apologized for its not being nicer and wondered aloud at . . . something Annie didn't hear, because she fell asleep before her head hit the pillow.

CHAPTER 29

When Annie finally woke up — she'd slept for twelve straight hours — Maude made scrambled eggs and bacon. She served up biscuits slathered with butter and just about the best peach preserves Annie had ever tasted. While Annie ate, Maude explained that Midway Station was on a working ranch in the heart of the Platte Valley. She and her husband had been hired on by Ben Holladay to keep the stage station that was at the midpoint of the route connecting Atchison, Kansas, and Denver. Hence the name, Midway.

The station itself reminded Annie of Clearwater, for it was a sturdy structure built of heavy timber. Just outside the front door and off to the right a three-sided shed was the closest thing to a barn on the property. Like Clearwater, a series of corrals rambled away from the station house. Unlike Clearwater, the yard around the

438

house was protected from roaming cattle by a fence.

"You should see it in summer," Maude said, of the narrow expanse of earth between her front door and the fence. "I've got a nice garden and a rosebush that blooms like nothing you've ever seen. And the blossoms smell like a bit of heaven."

Annie told her about the rosemary plant she'd nursed through the winter. And her Rhode Island Reds. For the rest of the day, she worked alongside Maude, while the older woman schooled her on everything from how to battle the constant threat of fleas to how to discourage flies to how to grow the best watermelon in the county.

"I'm grateful not to be living in one of them soddies, mind you — can't imagine the fight the sodbusters must have with varmints — but on the other hand, them deep windowsills are a good place to winter geraniums and such." Maude paused for a moment. "You obviously did all right with the snow. Sure makes for a long winter for us gals, all cooped up inside a house practically drifted over."

"George — that's the station keeper — said reading's the secret. We did plenty of that. I didn't mind it too much."

Maude just looked at her. Finally, she

said, "I don't mean to discourage you, honey, but you haven't made it through winter yet. It can blizzard all the way into early May out this way. You got any sewing projects stored up?"

Annie shook her head.

"Let me show you something." She trundled to a back room and came back with a box. Pulling the lid off, she picked up a quilt block. Someone had signed the center square. "I brought these with me from home when Henry and I came out in '54." She pointed to the name. "That's my sister, Bess." She picked up another block. "This one's our grandmother. The whole thing was Granny's idea," Maude said. "Called it the album block. Made from scraps of dresses." She pointed at a rose plaid. "That's Granny's favorite Sunday-go-to-meetin' dress. I never got them set together, but this year I told Henry I'm going to do it no matter what."

Annie looked through the stack of blocks, admiring the colorful scraps. A hideous chrome yellow dot elicited laughter.

"That one," Maude laughed, "makes me think of dear old Susie Bee, the pastor's wife. That woman was a caution. I once caught her taking stitches out after a group quilting. Come to find out, she actually *measured,* and if it was any less than eight stitches to an inch, out they came. 'I already basted it,' she said with a sniff. 'I invited people in to *quilt.*'

"Do you like to quilt?" She went on without waiting for Annie's reply. "I'm partial to piecing myself — evidenced by the half-dozen tops languishing at this very moment in the trunk in the bedroom. Of course what Henry doesn't know won't hurt him, will it? And someday when I'm gone my girls will be glad to have something their mama made them."

"How many children do you have?"

"Just the three girls," Maude said. "Henry and I weren't blessed with more. But he loves his girls. Oh yes, he does. Two went on to greener pastures, as they say. Pete stayed. She's her dad's own right-hand man."

"I've heard a little about Pete," Annie said.

Maude smiled. "From that handsome brother of yours?"

Apparently the woman didn't mind Frank's attraction to her daughter. Annie nodded.

"Don't know if you'll get a chance to meet her or not. She's not much for sitting around sewing. Can't cook worth a darn, either. Would you listen to me, babbling on and on and didn't even give you a chance to answer when I asked about quilting."

"I grew up chasing after my brothers," Annie said. "Only been to one quilting bee. That was last fall with the ladies at Fort Kearny. Guess I'm a bit like your Pete. I spent more time riding and doing farm chores." She paused. "After Mama died, it took me a long time to get the knack of cooking, but I finally did. I'm good at that." She ran her hand over the top of one of the quilt blocks. "These are lovely. I can see why you treasure them."

"You want to learn, I could teach you how," Maude said. "The basics, at least. That'd be a start. We could work it in before you have to make the run back to Clearwater. You are planning to make that run, right?"

"Lord willing and the creek don't rise," Annie said.

That evening, Maude showed Annie how to make an album quilt block, cutting pattern pieces from a pasteboard box, explaining things like *seam allowance, cutting line,* and *stitching line.* She put numbers on the pattern pieces so Annie would know exactly how to create the block. When Annie took her first few stitches, Maude declared her "a natural" because of her "dainty fingers."

"You wouldn't say that if you'd seen my first attempts at mending my brothers' shirts," Annie said. "And buttonholes? I'm still not sure I'm doing those right." Maude spent the next few minutes demonstrating a buttonhole stitch. Annie was so enthused about learning "the secret" that she hugged the older woman in gratitude. When it was time to take the eastward mail run, Annie regretted that Clearwater was a hundred miles away from the kind older woman.

The last morning over breakfast, Maude handed her a tightly rolled up bundle of fabric scraps. "You just tuck those right down in your boot," she said. "And every time you see those colors in your quilt, you'll remember Maude Lemay of the Midway Station."

Annie's second experience pretending to be a "midnight messenger" was no easier than her first. In fact, the horses were harder to handle, and the pace just as grueling, and the Willow Island station master just as unpleasant. Annie took pleasure in ignoring the old codger when it came time to mount up. She'd only been on the trail for a couple of hours this time, and so she did her best imitation of Frank and sprang unassisted into the saddle.

The rest of the stations passed by in a blur. The Plum Creek station master's wife provided a meal that Annie ate while moving. At Dobytown, daylight had silenced neither the piano nor the party. As she rode past, Annie wondered where Charlie Pender had spent the winter — and prayed Frank would never again set foot inside one of those saloons.

Once she'd left Fort Kearny, she began to worry about what kind of reception she'd get back at Clearwater. She remembered Billy's protest. *George will kill me. I can't let you do this.*

She was met by a veritable committee and had barely touched the earth when Jake trotted up to take the mochila. "Guess you proved what you said about being at least as good as Emmet," he said.

"You're feeling better," Annie said.

"Right as rain. There's a new rider come in yesterday, too. Name of Jimmy Bly." He leaped into the saddle and was gone.

When Billy began to lead the spent horse away, Annie walked with him, hoping he didn't realize that her steadying hand on the horse's flank was a subterfuge to keep herself upright.

Frank figured it out and hurried to her side. "Put your arm across my shoulders,"

444

he said, reaching around her waist.

"Just a little wobbly," Annie muttered. George hadn't said a word since she'd dismounted. He had, in fact, lingered by the station door with his arms folded across his chest. As Frank helped her toward the station, Annie said, "George looks really angry."

"Men get angry when they're terrified."

"What'd he have to be afraid of?"

"You can talk about that after you rest up."

As soon as she stepped onto the porch, Annie smiled up at George. "I made it. How's the mare?"

"Nice little sorrel colt," he said. "Guess you're mighty proud of yourself."

"As a matter of fact, I am." Annie tried to take the next step, but her legs wouldn't work. "I — um — I think —" Before she finished the sentence, George picked her up and carried her inside.

"What's next?" he asked, as he carried her toward her room. "Bronc busting?"

Annie leaned her head against his broad chest. "Sleeping." When he set her down on the edge of her bed, she croaked, "Please don't be angry."

"Get some rest," he said and left.

Annie gazed after him and then looked over at Frank. "He's angry."

Frank shrugged. "He'll get over it. You need anything?"

With a sigh, Annie sank down onto her bed. "Sleep."

With a nod, Frank pulled the door closed. Annie didn't bother to undress. Exhausted, she wriggled beneath the covers. She was just as done in as she'd been when she reached Midway Station. Just as eager to sleep. Just as glad to be finished. Hoping she'd never have to face the trail again. But something was different, too. Something inside. A new realization that, if she had to, she could ride again.

In fact, she could probably do just about anything — if she had to.

Annie woke to sunlight streaming in her shuttered window and a kind of soreness she'd never experienced. Every muscle ached. Even her hands hurt. She sat up in bed and stretched. Slowly. She smiled, remembering her first day at Clearwater the previous April. Then she'd been worried about what Mr. Morgan would *think* of a cook who slept half the day. This morning she was a little worried about what George would *say* when she first saw him. She thought she remembered his agreeing not to be angry. After all, he'd carried her to her room.

Slipping out of bed, she dipped her fingers in the water bowl on the washstand and dabbed at her eyes, wiping away the crust of a heavy sleep before retreating to bed just long enough to warm up a bit. Another leap out of bed and she dragged her petticoats and things back with her, squirming about beneath the covers until she had changed into them. She peeked out. Blew a slow breath, watching as the resulting vapor floated away.

Finally, she threw back the covers, raced to finish dressing, and hurried into the kitchen, skidding to a stop when she came face-to-face with George. For a long moment they stood still, just staring at each other. Annie realized she hadn't done her hair. She reached up and grabbed a hank of curls at the back of her head.

"Crow's nest," she said, and retreated into her room, grateful for the temporary warming effected by the kitchen stove. She took her time doing her hair, trying her best to decipher the expression she'd seen on George's face. She could hear him moving about in the kitchen. He was grinding coffee. That was a good sign, right? A man couldn't be too angry with a woman if he was making the coffee for her. Could he?

She lingered as long as she could, folding Frank's clothes and laying them on her bed, picking up the fabric Maude had given her and setting it atop her trunk. Finally, when she could smell the coffee boiling on the stove, she went back out to the kitchen. No sign of George. He'd left the oven door down. There was a plate in the oven covered with a towel. Beneath the towel, a slice of ham. Annie poured a cup of coffee and sat down to eat.

At midday, when George still hadn't ventured into the station, Annie walked down to the barn. Frank was standing outside a stall, admiring the new colt.

"George is over in the soddy," Billy said. "Polishing a harness."

"He didn't kill you," Annie teased.

"Thanks to Frank," Billy said.

"I told him we should all be proud of you," Frank said.

Once at the soddy, Annie rapped on the door before going in. When George didn't answer, she went in anyway. "Thanks for the coffee. And breakfast."

"You're welcome."

She perched on the windowsill, watching as George worked saddle soap into the leather. After a few moments, she said, "I guess you're really angry with me, hunh?"

He shrugged. "Why would I be angry? Just because you ran off on a fool's errand? Just because you risked your life? Just because you could have gotten killed over *scribbles on bits of paper*?"

He hadn't raised his voice at all. Still, Annie could feel him shouting. "The Pony Express is about the farthest thing from a 'fool's errand' a person could get, and I think you know that. And whatever scribbles I carried locked in those mail pouches, I'd like to think they were *important* scribbles."

"There's a lot of things in life that are important. Plowing's important. You want to take that over for me? Or maybe you'd rather take over for Hart when he leads the next column out on patrol. What about freighting? You want to try your hand at bullwhacking? A lot of people depend on those supplies getting delivered on time."

"Now you're just being silly."

He sputtered, "Y-you c-c-ould have d-died." He broke off. Dropping the harness, he stood up. He started to leave. Then he turned back and in one swift movement, gathered her into his arms and pulled her close — close enough that his scruffy beard tickled her cheek. Close enough that she could feel his heart pounding.

"S-see what y-you do to me?" He released her and stormed out.

CHAPTER 30

Moments after George released her and stormed out of the soddy, Annie made her way back to the station. If ever she needed another woman in her life, it was now. Her mind swirled from George to Lieutenant Hart and even, at times, back to the only other male she'd ever entertained romantic notions about, Luvina Aikens's brother, Calvin. Of course Calvin had been barely sixteen that time he tried to kiss her, and Annie had pushed him away shouting, "I'd rather be kissed by a horse!" The only thing she'd learned about romance from Calvin Aiken was to stay away from boys.

She didn't want to stay away from Lieutenant Hart — or George, for that matter. Did that mean she was falling in love? Was either man falling in love with her? They behaved nothing alike. Wade Hart visited the station, smiled at her a lot, and wrote those pretty notes at the bottom of some of

Lydia's letters. She'd never caught George looking at her — well, not except for that one time at the cotillion when he stared as if she was some odd creature he'd never seen before.

There was something about Wade Hart that made her feel uneasy. Love did that, didn't it? Until just now, she'd felt — homey — when she was around George. Especially now that she understood his ways. Why he was usually quiet, for example. And that beneath the sometimes-frightening, bearish exterior, there was a gentle side that brought chicks in from the cold to protect them and even named the milk cow. Everything was nice and settled with George — or had been, until a minute ago, when he scooped her up and stuttered about what she "did to him." What'd she do?

The whole time she swept floors and fixed lunch, Annie pondered the mysteries of men and romance, and by the time lunch was ready, she hadn't decided much of anything beyond a faint sense of comfortableness with the idea of being snuggled next to George. But love didn't mean feeling comfortable — did it? Wasn't love supposed to be wilder than that?

Annie's ponderings came to an abrupt halt when a gust of wind blew the storeroom door closed with a bang. She'd propped it open while she worked to take advantage of the spring breeze. Now, she realized the temperature had dropped. She went to the door, opened it, and peered west. She'd seen a wall of clouds like that before. While the crew shouted and chased about, closing the barn doors and securing corral gates, Annie shooed the chickens into the coop and closed the door, then hastened to where Elizabeth had been picketed and dragged her toward the lean-to George and Billy had put up.

Dried bits of hay and straw swirled through the air. The wall of rain hit just as Annie had tied the last hitch in the rope to secure Elizabeth in the shelter. Ducking inside the station, she ran to close all the windows and secure the shutters. It took all her strength to manage the last latch. She had just forced the front door closed, barred it, and turned to go to the back door when lightning struck the roof of the barn. A jagged tongue of fire shot down the roof. *George!* Her heart in her throat, Annie stepped outside, but she hadn't even crossed the back porch when a downpour doused the flames.

Billy ran out into the rain and peered up at the damage. George came around from behind the barn and joined him. In that brief moment of time, relief coursed through Annie — relief so strong it made her knees quake and her joints hurt. Unwilling to let George out of her sight, Annie stayed put. George looked toward the station, leaned in to say something to Billy, and jogged in her direction. He stepped just beneath the overhang, sweeping his soaked hair back out of his face as he called out, "Are you all right?" He practically had to shout to make himself heard above the rain.

"Yes," she hollered back.

For a long moment the two of them just stood looking at each other. And then George smiled. Nodded. "Good!"

"Coffee?" she hollered.

"Soon! Need to check a few more things!"

He ran back into the storm. Annie retreated to her room and changed into dry clothes. Back in the kitchen, she made coffee, humming while she worked. Whatever had gone on down in the soddy, George wasn't angry anymore. They were going to be all right.

As it had a year before, the spring rain splashed the prairie with welcome color and churned up mountains of mud. The crew tracked it in, customers tracked it in, and

Annie tracked it in, for there was simply no way to navigate without slip-sliding through mud and having it splatter the hem of her skirts. She was sweeping clods of dried mud into a pile in the main room one sunny May afternoon when Lieutenant and Lydia Hart rode in.

"We have news," Lydia said as she dismounted and hitched her horse. "I've already hired a girl to press our gowns for the cotillion. You'll come early again, I trust?"

"Let's talk about that over pie," Annie said. While she worked, she and Lydia chatted easily, laughing over the inconsequential dramas Cinda Collingsworth seemed incapable of avoiding and worrying aloud over the profound events going on in the East. When they finally sat down at one of the tables in the main room, the lieutenant pressed the point about the cotillion.

Annie had been thinking about the matter for a good long while now, but it was hard to face those blue eyes and say *no.* "You know I love to dance as much as the next woman." She looked across the table at Lydia. "And that gown — there are no words. But I just don't know. It's not like last fall, when things were winding down out on the trail." She glanced back at the lieutenant. "You know what it's like. We're heading into our busiest season. I've a flock of chickens to tend and a cow to milk and a garden to weed." She paused. Cleared her throat. "And when it comes right down to it, I'm not really a silk-and-sapphires kind of girl."

Scowling, Lieutenant Hart rose abruptly, marched to the open front door, and stared out toward the trail. Annie set her fork down. Lydia reached over and squeezed her hand. "Maybe not, but you're a rare gem. And a dear friend. And I'll never forget you."

Annie frowned. "That sounds dreadfully final."

Hart returned to the table. "We both have news — of a nature we felt we should share in person. As it happens, your attendance at the cotillion has taken on an even more important place in our lives because of recent events." He looked over at Lydia.

She took the cue to continue. Words spilled out. "Wade's finally getting his wish. He's been promoted to captain and ordered to Jefferson Barracks in St. Louis. And from there, to only God knows what thrilling action and future glory." Her eyes shone with tears. She forced a brighter-than-necessary smile.

The lieutenant broke in. "We'll depart the week after the cotillion. Which is why it's so important to both of us that you come. It'll be something of a farewell. At least for a while."

"I prefer to think of it as an until-we-meet-again," Lydia corrected. "Wade's going on to St. Louis by steamboat, but I'm staying in St. Joseph. There's plenty going on in Missouri to keep 'the Lady in the West' writing. In time, I will conquer the Rockies and see the Pacific Ocean. I may even adventure to the Sandwich Islands." Again, she squeezed Annie's hand. "I'll see you again, my friend — either when I visit that little cottage you're going to acquire in St. Joseph this fall, or here at Clearwater when I once again experience the delights of the Concord coach — hopefully without the disagreeable fellow passengers." She winked at Annie. "Perhaps I'll entertain myself this summer by trying my hand at writing a romance. A story about a Pony Express rider and a rancher's daughter. *A Girl Named Pete* has a nice ring to it, don't you think?"

It was, for a moment, as if the world paused with Annie and the Harts sitting at a table, three pieces of untouched pie before them. And then George's voice sounded from the back door and everything began again.

"Excuse me," he rumbled.

Annie started and jumped to her feet. She looked his way. A boy of perhaps ten had followed him inside.

George nodded at the lieutenant and Lydia, then put a hand on the boy's shoulder. "This young man and I have some trading to do."

A voice called from the back lot. "Napoleon Edward Casebolt, you coming to Oregon or should we just leave you here? Gid-ap there, Dude! Go on, now, Dimwit!"

Hearing the name *Dimwit* broke whatever spell had been suspended over the adults in the room. Annie and Lydia exchanged amused grins. Hart crossed the room to speak with George while the poor boy with the unlikely name ducked back outside to shout that he was coming and he'd catch up after he made the trade.

Annie hugged Lydia and offered her hand to Lieutenant Hart by way of farewell.

"Morgan and I have come to an agreement," he said. "He gets the first dance. I get the rest — save one for Frank if he's able to attend." When he bent to kiss the back of Annie's hand, his moustache tickled.

Mindful of a bit of grime beneath her

thumbnail, Annie gave an awkward curtsy. Again she hugged Lydia, then proceeded to clear the table while listening to George's friendly banter with the boy, who made it clear that he was "just plain Ed."

With all the ceremony of a Pawnee brave presenting George with a fine pelt, young Ed unrolled a snakeskin atop the counter. He'd killed the rattler "with his bare hands" and didn't really want to part with the prize, he said, but had decided he could take comfort in the knowledge that it was on display here at Clearwater. They could tell the story as much as they wanted, as long as they gave credit for the kill to Ed Casebolt of Oregon.

The boy pointed to a spot high on the wall behind the counter. "Right up there's where I'd put it," he said. "So's all your customers would see it."

George considered the suggestion before appearing to examine the snakeskin. With a little grimace, he looked up at the boy. "It's a fine specimen. What have you got to have for it?"

"Can't part with it for less than ten good pieces of horehound. Licorice'd do, I suppose, but I'm partial to the horehound."

Annie suppressed a smile and ducked into the kitchen, setting down the dirty dishes and then leaning against her worktable to listen. When Frank stepped in the storeroom door, she signaled him to be quiet and gestured toward the main room. He folded his arms and leaned against the doorframe to listen, his eyes alight with silent laughter.

"That's a mighty steep price," George rumbled. "Can't go more than eight on the horehound." He paused. "But I'll throw in a couple of lemon drops and put it all in a little cloth sack instead of paper. Better for the long road ahead."

The boy was quiet for a long while. Annie heard him shuffling his feet back and forth while he pondered the deal. Finally, with a dramatic sigh, he agreed. She peered around the doorframe just in time to see him extend a hand to George. They shook. Annie watched out the window as the boy tore off toward the trail in the wake of a wagon piled high with furniture. A calico-clad woman wearing a bright yellow bonnet walked alongside the wagon, two little girls dancing through the dust nearby.

When the boy caught up, the girls crowded around him. Annie smiled as he reached into the bag. She wondered if the girls would get lemon drops or horehound.

Looking in the mirror in her room, Annie

placed one palm to her midsection and took a deep breath. She turned sidewise and peered over her shoulder one way and then the other. She was no kind of seamstress, but she'd worked hard on the Prussian blue dress, and from what she could tell in the mirror, she'd done a good job. The dress felt right. And the blue ribbon woven into her braid was a nice touch. She hoped Lydia would understand about her wanting to wear her own clothes this time. The lace she'd taken off Mama's ancient ball gown had made a nice accent for the neckline. And Finnegan O'Day had been right about the buttons. The mother of pearl looked much better than the cheap metal ones she'd originally selected. She smiled at the memory of baking a lemon pie to pay for the nicer buttons.

With a last look in the mirror, she scooped her patchwork bedroll up. It had been lying atop the letter she'd received earlier in the day. With a quick glance at Luvina's frilly script, she picked up the letter, folded it up, and tucked it inside the cover of her Bible for safekeeping, all the while wondering how to think about the contents.

Dear sister, I write to lend my voice to Emmet's in the matter of our desire that you consider our home as yours when you return to Missouri. In these uncertain times, family becomes more important than ever. Incidents in St. Joseph must surely be sufficient warning that it is not the best place for a lady alone to reside. You will be heartily welcomed, your capable hands appreciated as we welcome a new Paxton into the world.

Annie still didn't know what to think about Luvina's odd invitation. It almost felt like she was hoping to acquire a free nursemaid. *You don't know Luvina well. Choose good thoughts instead of suspicious ones.*

George was waiting out front when she emerged from the station. The moment she stepped into the sunlight, he exclaimed, "You look beautiful."

Annie appraised his polished boots and crisp white shirt. "So do you."

Again, he lifted her into the saddle. They rode west — a bit off the trail to avoid the dust rising from the long line of wagons trundling along. Conversation wandered from Annie's wondering about the sick little boy George had carried back to his wagon the year before to the one who'd negotiated over a snakeskin.

At mention of Ed, George chuckled. "He's

a savvy little trader. I wouldn't be surprised if he ends up owning half of Oregon before he's my age."

"I don't know," Annie said. "The first thing he did when he caught up with his family was to dole out some of that hard-earned candy to his sisters. At least I assume they were his sisters. Two little tow-heads, from what I could tell by the braids hanging down their backs."

George shook his head in mock dismay. "Only ten years old and already subject to being taken in by a pretty face. I recant my prediction about his potential for driving the kind of bargains it takes to make a man rich."

Annie looked over at him. "Is that the voice of experience?"

"What d'ya mean? I drive a hard bargain. Last year was my best year yet trading with Badger and his clan."

"I was thinking more about the fancy furniture in my room. It just doesn't quite seem like something you really needed."

"I didn't really need a cow, either. But I've got one."

"That sort of proves my point, doesn't it?"

"I think I forgot the point. We're almost there. Don't forget to save me a dance."

"Already have," Annie said. "The first

one."

Long after midnight, long after reels and waltzes, long after endless glasses of punch and laughter and smiles, Annie bid Lieutenant Wade Hart and Lydia a warm good-bye. "Until next week," she said. "You promised to stop at Clearwater on your way east."

"We will," Lydia said. "I'll bring you a copy of the article I'm writing about saying farewell to Fort Kearny."

Annie took George's arm and, together, they walked to where their horses waited. George lifted her into the saddle, then fumbled with the straps to untie her bedroll while Annie tucked her skirts about her legs. The cotillion was still in full swing. Glancing in the direction of the laughter and music, Annie saw Cinda Collingsworth capture Wade Hart the minute he stepped back inside. George handed up the patchwork comforter, and Annie pulled it about her shoulders, holding it in place by pulling a single large button she'd attached to the binding through a leather loop affixed to another edge.

As they rode toward Clearwater, bright moonlight shone almost as bright as day. They rode in silence for a while, past several wagon trains circled around low-burning fires. Tomorrow was the first day of June. Annie gazed across the moonlit prairie, smiling as she imagined the wildflowers that would soon bloom.

"You asleep in the saddle, Miss Paxton?"

"Certainly not. I was entertaining flowery thoughts of wildflower bouquets arranged in my mama's cracked teapot."

"Your mother's. I wondered why someone would hang on to something in such bad shape." He paused. "I guess that just goes to show you can't judge a thing's value by how it looks."

Annie murmured agreement. "I have one of her old ball gowns, too. I don't dare try to wear it, but I can't seem to let it go."

"You never talk much about your mama."

"Neither do you."

George took a long, slow breath. He spoke of growing up in Philadelphia and always feeling himself the center of an unspoken tug-of-war between his adoring mother and his disapproving father. When he moved on to Rose's accident, he broke off. "But you already know about that. And how I ended up where I am. Tell me about your mama."

Annie did — what little she could remember. ". . . and so," she concluded, "I rescued the teapot off the trash heap behind our cabin and stowed it away until the day the prairie bloomed."

"You've kept it out, though," George said. "Up on that shelf by the window."

"It reminds me of all the good things about having a home."

George grunted softly. "Things like pretty dishes and window boxes and little white cottages with blue trim?"

Annie looked over at him. His face was shadowed by the brim of his hat. "Frank told you about that, did he?"

"It's a fine dream."

"It is," Annie agreed. "But since I've been here at Clearwater, I've realized that the very best of the good things about home aren't really things. The best things are the people you love. That's what makes a place feel like home."

They'd only ridden a short way when George pulled up. "You really mean what you said just now?"

"About . . . ?"

"What makes a place feel like home."

"I do. Why?"

He took his hat off. Cleared his throat. Finally, after taking a deep breath, he said, "I'll build window boxes. As many as you want. I'll paint the station white and add blue trim and shutters." His voice wavered. "I'd do anything for you, Annie — just to have you look at Clearwater and think, 'That's home.' I l-love you, Annie. P-please don't go back to St. Joseph. S-stay here. With me."

A blush warmed Annie's cheeks. For the briefest moment in time, it felt like someone was reaching inside her and rearranging things. In a good way. She looked toward Clearwater Station in the distance, the corrals and the buildings bathed in soft, bluish moonlight. And then she gazed at the man next to her. She thought of the first time she'd seen George Morgan as he staggered out the back door of the station and fell to his knees, yelling for Billy. She'd had no idea of the goodness hidden beneath the man's rough-hewn exterior. She thought of George carrying a sick child back to a wagon train for a worried mother. George trading for a snakeskin so a boy could have some candy. George caring for a wounded friend. Riding through the night to bring Frank home. Building a chicken coop and buying a cow and humming off key while he waltzed her around tables made from shipping crates. She didn't quite know when it had happened, but there was no doubt. She'd fallen in love with George Morgan. The realization swept over her like a refreshing spring rain.

Finally, she said, "You don't have to do any of that. The painting. The building. I don't need them."

"Y-you don't?" He nudged his horse closer.

Annie shook her head. "I already am home. Here. With you."

George leaned in. And this time, the moonlight message was love.

EPILOGUE

In July of 1861, telegraph crews moved west from Fort Kearny. Riots in St. Joseph resulted in the eastern terminus of the Pony Express being moved to Atchison, Kansas. By August, the "handwriting was on the wall" regarding the end of the Pony Express, and in October, the completion of the transcontinental telegraph line erased its *raison d'être*. Service continued into November, until all mail entrusted to the Pony had been delivered. The last run westward reached Sacramento, California, on November 18, 1861.

Farewell Pony: Our little friend, the Pony, is to run no more . . . Thou wert the pioneer of a continent in the rapid transmission of intelligence between its peoples, and have dragged in your train the lightning itself, which, in good time, will be followed by steam communication by rail. Rest upon your honors . . . Rest, then, in peace; for thou hast run thy race, thou hast followed thy course, thou hast done the work that was given thee to do.

— *Sacramento Daily Bee,*
October 26, 1861

Ann E. and George Morgan were remembered as founders of the town of Clearwater, which grew up around the road ranch. Ten years after their wedding, George began to build Annie's cottage, although *cottage* wasn't exactly the right word for the white, two-story, five-bedroom farmhouse that was the talk of the region. The house featured a broad front porch, blue trim, and an impressive complement of window boxes. Soon after its completion, the Morgans added a massive barn that became a favorite site for box suppers, socials, and dances.

Frank Paxton never returned to Missouri. After his last mail run, he volunteered to serve with a Nebraska cavalry regiment. Just before enlisting, he tracked down and purchased Outlaw, entrusting the once-magnificent black horse's care to an expert horsewoman known as Pete. While serving with the cavalry, Frank was befriended by

William Cody, and when Cody created his Wild West show he recruited Frank to perform as a Pony Express rider. In time, Frank convinced Pete to marry him. They settled down at Midway Ranch, where Frank received the unexpected blessing of a father figure and Pete's father gained the son he'd never had.

The Paxtons of Midway and the Morgans of Clearwater made it a point to visit each other often. After all, what was a hundred miles to two Pony Express riders once known as midnight messengers?

Emmet and Luvina Paxton were unable to have children because of the injuries Luvina sustained when her father's prize bull escaped his pen and went on a rampage. The Paxtons became everyone's favorite aunt and uncle, enjoying summer visits from their numerous nieces and nephews, contributing to various college funds, and supporting missionary causes around the world.

Lydia Hart not only saw the Pacific Ocean and the Sandwich Islands but went on to circle the globe and to publish several books about her adventures. She returned to Clearwater for a visit in 1881, marveling at the growing town and delighting in the moniker *Aunt Lydia* bestowed upon her by Ann's six children.

Lieutenant Wade Hart was mustered out of the United States Army as a Brigadier General. His distinguished service in the war put him in contact with many prominent political figures, and upon his return to the family home in Philadelphia, he enjoyed a long life of government service as an advisor to a succession of senators, cabinet members, and presidents.

AUTHOR'S NOTE

Dear Reader,

My storyteller's journey along the Pony Express trail has been a search for what it was like for the women living at those stations. It was born in my imagination decades ago when I read about "a woman on Plum Creek in Nebraska Territory" who "started a store across from a Pony Express station. She baked as many as 100 pounds of flour a day, sold bread at 50 cents a loaf and made as much as thirty dollars per day. She made cheese which she sold at 25 cents a pound and travelers paid as much as $2 for the good meals she prepared." While the historian in me may have doubted some of those statistics and wished for "independent verification," as I continued to learn about the history of my home state, I grew to admire the women whose efforts fueled nineteenth-century westward migration. It wasn't until many years after first reading

473

about that "anonymous" woman that I visited the Dawson County, Nebraska, historical museum and "met" Louisa Freeman, the woman who started that store across from a Pony Express station.

As I studied the Pony Express, I could not escape the question: Why has an entity that lasted for such a relatively short time (less than two years) retained such a prominent place in our national story? I think I've learned some answers to that question.

For one thing, the Pony Express was the NASCAR of 1860. Fast "cars," challenging "tracks," and courageous "drivers" all combined to make the Pony something people talked about, wrote about, and never forgot. If I'd been part of a wagon train making my way west at the rate of fifteen-to-twenty miles *a day* (not an hour, mind you), you can bet I would never have forgotten the breathtaking spectacle of a lone rider tearing across the landscape at breakneck speed. I would have done more than just admire his apparent fearlessness. I would have written about it in letters home and in my journal. In later years, when I looked back on the westward journey, I'd have remembered the Pony Express when I told my children and grandchildren bedtime stories.

Buffalo Bill saw to it that the Pony Express was immortalized by making it part of his Wild West production — the only view of the American West many Americans and Europeans would ever have. "Le Pony Express" featured prominently in one of the posters used to advertise the production when it toured Europe.

Beloved author Mark Twain did his part in *Roughing It,* the account of his own westward trek in 1861 wherein he described both the anticipation and, finally, the actual sighting of a Pony Express rider. Westerns and pulp fiction glorified the Pony Express. When the riders themselves began to reminisce about their youthful adventures, some extraordinary feats came to light. One rider's memoir inspired the scene where my fictional rider Frank Paxton is "saved by a bunny." Billy Fisher was twenty-one when Pony Express superintendent Howard Egan hired him and assigned him to ride between Ruby Valley Station and Schell Creek Station in Nevada. Fisher told of losing his way in a blizzard, getting off his horse to shelter against a cedar tree, and then beginning to get drowsy. "I was about to . . . take a good nap when suddenly something jumped on to my legs and scared me." A jackrabbit saved Fisher's life for, as Fisher said, "A man who goes to sleep in the snow might keep on sleepin', you know."

The more frustrating part of my research into this legendary phenomenon was the lack of information about the women. *I should make it very clear that there is no documentation of an Annie Paxton taking a moonlight ride in place of an injured rider.* Could it have happened? Why not? Did it happen? There is no record of anything like it. Then again, there are few records at all of the part the women played in the Pony Express. They were there, cooking and cleaning and raising children in sometimes incredibly difficult circumstances, but time and time again I caught only a whisper of them hidden behind words like *and family, and his wife,* or, in the case of the stations in Utah, *and his two wives and children.*

As is often the case in history, the women of the Pony Express are, for the most part, little more than anecdotes. This novel is my personal tribute to them.

Stephanie Grace Whitson
Lincoln, Nebraska, 2015
www.stephaniewhitson.com

READING GROUP GUIDE

1. When you first meet Annie, she's thinking about the twenty-third Psalm and apologizing to God because "I shall not want" doesn't seem to apply to her. She thinks *I do want. So much.* How would you answer Annie's question about the deeper meaning of those words? Is she failing in some way because she wants a different way? How can a believer reconcile contentment and desire?

2. What character flaw does Annie hope to help Frank overcome by encouraging him to "think good thoughts"? What do you think of her approach?

3. At the beginning of the book, Annie describes her idea of "home" in detail. When you think of "home," what kind of place to you envision? Have you had to learn to adjust expectations in regard to

the place you call "home"? What challenges did you face on that journey? What or who helped you most?

4. Do you think Lydia is a good friend to Annie? In what ways does the friendship benefit both women?

5. Did you learn anything new about the Pony Express or some other aspect of history from *Messenger by Moonlight*? If the story sparked any new questions about American history, share those — and the answers (assuming you sought them out).

6. What spiritual themes did you see woven into this story? Do you think the author was successful in her treatment of those concepts? Why or why not?

7. It's always fun to think about a film version of a story. Did any current actors' faces appear in your mind's eye as you read the story?

8. If the author were to write a sequel, when would you want it to begin? Whom do you want to know more about — besides George and Annie?

9. It's always important for a writer to know the backstory of each character. In fact, writers usually know a lot more about their characters than they can put into a relatively short book. Play with the idea of creating backstories for some of the minor characters. What kind of background would you create for Ira Gould? What about Luther Mufsy? Cinda Collingsworth?

10. If you had lived in 1860, would you be an Annie or a Lydia? Fearful or excited about going west? How do you think the reality of living in the "untamed West" would have challenged and changed you? What would you have loved the most? What would you have hated?

11. Frank responds to the parson and his message in a life-changing way. Have you ever known anyone who experienced a radical change as a result of someone else's personal testimony?

ABOUT THE AUTHOR

Stephanie Grace Whitson is a bestselling inspirational author of over twenty books. She is a two-time Christy Award finalist and the winner of an *RT Book Reviews* Reviewer's Choice Award for Best Inspirational Romance. When she's not writing, she enjoys taking long rides on her Honda Magna motorcycle named *Kitty*.

The employees of Thorndike Press hope you have enjoyed this Large Print book. All our Thorndike, Wheeler, and Kennebec Large Print titles are designed for easy reading, and all our books are made to last. Other Thorndike Press Large Print books are available at your library, through selected bookstores, or directly from us.

For information about titles, please call:
  (800) 223-1244

or visit our Web site at:
  http://gale.cengage.com/thorndike

To share your comments, please write:
Publisher
Thorndike Press
10 Water St., Suite 310
Waterville, ME 04901

ML
4/21